Julia Mary C. Ady

Madame

A life of Henrietta, daughter of Charles I. and duchess of Orleans

Julia Mary C. Ady

Madame
A life of Henrietta, daughter of Charles I. and duchess of Orleans

ISBN/EAN: 9783337334031

Printed in Europe, USA, Canada, Australia, Japan

Cover: Foto ©Andreas Hilbeck / pixelio.de

More available books at **www.hansebooks.com**

The Princess Henrietta of England.
Duchess of Orleans.

MADAME

A LIFE OF
HENRIETTA, DAUGHTER OF CHARLES I.
AND DUCHESS OF ORLEANS

BY

JULIA CARTWRIGHT
(MRS HENRY ADY)

AUTHOR OF
"SACHARISSA," "THE PILGRIMS' WAY," ETC., ETC.

"Madame, que les siècles entiers auront peine à remplacer et pour
la beauté et pour la belle jeunesse et pour la danse."
MADAME DE SEVIGNÉ.

"Cette princesse à qui tout avait concouru,
Pour lui gagner les cœurs, et se voir adorée,
Semble n'avoir paru,
Que pour estre pleurée."
EPITAPH ON MADAME.

LONDON
SEELEY AND CO. LIMITED
ESSEX STREET, STRAND
1894

CONTENTS

CHAPTER I

1644—1646

Birth of Princess Henrietta at Exeter—Her Baptism in the Cathedral—Flight of the Queen—Exeter relieved by the King—Besieged and taken by Fairfax—Escape of Lady Dalkeith and the Princess to France . .

CHAPTER II

1646—1655

Wars of the Fronde—The Royal Exiles in Paris—Death of Charles I.—The Princess Henrietta brought up a Roman Catholic—Attack on the Duke of Gloucester's Religion . . . . .

CHAPTER III

1655—1656

Education of the Princess Henrietta—Court *Fêtes* and Ballets—Visit of the Princess of Orange to Paris—Charles II. at Bruges . . .

CHAPTER IV

1657—1660

Marriage of Louis XIV.—Portraits of the Princesse d'Angleterre—Letters from Charles II.—The Restoration—Letters of Henrietta to her Brother

CHAPTER V

1660

Philip, Duke of Orleans, makes Henrietta an Offer of Marriage—State Entry of Louis XIV. and his Queen—Embassy of the Comte de Soissons to England—Death of Henry, Duke of Gloucester—Visit of the Princess of Orange to London—Reception of the Queen-mother and Princess Henrietta in England . . . .

CHAPTER VI

1660—1661

CHAPTER VII

1661

CHAPTER VIII

1661—1662

CHAPTER IX

1662

CHAPTER X

1663

CHAPTER XI

1663

CHAPTER XII

1664

CHAPTER XIII

1664

CHAPTER XIV

1664—1665

CHAPTER XV

1665

CHAPTER XVI

1665—1666

CHAPTER XVII

1666

CHAPTER XVIII

1666—1668

CHAPTER XIX

1668

CHAPTER XX

1668

CHAPTER XXI

1669

CHAPTER XXII

1669

CHAPTER XXIII

1670

CHAPTER XXIV

1670

CHAPTER XXV

1670

CHAPTER XXVI

1670

CHAPTER XXVII

1670

CHAPTER XXVIII

PREFACE

HENRIETTA, Duchess of Orleans, is so interesting
and attractive a figure in the history of the seven-
teenth century, and forms so important a link between Charles II. and Louis XIV., that it is strange
to find how little has been written about her in our
own time and country. All we have are a few
chapters in Mrs Everett-Green's *Lives of English
Princesses*, and in Miss Strickland's *Lives of the Four
Last Stuart Princesses*. Of these two accounts, the
former is by far the fullest and most accurate. But
the limits of her work naturally prevented Mrs Green
from doing justice to her subject, and there are
many notable omissions in her history of Madame
Henriette. She does not give any of the letters
which have been published in Daniel de Cosnac's
Memoirs, nor had she access to that portion of
Charles II.'s correspondence which is preserved in
the French Archives. A few fragments of these
letters, addressed by this monarch to his sister between 1660 and 1669, were printed by Sir John
Dalrymple in his *Memoirs of the Reign of Charles II.*,
and by Mignet in his *Négotiations relatives à la Succession d'Espagne*. But the greater part remained
unknown, to all but a few students, until some ten

years ago they were published by M. de Baillon, in
a volume entitled *Henriette Anne d'Angleterre, sa
vie et sa Correspondance avec son frère Charles II.*, a
work of considerable merit, which is now out of
print.   Even here, however, several letters of the
series are omitted, and Charles II.'s vigorous English
naturally loses much of its force and character by
being translated into French.   These letters, which
are now for the first time given to the world in their
original form, are ninety-eight in number, and have
been copied from the MSS. in *the Archives du
Ministère des Affaires étrangères*, by special permission obtained through M. Ribot, *Ministre des Affaires
étrangères*, from the *Commission des Archives diplo-
matiques* at the request of her Majesty's Ambassador,
the Marquis of Dufferin and Ava, K.P.   My thanks
are also due, in an especial manner, to M. Girard
de Rialle, *Ministre Plénipotentiare, Chef de la Division des Archives des Affaires étrangères*, for the great
kindness and courtesy with which he assisted my
researches.

These letters, as might be expected, are of rare
interest.   Their style is as lively as their contents are
varied.   They treat of the chief political events in
England during the first ten years after the Restoration, and are full of gossip about public and private
matters.   Charles II.'s first impressions of his new
Queen, his quarrels with the Duchess of Richmond,
the struggle of England and Holland for naval
supremacy, the fall of Clarendon and the intrigues
of Buckingham, the conclusion of the Triple Alliance, and the long negotiations that were carried on

secretly between the two kings, are all freely discussed. And, on the whole, they give us a better idea of this monarch's character than we had before. We see him, it is true, with all his faults and weaknesses, his incurable levity and cynical unconcern, his indolence and easy good-nature. But at the same time we see his remarkable abilities and keen sense of humour, the courage and spirit with which he could defend the privileges of his subjects and the rights of the British flag, and the deep and lasting affection which he had for his " dearest *Minette*," as he called the sister whom he loved so well.

Besides this valuable series of letters, several documents, from the collection of State Papers on French affairs in the Record Office, are now published for the first time, and help to throw fresh light on various incidents in the life of this English Princess.

Madame, to call her by the more familiar name, was herself an active and charming letter-writer. Her descriptions are of the most graphic kind, her language is clear and simple. " With all her divine qualities," writes the Bishop of Valence, " this Princess was the most human of creatures." She pours out her heart in the most unconstrained manner to her different correspondents. Whether her mood be grave or gay, whether she discusses important affairs of state, or sends a hasty note to a friend, her style is always bright and natural, full of life and spirit. Her wit brightens the most tedious controversies, and the generous warmth of her heart reveals itself at every page. In her graver moments she is full

of charm, in her darkest and most desolate hours
her words have a pathos which would move the
hardest heart.   It is impossible not to share her
joys, or to be touched by the tale of her sorrows.
We yield unconsciously to the might of her spell,
and own the power of a fascination which the ablest
men of the day were unable to resist.

Unfortunately, all Madame's letters to her mother,
Queen Henrietta Maria, have perished, and we only
possess a small part of her correspondence with her
brother, Charles II.   Forty-three letters from her
pen are all that I have been able to discover.   Of
these, seventeen addressed to Charles are preserved
in the collection of Royal MS. Letters in the library
of Lambeth Palace.   Nine letters to her brother are
among the French State Papers at the Record Office,
and one short note was lent by the Duc de Fitz-
James to the Stuart Exhibition.   A copy of a letter,
addressed to Sir Ellis Leighton, is in the French
Archives.   Eleven others, written by Madame to the
governess of her children, Madame de Saint Chaumont, or to the author himself, are given by Daniel
de Cosnac in his *Memoirs*.   Of the remaining four,
two, addressed to the Princesse Palatine and the
Cardinal de Retz, belonged to M. Monmerqué's collection.   The other two, addressed respectively to
Madame de La Fayette and the Maréchal de Turenne, are preserved in the Bibliothèque Nationale
and the Bibliothèque de Nantes.

Contemporary Memoirs and letters supply another
important source of information.   Here the wealth of
material at the biographer's disposal is almost inex-

haustible. There is hardly a French work of the period which has not something to tell of Madame. In Madame de La Fayette's *Histoire de Madame Henriette*, we have a detailed account of certain episodes in her life, written by an intimate friend, at her own suggestion, and partly from her own dictation. This book was first published in 1720, half a century after Madame's death. Since then it has gone through many editions. The last appeared in 1882, and had the advantage of an admirable Introduction from the pen of M. Anatole France, which deserves to be reprinted. Next in importance to Madame de La Fayette's *Life* is a far less known work, the *Memoirs* of Daniel de Cosnac, Bishop of Valence. As Grand Almoner in Monsieur's household, this prelate was closely associated with Madame in the most difficult moments of her life, and her figure occupies a large space in his reminiscences. Besides these, we have a whole host of contemporary records, dealing more or less directly with Madame's history. Père Cyprien de Gamaches and Madame de Motteville give us many interesting details regarding her early years. Mademoiselle de Montpensier, l'Abbé de Choisy, the Marquis de La Fare, M. de Beaumelle, Saint-Simon and the Princesse Palatine, who became the second wife of Monsieur, all speak of her triumphs and sorrows, and bear witness to her influence and popularity at the Court of Louis XIV. The letters of Madame de Sevigné and of Madame de La Fayette, of Bussy-Rabutin and of Madame de Scudèry repeat the praises of her charms and of her goodness, of the superior intellect

and cultivated taste which made her the ornament of
her age.   Jean Loret, the author of the *Muse Historique*, introduces her name at every page of his quaint
rhyming chronicle.   Benserade and Madame de Suze
addressed their courtly verses to her, as the leader of
beauty and fashion.   Racine and Molière dedicated
their great plays to her, as the most intelligent and
accomplished of princesses.

The correspondence of Colbert and Lionne, of
Temple and of Pomponne, of Buckingham and
Arlington, of Hollis and Montagu, reveal a new
aspect of her character.   There we see her conducting important negotiations between two powerful
monarchs, trusted with all their secrets, corresponding with their several ministers, and displaying a tact
and ability, a coolness and penetration, which amazed
grey-headed statesmen.

So brilliant and memorable was the part that
Madame played during the short twenty-six years of
her life.   That life, as we all know, was brought to
a close by a sudden and terrible death.   The eloquence of Bossuet has made its tragic circumstances
famous, and the suspicion of poisoning, that was
generally aroused at the time, has arrested the attention not only of her contemporaries, but of posterity.
No less than five different accounts of Madame's last
illness have been left us by persons who were at
Saint-Cloud on that fatal night.   Bossuet and the
Jansenist priest, Feuillet, Madame de La Fayette,
Mademoiselle and the English Ambassador, Ralph
Montagu, have all recorded their impressions of the
scene, and of Madame's actions and words during

those eight hours of mortal agony. But the best account is given by Cosnac, who, although absent himself, received a full report of Madame's death, either from his friend, M. de Saint-Laurens, or from some other member of Monsieur's household. He confirms the truth of the chief facts recorded by the above-named eye-witnesses, and describes, better than any one of them, the interview of Bossuet with the dying Princess, and the last words with which she passed out of this life, "to the infinite grief," wrote Cardinal Barberini, "not only of France, but of all Europe."

MADAME

CHAPTER I

1644—1646

OF all the royal ladies of the Stuart race, none has a stronger claim on our interest than Henrietta, Duchess of Orleans. The charm of her personality, and the romantic story of her life both attract us in a peculiar manner. Among the famous men and women of that famous century, there is no more gracious figure than that of this young Princess, who, born in the midst of civil war, and bred in poverty and exile, lived to play an important part in political life, and to become the brightest star of the most splendid Court in Europe.

Henrietta belongs so entirely to France by her education and marriage, that we are apt to forget the share we have in her. We think of her only as the wife of Louis XIV.'s brother, the Madame of Bossuet's *Oraison*, and need to be reminded that she was a Princess of England. Yet Mignard's portraits, for all their French prettiness, reveal her birth. The long, oval face, the straight, thin nose, the arched brows, the eyes and hair, all bear a strong likeness to the kingly features which Vandyke has immortalised. And in spite of the vivacity and sparkle which she inherited from her mother, her character, on the whole, was more that of a Stuart than of a Bourbon. She possessed, in a prominent degree, the

A

distinctive qualities of her illustrious ancestors. She had their remarkable abilities and their engaging manners, their love of culture and refined taste in art and literature. She had the same natural gaiety, the same love of amusement, the same scorn for conventionalities, the same impatience of etiquette and ceremonial. Her actions display the same impetuous feeling and carelessness of appearances, together with the same generous warmth of heart. At the same time, her character is plainly marked by that deeper and more serious vein, that strain of thoughtful and tender melancholy which was common to the best of the Stuarts. Above all, Henrietta possessed, in a supreme measure, that gift of drawing out sympathy and inspiring devotion in those about her, which was so striking a characteristic of her ill-fated race. She had many rivals, and not a few enemies, but no one was more faithfully served and more passionately beloved, or more deeply and enduringly lamented. And when a tragic fate brought her days to a close, at the very moment of her proudest triumph, she met her end with a courage and a gentleness not unworthy of a daughter of Charles I.

The romance of Henrietta's life begins from her cradle. She was born at Exeter in 1644, at a critical moment of the Civil Wars. Two months before, on the eve of the battle of Newbury, Queen Henrietta Maria had parted, for the last time on earth, from her husband. As the Parliament's forces increased in strength, and the war raged fiercely round Oxford, Charles had urged her to seek a quieter and safer retreat. From Abingdon, after taking leave of the King, Henrietta travelled by easy stages to Exeter, where she had decided to seek shelter under the protection of the Governor, Sir John Berkeley, one of the King's most trusted servants. Her health had been failing for some time past. She suffered from rheumatic fever, and was so ill on the journey that she doubted if she would ever reach Exeter alive. Here, however, she arrived about the 1st of May, and took up her abode at Bedford House, a residence belonging to the Russell family, which then occupied the site of Bedford Circus, between Southernhay and High Street. So great was the unhappy Queen's weakness, and so acute her suffering, that she had small hopes of surviving her child's birth, and the King, alarmed by the accounts of her condition which reached him, sent a pressing despatch to his chief physician, Sir Theodore Mayerne, begging him to hasten to Exeter without delay. " Mayerne," he wrote, " for love of me, go to my wife.—C. R." This urgent note produced the desired result. Mayerne, who was then in London, obeyed the summons, and reached Exeter on the 28th of May. About the same time, a French nurse, Madame Péronne, who had assisted at the birth of the young King Louis XIV. and that of his brother, and who had previously attended Henrietta Maria on similar occasions, was sent over by Anne of Austria, the Queen Regent of France, with a gift of money and clothes for the use of her distressed sister-in-law. At length, on the 16th of June, a little Princess was born.

The royal infant, a small and delicate babe, was at once given into the charge of Anne Villiers, the wife of Robert Douglas, Lord Dalkeith, eldest son of the Earl of Morton. This lady, a daughter of Sir Edward Villiers, half-brother of George, Duke of Buckingham, and ancestor of the present Earl of Jersey, had all the beauty and high spirit of her family. From the first she watched over her precious charge with the tenderest care, and was soon to give the highest proofs of her courage and devotion. The unfortunate Queen remained in a very precarious state. " I have seen the Queen," wrote M. de Sabran, the French envoy, who had hastened to Exeter, in spite of the troubled state of the kingdom, to pay his respects on this occasion. " She has given birth to a lovely little Princess, but is herself in a state of extreme weakness and suffering." To add to Henrietta's distress, Lord Essex now advanced against Exeter, and threatened to besiege the city. The Queen applied to him for a safe-conduct to Bath, but, instead of granting her request, the Parliamentary General replied " that if he escorted Her Majesty anywhere, it would be to London to answer to Parliament for the war." Thus reduced to extremity, Henrietta roused herself to take a desperate step. Weak and suffering as she was, she determined to make her escape from the beleaguered town, resolved that, whatever

risks she might have to run, she would never fall alive into
the hands of the rebels.

On the 28th of June, she wrote a touching letter to the
King, from her bed, informing him of her intention to make
her way to Falmouth, and there embark for France. She
knew well the perils to which she would be exposed, but for
his sake she was ready to dare all. "I will show you," she
wrote, "by this last action, that there is nothing which lies
so near my heart as your safety. My life is but a small thing
compared with that. For, in the present state of affairs, your
condition would be in great peril if you came to my relief,
and I know that your affection would make you risk all for
my sake. And so I prefer rather to risk this miserable life
of mine, a thing worthless enough in itself, saving in as far
as it is precious to you. My dear heart, farewell. The most
unhappy creature in the world, who can no longer hold a
pen." The next day Henrietta took a tender farewell of her
little daughter, and, commending this babe of a fortnight old
to the care of Sir John Berkeley and Lady Dalkeith, she set
out on her perilous journey, accompanied only by Sir John
Winton, her physician-in-ordinary, her Capuchin Confessor
Father Phillips, and one lady-in-waiting. Three miles from
Exeter they narrowly escaped falling into the hands of the
enemy. The Queen was forced to hide in a wretched hut, and
her companions heard the Parliamentary troopers boast they
would yet carry the Queen's head to London. But they succeeded in passing the enemy's outposts safely, and were soon
afterwards joined by the other members of the Queen's household, among whom were Lord Jermyn and the valiant dwarf,
Sir Geoffrey Hudson, who had left Exeter by different roads
to avoid suspicion. Thus attended, the Queen travelled to
Falmouth, with Sir John Winton walking by the side of her
litter the whole of the way. On arriving at the royal castle of
Pendennis, the Queen heard from Lady Dalkeith that the
infant Princess was suffering from convulsions, and at her
entreaty, Sir John returned at once to Exeter to attend her.
After a few days' repose, Henrietta Maria herself embarked on
board a Dutch vessel that was cruising in the bay, and on the
14th of July, set sail for France. But her adventures were not

yet ended. An English cruiser in the Parliament's service gave chase to the Queen's bark, and pursued it hotly as far as Jersey. There a shell struck the vessel, and for a short time it appeared in danger of being captured. Amid the consternation of her ladies, Henrietta alone retained her courage, and bade the captain blow up the ship, rather than allow her to fall into the hands of the rebels. Fortunately, a squadron of Dieppe vessels now appeared in sight, and under their friendly escort, the Queen's ship pursued its way safely to the French coast. Even then, the perils of the voyage were not yet over. Henrietta's journeys were proverbially unlucky. "Mam's bad fortune at sea" was often the subject of her son Charles II.'s merry jests to his sister. A furious gale sprang up in the night, scattering the French fleet in all directions, and driving the Queen's vessel on the rocks near Brest. Here Henrietta and her ladies landed in a small boat and took shelter in a fishing village on the coast, where the peasants gave them food and lodging. Soon, however, the news of the Queen's presence spread through the country, and the whole population flocked to welcome the daughter of Henri Quatre. Directly the tidings reached Paris, the Queen Regent sent carriages and doctors to meet the unhappy fugitive and received her with the most generous kindness.

"I am welcomed," Henrietta wrote to her husband, "on all sides with such marks of affection as surpass all imagination."

Meanwhile Charles I., as yet unaware of his wife's flight had hastened to her rescue, and fighting his way through the Parliament's troops, entered Exeter on the 26th of July. With him came the Prince of Wales, who was lodged at the Deanery, while the King took up his residence at Bedford House. Here he saw his infant daughter for the first time, and was moved to tears, when he clasped the unconscious babe in his arms and thought of her absent mother. The little Princess had suffered from repeated attacks of convulsions, but, under the care of Sir John Winton and her devoted nurse, Lady Dalkeith, she had survived, and good hopes of her progress were now entertained. Even before the King's arrival, he had sent orders that the child should be baptised according to the rites of the Church of England. In obedience with his commands, the christening of the infant Princess took place in the Cathedral, on the 21st of July.

A new font was placed in the nave, and a canopy of state erected in honour of the occasion. The Dean of Exeter, Dr Lawrence Burnell, officiated, and the Governor, Sir John Berkeley, Lady Dalkeith and Lady Poulett, acted as sponsors. The following entry, recording this event, is to be found in the registers of the Cathedral, one of the few in England which is also a parish church :—

"Henrietta, daughter of our Soveraigne Lord King Charles and our Gracious Queene Mary, was baptised the 21st of July 1644."

The name of Henrietta was apparently the only one then given to the royal infant. That of Anne was afterwards added by her mother, out of compliment to the Queen Regent, whose generous assistance and kindly forethought had proved of such timely help in her hour of need.

Charles now pursued his victorious march against Essex into Cornwall, but in September he again took up his quarters at Exeter and spent another week at Bedford House with his little daughter. Before his final departure, he assigned the excise duties of the city for the support of her household, and appointed Dr Thomas Fuller chaplain to the three-months-old Princess. Then he gave her his farewell blessing, and left Exeter to renew the campaign. During the following twelve months, the West of England remained comparatively tranquil, and in August 1645, the Prince of Wales paid his little sister a second visit and spent a month at Exeter. Hardly had he taken his departure, than the armies of the Parliament, under Fairfax and Waller, once more closed round the city. Lady Dalkeith, who had received orders from the Queen to remove the Princess, on the first approach of danger, made a vain attempt to take her charge to Cornwall. But it was too late, Exeter was once more surrounded by hostile forces, and the little Princess and her faithful servants found themselves again exposed to all the perils and hardships of a siege. Henrietta Maria, who from her retreat in France, watched the course of events in England with the keenest anxiety, was beside herself with grief and rage, when she heard of her child's situation. She heaped reproaches on Lady Dalkeith's name, and censured her conduct with so much severity, that Sir Edward Hyde took up arms in the innocent lady's defence and wrote to Lord Jermyn in the following terms :—

" In reply to your postscript concerning the Princess and her governess, I think it will break her heart when she hears of the Queen's displeasure ; which, pardon me for saying, is with much severity conceived against her. Your motto seems to be that an unfortunate friend is as bad as an unfaithful. I'll be bold to say, let the success be what it will, that the governess is as faultless in the business as you are, and hath been as punctual, as solicitous, and as impatient to obey the Queen's directions, as she could be to save her soul. She could not act her part without assistance ; and what assistance could she have? How could she have left Exeter, and whither have gone? She had just got the Queen's letter, when the Prince was last at Exeter, about the end of September ; she showed it me, and asked my help ; I durst not communicate, the season being not come which was pointed out by the Queen for her remove, which was when Exeter should be in danger to be besieged, which we had no reason to believe would be before winter was over. It was no wonder if they were not forward to leave that place till forced, since there they had complete subsistence, which nobody else had, and which they could not expect in any other place in England. No more remained to be done but to foresee the danger, and to provide in time for her remove. On the enemy's advance, we had reason to believe our troops, then little inferior in number, would have stopped them awhile, and, moreover, a report was just then raised that we were carrying the Prince of Wales to France, which caused fresh disturbance, and at Exeter itself, people would have formally protested against it, had not the Governor prevented them. In Cornwall, at the public sessions, a petition was framed by the judges that the Prince should be desired to declare that no adverse fortune should drive him out of the kingdom, but it was suppressed by Killigrew; even the servants spoke big and vowed what they would do, if the Prince's removal were undertaken. Was this the time to remove the Princess? Had it been done, all security for the Prince's safety would have passed away. The governess would have procured a pass to bring the Princess to Cornwall, had not letters been taken at Dartwell, by which the designs of transporting her transpired. You have now the whole story, and may conclude the governess could as easily have beaten Fairfax, as prevented being shut up in Exeter, from whence I hope she will yet get safely with her charge, to whom I am confident she hath omitted no part of her duty."

Clarendon's defence of Lady Dalkeith was as manly as it was honest, but many months were to elapse before the brave lady and her charge were to escape from the beleaguered city. Meanwhile, within the walls of Exeter, Dr Fuller spent his time in composing and printing quaint little tracts, for the future instruction of his royal pupil. The first of these, entitled *Good Thoughts in Bad Times*, was dedicated to Lady Dalkeith, in a long epistle which concludes with the words :—" But I am tedious, for Your Honour can spare no more minutes from looking on a better book, her infant Highness, committed to your charge. Was ever more hope of worth in a less volume? But O, how excellently will the same, in due time, be set forth, seeing the paper is so pure, and Your Ladyship the overseer to correct the press!" A copy of the book, bound in blue morocco, and adorned with the Princess Henrietta's cypher and coronet, was solemnly presented to the royal child, who received it, in the arms of Lady Dalkeith, at an audience to which Dr Fuller and the loyal ladies of the besieged city were admitted. The book, it is interesting to learn, was carefully preserved by the Princess, and although she did not long remain a member of the Anglican Church, she valued her kind old tutor's gift, and inscribed several passages in her own writing, on the title-page.

As the winter months wore on, food became scarce, and the inhabitants of Exeter were beginning to suffer from starvation, when, one day, a sudden flight of larks poured into the town, "an arrival," writes good Dr Fuller, "as welcome as quails in the wilderness." So plentiful was the supply that they sold for twopence a dozen, "and of this miraculous event," the divine adds: "I was not only an eye but a mouth witness." But the blockade continued, and the larks came no more. At length Sir John Berkeley, finding himself and his gallant comrades reduced to starvation, was compelled to surrender. On the 13th of April, the garrison marched out with the honours of war, and Sir John Berkeley himself escorted Lady Dalkeith and the Princess Henrietta to Salisbury. The *Mercurius Civicus* of April 23rd records, amongst other items of news from Exeter, that the Princess Henrietta, "the last of the royal offspring, but the first that was in any town, when it stooped to the obedience of the Parliament, came out with her governess, upon the entering of our force, and we hear, is gone with Sir John Berkeley to Oxford."

So the youthful Princess left her native town. She was never there again, but the loyal capital of the West treasured her memory fondly, and after Henrietta's death, Charles II., who never forgot that his sister was "an Exeter woman," presented the faithful city with a beautiful portrait of her by Sir Peter Lely. This picture, which represents Madame in the bloom of her lovely womanhood, still hangs in the Guildhall of Exeter, a precious memorial of her connection with the old Devon town.

By the terms of Sir John Berkeley's surrender, it had been expressly agreed that the Princess and her household, together with all her plate, money and goods, should be allowed to proceed to any place in the kingdom which her guardian might choose, and that a sum for their maintenance should be allowed by Parliament, until the King's pleasure as to the disposal of his child could be ascertained. Lady Dalkeith accordingly communicated with the King, and on the 18th of April, forwarded his decision to Sir Thomas Fairfax.

"I have prevailed with Mr Ashburnham," she wrote, "to acquaint you that I have His Majesty's allowance to remain, with the Princess, for some time about London, in any of His Majesty's houses. I have judged Richmond the fittest. This bearer will inform you of those particulars concerning the settlement of the Princess in that place, wherein I conceive your assistance and recommendation to the Parliament to be necessary, which His Majesty will acknowledge as a service, and I as an obligation to, Sir, your humble servant,

" A. DALKEITH."

Fairfax promptly forwarded this note to the Speaker Lenthall, begging that the honourable House might make its pleasure concerning the same known by the bearer, who was appointed to meet Lady Dalkeith at Salisbury on the following Thursday. But it proved to be the pleasure of Parliament that the Princess and her servants should be conducted, not to Richmond, but to Oatlands, where they all lived for the next three months, at Lady Dalkeith's expense. In vain this courageous lady addressed repeated applications to the Speakers of both Houses, to Sir Thomas Fairfax and to the Parliamentary Committee for the County of Surrey, then sitting at Kingston, begging that the allowance promised for the Princess's support might be paid. No notice whatever was taken of her request until the 24th of May, when, to her dismay, she received a message from the House of Commons, ordering that the Princess Henrietta should be brought up to London and placed with her brother and sister, the young Duke of Gloucester and the Princess Elizabeth, at St.-James's Palace, in the charge of Lady Northumberland, and that the whole of her present retinue should be dismissed. But Lady Dalkeith was determined never to part from the child until she could deliver her safely into the hands of her royal parents, and, nothing daunted, she addressed a spirited remonstrance to the Speakers of both Houses. The original of her letter to the House of Lords may still be seen in the Bodleian Library, and is as follows :—

" MY LORD,—Presently upon the surrender of Exeter,

while the Princess Henrietta, under my care, was on her way towards these parts, I presented your Lordship my humble desires to the Parliament, concerning the settlement of Her Highness with such allowance as to them should seem expedient, since which time, there having been nothing therein determined, I have been necessitated to renew those desires. I am not now so hopeful as I was, yet once more entreat that the honourable Houses would be pleased to consider that I received this trust from his Majesty; that I have his injunction, as will appear by this letter I have sent inclosed to your Lordship, not to leave the Princess, and that, by the article of Exeter which concerns Her Highness, you may also perceive she is to be disposed of, according to His Majesty's directions; that I have preserved Her Highness, not without many cares and fears, from a weak to a very hopeful condition of health, that I am best acquainted with her condition and constitution, that my coming into these parts was voluntary, that I have disbursed a great sum of money for the support of Her Highness and her family, since the treaty at Exeter, that I have, because the time is very precious in the condition I am in, endeavoured to anticipate all possible obstructions, which, I humbly conceive, did either arise from the charge or inconvenience of dividing the King's children into two families, or that they had not full confidence in me, or that there is some other exception to my person. To all which, I did humbly answer that I did cheerfully consent to remain with Her Highness at St.-James's, and to be subordinate to my Lord and Lady of Northumberland, and, from time to time, receive and follow their directions concerning the Princess, and to be continued no longer than, after the severest reflection upon my deportment, I shall appear without the least exception. All my desire is now to be continued about her person, quitting all power, without being any kind of burden to the Parliament, or inconvenience to my Lord and Lady of Northumberland, resolving to bring such an obedience as I hope shall make me acceptable. And I do very humbly conceive I have not at any time deserved ill of the Parliament, which does often make me hope this request will be granted, without which I am ruined, my interest and

inclination being both in this service.   But if this be not satisfactory, I have only these requests, that I may be reimbursed
the money I have laid out during my attendance and expectation of the Parliament's pleasure, and that I may have a pass
to send one to his Majesty to know his pleasure, without
which, in honour and honesty, I cannot deliver up his child.
And in the meantime (which cannot be long) I most humbly
entreat there may be a present order for a weekly allowance
for Her Highness and her family, which will enable me with
more patience to expect the reimbursement of my money.
Having nothing more but my earnest and humble instance
to have these communicated to both the honourable Houses,
if it be thought fit, I do most humbly entreat it may be by
a conference and a speedy signification of the Parliament's
pleasure.—I remain, my Lord, your Lordship's humble
servant,

" A. DALKEITH.

"OATLANDS, *the 28th June* 1646."

Another month passed and still no answer came.   Then
Lady Dalkeith, fearing to see the child torn from her arms,
resolved to carry her off, out of the reach of the Parliament.
She disguised herself in a shabby cloak and gown, placed a
hump of old rags on one shoulder to conceal her graceful
figure, and, dressing the little Princess in a ragged suit of boy's
clothes, walked to Dover with the child on her back.   None
of the household at Oatlands were in the secret, excepting
two servants named Lambert and Dyke, and a French valet
who passed as Lady Dalkeith's husband.   The only risk of
detection lay in the angry exclamations of the little Princess
herself, who resented the shabby dress she wore as much as
the name of Pierre, which had been given her for the time,
and told everyone they met on the road that she was not
Pierre, but the Princess, and that these rags were not her
real clothes.   Fortunately her baby language did not arouse
suspicion, and Sir John Berkeley, who, following at some
distance, kept his eye on the travellers all the way, saw them
safely on board the French boat for Calais.   Great was the
alarm at Oatlands when, on Friday, July the 25th, both Lady

Dalkeith and the Princess were found to be missing, but a few hours later the fears of the household were set at rest by the arrival of the following letter from her ladyship :—

"GENTLEWOMEN,—You are witness with what patience I have expected the pleasure of the Parliament. I have found it impossible to obtain any justice to Her Highness or favour to myself, or any of you. I was no longer able to keep her, which was the cause I have been forced to take this upon me. Be pleased to repair to His Majesty, all of you, or as many of you as think fit. I then am sure you will enjoy the blessing of serving Her Highness, which, believe me, is heartily wished by me. It will be a great mark of your faithfulness and kindness to your mistress, to conceal her being gone as long as you can, and it will make your past service more considered, and that to come more acceptable. And, trust me, your divulging of it will be of no advantage to you. Thus you may do it, seeming to expect her the day following after the receipt of this letter, and then come to deliver this other to Mr Marshall, after you have read it, and tell him—which is truth—that I have removed Her Highness to a better air, whither you may, if you will, follow her. All her wearing clothes, woollen or linen, you may distribute amongst you ; the little plate she hath, Mr Case will have a care of, her other things are to be continued with Mr Marshall. I am so confident you will behave yourselves kindly and faithfully to your mistress, that you may yet more oblige me to be, what you shall always find me, which is to you all, a very hearty, kind friend,   A. DALKEITH.

" *For her Highness the Princess Henrietta,*
          her gentlewomen."

The members of the household obeyed these orders implicitly, and the Parliament did not receive news of the Princess's flight for three days after her departure. By that time, Lady Dalkeith and her precious charge had reached France safely. The joyful news was quickly borne to Paris. Carriages were sent to meet Lady Dalkeith at Calais, and the little Princess, once more clad in her own clothes, was at length restored to her mother's arms. The

Queen wept tears of joy, as she once more clasped her long-lost child in her embrace, and kissed her again and again. Lady Dalkeith, herself worn out with fatigue and anxiety, and exhausted with her long journey on foot, fell seriously ill on her arrival at Saint-Germain, where the Queen was then residing. On her recovery she found herself quite a heroine. Her name was on every lip, her adventures became the theme of every cavalier, at the Court of the exiled Queen. The King, who had never heard of his little daughter's flight, until the news reached him from Paris, warmly expressed his deep sense of gratitude to her brave deliverer, in his letters to Jermyn and Culpepper. And Sir Richard Browne, John Evelyn's father-in-law, who was at that time the English Ambassador in Paris, writing home on the 17th of August, remarks :—

"I was yesterday at St. Germain, to kiss the sweet little Princess Henrietta's hands; the manner of the Lady Dalkeith's bringing Her Highness away from Oatlands, is a pretty romance."

In later years, this romantic episode was celebrated both in prose and verse. It supplied the poet Waller with a subject for a New Year's Ode, which he addressed, in 1650, "To my Lady Morton, at the Louvre in Paris." By the death of her father-in-law, Lady Dalkeith had lately become Countess of Morton, and after congratulating her on these new honours,

"To the fair Villiers we Dalkeith prefer,
   And fairest Morton now as much as her,"

he compares her exploits in turn with those of Judith in slaying Holofernes, and of Venus in saving Æneas from the flames of Troy. He recalls the adventures of her flight, and the disguise which she had assumed with so much success :—

"Where the kind nymph, changing her faultless shape,
   Becomes unhandsome handsomely to 'scape,
   When, through the guards, the river and the sea,
   Faith, beauty, wit and courage made their way."

And he winds up with a graceful compliment to the youthful Princess, for whose sake she had dared such perils by land and sea.

> " Born in the storms of war, this royal fair,
> Produced like lightning in temptestuous air,
> Though now she flies her native isle, less kind,
> Less safe for her, than either sea or wind,
> Shall, when the blossom of her beauty's shown,
> See her great brother on the British throne,
> Where peace shall smile, and no dispute arise.
> But which rules most, his sceptre or her eyes."

Twenty years afterwards, when Bossuet pronounced his famous *Oraison funèbre* over the widowed Queen of England, in the presence of her daughter Henrietta and her husband, the Duke of Orléans, he recalled this incident of Madame's childhood, in a well-known passage of his discourse.

"Princess, whose future destiny is to be so great and glorious! Must you be born in the power of the enemies of your race? Eternal God! watch over her! Holy angels, surround her with your unseen squadrons, and guard this illustrious and forsaken child. God did protect her, messieurs! Her governess, two years afterwards, saved her precious charge from the hands of the rebels, and although conscious of her own greatness, the child revealed herself, and refusing all other names, insisted on calling herself the Princess, she was safely borne to the arms of her royal mother, to be her consolation in misfortune, and to become the happy spouse of a great prince, and the joy of all France."

Two curious entries, in the domestic State papers of Charles II.'s reign, are interesting, as giving us the names of the faithful servants who assisted Lady Dalkeith in her escape, and afterwards suffered for their loyalty. The first, dated September 1663, is the petition of Elinor Dyke for arrears of wages due to her for six years service, £25. board wages at Exeter, and £7 for silver laced shoes for Princess Henrietta, "whom she attended into France, losing thereby her house and furniture for fifteen rooms, and now her pension of £60 is stopped, so that she has nothing left, and is beholden to the Countess of Berkshire for a house to live in." The second belongs to the year 1666, and is as follows :—"Thomas Lambert and Mary his wife, petition for the customs on 2000 pieces of Holland linen, to enable them to drive a trade in their old age. Were obliged to save their lives by leaving the country six years, for their diligence in convoying the Princess Henrietta, from her barbarous enemies to the Queen-mother in France, are injured by searches in their millinery ware and lace for French commodities."

CHAPTER II

1646—1655.

Wars of the Fronde—The Royal Exiles in Paris—Death of Charles I.—The Princess Henrietta brought up a Roman Catholic—Attack on the Duke of
Gloucester's Religion.

THE first scene in the chequered drama of the Princess Henrietta's life had ended happily. The storm-clouds which
threatened to burst on the royal infant's head, had been fortunately averted, but on the friendly shore [where she had
found shelter, there were still dangers and hardships enough
in store for her.

Nothing could exceed the warmth of the reception which
the English Queen had met with in her native land, or the
generous kindness with which she had been welcomed by her
sister-in-law, the Queen Regent of France. Wherever she
went she was treated with royal honours. The people of the
towns through which she passed, received her with acclamations
as a daughter of France, the Queen Regent and the young
King Louis met her at the gates of Paris, and brought her to
the Louvre in their state coaches. A pension of thirty thousand livres a month was granted her, and she was given rooms
in the Louvre and allowed the use of the palace of Saint-Germain
as a country residence. For some time she retained all the
state of a crowned head, kept up a large household of ladies
and gentlemen-in-waiting, and drove about in splendid equipages, attended by guards and running footmen. But little by
little, observes her niece, Mademoiselle de Montpensier, this
pomp diminished, until at length it disappeared altogether.
All the money she could spare was sent to her husband, and before long, all the plate and jewels she possessed were sold to

B

supply him with funds. In these early days of her exile, her
Court became the meeting place of those banished cavaliers
who had lost all for the King's cause. The Prince of Wales
had joined his mother in September 1646, and both Prince
Rupert and Lord Newcastle came to Paris, after their defeat
at Marston Moor. There, too, the poets and men of letters,
who had sung the praises of the Queen in happier days, now
sought shelter. There came Cowley and Denham, and the
fickle Waller, when he, too, had been driven into exile, for
plotting against his party. Others, such as Wilmot and
Henry Percy, Davenant and Culpepper, went to and fro
between France and England, hatching fresh schemes against
the Parliament, and carrying on an active intercourse between
the King and his exiled Queen. Henrietta Maria received
them all graciously, and had a smile and kind word for each.
In spite of the havoc which time and trouble had wrought
with her beauty, and the sad change which old friends, such
as Madame de Motteville saw in her once fair face, she still
kept much of her old charm. In her saddest moments, when
the tears were running down her cheeks at the thought of her
troubles, she would recall some amusing incident of her
adventures, and would make others laugh by her wit and
lively descriptions. She loved to tell her niece, Mademoiselle,
of the happy days which she had spent in England, and dwelt
on the beauty of the country and the splendour of her Court
at Whitehall.

At that time, the idea of a marriage between the young
Prince of Wales and his cousin, Mademoiselle, was already
entertained. This Princess, the only child of Henrietta
Maria's younger brother, Gaston, Duke of Orleans, by his
first marriage with Mademoiselle de Montpensier, had inherited the vast estates of the House of Guise from her
mother, and was the richest heiress in Europe. The pride
she felt in her rank and position, was further increased by the
consciousness of her youthful charms. In the Memoirs written
in her old age, she dwells with complacency on her fine figure,
dazzling complexion and fair hair, on the magnificence of
her attire, and the compliments that were paid her on all
sides. She had a sincere liking for her aunt of England,

"that poor lady who has no joy left her on earth," and was well pleased to accept the attentions of her young cousin, but had not the slightest intention of marrying him in his present forlorn condition. She describes Charles, then a boy of sixteen, as tall for his age, with a fine figure, dark complexion and a beautiful black head of hair. He knew very little French and had to employ Prince Rupert as an interpreter, so he could not make many fine speeches, but Mademoiselle allowed him to wear her colours of red, black and white, to sit on a stool at her feet at the theatre, hand her to her coach, and even hold a flambeau at her toilette. "Since, at that time, however, I thought of marrying the Emperor," she remarks, "I looked on the Prince of Wales merely as an object of pity."

But Charles left Paris to take command of the Royalist fleet, and the cabals and tumultuous scenes of the Fronde filled Mademoiselle's head with other schemes. Meanwhile, Henrietta Maria's position became every day more painful. Her husband was a prisoner in his own palace, and she was full of anxiety for her absent children. Her money was all spent, her plate and jewels had been sold, partly to supply the King, partly to help the exiled cavaliers, many of whom were reduced to the verge of starvation. Her son's servants came to her for their wages, and she was forced to dismiss her own, for want of money. Madame de Motteville, who paid her a visit at the Louvre, on the 14th of July 1648, found her in sore straits for lack of funds, and was filled with compassion when the Queen showed her a little gold cup, out of which she drank, and told her that this was the only coin which she possessed in the world. The French Royal Family were hardly in a better plight, for the flames of civil war had spread to their own land, and early in January the Queen Regent and her son left the Louvre secretly and retired to Saint-Germain, where they fortified themselves in the old château, while the troops laid siege to Paris. Their Majesties were in want of everything. Mademoiselle describes the hardships to which the Court was reduced. "Those who had beds had no hangings, and those who had hangings were without clothes." And Anne of Austria, hear-

ing of the Queen of England's destitute condition, sent her
word how gladly she would have relieved her, but that
"neither she nor the King had a single *sou*, and that she
knew not where to obtain either a dinner or a gown." Well
might Madame de Motteville remark : "In that year a terrible
star reigned against kings." Henrietta remained shut up
in the vast precincts of the Louvre, during the most tumultuous weeks of the Fronde, unmoved by the fighting that went
on in the barricaded streets, and the slaughter that took place
at her doors. And with her was her little daughter, who,
for the second time in her short life, now experienced the
horrors of a siege. The Queen's own thoughts were too
much absorbed in the terrible scenes then passing in England,
to reck of the riots and bloodshed outside. It was from the
Louvre, on the 6th of January, at the very hottest moment
of the struggle between the contending parties, that she
addressed the letters to the Parliament, asking leave to
come to London to see the King, her husband, before his
trial. But the House of Commons refused to receive her
petition, on the plea that she had been already voted guilty
of high treason, and since no couriers were now allowed to
enter Paris, the Queen remained for some time without
further news from England.

The same week that she sent her last appeal to the Parliament, the Cardinal de Retz, who was then all-powerful in
Paris, paid a visit to the Louvre, to inquire how the Queen
fared, in the midst of the strife raging around her. It was a
bitter winter's day, and the snow was falling fast. But he
found Her Majesty of England sitting by the bedside of her
little daughter. There was no fire in the room, and not a
stick in the house, for it was six months since she had received her pension, and the tradespeople had refused to supply
her. "You see," said the Queen, cheerfully, "I am keeping
my Henrietta company, since we have no fire, and the poor
child could not rise to-day." "You will do me the justice
to believe," wrote the Cardinal to a friend, "that Madame
d'Angleterre did not stay in bed the next day, for want
of a faggot." He described the scene that he had witnessed to the Parliament of Paris, and pleaded the cause

of the royal exiles so eloquently, that 40,000 livres were at once sent to Henrietta Maria, for her present use. "Posterity," the Cardinal remarks in his *Memoirs*, "will hardly believe that a Queen of England and a grand-daughter of Henri Quatre wanted firewood in the month of January, in the Louvre."

But worse sorrows were in store for the unhappy Queen. Rumours of the King's trial reached the members of her household early in February, but for some time his wife remained in ignorance of the terrible truth. She often expressed her confidence in the loyalty of the English nation, and spoke so hopefully of the King's release from captivity, that no one dared to undeceive her. At length, on the 18th of February, she sent a gentleman of her household to Saint-Germain, to endeavour to obtain tidings from England. Then Lord Jermyn broke the news to her. For some time she remained speechless, and those about her feared she would lose her reason. "Neither our words, nor yet our tears could rouse her from her stupor," writes her chaplain, Père Cyprien de Gamaches. "Curæ leves loquuntur, graves stupent." In that hour of agony, the little Princess Henrietta, he tells us, was the widowed Queen's only comfort, and the child's unconscious prattle did more to soothe her anguish than all other attempts at consolation. For her sake alone, did the Queen consent to remain in the world, and give up the intention, which she had at first announced, of spending the rest of her life in the Carmelite convent of the Faubourg Saint-Jacques. As it was, she retired there for several weeks, leaving her little daughter to the care of Lady Morton and Father Cyprian, who looked on the *petite princesse* as his own especial charge. From that day, Henrietta wore widow's mourning, and called herself *La reine malheureuse*, a name which she frequently used in signing her letters.

"She has often told me since," says Madame de Motteville, "that she wondered how she had been able to survive such a blow. She knew that life had nothing left to give her. She had lost not only a crown, but a husband and friend, whose loss she could never regret enough—good, just and wise, worthy of her love and of that of his subjects."

The same lady reports how, the very day after receiving the fatal news, the Queen bade her tell her mistress, the Queen Regent of France, that her lord the King had lost his life, because he had never been allowed to know the truth, and that she conjured her, by her love for her native land, to listen to those who told her the real state of things, before it was too late.

The Prince of Wales, who had been already recognised as King of England by the States-General, now joined his mother, and accompanied her to Saint-Germain, where she went in July, at the earnest request of Anne of Austria. The journey was not without its perils, and Evelyn describes how a mob of angry creditors surrounded the carriage in which the Queen and her little daughter sat, and how the young King, in deep mourning, rode by the side, with one hand on the door of the coach, to protect her from the insults of the populace. By the end of the month, however, some degree of tranquillity was restored, and the young King of France was able to return to Paris, where his first act was to pay a visit of condolence to his aunt. Charles II. was now received with royal honours at the Court, and showed a true spark of kingly feeling when, in spite of his mother's prayers and tears, he determined to make another effort to recover his crown. "Better to die in such an enterprise," he replied, "than to wear away life in shameful indolence." So he left Paris for Jersey, where he was proclaimed King by the loyal islanders, and, in the following May, landed in Scotland, to conduct the expedition which ended in the disastrous defeats of Dunbar and Worcester. That year proved a sadder one than ever for the widowed Queen. In September 1650 she received the news of her daughter Elizabeth's death at Carisbrook Castle, and two months later, her son-in-law, the Prince of Orange, died of smallpox at the Hague, leaving her eldest daughter, the Princess Royal, a widow at the age of nineteen. A week afterwards, this Princess gave birth to a son, who was one day to ascend her father's throne, and reign over Great Britain as King William III. The death of the Prince of Orange was a serious loss to the English royal family. Both the young King and the Duke of York had found a hospitable welcome at his Court in all their wanderings, and had been generously supplied with money and arms for their campaigns. Now his young widow was left alone to maintain the rights of her orphan boy against a rival faction, closely allied with the leaders of the military despotism in England, who had doomed her father to death.

And now, to add to Henrietta's sorrows, came the failure of Charles II.'s expedition and her anxiety on his account. News of his defeat at Worcester reached her, and for some time, she did not know if her son were alive or dead. "All the world," writes her niece, Mademoiselle, "went to console the Queen of England, but this only increased her grief, for she did not know if her son had been slain, or made a prisoner." The sudden arrival of the King, and the romantic story of his escape, had the effect of softening this haughty lady's heart, and she owns that her cousin's appearance and conversation impressed her favourably. His black curls had been cut off to complete his disguise, but his presence was manly and majestic, and he spoke French with ease. She hastened to congratulate him on his return, and as he led her back through the gallery that connects the Louvre and the Tuileries, he gave her an amusing account of his adventures after Worcester, of his concealment in the oak of Boscobel, and his escape to the coast. But what struck her fancy most, was the picture which he drew of the miserable life that he had led in Scotland, where he vowed there was not a single woman to be seen, and where the men were such barbarians that they actually held it sinful to play on the violin. "No wonder," she exclaims, "the poor King was glad to find himself again in a civilised country."

After that first meeting, Charles was a frequent visitor at the Tuileries, where Mademoiselle held receptions, and danced with her English cousin, to the music of her famous violins. She lent a willing ear to his soft speeches, and was well content to have this royal lover at her beck and call, but when Charles made her serious proposals of marriage, she rejected them with scorn. Her latest ambition was to become the wife of her cousin, King Louis XIV., and she replied that no one could expect her to stoop to a monarch who was one

only in name, when she might at any moment become Queen
of France. So she preferred to play the part of heroine in the
Fronde, and to join the Prince of Condé and his peers in their
revolt against the influence of the hated Cardinal. She held
Orléans against the royal forces, and appeared on horseback
with her ladies at the head of the troops. Then she returned
to Paris, to enjoy her well-earned laurels, and be hailed with
acclamations, by princes and people, as a new Joan of Arc.

"You are indeed another Pucelle," said the Queen of
England to her niece. "First you drove out the English, and
then you rescued Orléans." The sarcasm was by no means
displeasing to Mademoiselle, who liked above all to find herself a person of importance. But her triumph was of brief
duration. "*Corpo di bacco!*" the Cardinal exclaimed, when he
heard that Mademoiselle had ordered the guns of the Bastille
to fire on the King's troops. "That cannon-shell has killed
her husband." He was right. Neither Louis XIV. nor his
mother ever forgave the insult, and when the Court returned
to Paris, Mademoiselle was politely desired to vacate the
Tuileries and retire to her château at Saint-Fargeau.

Meanwhile, Queen Henrietta and her son had refrained
from joining either party, "with more prudence," Mademoiselle
observes, "than we should ever have shown." On her part, she
was violent in denouncing both their Majesties of England for
refusing to take her side. The Queen, on the contrary, employed all the influence she had with her brother Gaston, the
Prince of Condé, and his sister, the Duchess of Longueville, to
effect a reconciliation between them and the Queen-mother,
and was sincerely rejoiced when the civil war was at length
brought to a close. On the 21st of October 1652, the young
King Louis, now fourteen years of age, made his entry into
Paris, riding at the head of his guards, and his manly presence
won the hearts of the fickle populace, who welcomed him with
shouts of joy.

His first act was to recall the proscribed Cardinal, who
returned without delay, and once more took up the reins
of government, which he held undisturbed until his death.
Mazarin, however, was too wily a politician to lend his support
to the English monarch, and shortly after his return to power,

he publicly recognised Cromwell as Lord Protector, and sent an envoy to negotiate terms of peace with him. The blow was a heavy one to Queen Henrietta, who saw in this step an insult to her husband's memory, and the ruin of the hopes which she had hitherto cherished of her son's restoration. "Since my great trouble," she wrote to the Duke of York at the Hague, "I have felt nothing equal to this. God take us under His protection and give us patience to wait His time."

Anne of Austria, on her part, did her utmost to alleviate the sadness of her sister-in-law's position. She increased her pension, and insisted on her leaving the Louvre, to come and occupy a suite of rooms in the Palais-Royal, where she and her sons had now fixed their abode. Henrietta complied with her request, although she preferred the quiet of the Louvre, and resolved to find a spot, where she could retire at her pleasure. The nuns of Port-Royal invited her to take up her abode at their convent, in the Rue Saint-Jacques, but Henrietta preferred to found an independent community of her own. For this purpose, with the help of the Queen Regent, she bought a house on the heights of Chaillot, which had been originally built by Catherine de Medicis and granted by Henri Quatre to the Maréchal de Bassompierre. Here she invited ten or twelve nuns from the convent of the Filles de Marie, near the Bastille, to take up their residence, and obtained letters-patent from Anne of Austria constituting the house a royal foundation, under the protection of the Queen of England. This convent, which occupied the site of the present Trocadéro, and was destined to be intimately associated with several generations of Stuarts, now became Henrietta's favourite retreat. She retained a suite of rooms overlooking the Seine, and commanding a noble view of Paris, for her own use, and often retired there, with her ladies, for several weeks at a time. Here the Queen Regent also came to spend days of prayer and meditation, in her sister-in-law's company. Her example was soon followed by the Princesses and other ladies of rank, and Louise de La Fayette, once the object of Louis XIII.'s adoration, but now known as the Mère Angélique, became abbess of the new community. Here too, the Queen of England often brought her little daughter Henrietta. From

the moment of her birth, she had secretly vowed that this
" *enfant de bénédiction*," as she loved to call her, should be bred
in the faith of her own Church. Accordingly, she had early
entrusted her religious education to her French chaplain, Père
Cyprien de Gamaches, to whose *Memoirs* we owe the few
details we possess of Henrietta's early years. " As soon as
the first sparks of reason began to 'glimmer in the mind of
that precious child,'" writes the old father, "the Queen
honoured me with the command to instruct her, and took
the trouble herself to bring her to the chapel of the Louvre,
where I taught children the Christian doctrine!" Lady Morton
was always present at these instructions, and one day told the
little Princess, laughingly, "I think Father Cyprian's catechis-
ing is intended as much for my benefit, as for that of your
Royal Highness." The Princess, who already, Father Cyprian
tells us, showed signs of a remarkably quick intelligence, repeated the remark to her mother, who said, " My dear child,
as you are so devout yourself, why do you not try to convert
your governess ? " " Madame," replied the eager child, " I do
my best. I embrace her, I clasp my arms round her neck, I
say to her, ' Do be converted, Lady Morton. Father Cyprian
says you must be a Catholic to be saved. You have heard
him as well as I have. Do be a Catholic, *ma bonne dame*, and
I will love you still more dearly !'"

But in spite of Father Cyprian's arguments, and the
Princess's still more persuasive caresses, Lady Morton resisted all endeavours to shake her faith, and remained a
staunch Protestant. After her husband's death, in 1651, she
obtained leave from the Queen to go to England, where the
interests of her children required her presence. There she
died, three years later, of a sudden attack of fever, without
seeing her little Princess again.

Meanwhile, a report reached the Hague, that the Queen
intended to make her daughter a Catholic, and excited great
uneasiness in the minds of the Princess of Orange and of the
English refugees at her Court. Charles II. himself was considerably disturbed, and on his return to France, in 1651, he
took the first opportunity of remonstrating with his mother,
for acting in a manner thus contrary to his father's dying

wishes. The Queen resented this interference passionately, and Charles tried to shift the unpleasant task on Chancellor Hyde, who spoke freely to his mistress, and pointed out the evil it would do her son's cause, and the " irrecoverable ruin " it would be to the Princess herself, in the eyes of all England.

Upon this, the Queen urged, not without reason, the existence of the clause in her own marriage treaty, which provided that all her children should be brought up under her care, till their thirteenth year. This clause had been broken in regard to her other children, but the late King, she insisted, had promised her faithfully, that it should be observed in the case of this her youngest child. She further contended that, far from being injurious to the Princess's future, her education in the Catholic faith would prove of the greatest possible advantage to her future establishment, and spoke with so much passion and resolution, that Clarendon gave up his attempt as useless, and contented himself with obtaining a promise that the Princess should not be put into a nunnery. After this, the Chancellor advised his master to take no further steps in the matter at present, and pointed out that, for the next three or four years, his sister would be capable of understanding but little of religion, and that, by the end of that time, he might find himself better able to take her under his own care. Clarendon was afterwards blamed for giving his master this advice, but it is difficult to see what else could be done under the circumstances. " I could not give better counsel," he wrote to Sir Edward Nicholas, the King's secretary, " or I would. Not that I was satisfied with the resolution, or will not do all in my power to alter it, by any way under heaven ; yet, if by that time, the King have any place to put her in, it will easily be done ; if not, I know not what to say to it. Since I could never be suspected of kindness to that religion, and in that particular of your mistress, I think I did more than any other body, and I advised to have had somewhat done, when may be, it was seasonable enough, but I confess, when I spoke with the Queen and saw her passion and resolution in it, I could not advise the King what he could do, to remedy it, and then the less was spoken of it, for the present, I thought the best, till he might be able to do somewhat, which at present he could not. Tell me, I pray you, what could the King have possibly done in that business, if the Queen had been willing to have delivered her to him?"

These arguments were unanswerable. The exiled King had neither house nor home to offer his sister, and she depended for her bread on the French Queen Regent, who was a still more bigoted Roman Catholic than Henrietta Maria herself. Even the Duchess of Savoy, the Queen's elder sister, wrote to implore her to educate her daughter in the true faith; and to satisfy her relatives' anxiety on this point, Henrietta Maria caused Father Cyprian to publish the manual of instruction which he had drawn up for the Princess's use, and thus show the world that the child was brought up in the Holy Catholic Apostolic and Roman Church. A handsome copy of this book, bound in red leather and bearing the initials "H.A." stamped in gold on the cover, may be seen in the British Museum.

Unfortunately for the peace of the English royal family, Father Phillips, who had for many years held the post of Confessor to the Queen, died at the close of 1652, and was succeeded by Walter Montagu, Abbot of Pontoise. This ecclesiastic, a brother of the Earl of Manchester, had been won over by the Jesuits to the Roman Church during a visit to Paris, some years before, and had all the fiery zeal of a recent convert. He at once induced the two Queens to put a stop to the Anglican services which had been held by Dr Cosin, the exiled Bishop of Durham, in a hall of the Louvre, during Henrietta's residence there. The King and the Duke of York now attended the English Church services held at the house of Sir Richard Browne, who was still nominal ambassador on behalf of Charles II. And when, at the close of 1653, the young Duke of Gloucester, having been set free by Cromwell, joined his mother at the Palais-Royal, he attended those offices daily, on his way to his riding and dancing lessons. This excited the Queen's displeasure, and, urged by Abbé Montagu, she determined if possible to make a convert of this her youngest son.

Early in 1654, a Treaty of Alliance was concluded between France and England. One of the conditions on which Cromwell insisted, was the departure of Charles II. from France. Accordingly, in July, the King left Paris to take refuge at Cologne, and, fearing his mother would take advantage of his brother's youth, obtained a solemn promise from her, before his departure, that she would not attempt to pervert him. But hardly was his back turned, than the young Duke was exposed to a series of attacks, both from the Queen and Abbé Montagu. The boy was not yet fourteen, but, mindful of his dying father's last charge, he resisted these attempts in the most resolute manner. The Queen dismissed his faithful tutor, Lovel, sent him to Pontoise for a month with Abbé Montagu, and would have made him enter a Jesuit's college, if it had not been for the determined opposition shown by the rest of her children. The Duke of York stood by his brother manfully, and the Princess of Orange wrote in great concern to Chancellor Hyde of "the great misfortune likely to fall upon the family, by her brother Harry's being made a Papist." Her aunt, the good Queen of Bohemia, who loved her nephew as dearly as her own children, was no less distressed. "I was on Saturday last," she wrote to Sir Edward Nicholas, "with my best niece (the Princess of Orange), it being her birthday. I assure you that she is in much trouble for her dear brother Gloucester. I am sorry the King has so much cause for grief. I beseech God that He may speedily remedy it. I believe that my dear nephew Gloucester has a good resolution, but there is no trusting to one of his tender age. I confess I did not think the Queen, his mother, would have proceeded thus."

Clarendon told the Princess of Orange that he had never seen the King so awakened, as in this business. Even Charles's indolent nature was roused. He sent a spirited remonstrance to the Queen, and, on the 10th of November 1654, addressed a long letter to his brother, commanding him never to set foot in a Jesuit's college, and advising him to refuse to enter into any controversy with the Queen or Abbé Montagu.

"Do not let them persuade you," he concludes, "either by force or fair promises. The first, they neither dare nor will use, and for the second, as soon as they have persuaded you, they will have their end, and then they will care no more for

you. If you do not consider what I say unto you, remember
the last words of your dead father, which were, to be constant
to your religion, and never to be shaken in it, which, if you
do not deserve, this shall be the last time that you will hear
from, dear brother,—Your most affectionate brother,

"CHARLES R."

Still the Queen, with Anne of Austria's influence to support her, persevered in her endeavour. On the young Duke's
return from Pontoise, she tried the effect of caresses and tears,
assuring the boy of her tender affection, and promising him
wealthy benefices in France, and even a Cardinal's hat, if he
would only embrace the Catholic faith. But the young Duke
stood firm, and, after another long conference with Abbé
Montagu, sent his mother word that he would never leave the
Church of England. The Abbé replied, "Then it is Her
Majesty's command that you see her face no more." It was
Sunday morning, and the Queen was starting for Chaillot in
her coach, when her son fell on his knees before her, and
asked her farewell blessing. She turned angrily away, and the
boy went back heart-broken to his own room. Montagu, seeing his distress, asked him what the Queen had said to him, upon
which the young Duke replied sharply, "What I may thank you
for, sir, and what I now repeat to you. Be sure that I see
your face no more." He turned on his heel, and accompanied
the Duke of York to the English service at Sir Richard
Browne's chapel. On his return he found his rooms in the
Palais-Royal dismantled, and no dinner prepared for him.
His servants were dismissed, his horses turned out of the royal
stables. But the exiled cavaliers rallied round him. Lord
Hatton gave him shelter in his lodgings, and Lord Ormonde
sold his George, the last jewel that he possessed, to supply
him with funds for his journey. That night the young Duke
came back to the Palais-Royal, to take leave of the little
sister whom he loved so tenderly, before the Queen should
have returned from vespers at Chaillot. The poor little
Princess, hearing of her brother's intended departure, burst
into tears, and, dimly conscious that he had quarrelled with
her mother, cried out through her sobs, "Oh me, my brother!

Oh me, my mother! What shall I do? I am undone for ever."

So they parted, and the Duke, with his faithful companion Ormonde, set out to join the King at Cologne. On the way, he paid a secret visit to his sister, the Princess of Orange, who welcomed him with open arms. But the States-General had lately entered into alliance with Cromwell, and Mary dared no longer receive her brother openly. In her joy at seeing the young Duke, she persuaded him to prolong his visit, hoping the States would take no notice of his presence.

"I am extreme glad," wrote the Queen of Bohemia, who had hastened to meet her "sweet nephew," "the King permits him to see his sister and me. I hope he will suffer him to stay some time with my dear niece ; it will be a great contentment to her and no hurt to him. And I am sure our *Hoghen Moghens*—High-Mightinesses—will take no notice of him, as long as nothing is said to them."

But she was wrong, and soon Mary received a formal message from the States, requesting the young Prince's dismissal, and reminding her of the treaty which had been made with Cromwell. There was no help for it but to obey this ungracious order, and, much to the distress of his sister and aunt, the Duke started for Cologne.

"Sure," wrote the Queen of Bohemia in her vexation, "Cromwell is the beast in the Revelation, whom all the kings of the earth do worship. I wish him an end, and speedily."

CHAPTER III

1655—1656

IN the midst of all this strife and tumult, while civil wars were
raging without and family quarrels within, the young Princess
Henrietta grew up a bright and charming child. The Queen-
mother had spared no pains in her education, and Henrietta
certainly received more regular instruction, and proved far
more intelligent and accomplished than any of the other
princesses at the French Court. The education of princesses,
in those days, was, as a rule, singularly neglected. Monsieur's
second wife, Elizabeth Charlotte of Bavaria, declares that the
way in which the French princesses were brought up was a
positive scandal. "They are taught nothing and allowed to
do whatever they please, from the time they are seven until
they are twenty!" This at least could not be said of the
English Princess. Henrietta was naturally quick and clever,
fond of reading, and taking delight in music and poetry.
She sang well, played the guitar and harpsichord with
considerable skill, and danced with a grace and elegance that
attracted general attention, in those days when dancing was
looked upon as an important part of a lady's education.
Madame de La Fayette observes that this youthful Princess
had enjoyed the inestimable advantage of being educated as
a private person, and had thus acquired all the knowledge,
the sweetness and humanity in which royal personages are
too often wanting. The lessons of adversity had not been
wasted on Henrietta. "You could see by her very perfections
that she had been trained in the school of misfortune."

In her own home she was the pet and plaything of the whole household, especially of her eldest brother Charles, whose affection for his little sister was noticed by English residents at Paris, during the years which he spent in France. Those early days saw the foundation of that warm and constant love between the brother and sister which was to last to the end of Henrietta's life, and was probably the deepest and strongest element in Charles II.'s fickle nature. It was the same at the convent of Chaillot, where the Queen often took her child for long visits. The nuns welcomed her with delight, and nothing pleased her mother better than to see the young Princess waiting on the Abbess and the Filles de Marie, as they sat at table on great festivals. Visitors to Chaillot were charmed with the liveliness and grace of this engaging child. Madame de La Fayette and Madame de Sevigné both saw her there for the first time, and never forgot the pleasant impression which she then made. Another and more important personage, with whom the English Princess early became a great favourite, was her aunt, the Queen-mother of France. Anne of Austria invariably treated her young niece with the greatest kindness. Her heart was touched with sympathy for the lonely child, and, convinced that the retired life which her mother led could not be good for one so young, she would often come herself to the Palais Royal, and take her back with her to share in the amusements of her cousins, King Louis and his brother Philippe, the young Duke of Anjou.

The Court had now returned to the Louvre, and was gayer and more brilliant than it had been for many years past. The long-drawn troubles of the Fronde were over, the last rumours of civil war had died away, and, while the Cardinal held the helm of state in his firm hand, the young King gave himself up to amusement. *Fêtes* and balls were the order of the day. The King danced well, and took the greatest delight in the ballets and masques that had been lately introduced at Court. A perfect passion for masquerading had seized on the youthful members of the royal family. Mademoiselle took a childish pleasure in dressing herself up in various disguises, and her cousin, Monsieur, as the King's brother was now called, was never so happy as when he could put on a long mantle and skirts, and appear among his mother's ladies with patches on his face, and his handsome head dressed like that of a girl. On one occasion they both figured at a ball in the picturesque costume of the *paysannes de Bresse*, wearing skirts of silver tissue, trimmed with rose-coloured ribands, and stomachers and hats of black velvet with white, pink and flame-coloured plumes, and carrying gilded crooks in their hands. On another, they appeared in the habits of friars, an escapade which seriously displeased the Queen-mother. The King early showed a preference for those mythological and pastoral ballets which became so prominent a feature of his Court in later years. These ballets were in reality theatrical representations of a most elaborate kind, which were composed with the help of the best poets and musicians at Court, and performed with the utmost splendour of costume and scenery.

The Princess Henrietta was early invited to take her part in these brilliant entertainments. She first appeared at Court at the age of nine, at a magnificent ball given by Cardinal Mazarin, in February 1654, to celebrate the marriage of his niece, Anna Martinozzi, with the Prince of Conti. On that occasion the Cardinal's three younger nieces, the Mancini, who had lately arrived from Rome, made their first public appearance, but among the youthful guests none were more admired than the child-Princess of England, who was present with her brothers, the Dukes of York and Gloucester. The Court chronicler, Jean Loret, who so often sang the praises of Madame in after years, mentions her, that evening, for the first time in his metrical record, as a gracious *aurore* now about to dawn upon the world. Henrietta Maria still shrank from appearing in public at Court festivities, and would gladly have kept her daughter in seclusion for a few more years, but Anne of Austria overcame her sister-in-law's reluctance, and, at her prayer, the youthful Princess was allowed to take part in a grand ballet, entitled " The Nuptials of Thetis and Peleus," which was performed by the leading personages of the Court, at the Théâtre du Petit Bourbon, in April that year. The costumes were unusually splendid, the *mise-en-scène* most

costly and elaborate. The decorations were designed by
Torelli, the verses written by Benserade ; the music was
composed by Lulli, that wonderful Italian boy who had been
originally a valet in Mademoiselle's household, but had shown
so much genius for the violin that he had been taken into the
King's service. Comedians from Mantua had been brought
to Paris to assist in the performance. The Duke of York,
Monsieur, and his favourite, the Comte de Guiche, were
among the actors. Olympia Mancini, who engrossed the
King's attentions at that moment, represented Music. Louis
himself appeared in no less than five different parts, and
represented in turn, Apollo, Mars, a Fury, a Dryad and a
courtier. The beauty of the music and of the grouping was
exceedingly admired, and the King's elegance and graceful
dancing had never before been seen to so great advantage.
But the tableau that was most applauded was the one in
which the King appeared in his favourite *rôle* of Apollo, the
Sun-god, surrounded by the nine Muses, and uttered a long
speech, proclaiming himself the world's victor, before whom
all powers must quail, save only Love. Then the youthful
Princess Henrietta stepped forward, crowned with roses and
myrtle, as Erato, the Muse of love and poetry, and, holding a
lyre in her hands, repeated the following verses with the most
charming simplicity and grace : —

> " Ma race est du plus pur sang,
>   Des dieux, et sur mes montagnes,
>   On me voit tenir un rang
>   Tout autre que mes compagnes.
>   Mon jeune et royal aspect
>   Inspire avec le respect,
>   La pitoyable tendresse,
>   Et c'est à moi qu'on s'adresse,
>   Quand on veut plaindre tout haut
>   Le sort des grandes personnes,
>   Et dire tout ce qu'il faut
>   Sur la chute des couronnes."

The Court poet had, it must be acknowledged, touched a
more pathetic chord than usual, and the recital of these lines
by the orphan child, with her innocent face and winning air,

took all hearts by storm. The ballet naturally met with immense applause, and the King was so well satisfied with its success, that he repeated it several times in the course of the following winter. Among those present, there were not wanting courtiers, who whispered that the King might do worse than marry his fair young cousin. Such a union would have gratified the Queen of England's fondest wishes, and there can be no doubt that at one moment Anne of Austria seriously entertained the idea. The wish of her life, she said openly, was to see her son wedded to her own niece, the Infanta of Spain, but since the political situation seemed to render this impossible, she hoped that he would choose this amiable young English Princess for his wife. But Louis himself looked on his cousin as a mere child, and his eyes were dazzled by the more brilliant attractions of the Cardinal's nieces. Madame de Motteville relates an amusing instance of the way in which he already showed that he intended to be the master, and would brook no interference with his own pleasure.

During the winter of 1655, many small dances were given at the Louvre, and the Queen-mother invited the Queen of England to come in privately one evening, and see the King dance. She herself had been ailing for some days, and wore a cornette (mob-cap) and dressing-gown, to show that she was keeping her room, and only a few duchesses and young ladies, wives and daughters of the chief officers of the Crown, were admitted besides the ladies-in-waiting. In fact, says Madame de Motteville, the dance was merely given to show off the King's dancing, and to amuse the young Princess of England, who was just growing out of childhood and showing how charming she would soon become. The violins struck up, and the King, who at that time of his life was entirely devoted to the Mancini, offered his hand to the Duchess de Mercœur, the eldest, and as yet the only married one of Mazarin's nieces. Upon this, his mother, amazed at his want of thought, rose hastily, and whispered that he must lead out his cousin, the Princess of England. Here the English Queen, alarmed at the evident resentment of the King, interfered, declaring that her daughter had a pain in her foot and could

not dance. Anne of Austria replied, with some heat, that if
the Princess might not dance, neither should the King. So,
in order to avoid a scene, Henrietta Maria desired her
daughter to dance, although this was much against the young
Princess's will. The Queen-mother took her son gravely to
task, the next day, but Louis replied sulkily, that he did not
like little girls. "Yet the Princess," adds Madame de Motteville, "was at that time eleven years old, and the King sixteen
or nearly seventeen, but it is true that in appearance and
manner, he seemed more like twenty."

As a rule, however, the King treated his aunt and cousin
of England with all the respect and attention due to their
rank and misfortunes. In a letter to her son Charles, dated
November 8, 1655, Henrietta Maria speaks warmly of her
nephew's agreeable manners, and of the courtesy and defer-
ence with which he approached her. The other members of
his family were, unfortunately, not always so thoughtful in
their behaviour, and treated the poor Queen and her daughter
with scant consideration on more than one occasion.

The Princess Henrietta's name figures in the *Court Gazette*
repeatedly during the next few years. She accompanied her
mother to Rheims for the King's coronation, and was often
present at great religious functions at the principal churches
of Paris. But, except on these rare occasions, she led a
secluded life with her mother, either at the Palais-Royal and
Chaillot, or else at Colombes, a pretty country house on the
Seine, which Henrietta had bought for her summer residence.

In the winter of 1656, the quiet round of their lives was
suddenly enlivened by a visit from the Princess of Orange.
This Princess still remained the stay of her brothers and
their exiled friends. She supplied them with money, gave
Clarendon a house at Breda, and, since she could not receive
Charles in Dutch territory, met him at Spa or Breda, and paid
him visits at Cologne. In the summer of 1654 the brother and
sister took a journey up the Rhine to Frankfort, travelling
incognito, at least, as Charles remarks in a merry letter to his
aunt of Bohemia,—"It is so great a secret, that not above half
the town of Cologne know of it, but we do intend to foreswear
ourselves, till we be here again." In spite of the troubles

which had darkened her young life, the Princess Royal had kept her beauty and high spirits, and, when she could escape from political cares and be alone with her brothers, she was as gay and light-hearted as Charles himself. But the genuine affection which she had for her own family, made her anxious to heal the breach, that had been caused by the Queen's ill-advised attempts at converting her youngest son, and her chief object in visiting Paris was to effect a reconciliation between the King and his mother. Charles, however, who was entering into negotiations with the King of Spain, and had lately sent Ormonde on a mission to Madrid, did all in his power to stop his sister's journey. Still Mary persisted in her intention, and pleaded her natural anxiety to embrace the mother whom she had not met for thirteen years, and the sister whom she had never seen, and, after writing several angry letters, Charles gave way and bade her please herself. Accordingly, Mary started gaily on her journey, taking her new maid-of-honour, the Chancellor's daughter, Anne Hyde, in her suite, in the hope of softening the Queen's well-known antipathy to the girl's father, whose independent spirit and frankness of speech she could not forgive. They were met on the frontier by the Duke of York, who had been serving as a volunteer in Turenne's army against the Spaniards, and who now saw, for the first time, the fair maid-of-honour whose charms were soon to win his heart.

Meanwhile, great preparations were being made at Paris for the Princess Royal's reception, and Cromwell's emissaries were a good deal disturbed, fearing her visit might lead to a breach of the peace between England and Holland. "What should occasion her coming in so unseasonable weather at this time of the year, I know not," wrote one of them from Paris, "unless it be in the hope the French King will fall in love with her." The same suspicion had already crossed Mademoiselle's mind, but she observes, in her caustic manner that the times were not auspicious for such affairs.

The Princess was received at Paris with every possible honour. The whole Royal Family and the Cardinal went out to meet her at Saint-Denis, and brought her to the Palais-Royal with a great flourish of trumpets. "Her reception," wrote

Jermyn to Charles II., on the evening of the 4th of February,
"has been universally civil in all things and from all persons,
and, without any flattery, she doth make an impression it is
likelier to mend than impair. On Sunday she is to be at
Monsieur's ball, where there will be the best assembly this
Court can form, and we discover already that she will hold
her place very well. The Cardinal hath advanced great professions of civility to her, and inclinations of entering into the
interests of her son, which, perhaps, may be of important
advantage to him. I find a strong appetite in her to make
the confidence between the Queen and you more entire than
she supposes it to be, and I am infinitely joyed that the
Queen shall have so irreproachable a witness of her good
inclinations."

And the Queen herself added a few lines in her own hand,
expressing her gratification at the reception which had been
given her daughter.

" I leave better pens than mine to give you a description
of the arrival of your sister, the Princess Royal. She has
been received right royally, and she pleases everyone here
from the least to the greatest. She has been to-day so overwhelmed with visits, that I am half-dead with fatigue, which
is my excuse for not telling you more."

On the 18th she wrote again, rejoicing that the King of
Spain had declared war against Cromwell, and saying :—
" Your sister will tell you all she is doing here. I think she
is very tired of receiving visits from morning till night. As
for me, I am almost dead with them, but you who know
France, are well aware that, after the first few days, one is
left quiet enough."

During the next few weeks, the newly-arrived Princess
found herself in a whirl of gaiety, unlike anything that she
had ever seen before. Two days after her arrival, Monsieur's
ball took place in the Salle des Gardes, which was hung with
tapestries, and brilliantly illuminated. Anne of Austria
would allow no widows to dance at her Court, except in
private, so Mary looked on while the King opened the ball
with her young sister, and the *Court Gazetteer* again paints
the admiration that Henrietta's grace and youth excited.

> " La jeune infante d'Angleterre,
>   Qui semblait un ange sur terre,
>   Que menait le Roy très chrestien,
>   Dansa si parfaitement bien,
>   Que de toute la compagnie
>   Elle fut mille fois bénie."

On the 14th, the Princess of Orange was present at a comedy performed at the Louvre, and two days afterwards, she witnessed a ballet on the story of Psyche, composed by the King himself. But, the grandest of all the *fêtes*, this carnival time, was that given by Chancelier Seguier in her honour. The English Queen was not present, but both her daughters and her son James sat at the royal table with the Queen-mother and her sons. At the conclusion of the banquet, the Chancellor led his guests through a gallery, illuminated with 300 torches, to the ball-room; the King once more opened the ball with Henrietta, and when the violins struck up, each cavalier presented his lady with a richly-decorated basket filled with sweetmeats. Many similar entertainments followed, and Mary wrote in high glee to her faithful servants at the Hague :—" To tell you the truth, I have scarcely time to eat a morsel of bread. I am, however, impatient to tell you how well I am treated here, for I can assure you that I never, in all my life, received half so much civility." And to Charles II. she wrote a little later :— " I must tell you first, that I have seen the masque, and in the *entrée* of the performers, received another present, which was a petticoat of cloth of silver and embroidered Spanish leather, which is very fine and very extraordinary. I was, since then, at the Chancellor's, where the King and Queen and all the Court were, which was really extremely fine. Two nights ago, the King came here in masquerade, and others, and danced here. Monday next there is a little ball at the Louvre, where I must dance. Judge, therefore, in what pain I shall be! This is all I have to tell you, for I have been this day at the Carmelites and, to confess the truth, am a little weary. I have forgot for three posts to send you verses of my uncle's making, which I pray pardon me for, and for the dirtiness of the paper, which has been so, with wearing it so long in my pocket."

The impression which Mary herself made at the French Court, was extremely favourable. Her bright and genial manners, and her amiability and evident enjoyment of the *fêtes* which had been prepared for her, gave widespread satisfaction, and she was as popular with the people as with the Court. Anne of Austria treated her with the greatest distinction, and, when she paid a visit to the Louvre, made her sit down on a *fauteuil*, an honour usually reserved for crowned heads. "The Princess of Orange," observes a French contemporary, "outshone all our ladies, although the Court was never more crowded with handsome women, and if our Queen had permitted widows to dance, she would have done wonders." Mademoiselle, who somehow was apt to treat the English Royal Family in a very supercilious manner, was struck by the splendour of the pearls and diamonds which Mary wore, and the great affection with which she embraced her, when they met for the first time. She herself was still banished from Court, but she gave her aunt and cousins a sumptuous entertainment at her beautiful country house of Chilly, where all the princesses and duchesses in Paris were present. "The Princess Royal, Mary of Orange," she writes, "talked to me without ceasing, saying how desirous she had been to see me, and how sorry she should have been, to have left France, without having accomplished this desire, for the King, her brother, had talked of me with so much affection, that she had loved me before she saw me. I asked her how she liked the Court of France? She replied that she was indeed well pleased with it—the more so, because she had a horrible dislike for Holland, and that as soon as the King, her brother, was settled, she should go and live with him."

The Queen also took advantage of the occasion, to recall her discarded suitor to Mademoiselle's mind. "*Et ce pauvre Roi d'Angleterre ?*" she said to her niece, "are you so ungrateful, you will not even ask for news of him ? *Hélas !* he is so foolish that he will never cease to love you, and he bade me tell you when he left France, how sorry he was to go without bidding you farewell. Think, if you were married, you would no longer be subject to your father's caprices, you would be your own mistress, you would do what you pleased, and you would most likely be well established in England. *Ce pauvre misérable* will know no happiness without you! Had you married him, he and I would be on better terms now, for you, I am sure, would have taught him to live more happily with me."

Mademoiselle retorted, with some reason, that if the King did not live happily with his mother, he was not likely to live happily with her, and the subject was allowed to drop.

Henrietta Maria, as might be expected, did not let her daughter leave France without attempting to bring her over to the Church of Rome. She took her to several functions at the Carmelite convent, and at Chaillot, and enticed her into repeated discussions on the subject. But, however affectionate and submissive a daughter Mary proved herself in other ways, on this point she held firm. Contemporary writers all bear witness that, whatever amusements occupied her in the week, on Sundays she always made a rule of attending the Anglican Church service. She also refused to be present at a Court ball on the anniversary of her husband's funeral, a scruple which surprised the French ladies immensely, since the Prince of Orange had been dead five years. But Mary's love for her young husband had been deep and true, and, during her visit to Paris, she is said to have refused more than one offer of marriage. In the midst of her amusements, she did not forget her brothers. She succeeded in restoring a degree of harmony between Charles and his mother, and snatched time from her devotions in Holy Week, to write a hurried letter to her "deare brother of Gloucester," in which she promises him a pension of five hundred guilders a month, and tells him that she is sending off a suit of clothes which he had begged her to order in Paris. "And for the payment of them," adds this kind sister, "that shall neither be upon one month nor another, for you will find enough to do with your money besides that."

The arrival of that strange personage, Queen Christina of Sweden, at the French Court that summer, produced a renewal of *fêtes*, and the Princess of Orange lingered on with her mother till November, when the news of her precious child's illness made her hasten her departure. Fortunately the little Prince's malady proved to be only an attack of measles, from which he soon recovered, and his mother stopped on her journey home, to visit her brother Charles at Bruges. She took him a welcome present of 20,000 pistoles, since he was, as usual, reduced to his last penny, and all the money he received was too soon squandered on his pleasures. These years of inaction had already produced a disastrous effect on his habits and character. Madame de Motteville, who was fondly attached to his mother, paints the change for the worse, which she had noticed in this once hopeful Prince, with her usual frankness.

" The greatest heroes and sages of antiquity," she observes, " did not guide their lives by grander principles of action, than this young Prince at the opening of his career, but when he found that his struggles were doomed to failure, he sank into indifference, and bore the ills of poverty and exile with reckless nonchalance, snatching at whatever pleasures came in his way, even those of the most degraded kind. So he gave himself up to lawless passion, and passed many years, in France and other countries, in the utmost sloth."

CHAPTER IV

1657—1660

THE visit of the Princess of Orange brought a ray of sunshine into Queen Henrietta's sad life. After Mary's departure, the gloom seemed to settle down more deeply than before. The Queen's health was in a failing state, and her letters breathe a spirit of profound sadness. There seemed no prospect of a Royalist rising in England, and the hopes which Charles II. had entertained from his Spanish alliance were destined to end in smoke. Meanwhile Cromwell, seeing in Spain "the underpropper of the great Romish Babylon," formed a close alliance with Mazarin, and even sent a detachment of his Ironsides to join in Turenne's campaign against Spanish Flanders. "So," he wrote in his orders, "shall we be fighting the Lord's battles." This union between England and France greatly distressed Queen Henrietta, the more so that both her sons, the Dukes of York and Gloucester, had taken service in the Spanish army, and were fighting valiantly under the exiled Condé, against his own land of France. Charles II. himself served in the Spanish army during the winter of 1657, and a false report that he had been dangerously wounded in an attack on Mardyck reached Paris. In the following June, Dunkirk was taken by the French and English forces, after a gallant defence by the Spaniards. There was great consternation at the Hague and at Paris, for the Dukes of York and Gloucester were both in the van of the battle, and for some time, they were supposed to have been slain or made prisoners. In her distress and anxiety, the Princess of Orange took to

44

her bed, and the Queen-mother went through agonies of fear, until she heard that her sons had reached Bruges safely.

"You may imagine," she wrote to her eldest son, "how much I suffer and how ill I pass my time here."

It was a dark period in her life, and she had little heart for the balls and masquerades, the picnics and hunting-parties of the gay Court around her. Both in 1657 and 1658, the Queen and her daughter spent some weeks for her health at the waters of Bourbon, where they were joined by her brother Gaston, Duke of Orléans, and his family. The remainder of the year was spent chiefly at Colombes, or else in retirement at Chaillot, and the appearances of the young Princess at Court were few and far between. Mademoiselle de Montpensier mentions a *fête* given by Chancellor Seguier at the carnival of 1658, where the Princesse d'Angleterre was present, and, "poor child, seemed enchanted to be there, since she only goes to balls at the Louvre, as a rule." On that occasion, however, Mademoiselle thought it necessary to claim precedence of her young cousin, a proceeding which excited the Queen-mother's displeasure. Mademoiselle defended her action to the Cardinal, saying that she had taken Henrietta by the hand to avoid disputes, but Mazarin replied drily:—"It is said that you passed in to supper before her." Upon which Monsieur, who was always glad to oppose the Cardinal, took up the cudgels on Mademoiselle's behalf, and exclaimed:—"And if she did, she was perfectly right! Things must have come to a fine pass, if we are to allow people who depend upon us for bread to pass before us. For my part, I think they had better betake themselves elsewhere." The Queen-mother scolded the foolish boy for his impertinent speech, and the Cardinal tried to soothe Mademoiselle's offended dignity, by telling her that, in old days, the Kings of Scotland had given place to the sons of France, and that she might therefore, if she thought fit, dispute *le pas* with the Princess of England. Mademoiselle hastened to declare that she had always lived on the best of terms with her aunt and cousin, and had no wish to mortify the poor Queen in her present sad condition. But she took care to renew her claim at the first opportunity, and her jealousy of

her youthful cousin was noticed by the whole Court. All
these wrangles and unkind words were duly reported to
Henrietta Maria, who wept bitterly when she heard of her
nephew's speech, and tasted once more, to her cost, how salt
is the bread of exile.

Meanwhile, the question of the young King's marriage
became every day more pressing. The war that still continued between France and Spain had put an end to the
Queen-mother's hopes of his union with the Infanta Marie
Thérèse. Louis himself was devoted to the Cardinal's nieces,
and spent his time in their company. After Olympia's
marriage to the Comte de Soissons, in 1657, he transferred
his affections to her younger sister, Marie Mancini, who, on
her part, was passionately in love with him, and seriously
contemplated the prospect of becoming Queen of France.
The Queen-mother looked with dismay on her son's infatuation, and told the Cardinal that, as long as she lived, she
would never consent to such a *mésalliance*. In her alarm at
the possibility of such a disaster, her thoughts turned once
more to the young Princess of England, and she was heard
to say repeatedly, that she wished the King would make
choice of a bride who was his equal in rank, and so well suited
to him in all respects. For a time, the hopes of Queen
Henrietta revived, and these rumours reached Cromwell's
minister at the Hague, who reported that Harry Killigrew, a
talkative gentleman of Charles II.'s bedchamber, spoke confidently of "a marriage between the King of France and
Charles Stuart's sister in Paris." But Louis despised his
slight and delicate girl cousin, and never showed the least
inclination to choose Henrietta for his bride. "It was evident," observes Mademoiselle, "that the King was not pre-
possessed in her favour, although the Queen felt sincere
affection for her." Mazarin himself, anxious to strengthen
his political position, was inclined to marry the King to the
Princess of Savoy, and with a view to this alliance, the
Dowager Duchess of Savoy, or Madame Royale, as the eldest
daughter of Henri Quatre was still called in France, brought
her daughter to meet the King at Lyons, in November 1658.
The Princess Marguerite was very small and olive-skinned,

with no particular charm to recommend her. 'Sire," said
Marie Mancini, "you will never let them give you such an
ugly wife!" And the Queen-mother was heard to say, that
she thought the Princess of England would have made a far
better wife for her son. Whether Marie Mancini's influence
prevailed, or whether the secret proposals from the King of
Spain, which had reached Mazarin, put an end to his former
plan, it is certain that, after the first meeting at Lyons, the
King showed no further inclination to pay his addresses to
the Princess of Savoy. At the end of a few days, Madame
Royale left France, and the Court returned to Paris. The
Queen-mother told Mademoiselle that she was thankful to
get rid of the whole party, and the King became more
devoted than ever to Marie Mancini. It was even said that
he implored his mother on his knees to allow the marriage.
But Anne of Austria was inflexible, and even Mazarin dared
not sanction such a departure from inviolable tradition, and
told the King that if he persisted, it would be impossible for
him to remain his minister. Finally the Cardinal took the
wiser course of sending his nieces away. Louis shed tears as
he parted from Marie Mancini, but once she was gone, he
soon forgot her, and turned his thoughts towards the marriage
with the Infanta which was now decided upon. All through
that summer, negotiations of peace were carried on between
Mazarin and the Spanish Court. A truce was soon proclaimed, and in July, the Cardinal went to meet Dom Luis de
Haro at the famous Ile des Faisans, near Saint-Jean de Luz,
where the terms of the treaty were discussed during the next
four months.

The prospect of peace after so many years of protracted
hostilities between the two countries, was hailed with joy on
all sides. The English royal family shared in the general
rejoicing, and entertained hopes that once France and Spain
had made friends, the two countries would join in restoring
Charles II. to the throne of his fathers. But their expecta-
tions were again doomed to disappointment. The death of
Cromwell in September 1658, had not produced the change
of feeling, which the Royalists had expected to see in England,
and when Charles travelled to Fontarabia, to lay his claims

before the French and Spanish ministers, he was coldly
received by both parties. As a last means of softening the
powerful Cardinal, he offered to marry his niece Hortense,
the handsomest of all the Mancini, who, many years afterwards, became well known at his own Court as the Duchesse
de Mazarin. Even Queen Henrietta, who had violently
opposed her son's union with the widowed Duchesse de
Châtillon, as unworthy of his rank, eagerly embraced this
plan, as a last chance of enlisting Mazarin on his side. But
the wily minister replied that the King of England did him
too much honour, and that as long as a cousin of his own
remained unmarried, he must not stoop to think of a simple
demoiselle. This allusion to Mademoiselle's scornful rejection
of the exiled King's suit, was bitterly felt by his mother, and
the matter dropped. Charles returned to Brussels in a worse
plight than ever. His brothers lived at Breda, as pensioners
on the Princess of Orange's bounty, and he was compelled to
dismiss his servants and to pawn his plate. So great was
the poverty to which he found himself reduced, that he was
actually in want of clothes, and had to wear his coat thread-
bare.

The Treaty of the Pyrenees was finally signed on the 7th
of November 1659, and a month afterwards, Louis XIV.
started on a progress through the southern provinces of his
kingdom, accompanied by his mother and brother, by
Mademoiselle, Cardinal Mazarin and the whole Court.
Christmas was spent at Toulouse, and the early spring in
visiting the chief towns of Provence and Languedoc. By
April, Saint-Jean de Luz was reached, and at the same time,
the King of Spain and his daughter arrived at San Sebastian.
A series of prolonged conferences now took place, in which
all the details of the marriage contract, and the exact
etiquette to be observed at the wedding, were carefully
arranged. In her *Memoirs*, Mademoiselle has left us a
lively record of the wrangling over questions of precedence to
which this gave rise, and which in her eyes and in those of
Monsieur were of such inestimable importance. She has
also given us a minute account af the royal wedding, which
was solemnised twice over, first on Spanish, then on French

territory, on the 3d and 9th days of June. When the nuptial ceremonies had been at length concluded, the Court set out once more on its homeward journey.

While these splendid but tedious pageants were occupying the attention of all Europe, the young Princess Henrietta of England remained alone at Colombes, with her sad mother. She had witnessed the magnificent preparations made by her cousins for the royal wedding, and the dazzling display of robes and jewels destined to be worn on this occasion, before the Court set out on this memorable journey. Even her young cousins of Orléans, Mademoiselle's step-sisters, had been summoned to bear the new Queen's train on the wedding-day. Brought up, as Henrietta had been at the French Court, and accustomed to take a part in its festive scenes, from her earliest childhood, she may well have felt life at Colombes dull and lonely, and have sighed, a little wearily, over the perpetual round of services in the convent at Chaillot. She was fifteen years of age now, and full of youthful vivacity and brightness. We possess more than one description of her appearance, at this period of her life, which give a good idea of her budding charms. Father Cyprian is never tired of dwelling on the perfections of his "*petite princesse.*" He extols her rare beauty of face, her exquisite figure, the grace of her movements, her skill in dancing and playing musical instruments, her lively wit and excellent disposition. Others, beside the too partial old priest, now began to discover her attractions. The practice of writing portraits had lately become fashionable at Court. Mademoiselle began by composing her own, and gave a fairly correct, although decidedly flattering, description of her appearance and character. All the wits of the day followed her example. An accomplished lady of the Précieuses group, Madame de Brégis, wrote the following portrait of the Princesse d'Angleterre, in June 1658, when hopes were still entertained that she might one day be the bride of Louis XIV.

"To begin with her height, I must tell you that this young Princess is still growing, and that she will soon attain a perfect stature. Her air is as noble as her birth, her hair is of a

D

bright chestnut hue, and her complexion rivals that of the
gayest flowers. The snowy whiteness of her skin betrays the
lilies from which she sprang. Her eyes are blue and brilliant, her lips ruddy, her throat beautiful, her arms and hands
well made. Her charms show that she was born on a throne,
and is destined to return there. Her wit is lively and agreeable. She is admired in her serious moments and beloved
in her most ordinary ones ; she is gentle and obliging, and
her kindness of heart will not allow her to laugh at others, as
cleverly as she could, if she chose. She spends most of her
time in learning all that can make a princess perfect, and de
votes her spare moments to the most varied accomplishments.
She dances with incomparable grace, she sings like an angel,
and the spinet is never so well played as by her fair hands.
All this makes the young Cleopatra the most amiable Princess
in the world, and if Fortune once unties the fold that wraps
her eyes, to gaze upon her, she will not refuse to give her the
greatest of earth's glories, for she deserves them well. I wish
them for her, more passionately than I can say."

A year later, Sir John Reresby gives us a pleasant picture
of his own intercourse with this fascinating Princess. This
young Englishman had spent some months at Paris in 1654,
studying French and learning the guitar and dancing. He
tells us how, in those days, he often watched the King, the
Duke of York and Prince Rupert, playing at billiards in a hall of
the Palais-Royal. but how he dared not approach them, for
fear Cromwell might be told that he was paying court to the
exiled monarch, and take the opportunity to confiscate his
Yorkshire estates. In 1657, Reresby returned to spend the
winter at a pension in Paris, and then paid frequent visits
to the French Court, and went " as often as he durst " to pay
his respects to the Queen-mother of England, who received
him with especial favour, since he was related to several noble
French families, and had three cousins among the nuns in the
convent of Chaillot. That summer he went back to England,
but in November 1659, he once more arrived in Paris, which
he had before found so agreeable a residence. Now that the
dreaded Lord Protector was dead, his fears vanished, and he
lost no time in paying his respects to Queen Henrietta.

"As soon as I had put myself into some equipage," Sir John writes in his diary, "I endeavoured to be acquainted at the Queen-mother of England's Court, which she then kept at the Palais-Royal, which I did without any great notice taken of it in England, the King and Dukes being then banished into Flanders, and none of her children with Henrietta Maria, but the Princess Henrietta. Few Englishmen making there their Court, made me the better received, besides speaking the language of the Court and dancing passably well. The young Princess, then aged about fifteen years, used me with all the civil freedom that might be, made me dance with her, played on the harpsichord to me in Her Highness's chamber, suffered me to attend upon her, when she walked in the garden with the rest of her retinue, and sometimes to toss her in a swing made of a cable which she sat upon, tied between two trees, and in fine suffered me to be present at most of her innocent diversions. The Queen commanded me to be there, as often as I conveniently could. She had a great affection for England, notwithstanding the severe usage she and hers had received from it. She discoursed much with the great men and ladies of France, in praise of the people and country —of their courage, their generosity and good nature—and would attribute the rebellion to a few desperate and infatuated persons, rather than the temper of the nation. To give an instance of her care, in regard to our countrymen, I happened one day to carry an English gentleman to Court, and he, willing to be very gay, had got him a garniture of rich red and yellow ribbons to his suit. The Queen observing the absurd effect, called to me and advised me to tell my friend to mend his taste a little, as to his choice of ribbons, for the two colours he had joined, were ridiculous in France, and would make people laugh at him."

Another and still more welcome visitor, took advantage of the King and Cardinal's absence, to come to Paris. This was Charles II., who, on his return from Spain, paid a brief visit to his mother, in her country house at Colombes. His sister Henrietta alludes to this intended visit, in the first letter that we have from her pen. It bears no date, but the mention of the peace which had been proclaimed in November, shows that

it belongs to this period. Like all Henrietta's letters, it is
written in French, and the original, still bearing the seals and
brown silk ties that fastened it together, is preserved among
the Royal MSS. in the library at Lambeth Palace.

"I would not let Milord Inchiquin leave, without assuring
Your Majesty of my respect, and thanking you for the honour
you do me, in writing to me so often. I fear that this may
give you too much trouble, and I should be sorry if Your
Majesty should take so much for a little sister, who does not
deserve it, but who can at least acknowledge and rejoice in
the honour you do her. I hope the peace will give you all
the happiness you desire, and then I shall be happy, because
of the love and respect I bear Your Majesty. It is a cause of
great joy to me, since it gives me the hope of seeing you,
which is most passionately desired by your very humble
servant."

Soon afterwards, Charles arrived at Colombes, and his
presence had the good effect of removing the remains of the
ill-feeling that had so long divided him from his mother.
But Cardinal Mazarin would not give him leave to remain
long on French territory, and he soon retired to Brussels.
So the winter months passed gloomily. The situation remained unchanged in England, and the Cardinal's resolute
refusal to give her son the least encouragement, had deeply
distressed Queen Henrietta. To add to her troubles,
Mazarin took advantage of a quarrel which had arisen over
the government of Orange, to seize on that city, and this
ancient principality, from which the Princes of Orange had
long taken their title, was annexed to France. Henrietta's
attempt at intervention on her grandson's behalf, proved
ineffectual, but the boy Prince himself never forgave the
wrong, and from that moment, became the bitter enemy of
Louis XIV. Fortune seemed to have utterly forsaken the
cause of the Stuarts. Charles and his brothers were left to
drag on a miserable existence at Brussels or Breda, in the
utmost poverty, and without a friend to help them, but their
generous sister, Mary of Orange. Still the King, after his
wont, found means to enjoy himself, and a letter which he
wrote to his sister Henrietta from Brussels, on the 7th of

February, breathes his usual strain of light-hearted gaiety. This letter belongs to the series preserved in the *Archives du Ministère des Affaires étrangères* at Paris, and is one of the few which are written in French.

"I begin this French letter by assuring you, that I am very glad to be scolded by you. I withdraw what I said with great joy, since you scold me so pleasantly, but I will never take back the love I have for you, and you show me so much affection that the only quarrel we are ever likely to have, will be as to which of us two loves the other best. In that respect, I will never yield to you. I send you this letter by the hands of Janton, who is the best girl in the world. We talk of you every day, and wish we were with you, a thousand times a day. Her voice has almost entirely returned, and she sings very well. She has learnt the song *de ma queue.* 'I prithee, sweet harte, come tell me and do not lie,' and a number of others. When you send me the scapular, I promise to wear it always, for love of you. Tell Madame Boude that I will soon send her my portrait. Just now the painter is away, but he returns in a few days. Tell me, I beg of you, how you spend your time, for if you stayed long at Chaillot in this miserable weather, you must have been not a little bored.

"For the future, pray do not treat me with so much cere-mony, or address me with so many Your Majesties, for between you and me, there should be nothing but affec-tion.[1] C. R."

[1] "Je commence cette lettre icy en françois, en vous assurant que je suis fort aise de quoy vous me grondez ; je me dedis avec beaucoup de joye, puisque vous me querellez si obligeamment, mais je ne me dedieray jamais de l'amitié que j'ay pour vous, et vous me donnez tant de marques de la vostre, que nous n'aurons jamais autre querelle, que celle de qui de nous deux aimerons le plus l'un l'autre, mais en cela je ne vous céderay jamais. Je vous envoye celle-ci par les mains de Janton, qui est la meilleure fille du monde. Nous parlons tous les jours de vous, et souhaitons mille fois le jour d'estre avec vous. Sa voix lui est revenue quasi tout-à-fait, et elle chante fort bien. Elle m'a appris le chanson de ma queue. 'I prithee, sweet hearte, come tell me and do not lie,' et quantité d'autres. Quand vous m'envoyerez le scapulaire, je vous promets de la porter toujours pour l'amour de vous.

"Dites à Madame Boude que je luy envoyeray bientôt mon portrait. Pré-sentément le peintre n'est pas en cette ville, mais il reviendra dans peu de jours. Mandez-moi, je vous pris, comme vous passez votre temps, car si vous avez été

This letter, which breathes so tender an affection for his young sister and is in many respects so characteristic an effusion of the Merry Monarch, bears the royal seal, and is addressed on the fourth page "*For deare, deare Sister.*"

Four days after it was written, Monk entered London at the head of his army, and requested all the members of Parliament who had been driven out in 1648, to return to the House. A month later, the Long Parliament voted its own dissolution, and Monk entered into negotiations with the exiled King. Charles now joined his sister Mary at Breda, where he drew up the famous Declaration, proclaiming a general amnesty and religious toleration for all his subjects. His restoration was now morally certain, and from all sides congratulations and protestations of friendship came pouring in. The French and Spanish Kings, who had so lately declined to give him any promise of support, now vied with each other in the warmth of their expressions. Mazarin was foremost in his congratulations, and intimated his readiness to give the King either of his remaining nieces in marriage, while the High and Mighty States of Holland, who had treated the exiled Princes so harshly, now loaded them with presents and honours. "Whoever is King of England," they said in private, "were it the devil himself, we must be friends with him." English Royalists and foreign ambassadors alike hastened to Breda. Guns were fired and bonfires kindled, and before long the whole place was in an uproar of tumultuous rejoicing.

In the midst of all this turmoil, Charles found time to write another affectionate note to his sister at Paris. It is dated the 29th of April, and bears the inscription : "*Pour ma chere, chere soeur*" on the fourth page.

"I wrote to you last week, and meant to send my letter in Janton's packet, but she had already closed hers, so I had to give my letter to Mason. I have received yours of the 23rd, which is so full of marks of affection that I know not how to

quelque temps à Chaillot, par cette méchante saison, vous vous y estes un peu beaucoup ennuyée. Pour l'avenir, je vous prie, ne me traitez pas avec tant de cérémonie, en me donnant tant de Majestés, car je ne veux pas qu'il y ait autre chose entre nous deux qu'amitié."

find words in which to express my joy. In return, I must assure you that I love you as much as possible, and that neither absence, nor any other cause will alter the affection I have promised to bear you, in the smallest degree. Never fear that others who are present shall get the advantage over you, for, believe me, no one can share the love I cherish for you.

"I have sent to Gentseau to order some summer clothes, and have told him to take the ribbons to you, for you to choose the trimming and feathers. Thank you for the song which you have sent me. I do not yet know if it is pretty, as Janton has not yet learnt it. If you only knew how often we talk of you, and wish you were here, you would understand how much I long to see you, and do me the justice to believe that I am entirely yours.[1]   C. R."

On the 1st of May the new Parliament met, and after reading the King's letter, at once proclaimed " that, according to the fundamental laws of the kingdom, the government resides and ought to reside, in the King, Lords and Commons." Well might the widowed Countess of Derby write :—" The change is so great, I can hardly believe it. My letter of the 12th of last month would tell you of the hope we had of the restoration of the King. This one will tell you that, by the grace of God, the Parliament has done justice and recognised His Majesty. On the 1st of this month, the Houses of Lords and Commons unanimously consented to It. All are delighted,

---

[1] " Je vous écrivis la semaine passé, et croyait l'envoyer dans le paquet de Janton, mais elle avait fermé le sien, de sorte que j'étais contraint de donner ma lettre à Mason. J'ay la votre du 23e où j'ay trouvé tant de marques d'amitié que je ne savais trouver de parolles pour exprimer ma joye. En recompense, je vous assure que je vous aime autant que je le puis faire, et que ny l'absence, ni aucune autre chose, puisse jamais me detourner en la moindre façon de cette amitié que je vous ay promisé, et n'ayez point peur que ceux qui sont présent auront l'avantage sur vous, car croyez-moi, l'amitié que j'ay pour vous ne peut pas estre partaigée. J'ai envoyé à Gentseau de me faire des habits pour l'ésté, et je luy ay donné ordre de vous apporter le ruban, afin que vous choissiez la garniture et les plumes.

" Je vous remercie pour la chanson que vous m'avez envoyé ; je ne sçay pas si elle est jolie, car Janton ne la sçait pas encore.

" Si vous sçaviez combien de fois nous parlons de vous, et vous souhaitons icy nous diriez qu'on souhaite fort de vous voir, et faites moy la justice de croire que je suis tout à vous."

and have given evidence of their repentance for their past
conduct. The King has written three letters, to the two
Houses and to General Monk, who has conducted this affair
with a prudence that will cause him to be esteemed for all
generations. It is true that this passes human wisdom, and
that, in all humility, we ought to recognise in it the hand of
the Eternal : it is beyond our understanding, and can never
be enough admired."

A frenzy of enthusiasm now ran through the nation. The
King's presence was clamorously desired, and the Parliament
sent commissioners over to Holland, dutifully to invite his
return. They bore with them a gift of £30,000, and the
happy King called the Princess of Orange and the Duke of
York, to see the gold, which he had so sorely needed, spread
out before him. Gifts of money and pictures, a royal yacht
and a sumptuous bed, were humbly presented by their High-
Mightinesses of Holland, and the King was literally besieged
with deputations from all parts. On the 23d, he embarked at
the Hague, and the name of the ship which bore him, was
changed from the *Naseby* to that of the *Royal Charles*. On
the eve of his embarkation, the Queen-mother sent him a
touching little note from Chaillot, begging him to remember
those who had suffered for him and his father, and to satisfy
her anxiety by sending her news of his arrival as speedily as
possible. "My prayers," she adds, "go with you to England."

A week later, a courier reached Colombes to announce that
the King had landed safely at Dover, where he had been
received with acclamation, and was now about to make his
triumphal entry into London. The messenger also brought a
letter for the Princess, written by the King from Canterbury,
on the 26th of May.

"I was so tormented with businesse at the Hague, that I
could not write to you before my departure, but I left orders
with my sister (the Princess of Orange) to send you a small
present from me, which I hope you will soon receave. I
arrived yesterday at Dover, where I found Monk, with a great
number of the nobility, who almost overwhelmed me with
kindnesse and joy for my returne. My head is so dreadfully

stunned with the acclamations of the people, and the vast amount of businesse, that I know not whether I am writing sense or nonsense. Therefore pardon me if I say no more than that I am entirely yours.—For my dear sister." [1]

The present which the Princess shortly received, to her great delight, was a handsome side-saddle with trappings of green velvet, richly embroidered and trimmed with gold lace. She wrote back promptly from Colombes :—

" I have received the letter you have sent me by Mr Progers, and which has delighted me in no small degree, for to know that you have reached England, and at the same time that you have remembered me, has given me the greatest joy in the world. In truth, I wish I could express all that I feel for you, and you would see how true it is, that no one is more your servant than I am."

Her mother poured out her heart in the following note to her son, written from Colombes, at five o'clock on the morning of the 9th of June :—

" You may judge of my joy, and if you are torn in pieces over in England, I have had my share here in France. I am going this moment to Chaillot to have a *Te Deum* sung there, and on to Paris to light our *feux de joies*. We had them here yesterday. I think I shall have all Paris to congratulate me. Indeed, you would never imagine what joy there is here. We must praise God. All this is from His hand. You can see it plainly. I will not detain you any longer. God bless you. I send you a letter from Madame de Motteville, which M. de Montagu opened, he tells me, by accident. He is very sorry, and begs me to close it, but I shall send it as it is. You will forgive him."

Then came the news of the King's splendid reception in London, and his mother wept tears of joy, when she heard that he was once more lodged in his own palace of Whitehall.

" I stood in the Strand," wrote Evelyn in his journal, " and beheld it, and blessed God. All this was done without one drop of blood shed, and by that very army which rebelled

[1] This letter is given by Mrs Everett Green, from the original in M. Donnadieu's collection.

against him.   But it was the Lord's doing, for such a Restoration was never mentioned in any history, ancient or modern, since the return of the Jews from the Babylonish Captivity."

No one was more surprised than Charles himself.   "It is certainly a mistake," he said, with his usual irony, "that I did not come back sooner, for I have not met anyone to-day who has not professed to have always desired my return."

Far off in Paris, the long exiled and widowed Queen shared in the ecstasy of joy which thrilled the nation's heart.   The sorrows and humiliations of the past were forgotten in the rapture of the present.   All Paris thronged to the Palais-Royal.   The faithful friends who had sorrowed with her now came to rejoice in her joy.   The fickle courtiers, who had treated her with neglect and contempt in her dark hours, hastened to assure her of their regard, in the first flush of her revived prosperity.   Sir John Reresby, who was still in Paris, describes the extraordinary joy with which the news of the King's restoration was hailed, the bonfires and salutes which celebrated the happy event.   He was present at the noble ball given on this occasion, at the Palais-Royal, to which "everybody of the greatest quality was invited, and all the Englishmen in Paris had admittance."   At the Queen's command, Sir John himself led out the Cardinal's beautiful niece, Hortense Mancini.   He stayed on in Paris till the 2d of August, and tells us in his journal, how favourite a resort the English Queen's Court had now become, and how far more largely attended it was than that of the two French Queens, on their return to Fontainebleau.   "For our Queen's good humour and wit, and the great beauty of the young Princess, her daughter, made it more attractive than the solemn Spanish etiquette observed in the others."   Sir John adds that he himself received more honours from the Queen and Princess than he deserved, and finally went home with letters of particular recommendation to the King, from his mother and sister, which procured him a very favourable reception at Whitehall.

During the next few weeks, the Palais-Royal was besieged with English gentlemen, on their way home, all of whom came to beg for a few words of recommendation to the King, from the Queen or her daughter. Several notes of this description are to be found among the Princess's letters at Lambeth. On the 30th of June she writes:—

"After having only last week excused myself for troubling you so often with letters, you will think me quite incorrigible. You would certainly not have had to suffer from this fresh importunity, had not the bearer of these lines prayed me so earnestly that it was impossible to refuse. But I will not trespass upon your kindness, excepting to assure you that I am your very humble servant."

On the 30th of July, she writes again by Lord Dungarvan, who had begged the Queen for a letter to her son:—

"Even if you were likely to forget me, my importunity will certainly prevent that, but this time you would not have been troubled, had it not been for the prayer of my Lord Dungarvan. The Queen herself would have written had she not been ill, but, thank God! her complaint is not serious, since it was only caused by eating too much fruit. I hope you will excuse me this time, for I could not say no, since the bearer is a relative of Madame de Kinalmeky, and I will once more assure you, that I am your very humble servant."

On the 17th of August, the Princess appears to have sent as many as three notes to her brother, by different messengers, and, as she says merrily, the King may well declare that, in spite of all her promises of amendment, she is the most incorrigible of sinners. Two of the three are preserved at Lambeth, and were written from Colombes. The bearer of the first was an astrologer, who cast horoscopes after the fashion then prevailing at the Court of France, and amused great ladies with his conjuring tricks.

"I must write to you by M. Février, who is going to England, in the assurance that he will deceive more than half the kingdom. He even hopes to begin with you! We are soon going to Paris to see the entry of the Queen, which takes place on the 26th of this month. I would offer to tell you all about it, if my Lord St. Albans were not staying here over that time. He will acquit himself of the task far better than I can, although I am more than anyone your most humble servant."

The other letter was written at the request of Mr Fitzpatrick.

"This porter, Mr Fitzpatrick, has begged me earnestly to write to you, so that, although three letters in one day will make you think me very troublesome, I have already sinned so deeply in this respect, that I may as well venture it once more. Madame de Fiennes has just come in, and begs me to tell you that it is lucky for you she has not an army, for, had she one at her disposal, she would revenge herself on you for pretending that you have read her letters, when you have not even opened them !"

Madame de Fiennes, who was apparently on intimate terms with both the Princess and her brother, had been for many years one of Queen Henrietta's ladies-in-waiting, and had married the young Comte des Chapelles, a son of her mistress's old nurse. The disparity of age, as well as of rank, between the two, had excited great surprise in the French royal family, and Mademoiselle spoke with undisguised contempt of this "*fille de quarante ans*," who chose to marry a boy of two-and-twenty, simply for the sake of his good looks, and who now found herself related to all the Queen's waiting-women. But Madame de Fiennes was a clever woman, and, in spite of her marriage, she managed to fill her pockets, and retain her influence at Court. She was a great favourite of the King's brother, Monsieur, and remained sincerely attached to his future wife, the Princess Henrietta. When, in after years, she accompanied her mistress, the Queen-mother, to England, she kept Madame well informed of all that happened at her brother's Court, and acquired a great reputation for her witty letters and sharp sayings. But her too great freedom of speech proved the cause of many troubles, and the broils and intrigues in which she became involved did not add to the harmony of the royal family.

CHAPTER V

1660.

THE sudden change in the fortunes of the English Royal Family was naturally not without its effect on the future of the Princess Henrietta. One of its first results was to bring forward a suitor for her hand, in the person of Louis XIV.'s only brother, Philippe de France, commonly known as Monsieur.

To do Monsieur justice, it must be owned that he had fallen in love with his cousin, some time before her brother's Restoration. Mademoiselle complains repeatedly of his infatuation for ' *cette maison d'Angleterre*," and ascribes the influence gained over him by the Princess Palatine, Anne de Gonzague, wife of Prince Edward, the youngest son of the Queen of Bohemia, entirely to her skill in approaching him on his weak side, and promising to help on his marriage with Henrietta. Mademoiselle resented this obstinate passion of Monsieur the more, because, after her return to Court, she herself had seriously contemplated the idea of a marriage with him. The cousins had been brought up together. Mademoiselle, who was thirteen years older, had played and quarrelled with Monsieur from the days of his babyhood, and retained a certain liking for him all through her life. They bickered perpetually over the merest trifles, but, all the same, Monsieur admired his strong-minded cousin, and she, on her part, had acquired the habit of considering him as her own property. But her haughty and imperious temper, as usual,

stood in her way, and the Queen-mother, whom she was perpetually affronting, showed herself decidedly averse to the
marriage. Monsieur's evident inclination for his fair young
English cousin, on the contrary, was in the highest degree
agreeable to his mother, and when the King's marriage with
the Infanta had been finally arranged, she declared that her
only other wish was to see her younger son wedded to the
gentle Princess whom she loved as her own child.

Meanwhile, Queen Henrietta, anxious to see her daughter
settled, had made tentative proposals both to her nephew, the
young Duke of Savoy, and to the Grand Duke of Tuscany.
But neither of these seemed particularly desirous to wed the
sister of a crownless and penniless King. Besides which,
Cardinal Mazarin was bent on securing these Princes for the
two younger daughters of Gaston, Duke of Orléans, and had
laid his plans with his usual wiliness. So the English Queen's
advances were coldly received, and Mademoiselle tells us how
King Louis, who was fond of teasing his brother about his
impatience to get married, would often say as they sat
together in their coach on the way to Spain : "Come, cheer
up ! You will marry the Princess of England, for no one else
will have her. Monsieur de Savoie and Monsieur de Florence
have both declined the honour, so I am sure that you will
marry her in the end." It was not long, adds Mademoiselle,
before this marriage, which La Palatine was secretly arranging
for poor Monsieur, began to be freely discussed. For herself,
she owns, she could take no interest in the affair, although,
she hastens to add, that she had not the least wish to marry
His Royal Highness herself. And Gui Patin, that clever and
satirical doctor, whose letters are full of allusions to contemporary events, observes, about this time, that people say
King Charles of England is going to give his sister to the
young Duc d'Anjou, but that the proposal has aroused great
jealousy and discussion at Court.

The Cardinal's objection to the marriage was the real
difficulty, but from the moment of Charles II.'s restoration
all this was changed. Accordingly, no sooner had the Court
returned to Fontainebleau, than Monsieur hastened to pay
his addresses to the Princess, and took every opportunity of

declaring his intentions. A week after her arrival, Anne of Austria came herself to Colombes, and conducted Henrietta and her mother to Fontainebleau, to introduce them to the young Queen Marie Thérèse. A few days afterwards, on the 12th of August, Monsieur gave a grand ball at Saint-Cloud, which the King had lately purchased from Hervard, the Comptroller of Finances, and given his brother as a country residence. Both the Queen-mothers were present on this occasion, and Monsieur opened the ball with the Princess Henrietta. Her dancing was extremely admired, and the approaching marriage of the youthful pair became a common topic of conversation at the Court. On the 20th of August, Queen Henrietta wrote to her daughter of Orange that her sister's marriage was virtually settled, and that Charles II. had expressed his readiness to give his consent, although the formal demand had not yet been made. On the 24th, the Queen and Princess both came to Paris, to be present at the entry of the young Queen, and the next day, Henrietta Maria wrote the following letter to her son :—

"I arrived in this town yesterday, and, as soon as I was here, the Queen came to see me, and informed me that she came on behalf of her son, the King, to tell me that he joined her in begging me to do Monsieur the honour of giving him my daughter in marriage. They have decided to send an ambassador to present this request to you, and meanwhile, the Queen has given me many friendly messages, both for you and for myself. I replied that the King and herself did my daughter much honour, and that I would not fail to inform you of their wishes. 'I beg you to do this,' she said, 'until we are able to send an ambassador.' I believe that you will give me permission to say that you approve of this union. I assure you that your sister is by no means averse to the idea, and as for Monsieur, he is very much in love (*tout-à-fait amoureux*) and extremely impatient for your answer."

The marriage was naturally one after Henrietta Maria's own heart. Monsieur was twenty years of age, exceedingly handsome, and passionately in love with his cousin. On the death of his uncle, Gaston, Duke of Orléans, in February 1660,

the King had invested him with the Duchies of Orléans,
Valois, and Chartres, and the estates of Saint-Cloud, Villers-
Cotterets and Montargis. In age, rank and fortune he was
an eminently suitable match, "a husband," says Madame de
Motteville, "not to be refused by the greatest princess in the
world." And besides the natural pride which the *fille de
Henri Quatre* felt in the prospect of seeing her daughter
married into the royal house, this union would spare her the
pain of parting from her dearly-loved child, who need never
now leave France.

On the 26th of August, the entry of the young King and
Queen took place. The weather was brilliant, and the people
were enthusiastic. Eye-witnesses describe the scene as one
of the most splendid ever known in Paris. From the bal-
conies of the Hotel de Beauvais, close to an Arc de Triomphe
erected at the gates of St Antoine in honour of the occasion,
the English Queen and Princess, together with the Queen-
mother of France, looked down on the glittering procession,
as it paused to salute them in its course. They saw the
young Queen enthroned in her golden chariot, serene and
stately in her royal robes, with her placid face unmoved by
the shouts of the crowd. At her right hand rode the King,
followed by the flower of France's chivalry—glorious, says the
chronicler, in youth and majesty as the Sun-god himself—
while on her left, Henrietta saw her betrothed, riding a noble
white horse, and wearing a richly-embroidered suit, blazing
with jewels. Long was that spectacle remembered in years
to come, the brilliant harbinger of a still more brilliant period
in the history of France. The people had good reason to
shout for joy that day, for they applauded not only the
presence of their popular King, and the coming of a youthful
Queen, but the restoration of the long-wished-for peace and
the dawn of a new and better day. The summer morning
was full of triumph and gladness, bright hopes were stirring
in the air, and great things were expected from this young
and gracious King. And the youthful Princess, who watched
her royal lover ride by, amid the delirious shouts of the
multitude, may well have thought, as she stood on the
threshold of her wedded life, that for her, too, after all her

past troubles and dangers, a happier day was breaking, and that down the long vista of the years to come, love and joy were waiting to strew her path with blessings.

But there were shadows already on the sunny prospect, and in that triumphal procession there was more than one angry and discontented soul. "The quarrels over precedence have been endless," wrote Queen Henrietta Maria to her son, "and three dukes have been banished from Court because they refused to yield *le pas* to the foreign princes then in Paris." But the most tiresome, the most unreasonable of all, had been her own niece, Mademoiselle. On this occasion, she utterly refused to allow Princess Henrietta the place due to her rank, and contended stoutly that since, in Flanders, the Prince de Condé had taken precedence of the Duke of York, she, as a grand-daughter of France, need not give way to a daughter of England. "Up to this time," she writes, "I had only looked on the Princess as a little girl, without paying the least attention to her conduct, but now I felt that it was time to uphold the privileges and dignity of my rank." The result was a fine wrangle between Mademoiselle and her aunt, Anne of Austria, who scolded her niece roundly for her impertinence, and was extremely angry when Mademoiselle appealed to the Cardinal to defend her cause. The end of it all was, that Mademoiselle quarrelled with both her aunt and Monsieur, and refused to visit the English royal family, until Henrietta Maria, satisfied with the Court's decision in her daughter's favour, waived the point and allowed the Princess to give her haughty cousin the honours to which she pretended. Another cause of Mademoiselle's ill-temper, which, as she owns, made her feel extremely dissatisfied with herself at this time, was the revival of the old discussions over the King of England's marriage. Now that he was on his throne again, she would gladly have welcomed back her once discarded suitor, and, as she assures us, might have entered into negotiations with his mother through Madame de Motteville, had she been so minded. But since she had refused him in the day of exile and poverty, she was too proud to begin the wooing now. Charles on his part, had not the least intention of doing his imperious cousin the honour of asking her to be his wife a second time, and,

E

although her fortune would have been very acceptable in his still needy condition, he quite declined to act on the hints which Mademoiselle took care to give him.

"I greatly desire the marriage of Mademoiselle," wrote Lady Derby, in reply to a message from her sister-in-law, Madame de la Trémouille, "but the King has an aversion for it, on account of the contempt she has shown for him. I have spoken of her to the Marquis of Ormonde, but I meet with small encouragement." And again: "I have had Mademoiselle proposed, and I have some hopes. If the King thinks of riches, he could not have more than with Mademoiselle, which I would wish with all my heart, but I fear that, having been despised in his poverty, he would be unlikely now to contemplate such a match."

Lady Derby's words proved correct, and Mademoiselle was left to console herself with the bitter reflection that "she had acted like a fool, and had only herself to thank." Meanwhile, she had the mortification of seeing the *petite fille* she despised so much, already received by the young King and Queen as one of their own family. They came with Monsieur, two days after their state entry, to pay a visit to their aunt of England, at the Palais-Royal, and took the Princess in their carriage for a drive through Paris. Ten days later, the Cardinal gave one of his sumptuous festivals in honour of Monsieur's betrothal, and entertained both royal families at a banquet, where Roman singers delighted them with their melodies, and Spanish players acted a comedy in their presence. That evening, instead of arriving with the French royalties, Monsieur entered the room in the company of his future bride and mother-in-law, and as he led the fair young Princess, robed in pure white, by the hand, through the Cardinal's brilliantly-lighted gallery, an eye-witness describes her, as looking, for all the world, like his guardian angel.

Monsieur was now very impatient to hasten the marriage, and showed himself so ardent a lover, that his brother the King laughed at him openly, and teased him, by saying that he need not be in so great a hurry to marry the bones of the Holy Innocents. "It is true," observes the jealous Mademoiselle, "that the Princess was excessively thin, yet it must be owned that she was extremely amiable. There was a peculiar grace in all her actions, and she was so courteous, that everyone who approached her, was charmed." And Madame de Motteville, always careful and accurate in her descriptions, speaks of Henrietta in the following terms:—

"The Princess of England was above middle height; she was very graceful, and her figure, which was not faultless, did not appear as imperfect as it really was. Her beauty was not of the most perfect kind, but her charming manners made her very attractive. She had an extremely delicate and very white skin, with a bright, natural colour, a complexion, so to speak, of roses and jasmine. Her eyes were small, but very soft and sparkling, her nose not bad, her lips were rosy, and her teeth as white and regular as you could wish, but her face was too long, and her great thinness seemed to threaten her beauty with early decay. She dressed her hair and whole person in a most becoming manner, and she was so lovable in herself, that she could not fail to please. She had not been able to become Queen, but, to make up for this disappointment, she wished to reign in the hearts of all good people, by the charm of her person, and the real beauty of her soul. She had already shown much perception and good sense, and, although her youth had kept her hidden from public gaze, it was easy to see that, when she appeared on the great theatre of the Court of France, she would play one of the leading parts there."

Before the marriage could be celebrated, however, Henrietta Maria had determined to take her daughter on a visit to England. One object of her intended journey was to secure the payment of her own jointure, and of a dowry for the Princess. The other was to prevent the Duke of York's public recognition of his marriage with Anne Hyde, the Chancellor's daughter, and till lately maid-of-honour to the Princess Royal. This secret union, which had taken place in Flanders during the previous year, was a source of bitter annoyance to the royal family, especially the Princess of Orange and the Queen. The Duke was deeply attached to his wife, but he listened to slanderous reports, prompted by the malice and envy of her enemies, and after his return to

England, he refused to see the unfortunate Duchess, and allowed her to be kept a prisoner in her father's house. The Queen, who bore no good-will to Clarendon and his family, was loud in her denunciations of her daughter-in-law's conduct. She told Charles II. that she would leave no stone unturned, to annul a marriage that would bring so great dishonour on the Crown, and declared that if "the woman" entered Whitehall by one door, she would leave it by another. Henrietta Maria was anxious the Princess Royal should join her in Paris and proceed with her to England, but Charles, eager to enjoy the presence of the sister who had been so generous a friend in his days of exile, urged her to come straight to London. As usual, Mary found herself torn in pieces by these opposite entreaties, and wrote in pathetic terms to Charles, begging to be allowed to obey her mother. " For God's sake, agree between you what I have to do, for I know what it is to displease both of you. God keep me from it again!" But Charles insisted, and this time the Queen-mother had to give way, and to content herself with the prospect of a happy family meeting, before long, in England.

So this affectionate Princess set sail for England on the 20th of September, in high spirits at the thought of seeing her brother, and setting foot once more in her native land. But hardly had she started, than an express arrived with the sad news of the Duke of Gloucester's death. The blow was a heavy one to the Princess, who was tenderly attached to her youngest brother, and there was general lamentation in England over the early death of this promising young Prince.

"The Duke of Gloucester has been ill with small-pox," wrote Lady Derby, on the 12th of September (O.S.), "but by the grace of God the worst is over. He is a Prince of great promise." Five days later she wrote again :—" We lost His Highness the Duke of Gloucester, yesterday, after all the doctors had judged him out of danger. It is a great loss ; the Prince had a mind that cannot be too highly valued." On the 22d she alludes to Mary's arrival in England. "The Princess Royal arrived yesterday. She was on the sea when she learnt her bitter loss, which is one of the greatest the King and his people could sustain ; and we all individually feel it deeply. He had very remarkable qualities, which would have rendered him one of the greatest men of the age."

To the Queen, the shock of her youngest son's death was embittered by the remembrance of her last parting from him, and of the severity with which she had sent away the brave youth, whose face she was never to see again. His sister wept bitterly for her old playmate, and in a touching little note written from Colombes to her brother, the King, on the 10th of October, she thus alludes to their mutual loss :—

"Since I wrote to you, so cruel a misfortune has happened to us that, up to this hour, I have shrunk from mentioning it, and even now I hardly know how to find words to express what I feel. You know by your own sorrow, all the greatness of my own, and for the rest, I think the best is to keep silence, which I mean to do, when I have told you that what I most long for now, is to have the joy of seeing you. This, I hope, will be very soon, and then I can show you how truly I am your very humble servant. Everyone may say the same to you, but I am sure those are few who mean it as truly as I do."

The Princess of Orange had been received in London with great public rejoicings, and was welcomed as she deserved to be, by all who had shared her bounty and kindness during their years of exile. Now, only the Queen and Princess Henrietta's presence was needed to complete what Sir William Davenant called, "the matchless number of the Royal Race ;" and the poets who sang odes in honour of the Princess Royal began to ask, in their courtly strains, when her princely sister and her mother-queen would be here. Especial curiosity was felt with regard to the young Princess, whose charms had already made a sensation at the Court of France. The fame of her loveliness had been lately extolled by M. de la Serre, the Court Gazetteer, who, in a flattering portrait of Henrietta, dedicated to Monsieur, had pronounced that there was nothing under the sun to equal her. After praising her hair, her brow, her eyes, he goes on to say that the beauty of her soul can only be compared with that of her countenance. "She speaks so agreeably, that it is

as pleasant to hear her as to see her. In singing, who can
equal her? In other accomplishments she is unrivalled.
Who can express her goodness, grace, and sweetness and
wisdom? She possesses a thousand other qualities ; the
least among them all is that of being born a princess." It
was in high-flown terms of this kind, that the Comte de
Soissons, who arrived in England towards the end of October,
made a formal demand on the part of the King, his master,
and Monsieur, for the Princess's hand. Charles received the
ambassador graciously, and the terms of the marriage contract were drawn up. Some uneasiness was created in
Monsieur's mind, by a report that the Emperor Leopold II.
had sent an envoy to Whitehall to ask for Henrietta's hand,
and Lady Derby wrote to Madame de la Trémouille, that
Prince Rupert had just arrived, charged with the same errand.
Mademoiselle was furious when she heard this. That the
Emperor, whose alliance she had so ardently coveted, should
prefer a mere child to her, with all her wealth, was beyond
belief. Her jealousy would have been still fiercer, had she
known that two other royal suitors, to whose hand she had
aspired—the King of Portugal and the Duke of Savoy—were
about to make similar proposals to Charles II. Thus the
Princess, whom she had despised, was literally sought after by
many kings, " *recherchée de tant de rois*," as Bossuet says in his
Oraison, and as La Fontaine sings in the ode which he composed for Henrietta's marriage.

> " Que de princes amoureux
> Ont brigué son hymenée.
> Elle a refusé leurs vœux,
> Pour Philippe elle était née ;
> Pour lui seul elle a quitté
> Le Portugais indompté,
> Roi des terres inconnues,
> Le voisin du fier croissant,
> Et de nos Alpes chenues
> Le monarque florissant,
> Philippe est un bien si doux,
> Que c'est le seul qui l'enflamme,
> Sous les cieux que voyons-nous
> Qui soit du prix de son âme ?

> Les héritiéres des rois
> Ont souhaité mille fois,
> D'en faire la destinée ;
> C'est un plus glorieux sort
> Que de se voir couronnée
> Reine des sources de l'or."

But Charles II. was apparently satisfied with the marriage already arranged for his sister, and never seems to have entertained these more splendid proposals. On the 8th of November, the Comte de Soissons writes :—"As for the marriage of Monsieur with the Princess of England, I regard it rather as a family and domestic matter, than as an affair of state. The King talks so publicly about it every day, and sees all its advantages so clearly, that there is scarcely any doubt about the matter, but on the contrary, the utmost certainty that it will take place. The sight of the Princess will strengthen the King's resolve still more, for, as His Majesty loves his sister extremely, and knows that to give her to Monsieur, is to make her happy, he will never entertain any other thought, although the Emperor's cousin, who has just arrived here, and Prince Rupert, who still remains, have proposed a match with the Emperor for her, and certainly hoped to break off that of Monsieur. But the King of England knows, from his own judgment, that it is both the best for his own interests, and for the life-long happiness of the Princess, that she should marry Monsieur."

Meanwhile, the Queen and Princess were both on their way to England. They left Paris on the 29th of October, and were sped on their way by the French royal family, including Monsieur, who took a very reluctant leave of his future bride, and begged the Queen to bring her back speedily. The travellers were greeted with royal honours at Beauvais, where they spent All Saints' Day, and attended mass in the Cathedral. At Calais, they found the Duke of York awaiting them with a fine squadron of ships, and going on board his flag-ship, they set sail for Dover on the 6th of November. Unfortunately, there was a dead calm, and two whole days were spent in crossing the Channel. As soon as they were in sight of Dover, the King advanced to meet his mother, and welcomed her and his sister with the warmest embraces. At Dover Castle, the Princess Royal and Prince Rupert were awaiting them, and the whole of the Royal Family sat down to a banquet in the great hall, which was thronged with a crowd of eager people. Père Cyprien de Gamaches, who accompanied the Queen, gives an amusing account of the strange sights and novel experiences of this journey, which was a great event in his quiet life. The sight of the gallant ships hung with gay streamers, "thick as leaves on forest trees," the "marvellously loud and delightful thunder of the guns," the feast prepared on board by the Duke of York, and His Highness's kindness in providing him and the Queen's French servants with fish for their fastday, are all minutely recounted. But what gratified him most, was the dismay and horror on the faces of the townsmen of Dover, most of them Puritans and *Trembleurs* (Quakers), when he stood up boldly at the King's table to recite a Latin grace, and make "a great sign of the Cross." The act was hardly politic at such a time. Still less so was the celebration of high mass in the Castle Hall, at which he officiated on the following morning. But, in the enthusiasm of the moment, these things were allowed to pass unnoticed. The Royal Family drove through Canterbury to Rochester, where they slept, and then, by the Queen's express wish, instead of joining the royal barges at Gravesend, and making their triumphal entry up the Thames, they only took boat at Lambeth and crossed over to Whitehall.

"On the second day of November (N. S., 12th)," says the *Mercurius Redivivus*, "the Queen, the King's mother, and the Princess Henrietta came into London, for that the Queen had left this land nineteen years before, her coming was very private, Lambeth way, where the King, the Queen, Duke of York, Prince Edward (the son of the Queen of Bohemia), and the rest took water at Lambeth, crossed the Thames, and all safely arrived at Whitehall; and that night, in many places bells rang, and in some streets bonfires, and here and there shows of joy. Her coming, not through the city, was one great reason that no more joy was made, for many did scarcely know that indeed she was at Whitehall that night."

The river was thronged with boats, and Pepys, who spent sixpence on rowing up to the royal barge, complained he could see nothing, and went home out of temper, declaring that there were but three fires in the city, to welcome the Queen, and that "her coming did not please anyone." But Lady Derby gives a very different account to her sister-in-law. " I have to beg you a thousand pardons, for not having told you before of the Queen's arrival, which took place last Friday, to everybody's delight, with the acclamations of the whole nation. I saw her on her arrival and kissed her hand. She met me with much emotion and received me with tears and great kindness. You may imagine what I felt. Her Majesty charms all who see her, and her courtesy cannot be enough praised. She has constantly received visitors since she came, without having left her room."

The meeting between the widowed Queen and the Countess, whose lord had died in the King's service, was a pathetic incident in that day's festival, and the thought of all that had passed in the years since they had last met, may well have moved them both to tears.

The sight of the familiar scenes where the best days of her life had been spent, naturally stirred the Queen deeply. She wept at the sight of the Banqueting-hall, and called herself " *la reine malheureuse*." But to the young Princess, this visit to England was one of unmixed delight. No bitter memories came to darken her joy. All was fresh, new and bright. To find herself one of a merry family party was a novel and delicious experience. In the company of her kind elder sister and affectionate brothers, she forgot the gap which death had so lately made in their circle, and became as gay and joyous as of old. "The grief of princes," observed Lady Derby, " does not last long. They have so many things to occupy them, that they soon forget their sorrows." And life was smiling very radiantly just then on this Princess of sixteen years. She saw herself fêted and caressed on all sides, petted by her royal brother, and admired by the whole Court. " Our young Princess," wrote Lady Derby, " is all you said she was." Evelyn, who had hastened to kiss the Queen-mother's hand, was charmed with

the Princess's courtesy, and with the gracious manner with
which she thanked his wife "for the character she had presented her and which was afterwards printed." Even Pepys,
who declared that the Queen had lost all her looks and was
nothing but a little plain old woman, allows that the Princess
Henrietta is very pretty, although he objects to her fashion
of wearing her hair frizzed short up to her ears, and is of
opinion that his own wife, who stood near her, " well-dressed,
with the unwonted decoration of two or three black patches
on her face, did seem to him much handsomer than she."
One brilliant gentleman at Court, the same Duke of Buckingham, who had formerly dared to aspire to the hand of the
widowed Princess Royal, now professed himself the devoted
adorer of Henrietta, and loved her too well for his own peace
of mind. People flocked to see her in the streets and at the
palace gates. Balls and supper parties and theatrical entertainments were given for her amusement. During the few
weeks that she remained in town, she received the most
varied tokens of the admiration which her presence excited.
Soon the whole country was in love with the youthful
Princess. Sonnets were composed in her honour. Books
were dedicated to her. There is a singular dialogue, written
by one Thomas Toll, called "The Female Duel, or the
Ladies' Looking-Glass, representing a Scripture Combat,
about business of Religion, fairly carried on between a
Roman Catholic Lady and the wife of a dignified person in
the Church of England," which was inscribed to "our two
incomparable Princesses, one in affection, though different, it
may be, in some persuasion." The House of Commons sent
an address of congratulation on her arrival, with a present of
10,000 jacobuses, upon which Henrietta wrote a graceful
letter of thanks to the Speaker, begging him to excuse her
want of facility in the English tongue, but assuring him that
she had not lost her English heart.

The Comte de Soissons' secretary, M. Bartet, owned himself a victim to her charms, like everyone else, and gives us
more than one fascinating glimpse of the Princess, in his
despatches to Cardinal Mazarin. One day, it was the very
day after her arrival, when she was too wearied to appear at

her mother's reception, he was allowed to follow the Count, whom the King himself led into his sister's apartments. There he saw her in her *cornette* (mob-cap), wrapped in a cotton morning robe of a thousand colours, playing at ombre with the Duke of York and the Princess of Orange. "You can tell Monsieur,' he adds, "that he never saw her more beautiful in full dress, than she appeared to me at that moment. Even on the day when I saw him leading her through your gallery, and told her that she was as lovely as his little guardian angel, she was scarcely as fair as she looked, sitting there in her mob-cap and coloured print gown, at Whitehall."

Another time he adds a hurried postscript at the end of a letter. It is eleven o'clock at night and M. de la Feuillade has been sent to summon him to Whitehall. "He tells me the Princess has just won a bracelet worth 200 jacobuses, and that she spoke with him of the news from Paris, and how we hear Monsieur is very melancholy, and cannot sleep, and has grown quite thin in her absence, upon which he replied that the only remedy for his ills was in her hands."

The French Secretary apparently found his stay at the English Court exceedingly pleasant, and was well content to remain there, as he did, for some time after the Count's departure. The King's easy good-nature delighted him, and he was quite surprised to find how affably he treated M. de Soissons, living with him on the most cordial terms, just as any ordinary person might do, with an old friend. In his eyes, Charles was, what Lady Derby thought him when she met him on the stairs of her house—"the most charming Prince in the world."

The preliminary formalities had now been arranged, and the Secretary reports how, on the 22d of November, the Count had the honour of a royal audience, in which he repeated his demand and asked for the Princess's hand in marriage, on behalf of the King of France and Monsieur. "Sa Majesté Britannique," he adds, "granted the request in the most gracious manner possible, and afterwards spoke to the Count about our King, in a way not to be forgotten." By the marriage treaty, which had been agreed upon, Charles promised to give his sister a dowry of 40,000 jacobuses, and a further present of £20,000 towards the expenses of her marriage and as a token of his great affection, while Louis XIV. and his brother agreed to settle 40,000 livres a year on the Princess for her life, and to give her the Château de Montargis, magnificently furnished, for her residence. The arrangements necessary for the completion of the marriage contract were left to Lord St. Albans, who was sent to France to watch over the Princess's interests, and form her household. Charles showed his satisfaction with the French Ambassador, by presenting him with a valuable box, bearing his own portrait set in diamonds, and the Countess, his wife, Olympia Mancini, with a very handsome diamond ring. The Duke of Buckingham entertained the Count and his whole suite sumptuously two nights running, after which they left England, very well satisfied with the King and his Court. Hardly had they taken their departure than a great Italian Prince, the Marquis Pallavicino, arrived on a special mission from Charles Emmanuel, Duke of Savoy, to ask the King of England for his sister's hand. But he soon found out that he had come too late, and could only express his infinite regret, when he heard that the English Princess was already promised to another and less tardy suitor. Our friend Bartet chuckled not a little over the Italian *magnifico's* discomfiture, and was delighted when the Princess herself told him laughingly that the coming of Monsieur de Savoie's envoy had not in the least disturbed her night's rest. And he adds, with a spice of malice, "I know not what Mademoiselle, in her Palace of the Luxembourg, will say, when she hears of this."

CHAPTER VI

1660—1661

Death of the Princess of Orange—Illness of the Princess Henrietta—Her Return to
Paris—Her Marriage with Monsieur celebrated at the Palais-Royal.

"CHRISTMAS," writes Father Cyprian in the journal of his
visit to England, "is always observed in this country,
especially in the King's palaces, with greater pomp than in
any other realm of Europe." He goes on to describe the
ancient custom, then still in use, of bringing a branch of
the Glastonbury thorn, which blossomed on Christmas Eve,
to be solemnly presented to the King at this festival. Great
preparations were now made to celebrate Christmas at Charles
II.'s Court. After the long years of Puritan rule, the old
days of Merry England seemed to have come back once
more, and, in spite of Monsieur's urgent messages, the Queen
and Princess delayed their return to France, in order to spend
this time-honoured feast at Whitehall, in true old English
fashion. Suddenly, in the midst of these rejoicings, the
Princess Royal fell dangerously ill of smallpox. The
greatest alarm was felt, owing to the recent death of the
Duke of Gloucester, and the Queen-mother hastily removed
her darling child, Henrietta, to St. James's Palace, to avoid
infection. She herself was extremely anxious to remain with
her sick daughter, but her physician would not hear of this,
and the King, dreading the revival of his mother's attempts
to convert the Princess Royal at this critical moment, induced
her, for Henrietta's sake, not to expose herself to the risk of
infection.

On the evening of the 20th of December, the very day on
which her sister's illness was declared to be smallpox, Henri-

77

etta received an affectionate little note from her brother, who would not come to see her at St. James's Palace, since he was in constant attendance at the Princess Royal's bedside.

" The kindnesse I have for you will not permit me to loose this occasion to coniure you to continue your kindnesse to a brother that loves you more than he can expresse, which truth I hope you are so well persuaded of, as I may expect those returnes which I shall strive to deserve.   Deare sister, be kinde to me, and be confident that I am intirely yours.—C. R. For my Deare Sister, the Princesse Henriette."

Two days later there was a temporary improvement in the Princess Royal's condition, the fever diminished, the eruption came out fully, and Lord Craven, who paid her a visit, wrote to the Queen of Bohemia that good hopes of her recovery were entertained.   But, after the fatal practice of those times, the Court doctors seized the opportunity to bleed their patient repeatedly.   She became rapidly weaker, and feeling herself at the point of death, received the Sacrament, and made her will with perfect self-possession and clearness of mind.

" My last told you of the Princess Royal's illness," wrote Lady Derby on the 24th of December, " and now, with much grief, I have to tell you she is at the point of death, and I fear she may have passed away by this time.   Good people will be glad to know that on the third day of her illness, feeling some weakness, she asked for a cordial that she might have strength to receive the Sacrament, of which she partook with great devotion, and perfect confidence in her salvation, and when the King burst into tears, she spoke of death without fear or emotion.   She recommended to him her son, for whose sake alone she wished for life, if it was God's will, and the cordial having given her a little strength, she desired to make her will, which she did with great patience and in a very Christian spirit.   This was on Friday at 5 o'clock in the morning ; she was better on Saturday, and on Sunday they thought her out of danger."

Before the letter was closed, the dreaded news had come, and the next day Lady Derby added the following lines :—
" The Princess died at noon, and when she was not in convulsions was quite sensible.   I have just come from visiting the

Queen, who is much distressed. I saw her. The Princess changed her lodging from Whitehall to St. James's, where she is at present, and was very well yesterday. All these losses in the Royal Family grieve and shock their friends. May it please God to withdraw His hand, and preserve those who remain to us, and protect the King, and guide him through all dangers. In truth, our Princess was an excellent person. All the good and rare qualities she possessed were natural endowments, for she had had her own way from childhood, those about her having thought more of their own interests, than of what was good for her, or proper for her position." And the young Lord Chesterfield, whose mother had been the Princess Royal's most devoted attendant through-out her life, and who was himself present at her death-bed, speaks with admiration of her "unconcernedness, constancy of mind and resolution, which well became the grandchild of Henri Quatre."

The sudden death of this Princess, at the early age of twenty-nine, threw a gloom over the whole country. "This day," writes Evelyn in his diary, on that sad Christmas Eve, "died the Princess of Orange, which wholly altered the face and gallantry of the whole Court."

> "All things that we ordained festival
> Turn from their office to black funeral."

The corpse was removed to Somerset House, and after lying in state there during five days, was borne in solemn procession, on the night of the 29th of December, by the Duke of York and all the great officers of the Crown, to Westminster Abbey. There the Princess of Orange was buried, according to her dying wish, in the royal vault of Henry VII.'s Chapel, by the side of her young brother, Henry of Gloucester.

Hardly had the lamented Princess breathed her last, than pressing letters arrived from Monsieur, who, in his alarm on hearing of her illness, had sent over his own *maître d'hôtel*, to implore the Queen to bring away her daughter without delay. There was nothing to stop them now. The marriage pre-liminaries were satisfactorily arranged, and the difficult ques-

tion of the Queen's own jointure had been settled. The
Parliament agreed to make her a yearly allowance of £30,000,
while the King promised her an equal sum from his privy
purse, on the express understanding that she was to return to
England after her daughter's marriage, and take up her abode
at Somerset House. Only one thing more remained to be
done. This was the recognition of the Duke of York's marriage, on which point the Queen-mother had as yet shown
herself inflexible. Soon after her arrival in England, the
unfortunate Duchess had given birth to a son, whom the
Duke of York had recognised as his child, and the King as
heir-presumptive to the Crown. The calumnies, which had
been circulated to injure her character, were proved to be false,
and the King, who had throughout maintained his sister-in-
law's innocence, himself led the Duke into his wife's presence.
On her death-bed, the Princess of Orange had professed her
own deep regret at her unkindness to her late maid-of-honour,
and, following her example, the Queen now announced that
she was ready to forgive and receive her daughter-in-law.
Accordingly, in spite of her deep mourning, Henrietta Maria
gave a farewell audience at Whitehall, on the New Year's
Day, and when the Duchess, led in by her husband, sank on
her knees before her, she raised her graciously and kissed her.
The Princess Henrietta next embraced her sister-in-law, but
so great was the crowd, that the Queen, fearful of danger from
the smallpox then prevalent, desired her to leave the room.
" The Queen," says Clarendon, " received her daughter-in-law
as if she had approved the marriage from the beginning, and
very kindly made her sit down by her." The whole Royal
Family dined that day in public, after their habit on great
occasions, and Father Cyprian records how he and the King's
chaplain both had to force their way through the crowds who
thronged the doorways. To the priest's great delight, the
English minister stumbled and fell down, so that Father
Cyprian reached the Royal table first, and said the Latin
grace long before his rival could begin. This incident caused
much merriment among the gentlemen who stood behind the
King's chair, and they told his Majesty, that his chaplain and
the Queen's priest had run a race, to see who would say grace

first, but that the poor chaplain had been tumbled over, and so the priest had won!

On the following day, the Queen and Princess set out on their journey, and slept that night at Hampton Court, where the King joined them the next morning, and conducted them to Portsmouth. Here they embarked on board the *London*, a man-of-war commanded by the Earl of Sandwich, and, taking tender leave of Charles, set sail for France on the 9th of January. The grief of the Court was general at their departure, and Lady Derby speaks warmly of "our adorable Princess," and of the favourable impression which her simple and winning manners had made in England. She had formed a close friendship with Lady Derby's young married daughter, Lady Strafford, and had promised her a portrait of herself, in payment of a wager which she had lost. Her mother begs her niece, Mademoiselle de la Trémouille, a great friend of Henrietta's at the French Court, to remind the Princess of this, in case she should forget the honour which she had done her cousin. At the last moment, the Duke of Buckingham, unwilling to tear himself away from his adored mistress, obtained the King's leave to accompany the Queen to France. Unfortunately, Henrietta's usual bad luck did not fail to accompany her, and her journey this time seemed likely to prove more disastrous than ever. The day after her departure, a violent storm sprang up, and, owing to the pilot's negligence, the ship ran aground on the Horse Sand, and was compelled to put back into harbour. To add to the consternation of those on board, the Princess fell suddenly ill, and for some days it was feared that her illness would prove to be small-pox. The Queen was in an agony of grief, and Buckingham gave way to a passionate outburst of anger. Happily, at the end of a few days, her illness was pronounced to be a severe attack of measles. She was borne on shore, and during the next fortnight remained dangerously ill at Portsmouth. The King sent his own physician to attend his sister, but her attendants were firmly convinced that their "dear Princess" owed her life to her own resolution in refusing to allow the doctors to bleed her, as they had done in the case of her unfortunate brother and sister.

F

Monsieur sent another express to Portsmouth, and the
Queen-mother despatched one of her gentlemen, with anxious
inquiries after the Princess's health. By the 25th of January
she had sufficiently recovered to start on the journey. This
time the royal travellers reached Havre safely, and were
received with great enthusiasm by the people. The Queen
decided to remain there some days to give the Princess a
little rest, but by this time, Buckingham's attentions had become so annoying, that he was ordered to go on to Paris at
once, and inform Monsieur of the Queen's safe arrival. Since
the smallpox was raging at Rouen, the Queen would not pass
through the city, but accepted the hospitality of her cousin,
the Duc de Longueville, then Governor of Normandy, who
entertained the travellers royally, and escorted them to
Pontoise. Here they alighted at the ancient Abbey of St
Martin, and paid Abbé Montagu the honour of a visit. While
the Grand Almoner was doing the honours of his abbey, and
showing the Queen his pictures and treasures, a flourish of
trumpets was heard at the convent gates, and presently the
King rode up with his young Queen and Monsieur, who had
come from Saint-Germain to welcome the travellers on their
return. The King and Queen were full of kindness for their
aunt, while Monsieur could not contain his joy at the sight of
his long-expected bride. He could hardly take his eyes off
her, kissed her tenderly, and listened with delight to every
word that fell from her lips. It was late before the royal
party left the abbey, and the following morning Monsieur
returned again to escort his bride and her mother to Paris.
Their Majesties, accompanied this time by Mademoiselle and
the whole Court, and attended by a body of guards, met them
at Saint-Denis, and conducted them with great pomp to the
Palais Royal. A ballet entitled *L'Impatience des Amoureux*,
and full of playful allusions to Monsieur's suit, which the King
had prepared expressly in honour of the Princess's return, was
acted at Court that week. Gui Patin remarks on the performance, in his letters, and speaks of the rejoicings which hailed
the arrival of "the Queen of England and her fair daughter,
now about to wed the Duc d'Orléans."

After receiving visits from the Princes of the blood and

chief personages in Paris, the Queen and Princess retired to Chaillot, to spend the first days of Lent in seclusion, and to await the coming of the Papal dispensation, which was required for the marriage of first-cousins. There was some delay in obtaining this, owing to a technical error on the part of the French diplomatists, and the Papal brief did not arrive until the 9th of March. On that very day, Cardinal Mazarin died at Vincennes. He had long been failing, but clung with strange tenacity to life, and, as he lay slowly dying, in the midst of so many splendid and luxurious surroundings, he was heard to murmur with a sigh, as he looked around him : " And must I leave all this ? *Guenaud l'a dit.*" But the cynical philosophy of his nature soon revived. He told the King that he had no fear of death, and quoted the lines of his favourite Horace :—

> " Si fractus illabatur orbis
> Impavidum ferient ruinæ."

And when he was told by his attendants, that a comet, sure presage of coming evil, had suddenly appeared in the heavens, he observed, with his old irony : " The comet does me too much honour."

He had been more feared than loved, and few lamented him. " Mazarin is already forgotten," writes our satirical friend Gui Patin, " *Il est passé, il a plie bagage, il est en plomb, l'eminent personage.* And now people speak only of his will, of his gold, and of the millions which he has left behind him." And he goes on to wonder if, as is reported, l'Abbé Montagu, who was so high in Anne of Austria's favour, will be the next prime minister. " After having an honest Italian to reign over us for so many years," he adds, " it will be a singular good fortune if an Englishman is kind enough to govern France." The Court, however, paid the Cardinal the honour of going into mourning for a fortnight, and, to Monsieur's vexation, his wedding was again delayed. Meanwhile he was much annoyed by the attentions which Buckingham persisted in paying to the Princess, and Henrietta herself, seeing his displeasure, begged her mother to deliver her from the Duke's too openly-expressed admiration. The Queen laughed at the

notion, and told Monsieur that Buckingham merely made
himself ridiculous, and that the Princess only tolerated his
conduct because he was her brother's favourite. Monsieur's
jealousy, however, made him carry his complaint to the Queen-
mother of France, who wisely advised her sister-in-law to give
the King of England a hint, and beg him to recall the Duke.
This was soon done, and that troublesome personage left Paris,
not without many protestations of his hopeless but undying
devotion to the object of his worship. In Monsieur's present
frame of mind, it was plain that further delays would be in-
expedient, and in spite of the Lenten season, both the Queen-
mothers agreed that the marriage had better take place at
once. All state was dispensed with, owing to the near
approach of Passion-tide, and the deep mourning of the
English royal family, and the wedding was solemnised in
the quietest manner possible.

On Wednesday the 30th of March, the marriage contract
was signed at the Louvre, by the King and both the Queens
of France and Monsieur, on the one part, and on the other by
Lord St. Albans in his royal master's name. That morning, the
Princess Henrietta received absolution and Holy Communion
at Saint-Eustache, the parish church of the Palais-Royal,
while Monsieur performed his devotions at Saint-Germain
l'Auxerrois. In the evening, the betrothal took place in the
great saloon of the Palais-Royal, in the presence of the King
and Queen, and the two Queen-mothers. Mademoiselle and
her sisters, the Prince and Princess of Condé and their young
son the Duc d'Enghien, the Duc de Vendôme, another Prince
of the blood royal, the Prince and Princess Palatine, the Earl
of St. Albans and a few other lords and ladies of exalted rank,
were also among the guests. Mademoiselle tells us that the
dresses worn on this occasion were of rare splendour, and
that the bride herself was most richly adorned and elegantly
dressed.

At twelve o'clock on the following day, the marriage was
solemnised in the Queen of England's chapel by M. de Cosnac,
Bishop of Valence and Grand Almoner to Monsieur, in the
presence of the same illustrious company. That evening the
King and Queen supped with the bride and bridegroom at the

Palais-Royal, and the Queen of England did the honours with her accustomed grace and dignity. The following record of the marriage was inscribed in the register of Saint-Eustache :—

"On Wednesday, March 30, 1661, in the Château of the Palais-Royal, situated in our own parish, was celebrated before Monseigneur Daniel de Cosnac, Bishop and Comte de Valence et de Brie, by our consent and in our presence, the betrothal of the most high and mighty Prince Philippe, fils de France, Duc d'Orléans, the King's only brother, of the parish of St. Germain l'Auxerrois, and of the most high and mighty Princess Henrietta Anne of England, only sister of the King of Great Britain, our parishioner. And on the following day, the 31st of the said month, the marriage of the said lord and lady was solemnised in the Chapel of the said Palace, by the said lord Bishop, in our presence and with our consent, under the good pleasure of the King, of the Queen, His Majesty's mother, and of my said Lord the Duc d'Orléans, of the Queen Regent, of the Queen-mother of the King of Great Britain, of my said Lady, the Princess Henrietta Anne of England, in the presence also of Mademoiselle, of Mesdemoiselles d'Orléans, of M. le Prince and Madame la Princesse, of the Duc d'Enghien and many other princes and princesses and lords and ladies of the Court. This was done under a dispensation for banns unproclaimed, and for the time being prohibited by the Church, dated the 28th of the present month and year, signed by Contes, Vicar-General, by my Lord Cardinal de Retz, Archbishop of Paris, and sealed with the seal of the said Archbishop, the said dispensation making mention of the brief of Our Holy Father, the Pope, granting to the said parties a dispensation from the obstacle of the second degree of consanguinity and all others.

" (Signed) Louis : Anne ; Marie Thérèse ; Philippe ; Henriette Anne ; De Baufremont ; Antoine de Beaudoin, et Daniel de Cosnac, Evêque et Comte de Valence et de Brie."

The Court gazetteers now broke into pæans of joy, and celebrated this union of the lilies of France and the rose of

England, in torrents of rapturous song. They extolled the
loveliness of the bride and the virtues of the bridegroom, this
perfect marriage of rank and beauty, and prophesied years of
infinite bliss and harmony to the happy pair. La Fontaine
sang, in strains of truer melody, the charms of this bride of
sixteen summers.

> " Beauté sur toutes insigne
> D'un présent si précieux,
> Si la terre était indigne,
> C'est un don digne des cieux."

He told anew the wondrous story of her birth in the midst
of civil war and tumult, and of her escape across the seas.
He sang how soft Zephyrs had wafted her, and Loves and
Cherubs had followed her, to the shores of France, there
to become the delight of the Sun-King's court. He praised
not alone the beauty, but the wit and the grace which had
charmed her royal lover's heart.

> " Si sa beauté le surprit,
> Des graces de son esprit
> De jour en jour il s'enflamme,
> La Princesse tient des cieux
> Du moins autant par son âme,
> Que par l'éclat de ses yeux."

And he too foretold a destiny of immortal joys, awaiting the
wedded pair, and bade them live and love for ever, with that
constancy which can alone vanquish Time and Death.

> " Ils sont joints ces jeunes coeurs,
> Qui du Ciel tirent leur race,
> Puissent-ils être vainqueurs
> Des ans par qui tout s'efface !
> Que de leurs desirs constants,
> Dure à jamais le printemps,
> Rempli de jours agrèables.
> O couple aussi beau qu'heureux,
> Vous serez toujours aimables ;
> Soyez toujours amoureux ! "

On the day after the wedding, the King of France addressed the following letter of congratulation to his brother of
England :—

" *Monsieur mon frère,*—Since I have always considered the marriage of my brother with your sister, the Princess of England, as a new tie which would draw still closer the bonds of our friendship, I feel more joy than I can express, that it was yesterday happily accomplished ; and as I doubt not that this news will inspire you with the same sentiments as I feel myself, I would not delay one moment to share my joy with you, nor would I lose the opportunity of this mutual congratulation, to tell you that I am, my brother, very truly your good brother, LOUIS."

On his death-bed, Cardinal Mazarin, conscious it may be that he had been unwise in neglecting to secure the friendship of Charles II., had advised the young King to enter into a close alliance with England, a country which, in his opinion, was the natural ally of France. All through his reign, Louis XIV. remembered this piece of advice, and acted on the principle laid down by the dying Cardinal. The marriage of his brother with the sister of Charles II. was destined to form a strong bond of union between the two monarchs, and to produce great and lasting political effects. In these developments, the Princess Henrietta herself was soon to play an important part.

Madame at the Tuileries and Saint-Cloud—Friendship of the King for Madame—
Fêtes of the Court at Fontainebleau—*Ballet des Saisons.*

FROM the moment of Madame's marriage, her triumphs
began. The very day after her wedding, she received compli-
mentary visits at the Palais-Royal, from the whole Court, and
the exquisite beauty of her attire and the admirable grace
with which she entertained her guests, roused Mademoiselle to
envy and wonder. Up to this time, although she had occa-
sionally figured in great Court assemblies, she had been
seldom seen in private, excepting in her mother's apartments,
where she hardly spoke, and appeared shy and silent. Now
everyone who came to see her was surprised to find how
agreeable she could be. The charms of her conversation and
the graces of her person were the talk of the whole Court.
Everyone praised her, and soon no one could speak or think
of anything else.

"Never," exclaims that finished courtier and man of the
world, l'Abbé de Choisy, " has France had a Princess as attractive as Henriette d'Angleterre, when she became the wife of
Monsieur. Never was there a Princess so fascinating, and so
ready to please all who approached her. Her eyes were black
and brilliant, full of the fire which kindles a prompt response
in other hearts. Her whole person seemed full of charm.
You felt interested in her, you loved her without being able to
help yourself. When you met her for the first time, her eyes
sought your own, as if she had no other desire in the world
but how best to please you. When she spoke, she appeared
absorbed in the wish to oblige you. She had all the wit

necessary to make a woman charming, and what is more, all
the talent necessary for conducting important affairs, had this
been required of her. But at the Court of our young King
in those days, pleasure was the order of the day, and to be
charming was enough."

Another courtier who knew her well in these early days of
her marriage, the writer of a libel which afterwards made a
great noise, speaks of her fascinating manners in almost the
same terms. " There is a sweetness and gentleness about her,
which no one can resist. When she speaks to you, she seems
to ask for your heart at once, however trifling are the words
that she has to say. Young as she is, her mind is vigorous
and cultivated, her sentiments are great and noble, and the
result of so many fine qualities is, that she seems rather an
angel than a mortal creature. Do not think that I speak as
a lover, for if I could make you realise half the charm of her
wit and gaiety, you would agree with me, that she is the most
adorable object on the face of the earth."

But contemporary writers are unanimous on this point.
They all in turn praise her dark and sparkling eyes, her pearly
teeth, and enchanting smile, her complexion of lilies and roses,
the charm of her cultivated intellect. Even her detractors
own that she had the power of captivating all who approached
her. Her regular beauty, they say, was a surprise to those
who had known her in her younger days. Or else they
insist, with her successor, the original and sharp-tongued
Princess Palatine, that Madame had no actual beauty, but
so much grace, that everything she did became her. Her
chestnut hair was always dressed in a style that suited her
exactly. The slight defect in her figure was so artfully concealed that, as Mademoiselle remarks, she even managed
to make people praise its elegance, and Monsieur never discovered that she was crooked until after his marriage. " If
it had not been for that slight deformity," says de Beaumelle,
" she would have been a masterpiece of Nature. As it was,
there was no one at Court to compare with her."

A few days after the wedding, Monsieur took his bride to
his own residence at the Tuileries. " The thing was just and
according to God's laws," observes Father Cyprian, " but the

Queen was very reluctant to part from her dearly-loved
child, and the poor young Princess, who had never left her
mother, for a day, since her first arrival at Paris in Lady
Morton's arms, wept bitterly. The scene was a painful one,
and all the Queen's servants shed tears at the sight of her
distress. But the Queen retired to Colombes, and Madame
soon dried her tears and forgot her grief in the new and
brilliant life that awaited her. Her arrival at the Tuileries
was hailed by splendid wedding gifts from the different
members of the royal family, and became the signal for a
fresh round of festivities. The young Queen was in delicate
health, and too stiff and formal to take an active part in
society. Madame soon found herself the leader of the
fashionable world, and the Tuileries became the centre of the
Court. All the men were at her feet, all the women adored
her. Foremost among her admirers, was the King himself.
For the first time, he recognised the charms which in his
early youth he had refused to own, and declared aloud that he
must have been the most unjust of men, not to think Madame
the fairest and best of women. He paid daily visits to his
young sister-in-law, and took increasing delight in her company.

On Maundy Thursday, Madame took the Queen's place
in the solemn ceremony of washing the feet of the poor, in
the hall of the Louvre. On the 10th of April, she was present
with the whole Court at the marriage at Marie Mancini with the
Prince Colonna, Constable of the kingdom of Naples. Before
the Cardinal's death, he had given his niece Hortense in
marriage to the Marquis de la Meilleraye, who assumed the
title of Duc de Mazarin, and inherited the greater part of the
minister's wealth. At the same time, he had betrothed her
sister Marie to the Connétable Colonna, and the King's old
love left the country, where she had once hoped to reign, with
the consolation, that at least she was no longer the subject of
a monarch who had forgotten her. A week later, another
marriage, planned by the Cardinal, was celebrated. This was
that of Mademoiselle d'Orléans, the prettiest of *la Grande
Mademoiselle's* sisters, to the Grand Duke of Tuscany. A few
days afterwards, this Princess, whom Choisy describes as being

as lovely, but not as virtuous, as an angel, departed for her southern home, where she made herself and others miserable, until she succeeded in returning to France.

Immediately after these weddings, which were celebrated with great pomp, the King and Queen left Paris for Fontainebleau. Monsieur and Madame lingered in Paris, a few weeks longer, surrounded by a brilliant Court. Among the ladies who formed part of Madame's intimate circle, were several of the wittiest and handsomest women of the day. There was the widowed Duchesse de Châtillon, famous for her intrigues in the Fronde, and said to be the only woman who had ever touched the great Condé's heart. Bablon, as she is familiarly called in Henrietta's letters, had, at one time, caught Charles II.'s roving fancy, and had incurred Mademoiselle's jealousy, by boasting that she might one day be Queen of England. In this respect, her ambition had been disappointed, but she remained intimate with Madame and her royal brother, who kept a soft corner in his heart for his old flame. And there was the Duchesse de Créqui, and Mademoiselle de Mortémart, better known in after days as Madame de Montespan, and Madame de Monaco, daughter of the Maréchal de Gramont and sister of Monsieur's prime favourite, the handsome Comte de Guiche.

Two others there also were, who had known the Princess of England intimately before her marriage, and for whom she retained the same warm affection as in old days. One of these was the virtuous and gentle Marguerite de la Trémouille, the niece to whose friendship with Madame, Lady Derby so often alludes, but who was soon to marry a German prince, Duc Bernard of Saxe-Weimar, and leave France. The other was Madeleine de la Vergne, the young Marquise de La Fayette, who had been lately left a widow, and was one of the most intellectual ladies of the Court. As a girl she had amazed her tutors, and read Greek and Latin better than her instructor, Ménage. From these early days, she had been a favoured guest at the Hotel Rambouillet, and had enjoyed the friendship of Madame de Sevigné and Madame de Scudéry, while La Rochefoucauld was one of her most intimate associates. She had already published her first romance, *La Princesse de Montpensier*. In later days she was to become famous as the writer of *Zaïde* and of *La Princesse de Clèves*, and as the biographer of Henrietta herself. This accomplished lady had known the Princesse d'Angleterre from her childhood, and had constantly seen her in the convent of Chaillot. Although some ten years older than Madame, she remained her most intimate friend and confidant to the end of her life, and it speaks well for the lively young Princess, that she should have been so deeply attached to one whose tastes and habits were so different from her own.

All of these ladies were in the habit of spending their afternoons at the Tuileries. They drove out with Madame daily, to the Cours de la Reine, those pleasant avenues on the banks of the Seine, which had been laid out by Marie de Medicis, and were at that time the favourite resort of the gay world. On their return, Monsieur and a few of his intimate friends joined them at supper, after which the doors were thrown open and the men and ladies of the Court were admitted. Then cards and music, acting and *jeux d'esprit* were the order of the day, and the evenings were spent in the gayest and least formal manner. Monsieur was proud of the universal admiration which his young wife excited, and delighted to see her the object of so much homage. "Her conversation," says a contemporary, "was as animated as it was interesting, her naturally fine and delicate taste had been formed by the study of the best books, her temper was sweet and equable, such as it should be, to reign over the French. She had all the wit of her brother, Charles II., heightened by the charms of her sex and the wish to please. Her example inspired others with a taste for letters, and introduced a refinement and grace in the pleasures of the Court, which were altogether new."

At that time, Molière's *troupe* was giving frequent performances in the theatre of the Palais-Royal. The great dramatist had been originally recommended to Monsieur, by the Prince de Conti, and presented by the Duke of Orléans himself to the King. His *Précieuses* had been acted before the Court, in the last days of the dying Cardinal, and had been applauded by the whole society of the Hotel Rambouillet, whose extravagances were the object of the poet's satire. "In fact," wrote Ménage, after being present at one of these performances, and describing its extraordinary success, "we are doing what Clovis was told to do of old, by S. Rémi. We burn what we have adored, and we adore what we have burned." *Les Femmes Savantes* and *Sganarelle* met with a still larger share of popularity. The price of seats was doubled and the parterre was crowded. From the first, Madame honoured Molière with her patronage, and what was far more rare in those days, showed a degree of interest and sympathy in his creations, which no royal personage had yet done.

During the month of May, Monsieur and Madame paid a visit to the Queen of England at Colombes, and went on to Saint-Cloud. Now, for the first time, Madame found herself in this lovely home, which was to become so intimately associated with her name, where many of the brightest and some of the saddest days of her life were to be spent ; Saint-Cloud, that "*palais de délices*," which only nine short years later, was to witness the awful and memorable catastrophe of her death. The palace had been enlarged and embellished, on the occasion of Monsieur's marriage, by Lepante and Girard, the Court architects. The park and gardens had been laid out by the famous Le Nôtre, the cascades and *jets d'eau* were the work of Jules Mansart. The exquisite beauty of the spot lent itself admirably to the landscape gardener's hand. The terraces commanded a magnificent view over the winding Seine, and the distant towers of Paris, the noble avenues of plane trees led down to the banks of the river. Nature and art had combined to do their best, and the happiest results had been attained. Here the formal style of gardening was seen to perfection. Yew hedges and clipped trees, palisades and arbours, grass pyramids and amphitheatres met the eye at every turn. There were sunny parterres planted with orange trees, and adorned with statues of Greek gods and heroes, of fauns and naiads. There were shady nooks and cool retreats, where you could sit undisturbed on the hottest summer day and listen to the sound of running water. Such a bower there was, at the end of the lofty terrace, close to the Grande

Cascade, where Madame loved to sit, on balmy June nights, with some favourite companion at her side, enjoying the cool freshness of the air and the breath of the roses. But this time she only spent a few days at Saint-Cloud, for the Court was already at Fontainebleau, and there her arrival was impatiently awaited. This we learn from a graceful little note which the King addressed to her at Saint-Cloud. It is interesting, as one of the very few private letters we have from the pen of Louis XIV., and shows the pleasant terms on which he was with his young sister-in-law.

"FONTAINEBLEAU, *Friday.*

"If I wish myself at Saint-Cloud it is not because of its grottoes or the freshness of its foliage. Here we have gardens fair enough to console us, but the company which is there now, is so good, that I find myself furiously tempted to go there, and if I did not expect to see you here to-morrow, I do not know what I should do, and could not help making a journey to see you. Remember me to all your ladies, and do not forget the affection which I have promised you, and which is, I can assure you, all you could possibly desire, if indeed you wish me to love you very much. Give my best love to my brother.

"To my sister." [1]

Monsieur and Madame did not fail to respond to the cordial feeling expressed in this letter, and the next day they joined the Court at Fontainebleau. Here, in the graceful Renaissance palace of Francois I[er], on the edge of the forest, the King and his Court were spending the best months of the year. In these halls where the cipher of Diane de Poitiers may still be seen entwined with that of her royal lover, and the letters of Henri Quatre's name appear side by side with those of his *belle Gabrielle*, the fairest women and the bravest men of France took their pleasure and held high festival through the long summer days. And here, where Mary Queen of Scots had spent the brightest days of her life

[1] Both this note and another from Louis XIV., which is quoted at p. 258, were first published by M. Etienne Charavay, and are given by M. Anatole France, in his introduction to Madame de La Fayette's *Histoire de Madame Henriette.*

another Princess of the same royal Stuart line now came to
be the ornament and delight of the Court of France. Seldom,
it must be owned, had Court festivities offered a more attractive aspect, at any time or in any land. The youth and commanding personality of the King, his chivalrous manners and
courtesy to women, young or old, high or low, threw a glamour
on the scene, and lent a touch of romance to the most tedious
ceremonies. He would raise his hat to the meanest maid in
his household, and returned every salute with a majesty and
charm that went far to win the heart of his subjects. And
this was the May-time of his long and glorious reign. He
was twenty-two, and full of great hopes and of good intentions.
The Cardinal was dead, and he had been given no successor.
Louis was determined to be his own master, and had announced his intention to be King of France, not only in name,
but in fact. He applied himself to the management of state
affairs, with a resolution and a perseverance that amazed his
own mother, and commanded the respect of all about him.
He spent his mornings closeted with his ministers, and wrote
lengthy despatches to his foreign ambassadors, in his own
hand. Nothing was too minute to escape his attention, or too
remote to be outside his ken. The French envoy in London
stood aghast, when the King desired him to send him a list of
those persons in England who were noted for all sorts and
kinds of knowledge, both in the past and present, "such information," he added, " being necessary to the advancement of
my glory and service." And it is to be feared that the reply
of M. de Comminges, who had never heard of Shakespeare, and
was only dimly aware " of *un nommé Miltonius*, whose noxious
writings have rendered him more infamous than the very
assassins of their King," hardly enlightened His Majesty much.
But at all events, Louis was determined to be well served, and
to keep a watchful eye on every department of state affairs.
And he was equally determined to enjoy life, after his own
fashion. His brain was already busy with a thousand magnificent projects. He would create a Versailles to be the won-
er of the world, and leave the stamp of his own greatness
like on the architecture and the poetry of the age. The
greatest thinkers, the most gifted artists of the day, should be

drawn to his Court, and should help to add lustre to his name. Painters and poets, sculptors and musicians, dramatists and comedians, should minister to his pleasures. Lebrun and Mignard should adorn his galleries, Molière and Lulli should compose his ballets. He would make his Court famous in the eyes of the whole civilised world, and gild his very pastimes with a refinement and a distinction, such as no king before him had ever dreamt of.

Unfortunately as it happened, the wife who shared the Grand Monarque's throne was singularly ill-fitted to be the partner of this able and aspiring king. The marriage in which Anne of Austria saw the fulfilment of all her hopes, and which the Cardinal held to be the final triumph of his diplomacy, proved a signal failure in this respect. Marie Thérèse was dull, ignorant, and bigoted. She had been brought up in the most cramping traditions of Spanish etiquette, and had not a wish or thought beyond the narrow circle in which she moved. All her actions and movements were governed by the most rigid regard for ceremonial. She referred to Court Chamberlains for leave to embrace her father, and held out her skirt to be kissed by her own children. She fenced herself in, with a new code of minute regulations, and withdrew herself as much as possible from contact with any but her immediate attendants. Her time was divided between eating and dressing, cards, and church-going. She ate voraciously, and was greedily afraid lest her favourite morsels should be handed to others at table. She had a passion for cards, and played extremely badly, much to the satisfaction of her ladies, who won large sums from their royal mistress. But she had a kind heart, and was a pious and devout woman. It was her misfortune to be fondly attached to the husband with whom she had so little in common, and whose infidelities were destined to give her such deep and constant distress. Even in these early days of her wedded life, she already watched his conduct with jealous suspicion, and was alive to the first symptoms of neglect on his part. And now, to increase the King's sense of his wife's deficiencies, this young and brilliant Madame appeared suddenly on the scene.

It would have been hard to find a more complete contrast to

the Spanish Queen. Not only was the English Princess a thousand times more fair, but her beauty had all the life and gaiety that was lacking in poor Marie Thérèse. She hated the formal manners of the Court, and had only too little regard for conventionalities. On state occasions she bore herself with as much grace and majesty as anyone, but in private she threw etiquette to the winds and became the simplest and most natural of mortals. Her appearance at Fontainebleau gave a new zest to the pleasures of the Court. Everyone thought of Madame and tried to please her. And no one was more eager to anticipate her wishes, or more constantly at her side, than the King himself. His sister-in-law's high spirits and innocent gaiety delighted him. Her lively wit amused him. In her more serious moments her conversation was full of charm. He soon discovered that quick perception and real love of letters which she had inherited from her ancestors, and admired her accomplishments the more, from the keen sense which he had of the defects of his own education. Henrietta, on her part, was not insensible to the homage paid her by the royal brother-in-law who had so long refused to acknowledge her charms, and may well have preferred his society to that of her weak and effeminate husband. If, in the early days of her married life, Monsieur's passion may have blinded her eyes to his real character, by this time the illusion had already passed away, and Madame must have discovered, to her cost, the pettiness and emptiness of the Prince to whom a hard fate had bound her.

A more despicable specimen of humanity it would have been hard to find. The bad education which he had received had served to develop the worst side of his nature. From his earliest years, he had been sacrificed to his brother. It had been part of the policy of Cardinal Mazarin and of Anne of Austria, to keep him a child all his life, and bring him up with the most effeminate tastes, for fear he should follow the example of his uncle, Gaston of Orléans, and stir up troubles in the State. They had succeeded only too well, and "*le plus joli enfant de France*" had grown up a miserable dandy. His good looks were indisputable. He had fine black eyes, and a profusion of dark, curly hair, his features were very

regular, and his teeth very white. But he was small and
slight, and his personal appearance was rather that of a
woman than a man. His toilet occupied the chief part of
his time, and he devoted endless care and thought to the
choice of a plume or rosette. He powdered his hair,
rouged his cheeks, and loaded himself with ribbons and
jewels. His favourite amusement was to dress himself up
in women's clothes and to wear patches. He had been
brought up entirely by women, and loved nothing so well
as their society. But his excessive vanity prompted him to
seek admiration rather than to bestow it, and his selfishness
made him incapable of any lasting attachment. He was by
no means lacking in personal courage, but had far more dread
of soiling his clothes, and of exposing his complexion to the
sun, than of meeting the enemy in battle. This childish
vanity and frivolity marked all his actions. His tastes were
as effeminate as those of the King were the reverse. Mademoiselle relates how, while Louis was winning his first laurels
in the army before Dunkirk, his brother spent his time at
Calais, playing on the beach with the Queen's ladies, throwing
water over them, and buying the toys and ribbons which came
over from England. The delight which he took in Court
functions and ceremonies was extraordinary. Whether a wedding or a funeral, it was all the same to him, as long as he could
wear a flowing mantle, or a coat that glittered with diamonds.
Mademoiselle tells us how, when her father died, the King
said to her, "To-morrow you will see Monsieur in a trailing violet mantle. He is enchanted to hear of your father's
death, so as to have the pleasure of wearing one. It is lucky
for me that I am older than he is, or he would have been longing for my death!" And sure enough, she adds, "Monsieur
appeared the next morning in a mantle of a furious length!"
Although, at one moment, this Princess had certainly seriously
contemplated a marriage with Monsieur, she lived long enough
to congratulate herself on her fortunate escape. She had, at least,
enjoyed ample opportunities of knowing him, and had taken
his measure fully. "The more I knew of him," she remarks,
"the more I saw that he would never care for anything but
his own beauty and his own clothes, and that he was quite un-

able to distinguish himself by noble actions, or to take a leading part among men." "A woman," writes Saint-Simon, speaking of Monsieur, " but with all the faults of a woman, and none
of her virtues ; childish, feeble, idle, gossiping, curious, vain,
suspicious, incapable of holding his tongue, taking pleasure in
spreading slander and making mischief, such was Philippe of
Orléans, the brother of Louis XIV."

So contemptible a Prince was ill-fitted to be the husband
of a clever, high-spirited Princess. Before his marriage, he
had appeared to be passionately in love with Henrietta, but
Madame de La Fayette, who knew him intimately, doubted
if the miracle of inflaming his heart was given to any woman
upon earth. He himself often said, in later years, that, after
the first fortnight of his married life, he had never loved
his wife. And the second Madame gives it as her opinion,
that in his whole life Monsieur had never really loved any
woman. "His taste," she tells us, "was turned in other directions," and he lavished his fortune and affections upon the
most worthless minions.

Under these circumstances, it was hardly to be wondered
if Madame found pleasure in the companionship of the King.
His natural ascendency of character might well captivate the
fancy of a maiden barely yet seventeen years old. Here was
a Prince, full of great schemes and noble ambitions, ready to
share his dreams with her, and to seek her sympathy. The
mutual attraction which drew them together was heightened
by their mutual discontent. The friendship which sprang up
between them had all the flavour of romance. They wrote
verses that were read and applauded by the whole Court, and
sent each other little notes, innocent enough in themselves,
but which raised suspicion in other breasts. Significant looks
were exchanged, and mysterious whispers passed from one to
another. Courtiers ventured to express their regret that
Madame did not hold a more exalted place at Court, and to
hint that, had the King known her better a year or two ago,
he would have made her his Queen. But for the moment,
Monsieur was too well amused with the novelty of his own
position, and the importance which he acquired from his wife's
influence with the King, to show any signs of resentment.

The summer days slipped by, in a continual round of amusements. The mornings were devoted to business, the rest of
the day was spent in pleasure.

On hot afternoons, Madame would drive out, attended by
all the ladies of the Court, to bathe in one of the clear streams
which flow through the forest, and then ride back on horseback in the cool of the evening. The King himself, followed
by his suite, would come to meet her and escort her home.
Henrietta was a fearless rider, and never looked better than
when, mounted on her horse and wearing a gold-laced habit and
coloured plumes in her shady hat, she appeared at the head
of this brilliant cavalcade. Long after Madame was dead
and gone, the recollection of those joyous processions, winding their way through the leafy glades in the bright evening
light, lived among the fairest memories of the Sun-King's
Court. Or else the King would lead the way to the Her-
mitage de'Franchard, or some such picturesque spot in the
forest, where a dainty collation was served under the trees,
and the sound of horn and clarion woke the echoes of the
rocks. After supper, the royal party would embark on a
richly-decorated gondola and float down the waters of the
canal, to the strains of Lulli's wonderful violins, and the great
Condé, and other Princes of the blood, would hand refresh-
ments to the Queen and princesses. There were hunting
expeditions in the woods, moonlight serenades prolonged
far on into the night, and lonely rambles into the depths of
the forest. Strange were the sights the stars looked down
upon, strange the tales that were whispered under the spreading boughs of the ancient beeches. In all of these hunting
parties or moonlight walks, the King was Madame's companion. She shared all his tastes, and entered into all his
plans, with a spirit and a vivacity of which the poor, dull
Queen was utterly incapable. Together they arranged to-
morrow's *fête*, were it masque or water-party. Pastoral
plays were acted, ballets were danced in the open air under
the greenwood tree. "Never," writes Madame de Motteville, "had the Court of France witnessed festivities of so
varied a kind as were seen at Fontainebleau that summer-
time." Never had so bright an array of youth and beauty

been gathered around the Crown. All thought of care and sorrow was put away, and life seemed one long dream of delight.

Early in June, the Queen of England came to spend a few days at Fontainebleau. She was eagerly welcomed by Madame, and, on her departure, Fouquet, the Minister of Finance, gave a magnificent *fête* in her honour, at that splendid house, of which La Fontaine has left us so charming a description, in his *Songe de Vaux*. Monsieur and Madame were also present, and Molière's *Ecole des Maris* was performed for the first time. This was followed by a grand ball, given by Monsieur and Madame at Fontainebleau on the 11th of June, and a few days later by another, given in honour of Madame's birthday, by the Duc de Beaufort. On this occasion, the company danced under the trees of the park, which were brilliantly illuminated, and decorated with all manner of fanciful devices. A splendid *fête*, or rather succession of *fêtes*, was also given to Madame by her mother's old friend, the Duchesse de Chévreuse, in the gardens of her château at Dampierre, one of the finest country houses near Paris. The Queen-mother of France accompanied her son and daughter-in-law on this visit, and the information which she then received through Madame de Chévreuse and her friends, Colbert and Le Tellier, is said to have finally decided the fate of the unhappy Fouquet.

But the most memorable of all the *fêtes* held at Fontainebleau that summer, was the representation of the *Ballet des Saisons*. After many previous rehearsals, the final performance took place on the night of the 23rd of July, before the two Queens and the whole Court. The stage was raised on a grassy lawn, at the edge of the lake. The noble avenues on either side were lighted with thousands of torches, and the ornamental waters of the gardens were illuminated with fires of every hue. First came a troop of fair-haired maidens, who strewed flowers on the grass and sang praises of Diana, queen and huntress, chaste and fair. Then the curtain rose, and Madame appeared in classic draperies, wearing the silver crescent on her brow, and armed with bow and quiver. Ten of the loveliest ladies of the Court stood beside her, clad in

sylvan green, and danced around her, as they sang the following chorus in her praise :—

> " Diane dans les bois, Diane dans les cieux,
>   Diane enfin brille en tous lieux,
>   Elle enchante les cœurs, elle éblouit les yeux,
>   Glorieuse sans être fière,
>   Adorable en toute manière."

Then, decked out in fantastic costumes, and bearing ap-
propriate devices, came the different seasons of the year,
each in turn offering their homage at the shrine of Diana,
Flora and Ceres, shepherds and hunters, reapers and
vintagers all appeared in succession. Last of all, the King
himself entered, clad in the bright robe of Spring, and
followed by a troop of Lovers, with Joy, Laughter and
Abundance in their train. Before his face, the snows of war
and discontent melt away, the flowers return upon earth, and
the voice of the singing-birds is heard. So sang the chorus
in Benserade's flattering verses, as the King sank on bended
knee before Madame, and owned her Queen of Beauty, amid
the applause of the whole Court.

That night Henrietta's triumph was complete. She knew
not, alas! how short it was destined to be, brief as the
summer flowers or the midsummer night itself. Among the
actors in that ballet, there were many whose names are well
known in the story of the *Grand Monarque's* age. Monsieur
and his favourite, the Comte de Guiche, acted in one *entrée.*
In another, Madame de Monaco appeared with Madame de
Comminges, *la belle Césonie* of the Hotel Rambouillet, whose
husband was shortly to be sent as Ambassador to England.
Marie Anne, the youngest of the Mancini, soon to become
Duchesse de Bouillon, and afterwards celebrated by La
Fontaine as " *la mère des Amours et la Reine des Grâces,*" was
one of the Muses, and so, too, was Madame's English friend,
Miss Stewart, the future Duchess of Richmond, and object of
Charles II.'s admiration. And among these brilliant beauties
there was one of Madame's own maids-of-honour, a very
timid and blushing maiden, scarcely yet seventeen, who bore

the name of Louise de la Vallière. She appeared that night, among the nymphs of Diana's train, and her expressive eyes and lovely colouring attracted the notice of more than one courtier. But no one then dreamt the part that she was to play at Court, during the next few years.

CHAPTER VIII

1661—1662

THE Queen-mother of France was the first person who became uneasy at the King's devotion to his sister-in-law. She complained that Madame robbed her of her son's company, that her influence led him to neglect both his mother and his wife, and blamed her conduct severely. At her command, Madame de Motteville ventured to give the young Princess a word of warning. Henrietta listened to her mother's old friend with her usual gentleness, but laughed at her mother-in-law's fears, and refused to be guided by her advice. Her intimacy with the King became greater than ever. They spent whole days together, and took long rambles in the woods, which lasted until two or three o'clock in the morning. The young Queen's jealousy was awakened. She wept bitter tears, and alienated the King's affection by her reproaches. Monsieur, in his turn, took offence at the influence which Madame had acquired over the King, and carried his complaints to his mother. Anne of Austria, now thoroughly alarmed, begged the Queen of England to speak seriously to her thoughtless young daughter. But Henrietta Maria, conscious of the innocence of her child's intentions, refused to believe that her conduct was deserving of blame. None the less, from her retreat of Colombes, she watched the course of events anxiously. A touching letter which she wrote to Madame de Motteville at this time ends with the words :—
" You have with you, my other little self—*un autre petit-moi-*

même—who loves you well, I can assure you. I beg of you to remain her friend. I know you will understand what I mean."

Anne of Austria now desired Abbé Montagu to remonstrate with Madame, while she herself spoke gravely to her son, and entreated him to put an end to the scandal caused by his proceedings. Madame was indignant with her mother-in-law, and complained of her unjust accusations to the King. Louis consoled her with assurances of his unalterable friendship. But they both felt the need of greater caution, if family peace was to be preserved, and for the first time, Madame's eyes were ópened to the dangers which threatened her youth and inexperience. Henceforth she took care to show the world that the King was no more to her than a brother-in-law, for whom she had a sincere regard, and whose affection and good opinion she valued as they deserved. When, many years afterwards, Madame herself suggested the story of Bérénice as a subject for a tragedy, both to Corneille and Racine, the Court recognised the theme as inspired by her own experience. In this Roman Emperor, who sacrificed his feelings to a stern sense of duty, the servants of Louis saw the glorification of their master's conduct, and applauded the passage in which Titus bids the Jewish captive a long farewell, as the expression of the King's own sentiments. By way of diverting the Court's notice from Madame, Louis now chose her fair young maid-of-honour, the little La Vallière, as she was called, to be the object of his attentions, and paid her a homage which excited general surprise. The poor girl, gentle and modest as she was, soon fell desperately in love with this handsome and attractive monarch, who stooped to honour her with his notice. Louis himself, pleased to see the flame which he had kindled, soon returned her affection, and his feigned passion became all too real.

At the same time, Armand, Comte de Guiche, the bravest and handsomest man at Court, dared to lift his eyes as high as Madame, and professed himself her devoted servant. Madame de La Fayette speaks of him as a very fine and manly gentleman, infinitely superior to the idle gallants of the Court. Already he had proved his prowess on more than

one hard-fought field, and was burning to win fresh laurels.
With his proud bearing and his noble ambitions, he was, says
Madame de Sevigné, the very type of a paladin of old
renown. " I met the Comte de Guiche to-day at M. de la
Rochefoucauld's," she writes. " He seemed to me very clever,
and less supernatural than usual. We talked a great deal
together." There was something about him, she says, on
another occasion, unlike any one else. He seemed, indeed,
born to be a hero of romance. But he was too haughty and
independent to have many friends at Court. He had at an
early age been married, against his own wish, to a child-
heiress of the house of Sully, but he had never pretended to
love his wife, and although he had paid attentions to various
ladies in turn, no woman had hitherto touched his heart.
From his boyhood he had been Monsieur's chief favourite,
and it was in this capacity that he first became acquainted
with Madame. Even before her marriage, Buckingham had
foretold that the Count would fall in love with her, and it
must be owned that, in these early days of Henrietta's wedded
life, every opportunity of becoming intimate with her was
afforded him. The De Gramont family, to which he belonged,
stood high in the King's favour at Court. His uncle, the
famous Chevalier, had indeed incurred his royal master's
displeasure by his presumption, but his return to favour was
confidently expected, and in the meantime he had taken
refuge in England, and was honoured by Charles II.'s friendship. His father, the fine old Maréchal, commanded universal
respect, and was always treated with marked consideration
by Louis XIV. and the whole of the Royal Family. His
sister, Madame de Monaco, was Madame's chosen friend ; his
aunt, Madame de Saint-Chaumont, became the governess of
her children. Whether at Paris or at Fontainebleau, the
Comte de Guiche was daily in her presence. In the Court
ballets and masquerades this accomplished cavalier was
always one of the chief actors. They rehearsed their parts
together in private, they sang and danced together in public.
As long as the King devoted himself to Madame, the Count
had not ventured to confess his passion, but when Louis
became less assiduous in his attentions, De Guiche in his

turn grew bolder. One day, when he had come to rehearse a scene in the *Ballet des Saisons*, in which he and Madame were to appear together, he asked her if nothing had ever touched her heart, and when she gave him some merry answer, he rushed out of the room, declaring that he was in great danger. Another time, he confessed to Madame that he was the victim of a hopeless passion, and described the charms of his mistress in terms which left no doubt in the mind of others, that he spoke of Henrietta herself.

Even then, she failed to see his meaning, and the Count's adoration remained a secret to her alone. But one day, Monsieur took offence, and after angry words on both sides, the Count haughtily withdrew from Court. The King, who was secretly gratified at the new turn which events had taken, himself told Madame what had happened, and she learnt, to her surprise, that the Count had openly avowed his passion. At first, she acted with more prudence than might have been expected. She begged Madame de Monaco to desire her brother not to appear again in her presence, and refused to read a letter which he ventured to send her. But the seed was sown, and dissensions soon became ripe in Monsieur's household. He became sulky and jealous, and teased his wife about trifles. Next, he quarrelled with Madame de Monaco, who, to do her justice, had never encouraged her brother's pretensions, and that lady left Court for her husband's principality in the south. Vague reports of these unhappy disputes reached England, and Lady Derby, writing to Madame de la Trémouille, observes : " Rumour says that Monsieur is very jealous of Madame, and that he makes her a very bad husband, which I cannot believe. The Duke of York is very much the reverse ; there never was his equal, he and his wife being inseparable." Madame de la Trémouille and her daughter, however, plainly were not of those who thought ill of Madame, and Lady Derby remarks at the same time that nothing pleases her better than to know that the Princess continues to conduct herself with so much discretion and virtue.

Political intrigues now came to blend with love quarrels,

Fouquet's doom was sealed, not only because he had enriched himself at the expense of the State, but because he
had made insulting proposals to Mademoiselle de la Vallière.
On the 17th of August, this unfortunate minister gave the
famous festival which La Fontaine has described in such
glowing language.   A richly-decorated theatre was erected
under an avenue of pines, in the midst of orange groves and
fountains.　　Here Molière's new comedy, *Les Fâcheux*, was
performed with ballets and musical interludes between the
acts.　　At one moment, twenty *jets d'eau* shot up waters of
different hues to heaven.　　At another, long-haired naiads rose
out of the rocks, and an opening shell revealed the bewitching
form of the actress, Madeleine Béjart.　Madame, in whose
honour the *fête* was said to be given, was ill that evening, and
had to appear in a litter.　La Vallière was there among her
ladies, and the King's growing inclination became for the
first time evident to all.　Madame went home convinced that
her own influence with Louis was on the wane, and that her
shy maid of honour was rapidly taking her place.　The King
was visibly annoyed at the extravagant splendour and reckless profusion displayed by his minister, on this occasion.
More than one courtier had drawn his attention to the super-
intendent's device, a climbing squirrel, with the significant
motto "*Quo non ascendam?*" which adorned the ceilings and
mantelpieces of his house.　Four days afterwards, the Court
set out on a journey into Brittany, and Fouquet was arrested
at Nantes.　In vain his powerful friends tried to save him,
in vain La Fontaine implored the King's clemency, on behalf
of his Mœcenas, in the most poetic strains.　The nymphs
of Vaux wept bitter tears, but Louis could not forgive
the personal wrong which Fouquet had done him, nor
forget the millions which he had lavished on the gardens
of Vaux.　The fallen minister was found guilty of misuse
of public money, and condemned to drag out his miserable
existence in a long and hopeless captivity.　The King appointed Colbert his successor, and applied himself to effect
a thorough reformation in the disordered finances of the
state.

　　The Court returned to Fontainebleau for the autumn,

and there, on the 1st of November, the Queen gave birth
to a Dauphin. The event was hailed with rejoicing by
the whole nation, the fountains of Fontainebleau flowed with
wine during three days, and brilliant displays of fireworks
were given. The Queen-mother of England was invited to
become the royal child's godmother, and gave him the names
of Louis Toussaint, in memory of his birth on All-Saints' Day.
As soon as the Queen had recovered, the King accompanied
her on a pilgrimage to Our Lady of Chartres, and Monsieur
and Madame came to Paris. This long course of dissipation
had proved injurious to Henrietta's delicate health. She was
taken to the Tuileries in a litter, and tenderly nursed by her
mother during the next few weeks. Mademoiselle, who had
been kept away from Court by an attack of fever, was
shocked to see the alteration in her appearance. She was
transparently thin, coughed incessantly, and could not sleep
without opiates. For some time, her health was a cause of
great anxiety, and although, after Christmas, she began to
recover, she was ordered perfect rest during the winter months.
Jean Loret, whose *Muse historique* faithfully reflects the Court
gossip of the day, laments Madame's illness in his verses of
December 17th, and regrets that the gods who had endowed
her with so many gifts, had denied her the best of all, good
health.

> " Elle a douceur, elle a beauté
> D'agréments une infinité,
> Elle a naissance, elle a richesse,
> Pour elle on a grand tendresse.
> Voila bien des dons précieux,
> Mais la santé vaut encore mieux."

These alarms were shared by Henrietta's brother in
England, and an affectionate letter of inquiry, which he
wrote to his *chère Minette* on the 16th of December, is the
only one in the French Archives that belongs to the year 1661.
Lord Crofts of Saxham, formerly Captain of the Queen's
Guard, and now a gentleman of the King's bed-chamber, had
been sent to Paris, to bear his master's congratulations on the
Dauphin's birth, and had just returned with letters from the
Queen and Madame.

" I have been in very much paine for your indisposition, not so much that I thought it dangerous, but for feare that you should miscarry. I hope now you are out of that feare too, and for God's sake, my dearest sister, have a care of yourselfe, and beleeve that I am more concerned in your health than I am in my owne, which I hope you do me the iustice to be confident of, since you know how much I love you. Crofts hath given me a full accounte of all you charged him with, with all which I am very well pleased, and in particular with the desire you have to see me at Dunkerke the next summer, which you may easily beleeve is a very welcome proposition to me ; betweene this and then, we will adjust that voyage. I am sure I shall be very impatient till I have the happinesse to see *ma chère Minette* againe. I am very glad to finde that the King of France does still continue his confidence and kindnesse to you, which I am so sensible of, that if I had no other reason to grounde my kindnesse to him but that, he may be most assured of my frindship as long as I live, and pray upon all occasions, assure him of this. I do not write to you in French, because my head is now dosed with businesse, and 'tis troublesome to write anything but English, and I do intende to write to you very often in English, that you may not quite forgett it.   C. R.

" For my dearest sister."

One proof of Louis XIV.'s friendly feeling for his sister-in-law appeared in his readiness to make use of her, in his negotiations with her brother. The good understanding which he was anxious to maintain with England had been somewhat ruffled by an unfortunate incident. On the occasion of the Swedish Minister's entry into London, on the 30th of September 1661, the Spanish Ambassador, Baron de Watteville, thought well to take precedence of the French Ambassador, M. d'Estrades. A desperate fight took place on Tower Hill, in which the Spaniards, helped by the citizens, routed the French. Five Frenchmen were killed and thirty-three more wounded. The harness of the Ambassador's coach

was cut, and four of his six horses were stabbed.   As soon as
the news of what was happening got abroad, Mr Pepys, eager
to see the fun, ran to the City, and arrived to find that the
Spaniard had got the best of it and was gone through the
streets next to the King's coach, "at which it is strange to see
how all the City did rejoice, for we do naturally all love the
Spanish and hate the French."   But if the popular feeling was
all on the side of the Spaniards, that of the Court was well-
known to be on that of the French, and Charles II. and the
Duke of York were as sorry for M. d'Estrades' discomfiture
as Mr Pepys was overjoyed.   As for Louis, his fury knew no
bounds, and he ordered the Spanish Ambassador to leave
Paris, insisted on Watteville's immediate recall, and did not
rest content until he had obtained an ample apology and full
reparation from his father-in-law.   The same tenacity on all
points of honour led him to follow up his success in this
matter, by an attempt to induce Charles II. to dispense with
the customary salute yielded by ships of all nations to the
British men-of-war.   But on this point, he found his royal
brother less pliable than he expected, and in the following
letter to Madame, the King defends this time-honoured
privilege of his flag with true British spirit.

"WHITHALL.
"23 <i>Decem.</i>, 1661.

   "I receaved yours of the 27th so late this night, and the
post being ready to goe, that I have only time to tell you that
I extreamly wonder at that which you writ to me of, for
certainly never any ships refused to strike their pavilion when
they met any ships belonging to the Crowne of England.
This is a right so well known, and never disputed by any
kinge before, that, if I should have it questioned now, I must
conclude it to be a <i>querelle d'Allemand.</i>   I hope what you say
to me is only your feares, for I will never beleeve that anybody
who desires my frindship will expect that which was never so
much as thought of before, therefore all I shall say to you is,
that my ships must do their dutyes, lett what will come of it!
And I should be very unworthy if I quit a right and goe
lower than ever any of my predecessors did, which is all I

have to say, only that I am very glad to finde you are so well
recovered, and be assured, my dearest sister, that I am intierly
yours.   C. R."

Unfortunately the letter from Henrietta, which had pro-
voked this prompt and vigorous reply, has been lost, and we
find no further allusion to the matter in their future correspondence.

Madame's next letter was sent to London by the hands of
Mrs. Stewart, the widow of one of Lord Blantyre's sons, who
had taken refuge in Paris during the Civil War, and had
spent some years at the French Court.   Her daughter, Frances
Stewart, who had figured with Madame in the *Ballet des
Saisons*, had now been chosen, at Henrietta's recommendation,
to be maid-of-honour to Charles II.'s new Queen.   The
King's marriage with the Infanta of Portugal had been concluded in the course of the autumn, and Catherine of Braganza
was expected to arrive in England early in the following
spring.   So Madame, unwilling to let her friends appear at
Whitehall without a word of greeting to her brother, wrote
these few lines on the 4th of January 1662.

" I would not lose this opportunity of writing to you by
Mrs. Stewart, who is taking over her daughter to become one
of the Queen, your wife's, future maids.   If this were not the
reason of her departure, I should be very unwilling to let her
go, for she is the prettiest girl in the world, and one of the
best fitted of any I know to adorn a court.   Yesterday I
received your letter in reply to those I sent you by Crofts.
I cannot tell you what joy I feel at the mere thought of
seeing Your Majesty once more.   There is nothing in the
world I wish for more.   Believe me, when I say that I remain
your very humble servant."

Henrietta was now sufficiently recovered to leave her bed,
although she was still confined to her apartments.   Here,
reclining on her couch in one of those exquisite toilettes
which excited Mademoiselle's envy, she received visitors from
early morning till a late hour at night.   All manner of
amusements beguiled her days.   Ballets were danced, plays
were acted in her apartments.   A grand ballet on the glories

of the Royal House, which had been performed at the Louvre on the 7th of February, was repeated a week later, in Madame's rooms, the King, Queen and Monsieur taking leading parts. The Comte de Guiche had apparently made up his quarrel with Monsieur, for he also appeared as an actor, in the not inappropriate character of the Hour of Silence. As before, the whole Court crowded to the Tuileries. The King came there every day, drawn by his growing passion for La Vallière. Madame herself knew the reason of his frequent visits only too well, but neither of the Queens as yet suspected this new attachment. Accordingly they looked on Henrietta with increased bitterness, and she felt, with good reason, that it was very hard to be blamed, when the fault was not hers. Meanwhile, the Comte de Guiche sought to renew his old intimacy with Madame, through one of her maids-of-honour named Montalais. This girl, whose character ought to have debarred her from the place she held in Madame's household, was an *intrigante* of the first order. She had already discovered La Vallière's secret, and now tried to gain the Count's graces by inducing her mistress to lend an ear to his passionate appeals. When news of Madame's dangerous illness reached him, he had given way to an outburst of grief which excited the surprise of his friends. Henrietta herself, touched by the sincerity of his affection, no longer refused to receive the letters which he sent her, through her maid-of-honour. One day, becoming bolder, he ventured into her presence, in the disguise of a fortune-teller. No one recognised him but Madame, who was infinitely amused. After that, this bold lover repeatedly and openly defied public opinion, and made his appearance in Madame's rooms. The risks he ran for her sake gratified her vanity, and she was too young and thoughtless to see the folly of her conduct. Soon the Comte de Guiche's passion for Madame became the talk of the Court, and their names were linked together in the popular songs and satires of the day.

> " C'est la bergère d'Angleterre
> Qui à Saint-Cloud s'en va chantant,
> Est-ce si grand mal
> Que d'avoir fait un amant ? "

While Madame, like some innocent child, was playing with edged tools, the King's intrigue with La Vallière had assumed more serious proportions. So grave was the scandal, that one day Madame herself told her young maid-of-honour that she must leave her service. La Vallière, overwhelmed with confusion, acknowledged the truth of her mistress's reproaches, and left the Tuileries that night. The next morning the King was informed of his mistress's flight. There was a great hue and cry, and Louis himself set out to find her retreat. It was a week-day in Lent, and the eloquent Abbé Bossuet, whose sermons had attracted the Queen-mother's attention some years ago, was preaching at the chapel of the Louvre that day. The King's absence excited much surprise, and his wife was so uneasy that Anne of Austria found it difficult to allay her fears, and secretly avowed her conviction that something was amiss to Mademoiselle. At length, after a prolonged search, the unhappy La Vallière was discovered in a convent near Saint-Cloud, where she had taken refuge. The King himself brought her back to the Tuileries, and with tears in his eyes implored Madame to receive her. Henrietta consented, but not without considerable reluctance, and is said to have told the King, that in future she would consider La Vallière as his property, "*une fille-à-vous*."

On the 14th of March, Henrietta was at length well enough to appear again in public. She visited her mother at the Palais-Royal, and attended service at the Louvre, with the rest of the Royal Family. The eloquent Archdeacon of Metz did not preach on that occasion, and Madame did not hear Bossuet until some years later. Her mother, however, was constant in attending his Lent sermons at the Louvre, and shared the admiration with which the two French Queens regarded him. Monsieur and Madame were also often among his audience, and the King himself, in spite of the strangely opposite direction in which his thoughts were bent, was deeply impressed by the preacher's fervour. Not only did he appoint Bossuet Court preacher, but he wrote a letter with his own hand to the eloquent Abbé's white-haired father, congratulating him on having so distinguished a son.

Monsieur and Madame now moved to the Palais-Royal, in

order that Henrietta might be with her mother, during her *accouchement*. On the 21st of March, she accompanied the Queen-mother to another function at the Val-de-Grâce, the sanctuary founded by Anne of Austria in thanksgiving for the birth of Louis XIV., and on the 24th, she gave the Spanish Ambassador an audience in company with the Queen, her sister-in-law. Three days later, at an early hour on the 27th, she gave birth to a daughter. The event was premature, but passed off happily. Her mother was with her at the time, and before six o'clock, the King and the two Queens arrived to offer Madame their congratulations. Both parents, however, were greatly disappointed at the child's sex, and Madame, on hearing she had given birth to a daughter, is said to have exclaimed, "Then throw her into the river!" Her mother-in-law was much scandalised at these lamentations, and by way of consoling Madame, observed that if she had not given birth to a prince, her little daughter, who was but a few months younger than the baby Dauphin, might some day yet become a Queen. Her words were destined to prove true, although not in the sense in which they were intended, for the little Princess, who met with so cold a reception on her coming into the world, became the wife, not of the Dauphin, but of the King of Spain. In England the news was joyfully received, not only by the King, but by all who had seen and admired the Princess on her visit two years before. "We are very much surprised," wrote Lady Derby, "at the news you have sent of Madame's *accouchement*. She is young enough to have many sons and daughters, if she goes on as she has begun. I am astonished that the Queen, her mother, had not made all the necessary preparations. Mademoiselle, then, has lost her title!"

Henrietta now recovered rapidly, and on the 30th of April, according to custom, she appeared at St. Eustache with her infant to offer the *pains bénits*. The first news that she heard, on her return to society, was that the Maréchal de Gramont had obtained the command of the troops before Nancy from the King, for his son. The Count de Guiche afterwards discovered that he owed his removal from Court to the intrigues of a false friend, and, when he found that Madame was surprised at his abrupt departure, begged the favour of a parting interview. This Madame imprudently granted him, and the next morning, the Count left for his new post. Although Montalais had introduced him by a private staircase into Madame's presence, his steps had been watched by another of Madame's ladies, who reported what she had seen to the Queen-mother of France. Anne of Austria, furious with her daughter-in-law, immediately informed Monsieur, that his wife was in the habit of holding stolen interviews with the Comte de Guiche. In this emergency, Monsieur, to do him justice, showed more good sense than usual. He dismissed Montalais at once, and went to his mother-in-law for advice. Queen Henrietta spoke seriously to her daughter, and showed her the folly of her conduct. An explanation with Monsieur followed. Madame frankly told him all that had passed between her and his old favourite, upon which he embraced her kindly and declared himself to be quite satisfied. "Any other husband," observes Madame de La Fayette, "would have been more concerned." But Monsieur was not a man of deep feeling or strong passions, and vexed himself and others far more over petty trifles than serious troubles. The episode of the Comte de Guiche, however, was not yet ended, and many were the disastrous consequences of her own imprudence which Madame had yet to suffer.

CHAPTER IX

1662

THE winter of 1661-1662 was one of exceptional scarcity for the people of France. The severity of the season, following as it did on a bad harvest, and the high price of foreign corn, had produced an absolute dearth of bread. From all parts of the kingdom, the same cry of famine and misery was heard. The country groaned under the weight of excessive taxation, and the poorer classes were crushed by burdens that were too heavy for them to bear. Gui Patin, in his letters, draws a terrible picture of the suffering and destitution on all sides. Everywhere people are dying of want and disease, of poverty and despair. And he goes on, after his wont, to paint the startling contrast between the luxury and splendour of the Court *fêtes* on which the King wasted millions, while his subjects were literally dying before his eyes in the streets of Paris. But, even at the Court of Louis XIV., the poor were not without friends. That Lent, Bossuet pleaded earnestly on their behalf, from the pulpit of the Louvre, and warned the King solemnly not to turn a deaf ear to the cry of his oppressed people. And Louis, who was always easily moved, had taken measures to relieve the immediate needs of the poor at his gates. During these winter months, foreign corn was stored in the halls of the Louvre, and sold at cheap rates to the people of Paris, and thousands of loaves were daily given away at the doors of the Tuileries. The two Queens took an active part in these works of mercy, and the good Prin-

cesse de Conti sold her jewels, and gave alms to the hospitals.
More than this, a variety of financial reforms were effected,
and a reduction of four millions in the taxes, granted by the
King in the month of March, produced general satisfaction.
The return of spring, bringing with it, as it did, some allevia-
tion of the national distress, now became the signal for fresh
fêtes at Court. Louis XIV., having quieted his conscience
with these attempts at reform, gave free rein to his taste for
splendid amusements, and during the next few weeks, the
citizens of Paris were dazzled by a succession of magnificent
pageants.

On the 21st of May, the christening of Monsieur and
Madame's little daughter was celebrated with royal pomp in
the Chapel of the Palais-Royal. Abbé Montagu officiated, in
the absence of Monsieur's Grand Almoner, the Bishop of
Valence. The King, the Queen, and Henrietta Maria, were
sponsors, and the babe received the name of Marie Louise.
The same day, a tournament was held in the great square of
the Tuileries, and the gentlemen of the Court rode at the
ring, after the fashion of the knights of olden time, to the
sound of trumpets and the clang of cymbals. This was only
a prelude to the famous Carrousel that was held on the same
square, on the 1st of June, and which gave its name to the
quadrangle between the Louvre and the Tuileries. On this
occasion, the knights appeared in the costume of different
nations. The King rode at the head of the Roman squadron,
Monsieur led the Persians, while the Queens and Princesses,
seated under a gorgeous canopy of cloth of gold, looked on at
the tournament, and gave prizes to the victors with their own
royal hands. A month later, the King gave a stag-hunt at
Versailles, where Madame appeared on horseback, at the head
of a party of ladies clad in grey hats and plumes, and rode
more fearlessly than any of her companions. But she spent
most of that summer either at Colombes, or else at Saint-
Cloud, in the company of her mother, who was now about to
take leave of her fondly-loved child and return to England.
On the 25th of July she left Paris, and was escorted on her
journey as far as Beauvais by Monsieur and Madame. Here
Henrietta and her mother parted, not without many tears, and

Monsieur took his wife to Chantilly, where the Prince de Condé entertained them royally, during the next few days. The hero of Rocroi had always been a kind friend to the English royal family, and was proud to do Madame the honours of his beautiful home of Chantilly, which Madame de La Fayette calls the loveliest of all the places that the sun shines on. The great soldier, who seldom showed himself at Court, liked to collect his friends about him for hunting parties and theatrical performances, and show them the pictures and other treasures which adorned the galleries of Chantilly. The nobleness of his character attracted thoughtful natures. He was an intimate friend of Bossuet, whom he had known in his student days, and Madame de La Fayette was one of the very few ladies with whom he ever cared to converse. After this pleasant visit, Monsieur and Madame joined the Court at Saint-Germain, where they had rooms in the Château Neuf, the palace which Henri Quatre had built in the midst of terraced gardens on the banks of the Seine, close to the ancient castle of the French Kings. There they spent the rest of the summer, with the occasional diversion of a visit to their own house at Saint-Cloud, until the approach of the winter found them once more settled at the Palais-Royal, which now became their permanent town residence.

All this time, Madame kept up a frequent correspondence with her mother, whose presence in England accounts for the King's silence during the greater part of this year. Charles was never fond of writing letters, and the regularity with which his mother and sister exchanged letters was a good excuse for the laziness to which he so often pleads guilty. All we have in the first half of 1662 is one letter, written on the 23d of May, from Portsmouth, two days after his wedding. The Infanta landed at Spithead on the 20th, and the marriage was performed by the Bishop of London on the following day at Portsmouth. Charles was agreeably impressed with his Portuguese wife, but by no means gratified with the manners of her suite. These " Portingall ladies," as Lord Chesterfield calls them, with their huge foretops, their monstrous fardingales or guardinfantas, and their ridiculous notions of propriety, made themselves sufficiently " unagreeable " from the first

They refused to go out of doors, for fear they might be seen
by men, and would not even consent to sleep in any lodgings,
without first ascertaining if they had been previously occupied
by any of the other sex. And they and their priests buzzed
round the Queen, Charles complains, like so many hornets.

"I cannot easily tell you," wrote the King to Clarendon,
"how happy I think myself; and I must be the worst man
living, which I hope I am not, if I am not a good husband.
I am confident never two humours were better fitted together
than ours are. We cannot stir from hence till Tuesday, by
reason that there are not carts to be had to-morrow to
transport all our *guarda infantas* (there were a hundred
members in the suite), without which there is no stirring; so
you are not to expect me till Thursday at Hampton Court."

To Henrietta he wrote in a similar strain.

"My Lord of St. Alban's will give you soe full a description
of my wife as I shall not go about to doe it, only I must tell
you I think myselfe very happy. I was married the day
before yesterday, but the fortune that follows our family is
fallen upon me, *car Monseigneur le Cardinal m'a fermé la
porte au nez!* But I flatter myself I was not so furious as
Monsieur was, and shall let this passe. I intend, on Monday
next, to go towards Hamton Court, where I shall stay till the
Queene (Henrietta Maria) comes. My dearest sister, continue
your kindnesse to me, and beleeve me to be intierly yours,
                                        "C. R."

"And yet," wrote Lord Chesterfield, who knew his master
too well, "I fear all this will hardly make things run in the
right channel. If it should, our Court will require a new
modelling." His misgivings proved only too correct.

During the next two or three months, the King was
entirely taken up with his wife. Her sweetness and naiveté
pleased him; her very ignorance tickled his fancy. He forgot
his mistress for the time, and was as well amused as a child
with a new toy. But, before long, Lady Castlemaine resumed
her old influence, and, when he insisted on forcing the Queen
to receive her at Court, Clarendon had to remind him how

strongly he had blamed the conduct of Louis XIV., in allowing La Vallière to live under Madame's roof, and appear in his wife's presence. Charles had even been heard to say that "he should never be guilty of such a piece of ill-nature, for, if ever he could be guilty of keeping a mistress after he had a wife, she should never come where his wife was."

His next letter to Madame, curiously enough, contains an allusion to the French King's behaviour on this point, but this time he wisely abstains from making any comparison with his own, and does not allude to his wife, although he speaks of his mother with the tenderest affection.

> " WHITHALL,
> " 8 *Sept.* 1662.

" I am soe ashamed for the *faute* I have committed against you that I have nothing to say for myselfe, but ingenuously confesse it, which I hope in some degree will obtaine my pardon, assureing you for the time to come I will repair any past failings, and I hope you do not impute it in the least degree to wante of kindnesse, for I assure you there is nothing I love so well as my dearest Minette, and if ever I faile you in the least, say I am unworthy of having such a sister as you! The Queene has tould you, I hope, that she is not displeased with her being heere. I am sure I have done all that lies in my power to lett her see the duty and kindnesse I have for her. The truth is, never any children had so good a mother as we have, and you and I shall never have any disputes but only who loves her best, and in that I will never yield to you. She has shewed me your letters concerning your quarrell with the K., and you were much in the right. He has too much ingenuity not to do what he did. If I had been in his place I should have done the same. The Chevalier de Gramont begins his journey to-morrow, or next day; by him I will write more at large to you. I am doing all I can to gett him a rich wife heere. You may thinke this is a jeste, but he is in good earnest, and I believe he will tell you that he is not displeased with his usage heere, and with the way of living; and so farewell, my dearest Minette, for this time.—I am intierly yours,

C. R."

The quarrel with the King, to which Charles alludes, was a fresh dispute, which had been caused by La Vallière's continued presence in Madame's household. The King's *liaison* with her was now a recognised fact at Court. Every *fête* which the King planned, was in reality given in her honour. She was the true queen of love and beauty who presided at the famous Carrousel. Another might occupy, the throne, or hand the victor his prize, but La Vallière was the mistress before whose eyes her royal lover rode at the ring. Clarice, as the courtiers called her, was the soul of all the *fêtes*. Poems, full of veiled meanings, were written on the loves of the King, and recited before the unconscious Queen. And when, in masquerade or ballet, the Court poets put verses in La Vallière's own lips that told her love, when she recited Benserade's lines :—

> " Et je ne pense pas que dans tout le village,
> Il se rencontre un cœur mieux placé que le sien,"

the applause of the listening courtiers showed that the poet's meaning had not been lost upon the audience. Only Marie Thérèse still remained ignorant of her husband's unfaithfulness, and it was not until a year later, when the Comtesse de Soissons revealed the truth to her, that she became aware of the full extent of her wrongs. She still looked upon Madame as her sole rival, and hated her accordingly. Naturally, Henrietta resented this injustice, and repeatedly begged the King to remove his mistress from her household. It was hard, to say the least, that she should be hated for the fault of another. At length Louis acknowledged his mistake, and La Vallière was given separate apartments, and appeared no longer among Madame's ladies. And when, in the spring of 1663, her condition rendered further concealment impossible, she moved to the Palais Brion, a house in the gardens of the Palais-Royal, which the King gave her as a residence.

During the latter half of 1662, negotiations between France and England were carried on with great frequency, and Louis attained what had long been a chief object of his policy, the cession of the port of Dunkirk. At the time of Madame's marriage this had been already proposed, but Charles then shrank from the unpopularity which such a measure could not fail to entail. Now, however, his throne appeared to be more secure, and his want of money was greater than ever. Accordingly he agreed to sell Dunkirk to France for the sum of five million French livres. "The King of England," writes Bussy de Rabutin, "has turned into a shopkeeper. He has sold us Dunkirk, and I hope we shall buy London to-morrow!" And the French Secretary describes Charles II.'s satisfaction, when the first three millions of money were sent over in boats, and he rode to the Tower, to see the newly-arrived gold deposited in his coffers.

In October, Ralph Montagu, the second son of Lord Montagu of Boughton, was sent to Paris, with two letters addressed to Madame, the one for her eyes only, the other, which was written in French, intended to be shown to Louis XIV. In both, Charles declares his wish to conduct future correspondence on state affairs with the King, through his sister, rather than through their respective Ambassadors, and expresses his opinion that, by this means, both countries are likely to be drawn more closely together.

"WHITHALL,
"26 *Oct.* 1662.

"I shall not neede to say much to you by this bearer, Mr Montagu, he is so well instructed as he will informe of all that passes heere. I will only tell you that nothing but pure necessity and impossibility hath kept me hitherto from paying what I owe you, but I will now put it into so certayne a way, as you shall begin to see the effects of it very speedily, and I assure you it hath more troubled me the not being able to pay it then the wante of that summe can be to you. The man that makes the *lunetts d'aproche* has been very sicke, which is the cause I have not sent you one all this while, but now he promises me one very speedyly. I will say no more to you at this time, because I will not prevent this bearer in what he shall say, only I will trust nobody but myself in telling you how truely I am yours,   C. R."

" LONDON,
"*26th Oct.* 1662.

" I avail myself of the permission which you have given me, to assure you of the continuation of those sentiments which you approve, and of my intentions to employ all the means that are most likely to attain the fulfilment of our wishes. Nothing can better serve this end, than a close friendship between the King, my brother, and myself, and I assure you that this consideration was my chief reason in making this last Treaty, for an intimate alliance between us. In this I am persuaded that we shall have the advantage of your intervention, and if you think fit to propose that we should communicate our thoughts to each other through you, I shall be very glad, knowing how much this mutual confidence will assist in promoting our friendship. I have desired this bearer to inform you and the King, my brother, of the present state of our affairs, and of the object I pursue. He will assure you of all the imaginable respect which I cherish for your person, and of my wish that you should become the witness and mutual pledge of the friendship that binds me to the King, my brother   I leave all further particulars to this porter. [1]   C. R."

The King's next letter mentions the payment of Madame's long-delayed dowry, and the recent Anabaptist riots. He

" LONDRES,
" *ce 26th Oct.* 1662.

[1] " Je me sers de cette liberté que vous avés agreé, pour vous asseurer de la continuation des sentimens que vous aprouvés, et de mon dessin d'employer tous les moyens les plus convenables pour faire reussir nos desirs, a quoi je ne considére rien de plus utile que l'amitié intime entre le Roy mon frere et moy, et je vous asseure que cette consideration m'a persuadé fortement a faire ce dernier traité pour lier une correspondence fort estroitte entre nous, enquoy ie suis fort persuadé de vostre intervention, et s'il vous plait de luy proposer que nous puissions communiquer nos pencées par cette voye particuliere de nos mains, i'en seray fort aise, connoisant combien cette confiance réçiproque contribuera a entretenir nos amities, j'ay donné charge à ce porteur de vous entretenir et le Roy mon frère de l'estat present de mes affaires, et de la poursuite que ie me propose. Il vous asseura de tout le respect imaginable que j'ay pour vostre personne, et du desire que j'ay, que vous soyés tesmoin et caution commune de l'amitié entre le Roy mon frere et moy, me remettant particulierement a ce porteur.

" C. R."

also alludes to a request made by Monsieur, on behalf of two
of his favourites, the Prince de Chalais and his brother-in-law,
Alexandre de la Trémouille, Marquis de Noirmoustier. These
two young noblemen had been engaged in a recent duel, which
arose from some foolish quarrel at the Palais-Royal. One of
their opponents, a brother of the Duc de Beauvilliers, had been
slain, and Chalais and Noirmoustier had fled, fearing to incur
the heavy penalties to which they were liable. The practice
of duelling had of late years become so common among the
gilded youth of France, that Bossuet had denounced it in one
of his Lent sermons before the King, and Louis had determined to put a stop to it by stringent measures. He now
absolutely refused to pardon the culprits, and, as a last resource,
Monsieur tried to enlist his royal brother-in-law's good offices
on behalf of his friends. Charles, with his usual good nature,
promised to do his best, and sent an envoy across to Calais,
to bear his request to Louis XIV., who was then inspecting
the frontier fortifications. The King, however, was inflexible,
and spoke so strongly to his brother, that Monsieur did not
even venture to allow the English envoy to address him on
the subject. Chalais died in exile, and his brother-in-law, who
had only served as his second in the duel, was allowed to
return to France the following year, but never again to show
his face at Court. In April 1664, at Monsieur's request, he
obtained the command of an English regiment at that time
serving in Portugal, and was slain in a battle against the
Spaniards.

"LONDON,
"4 of Nov. 1662.

"I will not trouble you with an answer concerning the
business of Noirmoutier and Chalais, because I have done it
to Monsieur, so as I refer you for that matter to his letter;
the chiefe businesse of this letter shall be to tell you that I
am now settling a certaine funde for the payment of what I
owe you, which I assure you had not been so long undone
but that my condition has been such hetherto, as there was
no possebility of doeing it till now, and I promise you it has
given me very much trouble and shame, that I could not per-

forme what I so much desire, and to one I love so well as you. By my next you shall have a more certaine accounte, and I dout not but to your satisfaction. You will have heard before now of the alarums we have had from the risings heere of the anababtists, but our spyes have played there parts so well amongst them, as we have taken many of them, who will be hanged very speedily, so as I believe for this time, there designes are broken. This is all I shall say to you at this time, but be assured that I will alwais have as much care of all your interests, as of his who is intierly yours,   C. R."

" WHITHALL,
" 21 Nov. 1662.

" I shall despatch my Ld Garret to-morrow with my compliments, to meete the K. of France at Calais, by him I will make my ernest desires for Noirmoutiers' and Chalais' pardon, and in case I cannot obtain it for both at least that I may have it for Noirmoutier, as the least fauty. The Queene read to me last night your letter, in which you feare that there is two of yours miscarried. I hope they are only lost by the post, for I never receaved any from you, upon the subject you mention. What is past, there is no helpe for, but for the future, write nothing by the post, but what you would have know, for to my knowledge the letters are very often opened, this messenger is in such hast to be dispatched as I will say no more but that I am intierly yours,   C. R."

These complaints of the insecurity of the post, between the two countries, were constantly repeated by the Ambassadors on both sides of the Channel. "Letters are opened more cleverly here," Comminges writes to his master, "than anywhere else in the world. *Cela a le bel air.*" There was, at that time, only one postal delivery during the week, both in Paris and London, and even this was constantly delayed by bad weather and accidents on the way. Sometimes no packet could cross the Channel for a whole week at a time; sometimes, as we find from Charles' letters to his sister, the boat was upset and the courier drowned! But still, although special messengers were despatched on all important business, the King and Madame continued to write to each other by the mail, and most of Henrietta's letters were sent by the "*ordin-aire*" which left Paris on Sundays.

Her next letter contains another request, this time on behalf of an old friend of her brother's. The lady whom Henrietta calls by her pet name, Bablon, was none other than that famous heroine of the Fronde, Madame de Châtillon, whose black eyes had so long made her the object of Mademoiselle's envy. This letter is now preserved among the papers on French affairs at the Record Office, and bears the following inscription :—"Madame, to His Majesty, in favour of Madame de Chastillon."

"PARIS,
"*ce* 20 *Novembre* 1662.

" I am almost glad to give you an opportunity of doing Bablon a service. She has begged me to recommend her affair to you, and I assure you, that I do it most willingly, for I am very fond of her, and know that she is much attached to both of us, which is a good reason why you should do your best for her, even if you have forgotten old days. Bablon and I, we both of us thank you beforehand, since we have no doubt that you will do what we ask. If you want more news, Vivonne will give it you. He is a great friend of mine, and I have told him to tell you all you wish to know. I am sure that he will do this, if you say that it is my wish. I have not written to you, since I received your letter by M. de Montagu. I will only say that I am very well satisfied with what you have done, and if I have not told you so before, it is because I am afraid of wearying you as much with my thanks as I had done with my prayers before. This is all I will say, excepting that I am, your very humble servant."

We do not learn the precise nature of Bablon's request, but, from the King's answer, there can be little doubt that it was a petition for some lucrative privilege, which would bring gold into the pockets of this needy and extravagant lady. The Duc de Vivonne, who was the bearer of both letters, and of whom Madame speaks so warmly, was a very accomplished person, a great favourite with Madame de

Sevigné and her friends, and brother to one of Henrietta's maids-of-honour, Mademoiselle de Mortémart, afterwards Madame de Montespan."

"You may easily beleeve that any request which comes from Bablon will be quickly dispatched by me. I am striving all I can, to take away the difficulties which obstruct this desire of hers, which in truth are very greate, all those thinges being farmed, and 'tis not hard to imagine that people on this side the watter, love there profit as well as they do every where else ; I have sent to inquier farther into it, and within five or six dayes will give you an account, for I am very unwilling not to grante Bablon's desires, especially when they come recommended by you. In the meane time I referre you to this bearer, Mon^r Vivonne, who will tell you how truly I am, yours.   C. R."

One more letter of Madame's belongs to this year. It was written from Paris on the 14th of December, and sent to her brother, by the hands of Monsieur de Comminges, the new Ambassador to England.

"I have not troubled you often with letters lately, but when an Ambassador starts, it is necessary to write, and I should not make those excuses for doing my duty, if I were not afraid you might think yourself obliged to answer me, and were not also conscious of my natural inclination to be troublesome. I am telling the Queen my mother all the news I have, and which I know she will tell you, for which reason I do not write it here. I should have done myself the honour of writing to the Queen your wife, but as she would not understand a word I said, I prefer begging you to tell her, that this is the reason why I do not trouble her. And I feel sure that a compliment coming from yourself, will be better received than one from me, although there is no one who honours her more than I do. I will only add that I am your very humble servant."

CHAPTER X

1663

THE Court spent Christmas at Paris, engaged in a continual
round of gaiety. Even the death of the King's infant
daughter, Madame Anne Elisabeth de France, which happened very suddenly, on the 30th of December, was not
allowed to interrupt their course, for more than a few days.
The little Princess was only a few weeks old, when she died,
a victim to the ignorance of the Court physicians who, as
usual, insisted on bleeding her. "Princes," remarks Gui
Patin, "are invariably unfortunate in doctors," and the
mortality of the King's children was indeed remarkable, four
out of the five dying in their infancy, "hurried out of this
world," in the second Madame's expressive phrase, "by the
Court physician's ignorance." But the King, absorbed in his
passion for La Vallière, had no leisure for grief. Twelfth
Day was celebrated at the Louvre, by a splendid representation of Molierè's *École des Femmes*, followed by a concert of
Lulli's violins. The same play was repeated during the
Carnival, on the occasion of Mademoiselle de Valois' marriage,
and on Easter Tuesday, at a *fête* given by Madame. She had
from the first expressed the warmest admiration of Molière's
clever comedy, and the poet inscribed the work to her, in a
dedicatory epistle, printed in March, 1663. On the 8th of
January, the *Ballet des Arts* was performed at the Palais-
Royal. The words were written by Benserade, the music
was composed by Lulli. Madame herself, assisted by the
Duc de Saint-Aignan, had chosen the costumes and arranged

I

the different *entrées*. The various arts of peace formed the
subject of the opening scenes. First of all came a fancy
picture of pastoral life, one of those idyllic scenes in which
the Court of Louis XIV. delighted. The King appeared
dressed as a shepherd *à la Watteau*, feeding his flock by the
streams of Arcady. Then Madame entered, attended with
four youthful *bergères*, all clad in flowery hats and ribbons of
the brightest hues. The loveliness of the group attracted
general admiration. Henrietta's four attendants were Mademoiselle de La Vallière, Mdlle de Mortémart, then about to
become the wife of the Marquis de Montespan, Mademoiselle
de Saint-Simon, whom her brother describes as " perfectly
good and beautiful," and who soon afterwards married the
Duc de Brissac, and finally Mademoiselle de Sevigné, who, on
this occasion, made her first appearance at Court, while her
happy mother looked on with a pleasure which she could not
conceal. The presence of this beloved child gave every *fête*
a fresh charm. For her sake she becomes young again and is
ready to cry *Vive le Roi !* when Louis XIV. himself dances
with her beautiful daughter.

As Madame stepped forward, surrounded by these fair
shepherdesses, the chorus took up the following verses in her
honour, and in the last lines the Court recognised a delicate
refutation of the libels which insolent tongues had dared to
bring against her.

> " Quelle bergère ! quels yeux,
> A faire mourir les dieux.
> Aussi comme eux on l'adore.
> Elle est de leur propre sang,
> Mais sa personne est encore
> Bien au-dessus de son rang,
> Des jeunes lis et des roses,
> Toutes nouvellement écloses,
> Forment son teint delicat.
> Enfin les plus belles choses,
> Près d'elle n'ont point d'éclat.
> C'est une douceur extreme ;
> Et pour en dire içi le mal comme le bien,
> Il est vrai tout le monde l'aime ;
> Mais après son devoir, ses moutons et son chien,
> Je pense qu'elle n'aime rien.

After this dream of Arcady came different tableaux, representing the arts of sculpture and painting, of printing and medicine. Then Mars and Bellona appeared on the scene, and Roman legionaries chanted warlike songs. Last of all Madame returned, this time as Pallas Athenè, robed in classic draperies, with helmet on her head, and spear and shield in her hand. The same four maidens attended her, this time not as *bergères*, but as Amazons in armour, and danced a stately measure round their heaven-born Queen.

This was the famous ballet, which Madame de Sevigné recalls with such infinite delight, the ballet of all ballets in her eyes. Writing to Madame de Grignan in her far-off Provençal home, seventeen years afterwards, the old memories rise vividly before her. Once more she sees that brilliant group, those faces whose loveliness she can never forget. "*Ah! quelles bergères et quelles amazones!*" she exclaims, and then she breaks off abruptly, and drops a tear for poor Madame. "*Madame, que les siècles entiers auront peine à remplacer, et pour la beauté, et pour la belle jeunesse, et pour la danse.*" The *Ballet des Arts* was a great success at the time, and was repeated no less than five times in the course of the winter, either at the Louvre or at the Palais-Royal. On the 31st of January, Madame gave a grand *bal masqué*. Even the Queen-mother consented to appear masked, and the jewels and costumes worn were of such extraordinary splendour, that Ralph Montagu declared he had never seen anything to equal them. He went back to London in February, well pleased with his visit, and gave the King glowing accounts of the *fêtes* at Paris and of Madame's charms. Charles asked nothing better than to make Whitehall as gay a place, and if, at his Court, there was no one to equal Henrietta in grace and liveliness, he managed to amuse himself and others sufficiently well, as it appears from his next letter.

"WHITHALL,
"9 *Feb.* 1663.

" Mr Montagu is arrived heere, and I wonder Monsieur would lett him stay with you so long, for he is undoubtedly in love with you, but I ought not to complain, he haveing given

me a very fine sword and belt, which I do not beleeve was out
of pure liberality, but because I am your brother, he tells me
that you passe your time very well there. We had a designe to
have had a masquerade heere, and had made no ill designe in
the generall for it, but we were not able to goe through with
it, not haveing one man heere that could make a tolerable
entry. I have been perswading the queene to follow Q-
mother of France's example and goe in masquerade before
the carnavall be done, I beleeve it were worth seeing my L^d
St Albans in such an occasion. My wife hath given a good
introduction to such a businesse, for the other day she made
my Ld Aubigny and two other of her chaplins dance country
dances in her bed chamber. I am just now called for to goe to
the Play, so as I can say no more at present but that I am
intirely yours,   C. R."

My Lord Aubigny, the churchman who danced for his
royal mistress's pleasure on this occasion, was l'Abbé Lodovico
Stuart d'Aubigny, the fourth son of the Duke of Richmond
and Lennox, who had been lately appointed Grand Almoner
to the Queen. He is probably the dignitary to whom Charles
II. alludes as M. le Cardinal in a former letter, although he
steadily refused to accept a Cardinal's hat, for which dignity
he was repeatedly recommended.

On the 16th of February, an envoy was despatched to
Paris, to remove certain difficulties which had arisen over the
entry of the new Ambassador, M. de Comminges. The King,
after his habit on previous occasions, sent two letters by the
bearer, Sir John Trevor, to Madame, one written in French,
the other in English.

"LONDON,
"16 Feb. 1663.

" The great wish that I have, not to leave any doubt in the
King my brother's mind as to the perfect friendship that
exists between us, has induced me to send this gentleman, Sir
John Trevor, to satisfy him as to my reasons with respect to
M. de Comminges' demand for an audience. I have also
charged him, to let you know them, wishing that you should
understand, how anxious I am to satisfy the King, my brother,

in all points, as far as the welfare of my Kingdom allows. The difficulty in question, involves the maintenance of regulations which greatly concern the peace and safety of the city of London. I beg you to believe this, and to endeavour to explain my intentions in the right way, since I desire nothing more anxiously, than to retain the perfect friendship of the King my brother, and to prove to you how much I cherish the honour of your own,   CHARLES R."[1]

" WHITHALL,

" 16 *Feb.* 1663.

" I send this bearer, Sir John Trevor, to the King my brother, about a business which, though it may seeme at first to be of a very slite nature, I assure you it may prove of dangerous consequence to me. He will informe you of the particulars, and then you will see that it cannot be of any consequence to France, only may be of a very ill one to me. The parliament is to meete againe after to-morrow, which gives me so much businesse to prepare all thinges for that purpose, as I hope you will excuse me if this letter be a little shorte. I have sent Mon[r] Vanderdoes *à la foyre de St Germain* to buy little thinges to play for heere. I had not time to write to you by him, as he desired, and I thinke you know him so well, as it will be sufficient to introduce him into your presence when he comes, and so my dearest sister farewell for this time.

"C. R."

The Foire de Saint-Germain was at that time an event of

" DE LONDRES,

"*ce* 16. *Fevrier* 1663.

---

[1] " Le grand desire que i'ay de ne laisser aucune ombrage dans l'esprit du Roy mon frère, a l'esgard de l'amitié parfaite establye entre nous, m'a persuadé de luy envoyer ce gentilehome, le Sr Trevor, exprès pour le satisfaire de mes raisons sur la demande que fait Mon[r] de Cominges son Ambassadeur pour son audience. Je l'ay chargé aussi de vous en faire parlé, ayant la mesme envie, que vous demeuriez, persuadée de mon désir de satisfaire au Roy mon frère, en tout ce que le bien de mon estat peut permettre, et la difficulté dont il est question, n'a autre veue que celle de conserver un réglement, qui regarde fort la paix et la sureté de la ville de Londres. Je vous supplie d'en estre persuadée et de contribuer a faire bien entendre mes intentions en cette occasion, ne desirant rien plus fortement que de conserver la parfaite amitié du Roy mon frère, et de vous donner des preuves de combien je chéris l'honneur de la vostre.   CHARLES R."

great importance in the gay world of Paris. It was held
yearly, on the market place close to the ancient church of
Saint-Germain des Prés, and lasted from the 3d of February to
the last week of Lent. During these seven or eight weeks, the
Fair became the meeting-place of the whole Court. Royal
ladies drove there in hired coaches, with servants in grey
liveries, by way of remaining incognito, and made purchases
in the bazaars, tried their luck at lotteries and games of
chance, admired the tricks of the Indian jugglers and performances of strolling players, or had their fortunes told by gipsies
and astrologers. Rows of shops lined the streets, which were
as many as nine in number, and merchants of all nations
offered their wares for sale. Persian carpets and Venetian
brocades, costly tapestries and rare gems, old lace and ivories
and bronzes, lacquered cabinets from Coromandel and Japan,
mirrors and perfumes were bought and sold there. Mademoiselle, who was in the habit of going to the Fair every day,
in order to make purchases for herself and her friends, confessed to Cardinal Mazarin that there were only three things
which she really missed during her exile from Court—her daily
rides on the Cours de la Reine, the evening masquerades, and
the Foire de Saint-Germain. At night the streets were illuminated with torches, and the splendour of the bazaar, and rich
attire of the ladies present, made the scene very brilliant. In
these early years of Louis XIV.'s reign, this annual fair had
attained a world-wide reputation. Strangers from all countries came there to see the sights and pick up curiosities,
and English ladies especially, always eager to know the
"fashones" and have pretty things from France, were fond of
sending commissions to their friends for "trinkets and fannes,
little wooden combes," or "dainty silver brushes for cleaning
the teeth," which were among the latest novelties of Paris.

This year, the presence of the Court and of a royal visitor
in the person of the Prince of Denmark, gave fresh lustre to
the Carnival gaieties. Poor Mademoiselle, who had incurred
the King's displeasure by her refusal to marry the King of
Portugal, and had again been ordered to retire to her estates,
heard with a sigh of the masques and balls at Court. Two
weddings were also celebrated with great pomp—one was that

of M. le Prince's eldest son, the Duc d'Enghien, to a daughter
of the Princess Palatine, the other that of her step-sister,
Mademoiselle de Valois, to the Duke of Savoy, one of the few
royal personages, whom she herself had thought worthy of her
hand.   Another marriage, still more interesting in Madame's
eyes, took place in the spring of 1663.   This was that of her
old friend Madame de Châtillon, to the Duke of Mecklembourg.   Charles II. pitied her for going to live in Germany, but
the new Duchess had expressly stipulated for leave to spend
as much of her time in France as she chose, and soon made
her appearance at Court again.   " People say," remarks Gui
Patin, " that the Duke of Mecklembourg has sent three things
back to the King—his collar of the Saint-Esprit, his wife and
his religion," alluding to the Duke's prompt return to the
Lutheran faith, which he had abandoned during his residence
in France.

Lent brought a brief lull in this round of amusements, and
for a time, sermons and services took the place of balls and
comedies.   The two Queens were assiduous in their devotional
exercises, and the ladies of the Court followed their example,
by frequently attending functions at Val-de-Grâce or Chaillot,
or making pilgrimages to the Dominican shrine on Mount
Valèrien.   Easter was about to bring a renewal of *fêtes*, when
the Queen-mother fell dangerously ill.   For some weeks her
life was in danger, and she was tenderly nursed by the King,
whose devotion to his mother, both by day and night, touched
Madame de Motteville deeply.   He listened with remorse to
her reproaches, and even promised to reform his ways, but no
sooner had the Queen recovered, than these good intentions, as
might have been expected, were forgotten.   After taking a pilgrimage to Chartres, in fulfilment of a vow which he had made
during his mother's illness, Louis XIV. renewed his *liaison* with
La Vallière, and in the autumn of that year his mistress gave
birth to a son.   Suddenly, towards the end of May, the King,
who had gone to Versailles for a few days, caught the measles,
and became dangerously ill.   There was consternation both in
the Court and country, and the fever ran so high, that for three
days his life was despaired of.   Happily, by the end of that
time, the attack passed off, and the royal patient recovered as

rapidly as he had sickened. " I am still shaking with fright," wrote his minister, M. de Lionne, to England. "On Friday, His Majesty's life was in danger, up till twelve o'clock. On Saturday afternoon, he was at work with his secretaries as usual." Madame showed her wonted courage in the general panic, and went to see the King at the height of his illness, fearless of the risk to which she exposed herself. The news of the King's danger had time to reach London, and Charles II. hastened to send a messenger of inquiry to Versailles. The following letters to his sister contain allusions to this event, and mention Lord Bristol's attempt to bring a charge of high treason against Clarendon in the House of Lords. The session had been a stormy one, but on the whole Charles congratulated himself, that it had passed off better than he had expected, and begged his sister not to be disturbed by contrary reports.

Madame had been greatly concerned at this attack on her brother's old and tried servant, and the whole proceeding had excited much attention in France, where the independence of English members of Parliament was a matter of constant amusement. Comminges cannot contain himself, and writes that he is at his wit's end, when he sees Lord Bristol, the man who has ventured to bring these charges against the Lord Chancellor, and what is more, the father-in-law to the King's own brother, walking about as usual, and playing on the bowling-green, without fear of the Bastille. He concludes that England will very soon be tired of Monarchy, and will set up another Commonwealth, and is more than ever puzzled over this strange constitution, which, according to him, owed its origin partly to the book of Daniel and the laws of the Medes and Persians, and partly to William the Conqueror.

" WHITHALL,
" 5 <i>March</i>, 1663.

" I writt to you yesterday by de Chapelles (the husband of Madame de Fiennes), who will tell you what a cruell cold I have gott, which is now so generall a disease heere, after the breaking of the frost, that nobody escapes it, and though my cold be yett so ill, as it might very well excuse my writting, I thought it necessary to lett you know that the Queene, my mother, findes an absolute ease of the headache which she had all night, by being lett blood this afternoone, and she findes so greate benefitte by it, as I hope her cold will in two or three dayes be gone, espetially if the wether continue so faire and warme as it is to-day. Excuse me that I say no more at this time, for really this little holding downe my head makes it ake, my dearest sister I am intierly yours. C. R."

"WHITHALL,
"28 *March*, 1663.

" You may be sure, that I would not have missed so many posts, but that I have been overlayd with businesse. I give you many thanks for the concerne you shew in my L^d of Bristol's businesse ; you see I have had reasonable good successe in that matter, I have only failed in not takeing him, but you know how hard 'tis to finde out one who is cunning enough, in so great a towne as this. I was very neere it once or twice, I am iust now informed that he is gon out of England, how true 'tis I cannot tell, but that shall not make me the lesse watchfull against his mischiveous purposes, nor make me lesse diligent in seeking after him. The bill passed in the house of commons for the repeale of the Trieniall bill, and all thinges goes on in both houses as I can wish, I am to much Madame de Châtillon's servant, to tell her that I am glad that she is married into Germany ; if she knew the country, that's to say the way of liveing there, and the people, so well as I do, she would suffer very much in France, before she would change countries, but this is now past, and I shall desire you to assure her that, upon any occasion that lies within my power, I shall ever be ready to serve Bablon. I thanke you for the wax to seale letters, you sent me by de Chapelles. I desire to know whether it be the fashion in France, for the wemen to make use of such a large sise of wax, as the red peece you sent me ; our wemen heere finde the sise a little extravagant, yett I beleeve when they shall know that 'tis the fashion there, they will be willing enough to submit to it, and so I am yours. C. R."

" You must not by this post, expect a long letter from me. this being Jameses (the Duke of Monmouth's) marriage day, and I am goeing to sup with them, where we intend to dance and see them a bed together, but the ceremony shall stop there. The letters from France are not yett come, which keepes me in paine, to know how Queene-mother does, I hope James Hamilton will be on his way home before this comes to your handes. I send you heere, the title of a little booke of devotion, in Spanish, which my wife desires to have, by the derections you will see where 'tis to be had, and pray send two of them by the first conveniency. My dearest sister, I am intierly yours."

" Hamilton came last night to towne, and was so weary with his journey, as he was not able to render me a full account of all that you commanded him, yett he hath sayd so much to me, in generall, of the continuance of your kindness to me and the obligations I owe you, that I cannot tell how to expresse my acknowledgements for it. I hope you beleeve I love you as much as 'tis possible, I am sure I would venture all I have in the world to serve you, and have nothing so neere my harte, as how I may finde occasions to expresse that tender passion I have for my dearest Minette. As soone as I have had a full account from Hamilton, of all you have trusted him with, you shall heare farther from me, in the meane time be assured that all thinges which comes from you, shall never go further than my own harte, and so for this time, my dearest sister, adieu. C. R."

" If I do not write to you so often as I would, it is not my *faute*, for most of my time is taken up with the business of the Parlament, in getting them to do what is best for us all, and keeping them from doeing what they ought not to do. and though I finde by Hamilton, that there is greate in-

deavours used in France, to persuade all men there, that
this parlament does meane me no good, yett, you will see,
before they parte, that they will shew there affections to me,
by helping me in my revenue. I hope you have, before this,
fully satisfied the King my brother of the sincerity of my
desire to make a stricte alliance with him, but I must deale
freely with you, in telling you that I do not thinke that his
ambassadore heere, Monr de Cominges is very forward in the
businesse. I cannot tell the reasons which make him
so, but he findes, upon all occasions, so many difficultyes, as I
cannot chuse but conclude, that we shall not be able to
advance much in that matter with him, therfore I am
hastening away my Ld Hollis with all possible speede, to let
the King my brother see that there shall nothing rest, on my
parte, to the finishing that entier frindship I so much desire ;
my wife sends for me iust now to dance so I must end, and
can only add that I am intierly yours.   C. R."

" WHITHALL,

" 25 May, 1663.

" I receaved yours by your expresse yesterday, and dispatch this bearer, my L^u Mandeville, imediately to know how
the King my brother does. You may easily beleeve that the
newes surprised me very much, and by the sircumstances you
write to me of his sicknesse, it apeares to be very dangerous,
which keepes me in continuall paine till I heare from you
againe, and the disease is such as before this time the matter
must be desided one way or other. I shall not say any
thing now to you, upon any other subject, till I know what
becomes of this, only to tell you that there is nothing
in this world I thinke my selfe so happy in, as to see the
continuance of your kindnesse to me, and I beg of you to be
assured that I am as sensible of it as 'tis possible, and that
nothing can alter me from being intierly yours.   C. R."

" WHITHALL,

" 25 May, 1663.

" Though I send my Ld Mandeville, on purpose to see how
the K. of France does, yett this bearer haveing made such diligence hither, I beleeve will be first with you, therfore I add

these few lines, only to thanke you for giveing me so timely
notice of this ill accident, and to desire you upon any change,
that you will advertise me of it, which is all I have to say for
this time, but that I am intierly Yours.   C. R."

" WHITHALL,
"24 June, 1663.

" I shall not say much to you, by this bearer, my Ld Hollis,
in writting, because I have ordered him to entertaine you at
large, upon all I have trusted him with, by which you will see
the kindnesse and confidence I have for you, for I am sure I
will never have a secret in my harte, that I will not willingly
trust you with, and there is nothing I will endeavour more,
then to give you all sortes of testimonyes, how truely and
passionately I am Yours.   C. R."

Intrigues of De Vardes and the Comtesse de Soissons—Illness of Queen Catherine
—Lord Hollis sent as Ambassador to France — The Quarrel of the
Coaches—Madame becomes the true Ambassador.

CHAPTER XI

THAT summer, the Queen-mother's long illness kept the
Court in Paris till the end of July. She herself never left
the Louvre until, on the 11th of August, four months from the
day on which she was first taken ill, she went to Notre Dame
with her daughter-in-law, Marie Thérèse, to return thanks for
her recovery. The King and Monsieur and Madame beguiled the time by frequent excursions to Versailles or Saint-
Cloud. Sometimes a few days were spent at Vincennes or
Saint-Germain, where the ladies of the Court amused themselves with the strangest variety of sports. At one time
swinging was the fashion, at another tobogganing, then colin-
maillard or hide-and-seek. When Monsieur and Madame
paid a second visit to Chantilly that autumn, a stag-hunt by
torchlight was invented by way of novelty for Henrietta's diversion. Boating was another of her favourite pastimes. On
fine summer days, Madame and her ladies would row on the
Seine, in a richly-decorated barge, which Charles II. had lately
given his sister.

On May 11, 1663, we find that a certain George Platt
received "the sum of £4 for his own expenses and those of ten
watermen, who conveyed the Princess d'Orléans' barge to
Paris." Another waterman, Ben Huskins by name, was paid
10s. for work done to the said barge, by order of Sir George
Carew. This barge was painted blue, the cushions and hangings were of blue velvet, embroidered with gold. "The whole
most royal and gallant in appearance, "a fitting present," said

the *Court Gazetteer*, " from the King of the sea to his fair sister." Both the French Queens, Marie Thérèse and Anne of Austria, often borrowed Madame's barge for their trips on the Seine, and the Court poets were never weary of praising its beauty and swiftness. Happy they who set foot on this magic bark, they sang, for their journey cannot fail to prosper, and Loves and Zephyrs will waft them gently to the desired haven.

A graceful writer at the Court, who was also one of Henrietta's most faithful friends, the Comtesse de Brégis, gives a poetic description of one of these water-parties, in the summer of 1663, when Monsieur and Madame, or, as the writer prefers to style them, Prince Orondate and Princess Statira rowed up the Seine, to spend the day at Saint Cloud. There, they happened to meet a party of English travellers. Madame, with her usual grace, insisted that these subjects of the King her brother should become her guests, and herself did them the honours of the palace. They saw the rich suite of rooms which she occupied, her boudoir with its lacquered walls and Indian cabinets, the allegorical frescoes of the ceilings, and the chapel with Mignard's altar-piece. Then 'the English strangers passed into the gardens, watered by a thousand crystal streams, and saw the wonderful *jet d'eau* which seemed to lose itself in the skies, and to descend in showers of sparkling dew-drops, over woods and lawns. Both Monsieur and Madame conversed with their guests with the utmost kindness and freedom, and invited them to sit down to a collation spread in the gardens. At nightfall, the whole party rowed down the river to Paris. Madame, enchanted with the beauty of the starlit heavens, bade the rowers lay by their oars, and let the boat drift slowly down the stream. So, with pleasant talk and song, they floated under the stars, until the current became more rapid, and the bridges of the city came in sight. All too soon the end of the journey was reached, and the travellers went on their way, bearing with them a delightful memory of the most charming of princesses. On such occasions Madame won all hearts. As Cosnac and Madame de La Fayette say, there was no one like her.

Unfortunately, this irresistible attraction was the source of perpetual trouble. The Comte de Guiche was gone, it is true. Madame had vowed that she would never see his face again, and had begged the King, his master, to ask him for the letters which she had written to him. Louis, who himself joined the army in Lorraine that autumn, complied with her request, and was so well pleased with the frank and honourable way in which the Count behaved, that he pardoned his past indiscretions, and honoured him with repeated marks of his regard. The campaign ended with the surrender of the town of Marsal, and the Count obtained leave to go and fight against the Russians, in Poland, where he distinguished himself by prodigies of valour, and was severely wounded in one hard-fought battle. A bullet struck him on the chest, and a case containing Madame's portrait, which he wore next to his heart, was shattered into atoms.

Meanwhile, at home, there was already more than one pretender to the place which he was supposed to hold in Madame's heart. The Duc de la Rochefoucauld's eldest son, the Prince de Marsillac, had long been desperately in love with her, and although he received little or no encouragement, the extravagance of his behaviour excited Monsieur's jealousy, to such a pitch, that his father was forced to send him away. Then M. d'Armagnac, a member of the ducal house of Lorraine, and Grand Écuyer de France, annoyed her with his attentions, and would not see how disagreeable they were, until the Archbishop of Sens interfered at Madame's request. But the most persevering, and by far the most dangerous of her adorers, was the Marquis de Vardes, one of the ablest and most unscrupulous men at Court. As first gentleman of the bed-chamber, he had won the King's ear, and his ready wit and polished manners made him acceptable in the brilliant coterie to which Madame de Sevigné belonged. His epigrammatic sayings, and the dexterity with which he turned awkward situations to his advantage, were proverbial. "*De Vardes!*" exclaims Madame de Sevigné, "*Toujours De Vardes!* He is the gospel according to the day!" This thorough villain, whose intrigues with both the Comtesse de Soissons and Madame d'Armagnac, the Grand Écuyer's wife, had been well-known, now determined

to make Madame his mistress, and laid his designs with the
utmost skill.   He began by blackening his absent friend, the
Count of Guiche, in her eyes.   Next, he took care to excite
Monsieur's jealousy by drawing attention to Marsillac's follies,
and having thus cleared the ground of these two rivals, he
tried by every art in his power, to ingratiate himself into
Madame's favour.   Henrietta became his dupe, only too
easily.   She lent a willing ear to his artful insinuations,
honoured him with her confidence, and even showed him her
brother Charles II.'s letters.   While the Court talked openly
of De Vardes' successful intrigue, Madame herself looked
upon him as the lover of the Comtesse de Soissons, and had
not the least suspicion of the man's infamous designs.   But
one day, when news of the Comte de Guiche's heroic exploits
in Poland reached the Court, Madame, touched at the thought
of the dangers to which her old lover was exposed, said in
De Vardes' hearing, "I believe I care more for the Comte de
Guiche, than I knew before." From that day, De Vardes
saw that his plans had failed, and in his anger and hatred
vowed to ruin both Madame and her absent friend.   Above
all, he resolved to destroy the King's confidence in his sister-
in-law, and during the next few months, he took every opportunity of poisoning his master's mind against this innocent
Princess.   He told Louis that she carried on a treacherous
correspondence with her brother, and spoke of her as a very
dangerous and intriguing person, while on the other hand, he
inspired Madame with distrust of the King, and did his best
to make mischief between them.   Traces of these suspicions
appear in Madame's letters to her brother, during this year,
and we see how much her daily life was embittered by these
miserable intrigues.   But she knew that in him she had at
hand one friend, to whom she could always turn, whose
sympathy was always ready, and whose powerful help was at
her service, in her worst troubles.

On the 22d of July, 1663, she wrote to him from Paris.   "The
courier I had sent you, came back two days ago, and brought
me the worst news I could possibly receive, in telling me that
my hopes of seeing you were, after all, to be disappointed.
Everyone here does not share my feelings, and the highest

are as much pleased as I am grieved. I should indeed be inconsolable, if you had not led me to hope that your intended visit was only postponed. I will cling to that hope, and still believe that you keep a little love for your poor Minette, who certainly has more for you than she can express. You tell me, that someone has spoken ill of a certain person, to the Queen your wife. Alas! is it possible that such things are really said? I, who know your innocence, can only wonder! But to speak seriously, I beg you to tell me how the Queen has taken this. Here, people say she is in the deepest distress, and to speak frankly, I think she has only too good reason for her grief. As to this kind of thing, there is trouble enough here, not as with you through the Queen, but through mistresses. I have told Crofts all particulars. If you are curious to know them, he can tell you. Adieu, I am more your servant than anyone in the world."

The King was probably too hardened a sinner in this respect, to feel much remorse at this remonstrance from his favourite sister, but it is worthy of note that just at this time he paid considerable attention to his wife, and, much to Pepys' surprise, appeared in the Park, riding hand in hand with the Queen, "looking mighty pretty in her white-laced waistcoat and crimson short petticoat." Lady Castlemaine was there too, "looking mighty out of humour, and wearing a yellow plume of hat, which colour," observes Pepys, "all took notice of." But the King took no notice of her, "nor did she so much as smile or speak to anybody." At the end of July, Charles accompanied his wife to Tunbridge Wells, to drink of what Comminges calls "the waters of scandal," since he remarks, "most of the Court seem to leave their reputation behind them there." Pepys began to wonder if this coldness to Lady Castlemaine were not caused by the King's fancy for the Queen's new maid-of-honour, "pretty Mrs Stuart," who "with her hat cocked and a red plume, her sweet eyes, little Roman nose and excellent taille," is, he thinks, the greatest beauty he has ever seen. It would be interesting to see how Charles tried to justify himself to his sister. Unfortunately, his answer to Madame's letter of July 22d is missing, and the next letter we have is a short note about a present of

K

horses, which he was anxious to send Monsieur. Charles always managed to remain on friendly terms with his brother-in-law, however much he disliked and despised him in his heart. He loses no opportunity of sending him a civil message, or doing him a kindness, and Monsieur in return addressed frequent letters to the King of England. Many of these, sealed with black and fastened with elegant pink silk, are still preserved at the Record Office, but they are, for the most part, of a purely formal character.

> "WHITHALL,
> "25 *Aug.* 1663.

"I have kept this bearer, Haughser, some dayes, in hopes to have founde some good horses, to have made a present of them to Monsieur, but in ernest they are so harde to be founde heere, as I have not been able to finde any that I like; however, I have sent 4 which I desire you to give them to him, in your name, for I do not think them worth a formall present, and such as they are, I assure you, I have chosen them out of twenty. This being the only businesse of this letter, I shall end it with desiring you to continue your kindnesse to me, which I esteeme above all thinges, and be assured that I am and ever will be intierly yours.   C. R."

The autumn was spent partly at Vincennes, and partly at Monsieur's country-seat of Villers-Cotterets, a royal château built by Francis I., in the midst of the vast forests near the town of Laon. By the end of October, the Court was back in Paris, and during the winter months Madame kept up a brisk correspondence with her brother. One result of De Vardes' intrigues was to excite perpetual jealousies and quarrels among the ladies who surround ed Henrietta. Madame d'Armagnac and Madame de Montespan laid their heads together to try and banish Madame de Mecklembourg, and actually induced Monsieur to forbid his wife to receive her. Madame, naturally indignant at this arbitrary act, appealed to the King, who took Madame de Mecklembourg's part, upon which Monsieur sulked after his wont, and carried his complaints against his wife to the Queen-mother, who still looked coldly on her daughter-in-law. Charles II. took

great interest in the dispute, since it concerned his old friend
Bablon, and expressed his sympathy with his sister in two
different letters. His own wife was just recovering from the
dangerous illness, which had threatened, at one moment, to
end her life. The feeling shown by Charles on this occasion,
surprised the whole Court, most of all the French Ambassador,
who wrote home, that he had never seen His Majesty so
deeply affected. "None the less," he adds, "he supped with
Lady Castlemaine, and had his usual talk with Mrs Stuart, of
whom he is excessively fond." Comminges, however, was of
opinion, that the Queen owed her life entirely to her husband's
courage in dismissing the Portuguese attendants, who surrounded her bed with lamentations, and kept her awake
during two whole nights, first making her draw up her will,
and then take leave of them all. A French gentleman, M. de
Cateux, was sent over, with messages of condolence and
inquiry from Louis XIV., and had returned to Paris, with the
news that the Queen was now pronounced to be out of
danger. A few days afterwards, Charles wrote as follows :—

"WHITHALL,
"2 Nov. 1663.

"I could not write more to you by Mon^r Cateux, haveing
then the collique, which troubled me very much, but I thanke
God 'tis now perfectly over, and pray make my excuse to the
King of France and Monsieur, that I write to them in an
other hande, for, seriously, I was not able to make use of my
owne, Mr Montagu did shew me your letter concerning the
businesse you had about Mad. de Châtillon, and without being
partiall to you, the blame was very much on the other side. I
was very glad that the King tooke your parte, which in
iustice he could not do lesse, I do more wonder that other
people who had more yeares did not do the like, and then
Monsieur would not have continued so much in the wrong.
You will have heard of the unluky accident that befell the
French Ambassadour at my Ld Maior's feast, I was very much
troubled at it, my Ld Maior has been since with him, to give
him all imaginable satisfaction, and I hope he is now fully
persuaded that it was a meere misfortune, without any farther

intent, though I must tell you, that the Ambassadore is a man very hardly to be pleased, and loves to raise difficultyes even in the easiest matters.

"My wife is now out of all danger, though very weake, and it was a very strange feaver, for she talked idly fouer or five dayes after the feaver had left her, but now that is likewise past, and desires me to make her compliments to you and Monsieur, which she will do her selfe, as soone as she getts strength, and so my dearest sister, I will trouble you no more at this time, but beg of you to love him who is intierly yours.

"C. R."

The unlucky accident to which the King alludes, was an affront, which Comminges conceived to have been intentionally done him, at a Guildhall dinner, where he had been a guest. Owing to some mistake, the Lord Chancellor and several of the Council were already seated at table, when the Ambassador arrived, and, since they made no apology, Comminges retired highly affronted at what he terms "*cette incivilité grosse et barbare.*" He refused to accept the ample apologies tendered by the Lord Mayor, and would not be satisfied until the King himself had expressed his sincere regrets for this unfortunate occurrence, and had gratified him by remarking that the bad manners of the English towards foreigners were already but too well known.

In his next letter Charles mentions the marriage of his favourite, the Chevalier de Gramont, who had found in his *belle* Hamilton, if not the rich wife he sought, a lady of rare beauty and virtue.

"WHITHALL,
"11 *Nov.* 1663.

"I have nothing to say to you by this bearer, Lusan, but to tell you that I have dispatched all, on my parte, in order to the mariage, and I hope the young couple will be as happy as I wish them. This bearer tells me, that all thinges are now adjusted, concerning the dispute about Madame de Châtillon, for whome, you know, I had more than an ordinary inclination, and pray remember my service to her, and tell her that upon all occasions I shall alwais declare my selfe on her side. I have no more to add, but that I am intierly yours.

"C. R."

On the 13th of November, Madame wrote the following note to her brother, recommending some petitioner, who craved for redress, to his notice. "The bearer, whose daughter has been carried off, has begged me to ask you, to see that he may obtain justice, and, indeed, he has so much right on his side, that I doubt not, but that you will be able to help him. This being the sole object of my letter, I will only assure you that I am your humble servant." We find no reply to this appeal in the King's letters, and Charles probably contented himself with referring the matter to one of his ministers.

"WHITHALL,
"20 *Nov.* 1663.

"I shall say little to you by this bearer, le Chevalier de Clairemont, because I will dispatch Mon^r d'Araquin, in a day or two, only by way of advance, I thanke you and Monsieur for the great part you take in the recovery of my wife. She mends very slowly, and continues still so weake as she cannot yett stande upon her leggs, which is the reason she does not thank you herself, but she does constantly desire me to do it both to you and Monsieur, and so, my dearest sister, farewell for this time. C. R."

"WHITHALL,
"10 *Decem.* 1663.

"I have receaved yours, in which you take notice of the receite of myne, by the Marquis d'Araquin, and you shall see that I will be very punctual in writing to you every weeke. I am now dispatching the judges into Yorkeshire, to try those rogues that had the late plott, and I beleeve a good many of them will be hanged, and, to prevent all further mischief of that kinde, I am in deliberation of raysing two regiments of horse more, of 500 men a peece, the one to lye in the north, and the other in the west, which will, I doute not, for the future, prevent all plotting. My wife is now so well, as in a few dayes, she will thanke you herselfe for the consernement you had for her, in her sicknesse. Yesterday, we had a little ball in the privy chamber, where she looked on, and, though we had many of our good faces absent, yett, I assure you, the assembly would not have been disliked for beauty, even at Paris it selfe, for we have a great many yong wemen come up, since you were heere, who are very handsome. Pray send me some images, to put in prayer bookes. They are for my wife, who can gett none heere. I assure you it will be a greate present to her, and she will looke upon them often, for she is not only content to say the greate office in the breviere, every day, but likewise that of our Lady too, and this is besides goeing to chapell, where she makes use of none of these. I am iust now going to see a new play, so I shall say no more, but that I am intierly yours.   C. R."

Madame hastened to comply with her sister-in-law's request, and sent her a handsome selection of the "pretty pious pictures," which Pepys admired, when he visited her Majesty's bed-chamber.

The King's next three letters are devoted to a fierce struggle, which arose over one of those knotty points of precedence, to which Louis XIV. attached such great importance. The new English Ambassador, Denzil, Lord Hollis, had been sent to Paris in June 1663, but, before his public entry could take place, there were several difficult questions to be settled. The point which excited most discussion, was his claim to take precedence of the Princes of the blood, a right which Louis XIV. absolutely refused to acknowledge. Charles, on his part, was equally resolute in the maintenance of a right which had been invariably claimed by his father's ambassadors, and the quarrel of the coaches, as it was termed, was prolonged during several months. At length Madame, after vainly trying to effect a compromise, suggested that the public entry should be given up, but that the Ambassador should be presented to Louis XIV. at Saint-Germain. This actually took place in the following March, much to the satisfaction of both parties, who agreed in giving Madame credit for having, by her tact and skill, succeeded in settling a question which, but for her, might have been attended with serious consequences.

"WHITHALL,
"28 *Decem.* 1663.

" I did not write to you the last post, it being Christmas
eve, and I was preparing my selfe for my devotions, but I bid
J. H. (James Hamilton) make my excuse to you, since which
time, I have seene both your letter to thé Queene, and my L^d
Hollises to the secretary, concerning the .pretention of the
Princes of the blood, about my Ld Hollises entry, and truly I
thought that I had found out a very faire expedient to avoyde
all dispute, in proposing that there might have been no entry
at all, but that he might have gone derectly to his audiance,
which, considering all former presadents, who are cleerly on
our side, ought not to be refused on the side of France; for I
finde, by the recordes of Sr Thomas Edmonds, my Ld Scuda-
more and the Earle of Lesester, who were all three Ambassa-
dors in France, the two latter being now alive, that it was
cleerely desided on their side. 'Tis true, that when the princes
of the blood saw they could not gett there pointe, they forbore
sending ther coches, and I hope when the King my brother
sees that it has been alwais the coustume, that he will not
insist to bring in a new methode, which is so contrary to right
and reason. I wonder very much that the P. of Condé should
say, that ever I yeelded the presedence to the King of Spaine,
and I thanke you for holding up our right so handsomly as
you did, for I assure you I am so farr from that, that I will
not yeelde it to any King whatsoever. But to returne to the
former matter, I do not finde that Mon^r de Lionne has made
anything apeare on there sides, to my Ld Hollis, only the
mayne argument is, that the King of Spaynes ambassadore
and some others have submitted to it, which is no rule at all
to me, for they have no power to give away my right, and it
would be a very unreasonable argument, that because others
will parte with there right, therfore I must parte with myne.
I enlarge myselfe the more upon this matter, that you may be
fully informed of the truth of it, and know what to say in it,
there is nobody desires more to have a strict frindship with
the K. of France than I do, but I will never buy it upon
dishonorable termes, and I thanke God my condition is not
so ill, but that I can stand upon my owne leggs, and beleeve

that my frindship is as valuable to my neighbours, as theres is
to me.   I have reason to beleeve that the french Ambassadore
heere, is no greate frinde to this place, otherwise these had
been much more advanced in the stricte aliance with France,
then there is.   I am certain his informations thither are not at
all to our advantage, and now and then very farr from the
truth.   I say this, that you may know, that I have the same
good inclination for a true frindship with the King there, I
ever had, and that it is not my faut if it do not succeede,
according to my inclinations and desire.   I thinke this letter
is of a sufficient length, therfore I will conclude with assuring
you that I am entierly yours.   C. R."

" WHITHALL,
" 4 <i>Jan.</i> 1664.</div>

"I have sent this post the extracts of the letters to my
Ld Hollis, by which you will see how much reason I have to
stande upon the right my father had, touching the precedency
of my ambassador's coach, before those of the Princes of the
blood there ; I do assure you I would not insist upon it, if I
had not cleerely the right on my side, for there is nobody
that hates disputes so much as I do, and will never create
new ones, espetially with one whoes frindship I desire so
much as that of the King of France, but on the other side,
where I have reason, and when I am to yeelde, in a pointe by
which I must goe lesse then my predesessours have done, I
must confesse that consernes me so much, as no frindshipe
shall make me consent unto.   I am very glad that le Conte
de Gramont is so well received there, and I hope he will
receave the effects of it.   My wife thankes you for the care
you have in sending her <i>les images</i>.   We are both going to
supper to my Lady Castlemaine's, so I have no time to add
anything to this letter, but that I am yours entierly.

"C. R."

" WHITHALL,
" 18 <i>Jan.</i> 1664.</div>

I am very glad that I received yours of the 19th before
that which the Comte de Gramont brought.   You see that I
have reason to insiste upon a matter, which is so cleerely my

right, and whensoever I tell you anything which afterwards proves not to be so, I must be very much consoned (cozened) my selfe, for I will never deceeve you, but I will say no more on this subject, being confident that the examples I sent, will put an end to all dispute, and then my Ld Hollis will enter upon his negociation, and proceede with greater francknesse and ingenuity than your ambassadore does heere, by which you will perceave that the delay has not layne on this side ; and I cannot chuse but tell you, betweene you and me, that this Ambassadore is good for nothing, but to give malicious and wrong intelligence. I finde J. Hamilton in greate paine about the letter you writt to him, and that he should be re-presend there as a person who strives to put division upon all occasions between France and us. I do assure you he is very farre from it, and pray upon any proper occasion do him the justice, as to disabuse them there. My Ld Fitz-harding has acquainted me with your letter, concerning Mon^r de Turenes' niece. I think you beleeve that the relation she has to him, would make me very glad to serve her upon any occasion, but I am affraide I shall not be able to do her the service I could wish, for I finde the passion Love is very much out of fasion in this country, and that a handsome face without mony has but few galants, upon the score of marriage. My wife thankes you very kindly for the images you sent her, they are very fine ones, and she never saw such before. I have not had yett time to talke with the Conte de Gramont, he is so taken up with his wife, as I have scarse seen him these two days that he has been heere, but that fury continues not long, and I beeleve he will be as reasonable in that point as most men are, and then I will give you a farther account of our conversation, and so I will end my letter with assure-ing you that I am intierly yours.　　　　　C.R."

Mademoiselle de Duras was the niece of Maréchal de Turenne, whom Madame had recommended the King, through Lord Fitzhardinge, as her brother's faithful servant Charles Berkeley had now become. This young lady, one of Henri-etta's maids-of-honour, apparently thought of going to England to join her brother, Louis de Durfort, captain of the Duke of

York's guards. Eventually, however, she seems to have given up her intended journey, and certainly did not succeed in finding an English husband, for she died unmarried in 1679.

" WHITHALL,
" 17 <i>March</i> 1664.

"I did not write to you the last post, because I had so much business in order to the parlament, as I had no time. This day I receaved a letter from my Ld Hollis, in which he gives me an accounte of his audience, which I am very well satisfied with, and his whole treatement there, and pray lett the King my brother know how well I am pleased with it, and that upon all occasions I will strive, if it be possible, to out doe him in kindnesse and frindship. He tells me, likewise, how much I am beholding to you in all his businesse, which I assure you I am very sensible of, and though it can add nothing to that entier kindnesse I had for you before, yett it gives me greate joye and satisfaction to see the continuance of your kindnesse upon all occasions, which I will strive to diserve by all the endeavors of my life, as the thing in the world I value most. The Queen showed me your letter about the operation done upon Melle Montosier, and by her smile, I beleave she had no more guesse at the meaning than you had at the writing of the letter, I am confident that this will be the only operation of that kinde, that will be don in our age. It may be you will understand this no more than what you writt in your own letter, but I do not doute you will very easily gett it to be explayned, without going to the Sorbone, therefore I neede add no more, but that I am intierly yours.

"C. R."

Lord Hollis himself was the first to acknowledge his obligations to Madame. "I must do Madame right," he wrote home, " who, only by her dexterity and wisdom, carried on and managed all this business, and brought it to that point where it now is." The stern Puritan had bowed to Henrietta's charms, and a little later on we find his royal master laughingly telling his sister that my Lord Hollis is undoubtedly in love with her, and that his wife is already beginning to grow jealous. Unfortunately the new Ambassador was of too punctilious and too irascible a nature to prove a successful diplomatic agent, and if Comminges vexed the easy-going King by his readiness to take offence over trifles, Hollis gave Madame constant trouble by his "uncertain humours" and quarrels over points of etiquette. The result of the mutual distrust with which both Kings regarded their Ambassadors, was that Henrietta became their regular channel of communication, and during the next few years, all the most important correspondence between Charles II. and Louis XIV. passed through her hands.

Fêtes at Paris and Versailles and Fontainebleau—Court Intrigues—Disputes between Lord Hollis and the French Ministers—Negotiations with Holland.

THE winter months of 1664 were marked by the usual *fêtes*,
both at the Louvre and Palais-Royal. On the 19th of
January, Molière's new play, *Le Mariage forcé*, was acted at
the Louvre, and repeated, by Madame's desire, at her house a
month later, with musical interludes and dances. The King
himself appeared in Egyptian costume, in one of the ballets,
and he and the Queen and Monsieur all took parts in the
Ballet des Amours Deguisés, which was performed at the
Palais-Royal, on the 6th of February. Madame de Montespan
and Mademoiselle de Sevigné both appeared in the character
of nymphs, but Henrietta herself was prevented, by her state
of health, from taking any active part in the performances.
Neither was she able to be present at the six days' *fête*
given by the King, early in May, in the gardens of Versailles.
A succession of tournaments, masques, and comedies delighted
the eyes of the Court. Molière's *Princess d'Elide* was composed expressly for that occasion ; his *Mariage forcé* was repeated, and the three first acts of Tartuffe were performed
for the first time. Lord Hollis, in a despatch of the 12th
of March, mentions an accident which Madame had met with,
at a *bal masqué* given by the Queen-mother to please her son,
in the Carnival week. "The Court," he writes, "removes
hence very suddenly to St Germain, and after to Fontainebleau for all the summer, that the building of the Louvre may
be followed. I think Madame's keeping her bed, put it off for
some days, which is to be yet for five days longer, by reason

of a fall she had, Tuesday night at the Louvre, by her foot catching in a ribbon which hung down at her masking gown, and that, very heavy with jewels, might have made the fall very dangerous against the silver grate upon which she was coming, if a gentleman (M. Clérambault, I think) had not stayed her. But, God be thanked, she hath not the least hurt, only the trouble of always lying, and not putting her foot to the ground for nine days."

As soon as Madame was able to move, she and Monsieur went to Saint-Cloud, taking the Queen-mother with them, in King Charles's beautiful barge. There her health improved, and towards the end of May she joined the rest of the Court at Fontainebleau. Mademoiselle, whose quarrel with the King had been made up now, appeared on the scene once more, and describes a brilliant *medianoche*, or midnight *fête* on the canal, that took place one midsummer night. The *fête*, she remarks, was really in honour of La Vallière, who now took daily promenades with the King, in the eyes of the whole Court. But Madame was also present, and it was noticed that neither Madame d'Armagnac nor Madame de Montespan were among the guests, an omission which gave great offence to Monsieur, and was regarded as a proof of the King's secret understanding with his sister-in-law.

Madame was at that time in constant correspondence with her brother, and Louis XIV. found her mediation too useful to dispense with her services. The following letters from Charles II. belong to this period :—

"WHITHALL,
"24 *March* 1664.

"The Parlament has sat ever since Monday last, and if they continue as they have begun, which I hope they will, I shall have great reason to be very well pleased with them. The Lords' house has refused all sortes of adresses from my L^d of Bristol, upon the account of his disobeying my proclamation, and not rendreing himselfe, as he is therein commanded, and this day his wife brought a petition to the house doore, but could not gett one of the Peeres to deliver it ; the other adresse, which he sent the first day of the meeting, was sent

sealed to me, without ever being opened, and the truth is, 'tis
rather a libell than a petition; what his next eforte will be, I
cannot tell, but I beleeve he will add to those crimes and
follyes he has already committed. As it is, he has put it out
of any of his frindes power, to mediate for him. The house of
Commons are now upon breakeing that wilde act of the
Trieniall bill, which was made at the beginning of our troubles,
and have this day voted it, so that now it wants nothing but
puting it into forme. The truth is, both houses are in so good
humour, as I do not doute but to end this sesion very well.
By the letters I have receaved from my Ld Hollis, he has, by
this time, demanded commissioners to treate with him, and
I hope that treaty will go on, to all our satisfactions; I am
sure there shall be nothing wanting, on my parte, to bring it to
a good conclusion. My Ld Hollis writes such letters of you,
as I am affraide he is in love with you, and they say his wife
begins already to be jealous of you. You must excuse me,
as long as the parlament sitts, if I miss now and then a post,
for I have so much businesse, as I am very often quite tired,
and so, my dearest sister, I am intierly yours.   C. R."

"WHITHALL,
" 19 *May* 1664.

" I have ben all this afternoon playing the good husband,
haveing been abroade with my wife, and 'tis now past twelve
a clocke, and I am very sleepy. I thought I should have had
a word from you, about this accident which fell out betweene
our nephew and Mon^r d'Estrade at the Hage; the secretary
I cannot well tell what to say upon the matter, but me thinkes
hath written both to my lord Hollis and Mr Montague about it.
it is a strange thing, that at the same time that the Princes of
the blood in France, will not yeelde the place to my ambassadore there, that the french ambassadore at the Hage
should goe out of his way, to make a dispute with my nephew.
I would be glad to know your opinion upon this businesse,
for it concernes you, in all respects, as much as me. I hope
you will pardon me for haveing mist writing to you so many
posts, but the truth is, I had very much businesse at the end
of the parlament, which hindreed me, and I hope you will

thinke my paines not ill imployed, when I shall tell you that never any parlament went away better pleased then this did, and I am sure that I have all the reason in the world to be well satisfied with them, and when they meete againe, which will be in November, I make no dout but that they will do all for me that I can wish, and so good night for I am fast a sleepe. C. R."

The incident at the Hague to which Charles alludes was a quarrel between Monsieur d'Estrades, formerly Ambassador in England, and the boy-prince, William of Orange. Their coaches had met in the Foreholt, and the French Minister had refused to give way to the Prince. A great crowd had assembled, but fortunately the contending parties did not get beyond angry words, and the tumult that appeared imminent was avoided.

The King's next letter gives us the first intimation of the war that was shortly to break out between England and the States-General. Charles himself had no liking for the Dutch, and his personal animosity against Jean de Witt, had been increased by the Grand Pensioner's refusal to invest the young Prince of Orange with the dignity of Stadtholder, formerly held by his father. Great jealousy of the Dutch was also felt by the English merchants. The newly-formed African Company complained loudly of the injuries inflicted by Dutch seamen on their settlements, and at the close of the session an address had been presented by both Houses of Parliament to the King, begging him to demand reparation from the States. Sir George Downing was accordingly despatched to the Hague, but the temper of both nations was too warlike for much prospect of peace to be entertained on either side, and before long, open hostilities were commenced.

"WHITHALL,
"2 *June* 1664.

"This bearer has been so long resolving to leave this place, that I did not beleeve he would goe, till I see now his bootes are on, and he has taken his leave of me, and he gives me but a moment to write this letter, for 'tis not a quarter of an houer since he was looseing his mony at tenis, and he should have been gone, two howers agoe. I am affraide he comes very light to you, for though his wife has her loade, I feare his purse is as empty, haveing lost very neare five thousand pounds within these three monthes. You will heare of the misfortune I have had at Tanger. We are not very certaine that the governer is dead, but I am very much affraide that those barbarous people have given him no quarter; whosoever, he is taken, and 'what is become of him God knowes. Sᵣ George Downing is come out of Holland, and I shall now be very busy upon that matter, the States keepe a great braging and noise, but I beleeve, when it comes to it, they will looke twise before they leape. I never saw so great an appetite· to a warre as is, in both this towne and country, espetially in the parlament-men, who, I am confident, would pawn there estates to mainetaine a warre, but all this shall not governe me, for I will looke meerly what is just and best for the honour and good of England, and will be very steady in what I resolve, and if I be forsed to a warre, I shall be ready with as good ships and men, as ever was seene, and leave the successe to God. I am just now going to dine at Somerset House with the Queene, and 'tis twelve o'clocke, so as I can say no more, but that I am yours.

"C. R."

On the 22d of June, Madame wrote from Fontainebleau as follows: ⸶ I have already written to you several times, on the little affairs, which concern my Lord Hollis. I really think you must send him imperative orders to conclude them, if things are not to remain, as I am told they now are. For from him, I do not hear the least thing, since I told him that I did not think him right to vex himself so much over points of no importances. It is the justest thing in the world that he shall have certain privileges, but since these are not according to the custom of the country (*à la mode du pays*), and the King offers to deprive Comminges of them, to my mind there is nothing more to say. Milord Hollis is offended because Lionne (the Secretary of State) has not addressed him as your Excellency. As a matter of fact, he had always done this, but since the other never styled him so in return, he grew tired and gave it up. The same thing has happened with M. le Chancelier. They agreed to adopt this style, and M. le Chancelier having addressed Milord Hollis as Your Excellency, he replied by a simple *Vous*, which enraged the other to the last degree. Nothing, however, advances, and I am in despair to think all should be at a standstill for such trifles. I am called to go to the comedy, and can only assure you that I am your very humble servant."

In another letter, now missing, Madame gave her brother a description of her little girl, who was now a lovely child of two years old, and, she declared, exactly like Charles himself. She also informed the King that she had invested a sum of money, on behalf of this little Mademoiselle, in the newly-formed French East India Company, which Louis XIV. had taken under his royal patronage, and which at that time attracted much attention both at Court and in the country. In reply, Charles wrote his sister a merry letter, laughing at the notion of his niece's striking likeness to himself, which he is sure, exists only in her mother's fancy, and expressing great incredulity over the prospects of the new East India Company. The letter is not preserved in the French Archives, but belonged to M. Donnadieu's collection, and was first published by Mrs Everett-Green.

"This bearer, Mr Walters, being one of my servants, and having asked me leave to go into France to see the country, I would not let him kiss your hands, without a letter. I see you are as hot upon setting up an East India Company, at Paris, as we are here upon our Guinea trade. We are now sending away eight ships thither, to the value of £50,000, and I have given them a convoy of a man-of-war, lest the Dutch in those parts might do them some harm, in revenge for our taking the fort of Cape Verde, which will be of great use to our trade. I hope my niece will have a better portion than what your share will come to, in the East India trade. I believe you might have employed your money to better uses, than to send it off so long a journey. I hope it is but in a compliment to me, when you say my niece is so like me, for I never thought my face was even so much as intended for a

L

beauty. I wish, with all my heart, I could see her, for at this
distance I love her; you may guess, therefore, if I were upon
the place, what I should do! I am very sorry that Lord .
Hollis continues these kind of humours; I have renewed, by
every post, my directions upon it, and have commanded him
to proceed in his business, and not to insist upon trifles. I
am newly returned from seeing some of my ships, which lie
in the Hope, ready to go to sea, and the wind has made my
head ache so much, as I can write no longer, therefore I can
say no more but that I am yours.   C. R."

Another short letter, dated the 19th of June (O.S.), was
written after receiving Henrietta's complaints of Hollis, and
probably a day or two before the above.

"WHITHALL,
" 19 *June* 1664.

" I writt to you yesterday by the post, whereby you will
have a full answer to yours, I shall therefore say little to you
now, only that I am so confident both of your kindnesse to
me and of your discretion, as I shall ever put the greatest of
my secretts into your hands. The cheefe businesse of this
letter is to accompany this bearer, Mon^r Le fèvre, my apoti-
cary, who I send to Paris about some businesse which concernes his trade. I will only add that I am Yours.

"C. R."

Ten days later, Charles resumes his account of the Dutch
negotiations, which were still continued, in spite of occasional
hostilities, between the ships of both nations, off the coast of
Guinea. The "sudden gust" of royal displeasure, to which
the Duc de Navailles owed his disgrace at the French Court,
was a fresh result of the intrigues of De Vardes and his cast-
off mistress, the Comtesse de Soissons. After vainly endeavouring to ruin La Vallière, in the King's eyes, the
Countess had revealed her secret to the Queen, and had told
Louis XIV. that Madame de Navailles, the first lady-in-
waiting, was Her Majesty's informant. The King promptly
dismissed that lady from her post, and when her husband
ventured to remonstrate, he was included in his wife's dis-

grace. Both the Duke and Duchess, Mademoiselle informs us, were persons of irreproachable virtue, but too frank to retain the King's favour long, and their removal was deeply regretted by the two Queens, and, indeed, by all persons of merit.

4.

" WHITHALL,
" 27 *June* 1664.

" The last letter I writt to you, I had so great a paine in my head, as I could not make an end of my letter. I did intend to have tould you then, of the Holland Ambassadore's being arrived heere; he had two private audiences before his pub-lique one. If his masters be but as aprehensive of a warre with us, as he in his discourse seemes to be, I may expect to have very good conditions from them, and I have reason to beleeve by the letter they writt to me, there feares are no lesse at home. For, after takeing great paines to assure me of the great affection they have for me, they desire by all meanes that I will not lett my ships, which I am prepareing goe out to sea, least, by the indiscretion of some of the captaines, the quarrell might be begun. And they promise me, that they will not send out more men of warre, but such as are of absolute necessity to looke to the East India fleete and fishermen, and they desire me, that I would likewise give it under my hande, that those ships which I sett out may not fight with theres. You may guesse, by such a simple proposition, whether these people are not affraide! I have made no other answer to all this, but that I do intend, very speedily, to dispatch Sr George Downing into Holland, and by him, they shall have a returne of all this. I am very sorry for Mon{r} de Navaile's misfortune, I see Madame de Fiennes will rather venture the stormes at sea, then those suden gustes with you at land! I do not doute but that your wether there, is as hott as ours heere, no body can stirre any where, but by watter, it is so very hott and dusty. I am iust now cald away, by very good company, to sup upon the watter, so I can say no more but I am entierly Yours.

"C. R."

Birth of the Duc de Valois—Intrigues of De Vardes—Letters of Charles II. and Renewal of Negotiations—Madame endeavours to recover her Father's Jewels.

ON the 16th of July, Madame gave birth to a son at Fontaine-bleau. The event was hailed with acclamation throughout the country. There were bonfires and rejoicings all over France. Even Gui Patin, who had no love for the Royal Family, records the little Prince's birth with great satisfaction, and expresses fervent hopes for the welfare of the new Duc de Valois, as he was called. The Queen-mother was especially pleased, as her only other grandson, the young Dauphin, was a very sickly child ; and Monsieur, who had long complained of being without a son, could not contain his delight. He hastened to send the good news to England, and addressed the following note to Charles II. :—

" From FONTAINEBLEAU,

" 16 *July*.

" I should fail of the duty which I owe Your Majesty if I did not hasten to inform you, that your sister was this morning safely delivered of a fine boy. The child seems to be in excellent health, and will, I hope, grow up worthy of Your Majesty's friendship, which I ask you to bestow upon him. I wish you the same joy with all my heart. I send Boyer, my first *maître d'hôtel*, to you with this."

The same day, Hollis sent what he calls "the blessed newes" home by the hand of a private gentleman, Mr Roper, who offered himself as messenger on this auspicious occasion.

"Wednesday night, 16 *July.*

"When I writt to you this morning, I did not think to have done it again so soon. God be praised that I have so good an occasion! It is to let His Maiesty know, that Madame was this morning, between 9 and 10 of the clock, happily delivered of a sonne, a Duke of Valois. She had but an houre's labour, and is exceeding well, as any in her case, so newly brought to bed, can be. God be praised for it! The King and two Queens were all the while present. All the Court infinitely joyed, as I doubt not but you will be in England."

Louis XIV. was equally warm in his congratulations. He settled a pension of 50,000 crowns on his infant nephew, and wrote the following letter to Charles II., which was sent by the hands of Abbot Montagu, who started at once for England to take the news to Queen Henrietta :—

"We have, this morning, received the accomplishment of our wishes, in the birth of a son, whom it has pleased God to give to my brother ; and what renders this blessing the more complete, is the favourable state of health both of mother and child. With all my heart, I congratulate Your Majesty, and to understand my joy, you need only be pleased to consider the greatness of your own, for my tenderness towards my brother and sister is not less than even that of Your Majesty."

As for Madame, her joy was unbounded, and the fulfilment of this ardent desire was some consolation for the troubles which she had endured of late. A short time before her son's birth, the Comtesse de Soissons, who was then seriously ill, had sent for her and revealed De Vardes' treachery. At first Madame could hardly believe the extent to which she had been deceived. In the kindness of her heart, she thought only of consoling her sick friend, and assured her that no deeper feeling than that of mutual regard could ever exist between herself and De Vardes. But, by degrees, her eyes were opened to the full extent of the man's baseness. The Comte de Guiche had just returned from Poland, and had received the King's permission to appear at Court, if he did

not actually enter Madame's presence. He soon discovered
how treacherously De Vardes had behaved, and challenged
him to confess his guilt or fight. De Vardes, finding himself
attacked on all sides, implored Madame to see him, and,
although she had as yet received no visitors, in her anxiety to
discover the truth, she granted him an interview, three weeks
after the Duc de Valois's birth. De Vardes brought her a
letter from the Comte de Guiche, which she refused to read,
very wisely as it proved, for the miserable wretch had already
shown it to the King. Then he threw himself at her feet, and
implored her pardon. But Madame would make no promises,
and, in spite of his prayers and tears, she dismissed him indignantly from her presence. Hardly had he left the room,
than the King appeared, and Madame told him all that had
passed. " She saved herself from the pitfalls which surrounded
her," observes Madame de La Fayette, " by always speaking the
truth, and it was to this perfect sincerity that she owed the
King's friendship." Louis begged his sister-in-law to leave the
matter to him, and promised to punish De Vardes as he deserved.

Madame consoled herself by writing a long letter to her
mother, giving a full account of the intrigues of which she had
been the victim, and Charles II. hastened to assure her of his
affectionate sympathy. His congratulations on her son's birth
had been delayed by a sudden attack of fever, brought on by
his imprudence in laying aside his wig and pourpoint, one hot
day, when he had gone with the Queen to see the fleet before
it sailed out of the Thames. But on the 14th of July (O.S.)
he wrote :—

" My feaver had so newly left me, and my head was so giddy,
as I could not write to you on monday last, to tell you the
extreame joye I have at your being safely brought to bedd
of a sone. I assure nothing could be more welcome to me,
knowing the satisfaction it must be to you, and all your
concernes shall ever be next my harte. I thanke God I am
now perfectly quitt of my feavour, though my strength is not
fully come to me againe, for I was twise lett blood, and in
eight dayes eate nothing but watter-grewell, and had a greate
sweat, that lasted me almost two dayes and two nights. You

may easily beleeve, that all this will make me a little weake!
I am now sending Sr George Downing into Holland, to make
my demandes there, they have never yett given me any satisfaction for all the injuryes there subjects have done myne,
only given good words and nothing else, which now will not
be sufficient, for I will have full satisfaction, one way or other.
We have six East India ships arrived heere this weeke, which
bring us newes of a great losse the hollanders have receaved
there, three of there ships, which trade to Japon, being cast
away, whereof two richly laden, and besides this, they had sent
24 saile upon some designe in China, who are all blocked up
in a river in that country, so as they cannot escape. This will
coole the courage of the East India company at Amsterdam,
who are yett very impertinent. I am just now come from
seeing a new ill play, and it is almost midnight, which is a
faire howre for a sicke man to thinke of goeing to bed, and so,
good-night.   C. R."

A week later he despatched the following letter by Boyer,
Monsieur's *maître d'hôtel*. The man had been sent to England
on more than one previous occasion, and was frequently employed by the King and his ministers, to supply them with
French wines.

> "WHITHALL,
> "22 *July* 1664.

"The Queene shewed me yesterday your long letter, in
which I perceive you have been very ill-used, but I am very
glade to finde that the K. is so kinde and iust to you. I did
not thinke it possible that some persons could have had so ill
a part in that matter, as I see they have had by your letter.
I shall have by this a better opinion of my devotion for the
time to come, for I am of those bigotts, who thinke that malice
is a much greater sinn then a poore frailety of nature I shall
send James Hamilton to you and *Monsieur*, in two or three
dayes, to performe my compliments, I must give Boyer that
time before him, because I beleeve my messenger is the better
rider-post, and so might be at Paris before him. My wife
thinkes that Boyer is very like a faire Lady of your acquaintance, he will tell you who it is. I will say no more to you at

present, because I shall write more at large to you by J.
Hamilton, only againe I must give you joye for your sonne.

" C. R."

Madame recovered in time to be present at the *fêtes* which
were given in honour of the papal legate, Cardinal Chigi.
This dignitary had been sent to offer the Pope's apologies to
Louis XIV. for an insult which the servants of his Ambassador,
the Duc de Créqui, had received in the streets of Rome, and
which had caused a suspension of diplomatic relations between
France and the Vatican, during the last two years. Besides
the papal excuses, His Eminence brought with him pictures
by Titian and Lionardo, for the Most Christian King's acceptance. He was received with great honour, and entertained
with a series of festivities. First a ball was given, then a
tragedy of Corneille was performed. After that, the Queen-
mother gave a collation, and presented the Cardinal with
twenty-four elegant baskets of fruit, tied up with coloured
satin ribbons. One day His Eminence was present at a
review of the King's guards, another day he went out hunting
with His Majesty and killed three hares and a partridge, after
which he assisted at an orchestral performance in the royal
chapel. On the 13th of August the Court went to Vincennes.
"The King, Queens and Madame," wrote Hollis, "are at
Vincennes, Monsieur is here at the Palais-Royal, and the two
children ; and so I find they mean to continue, till Madame
and he go to Villers-Cotterets, which they do some ten days
hence, where, she saith, she will stay a month, but I hardly
believe it. She looks as well as ever I saw her look in my
life, that is, as well as possible ; and is grown so fat, that my
compliment to her yesterday was, it was well she had good witnesses, else nobody would believe she had brought forth such a
lusty young duke, to see her in so good a plight so soon, and
the young duke is as lusty and fine a child as ever I saw."

But the agitation of mind which Madame had lately
suffered, had tried her strength sorely, and she became so
ill at Villers-Cotterets, that the doctors ordered her complete
rest, and a course of asses' milk. Gui Patin observes in a
letter that September :—" The Duchess of Orléans has been

ill at Villers-Cotterets. She is frail and delicate, and belongs to those of whom Hippocrates speaks, as inclined to phthisis. The English, as a nation, are especially subject to this illness, which we call consumption." But Henrietta was too much accustomed to excitement, to allow herself any lasting repose. During the last week of their residence àt Villers-Cotterets, Monsieur and Madame gave a brilliant *fête* to the Court, and the King, the Queen and the Prince de Condé were all present at a second representation of *Tartuffe*. In October the Court paid a visit to Versailles, where the King was anxious to see the progress of the new works, which were eventually to transform his father's hunting-box into the finest palace of Europe. From here, Madame addressed a letter to her brother on the subject of certain jewels, which had formerly belonged to Charles I., and were now discovered in the possession of some French jewellers.

"24 *October* 1664.

" I have always delayed to inform you of a discovery that I made six months ago, of certain jewels which are said to have been stolen from the King, our father, and I should not mention it now, only that the Ambassador has lately been informed of it, and will no doubt have written to you. Since this is the case, I can no longer give you the surprise which I had planned, so I will tell you that the suspected parties, who have been arrested by my orders, confess to having once had the jewels in their possession, but as they have now passed into different hands, there will, I fear, be some difficulty in recovering them. But, cost what it may, I am determined they shall not escape me, and I hope before long to restore them to you. There is a very handsome hat-band of diamonds, also a garter, a great many rings, and a portrait of Prince Henry, set in very large diamonds. The Queen will be able to tell you whether she remembers them, for the King had nothing which she did not know of. I have nothing to say in reply to your last letter. I have so often spoken to you on the same subject, that it would be troubling you to begin again. To give you some news, in return for what you tell me about the Queen's building (Somerset

House), I must tell you that the King is making a grand building here, which will adorn the place very much, and which joins the fore court in the shape of a triangle. The best of it is, that it will cost him nothing, for he gives the ground to several persons of quality, who will build at their own expense, and will be very glad to have houses on this site. This is all that I have to say to you."

The subject which Madame had so often mentioned to the King, was probably the Ambassador's troublesome conduct. Knowing, as she did, Lord Hollis's susceptible temper, she wrote to him at the same time: "M. de Montagu has shown me the letter which you wrote to him concerning certain jewels, which are said to have been stolen from the King, my father. I heard of this some time ago, and have taken all necessary measures to recover them, in order that I may restore them to the King, my brother. The King has promised to make all the arrests that are necessary for my purpose, and if I have said nothing to you, it is because I hoped to give the King, my brother, an agreeable surprise. I send you the letter which he wrote in answer to the paper I sent him, of which M. de Montagu has informed you, for I am well content that you should know all that may pass through my hands, being, as it were, an anticipation of your charge. You are reasonable enough to know that we must obey our masters. For the rest, you may be satisfied that I shall only take what action is necessary, and shall always inform you of all that I do. Let me end by assuring you of my profound esteem."

Hollis's dignity was quite satisfied by this explanation, but he wrote home, saying it was fortunate that he had got wind of the matter, for Madame would certainly have been deceived. The business, however, proved a more complicated one than he had imagined. The jewels, including a very fine sapphire, and a wonderful crystal ship enriched with pearls and rubies, besides various curious tapestries, had all belonged to Charles I. Cardinal Mazarin had purchased some; others had been hidden away in thieves' quarters, and had been either sold or stolen during the Commonwealth. But they had passed through so many hands, that it was impossible to

prove anything with certainty, and, after a prolonged correspondence, the matter dropped.   Charles II. showed less
eagerness to recover his property than his sister and ministers
did.   Meanwhile, the prospect of the Dutch war was engaging
the King of England's time and thoughts.   His chief object
was to detach France from her alliance with the States.   In
1662, Louis XIV. had signed a treaty, by which he pledged
himself to assist the Dutch in case of war, with a view to
facilitate his own schemes of conquest in Flanders.   This
made Charles the more anxious to discover what he had to
expect from his brother of France, and, as usual, the chief
part of the correspondence passed through Madame's hands.
On the 23rd of August, Charles wrote as follows :—

"I tould you in my two last that I would write to you
more at large upon the subject of your two letters by the
Conte de Gramont and James Hamilton.   The truth is, I am
sorry to see you beleeve that the faute is on our side, that the
aliance with France is not farther advanced; 'tis true there
has been very unlucky accidents which have fallen out, that
have retarded it, as the dispute with the princes of the blood
at my Ambassadore's entry, and, since that, others of the like
nature, but if the ambassadores on both sides have had the
misfortune to render themselves unacceptable where they
negociate, why must it be thought their masters' faute?   I
assure you, if I had made that the rule, I must have long
since concluded that France had very little inclination to
advance in the treaty, but you shall see now that my L^d
Hollis will goe on very roundly in the matter, so as there
shall be no neglect on our part, and when the generall treaty
is concluded, it will be then the proper time to enter upon
the particular one, of that kindnesse and frindship which I
have always desired there should be betweene the King, my
brother, and my selfe.   But, now that I am upon this matter,
I must deale freely with you, and tell you that nothing can
hinder this good aliance and frindship which I speake of, but
the King, my brother's, giving the Hollanders some countenance in the dispute there is betweene us.   I assure you, they
brag very much already of his frindship, and it may be they

would not be so insolent as they are, if they had not some
such hopes. My Ld Hollis will give you a true state of that
businesse, wherein you will finde how much the Hollanders
are in the wrong. I meane the two companyes of the east
and west India, against whome my complaints are, and the
States hitherto have given them more countenance and assistance than they ought to have done. I must confesse I would
be very glad to know what I may expect from France, in
case the Hollanders should refuse me all sorte of reason and
iustice, for upon that, I must take my mesures accordingly.
I am very glad that the King, my brother, is so kinde to you,
there can be no body so fitt to make a good correspondent
and frindship betweene us as your selfe, I take the occasion
of this safe messenger to tell you this, because I would not
have this businesse passe through other hands than yours, and
I would be very willing to have your opinion and counsell
how I shall proceede in this matter, I do not doute but you
will have that care of me, that I ought to expect from your
kindnesse, and as you are an Exeter woman; and if you are
not fully informed of all things as you complayne of in your
letters, it is your own faute, for I have been a very exact
correspondent, and have constantly answered all your letters,
and I have directed my Ld Hollis to give a full account of
our dispute with Holland, if you will have the patiance to
heare it. I shall sum up all, in telling you that I desire very
much to have a strict frindship with France, but I expect to
finde my account in it, as 'tis as reasonable that they should
finde theres, and so I shall make an end of this long letter, by
assuring you that I am intierly yours.   C. R."

Madame's reply is missing, but on the 19th of September
the King resumed the subject in another letter, of which only
a fragment remains. If France, he repeats, desires his friendship, "there is nobody so proper to make it as yourself, and
I am sure I will put all my interest into your hands, and then
you shall be the judge who most desires the good alliance. . .
The feeling here against Holland is extremely strong, and I
find myself almost the only man in my kingdom who doth
not desire war. I do expect with impatience to hear some-

thing from you on the subject of my long letter, that I may know what I may depend upon. I am confident the conjuncture will be such, before long, wherein I may be useful to France, and I tell you freely, I had much rather make my frindship where you are, and with those I know, than with others. But it will be impossible for this nation to be idle when they see their neighbours busy, and I cannot deny to you, that it agrees with my humour likewise. I write thus freely to you that you may know the truth, for I assure you, I consider your interest in it, and so good-night, my dearest sister, for 'tis late. Pray make my compliments to Monsieur, and though I do not trouble him often with letters, there is no one more truely his than I am.—C. R."

A month later, on the 17th of October, he wrote again :—

" I have deferred thus long to answer yours, that I might as well do it, to your satisfaction as my owne, for being very well satisfied with the King, my brother's, expressions of kindnesse, I was very willing to finde that the methode proposed by him, would with most expedition have brought us to the end we both desire. I do in the first place desire you to use your interest and creditt to remove all jealousyes of any change in me, or that I am lesse warme in my inclinations towards a firme frindship with france, then I have professed to be. Those apprehentions will in the ende be founde to be without grounde, and if I were naturally inclined to suspition I have more cause to beleeve the change may be there ; I do assure you, there is nothing more in my wish and indeavour, then that this present treaty may be finished, that we may the better and the sooner and with lesse noyse, thinke of a more strict and usefull frindship. I called for the treaty of 1610 (which, in the confusion the late time hath cast all our papers, could not be presently founde), and have perused it my selfe and by my selfe, and finde the whole so unapplicable to this conjuncture, and that in truth scarce any article of it hath ever been observed on either side, and that the whole traffique and commerce (which is quite an other thing from what it was then) is referred to former treatyes, the copyes whereof are lost, or cannot yett be founde, that much more time must inevitably be spent in makeing that treaty inteligible and practicall then will serve to finish this, which, in my opinion haveing been so lately, can take up very little time before it be againe concluded, and if my Ld Hollis (who upon my creditt is very well affected to this worke in hande, and hartily desires a very fast frindship betweene us, though in matters relating to himselfe, he may possibly be formal and punctuall enough) hath made any unseasonable addition to what he proposed at first, the King may reject it, what I desire being no more than that the Duch may not enjoy any priviledges in France, which shall be denyed to my subjects, which is a preference I am sure the King will never give to them. In a word, it is in the King, my brother's, power to have what kinde of correspondence, or what kinde of frindship he will with me, and if I do understand his or my owne interest and designes, a very fast frindship is good and necessary for us both, and it cannot but be a manifestation to him of the sincerity of my intentions, that I ingage you to undertake for it, which sure I would not do, if they were otherwise. I have written my harte to you, which I will not undertake to do so in french, but you may have this translated, and so, my dearest sister, I am yours.   C.

" Since the writing of this, I have receaved yours of the 21st, with a copy of the treaty of 1610, the same I mention to have read heere, with the procés-verbal of the ceremonyes passed at my Ld Gorings swering this, and all other treatyes then subsisting between France and us, which, as I have sayde, cannot come home to the present case now before us. This makes me still remaine in the conclusion, that we must lay for a foundation the project my Ld Hollis hath now given in, and add to it other private articles of mutuall defence and succour, as may be easily agreed upon betweene us, and this will not be a worke of much time, if our mindes be according to our professions, and so I am yours.   C. R.

" Pray lett le Nostre goe on with the modell, and only tell him this adition, that I can bring water to the top of the hill, so that he may add much to the beauty of the desente by a cascade of watter.   C. R."

Charles's next letter was sent by the hand of the Comte de Gramont, who was on his way to his own country, with his fair English wife and their young child. Two months before, Comminges had written to Lionne: "M^dme la Comtesse de Gramont gave birth yesterday to a son, as handsome as his mother and as gay as his father. All the Court rejoices with them, but I think the prospect of returning to France has done more to wipe out the wrinkles from the Count's brow, and bring back the lilies and roses to his cheeks."

Charles speaks warmly of both the Count and Countess, in his two following letters :—

"WHITHALL,

"23 *Oct.* 1664.

"I hope you will be well satisfied with the last letter I writt to you, for in it I sayd nothing but what came from my harte, and as I then tould you, I do now againe, that if I did not intend what I write, I would not adresse it to you. The Comte de Gramont will give you this, and he will tell you how kind I am to you. I pray be kinde to him, and to his wife, for my sake, and if at any time there be an occasion to send hether one of his talent, there is nobody will be more wellcome to me than him. I will say no more to you now, because this letter will be long upon the way, only againe recommend them bothe to your protection, and desire you to beleeve that I am intierly Yours.   C. R."

"WHITHALL,

"24 *Oct.* 1664.

"I writt to you yesterday, by the Comte de Gramont, but I beleeve this letter will come sooner to your handes, for he goes by the way of Diepe with his wife and family, and now that I have named her, I cannot choose but againe desire you to be kinde to her, for besides the meritt her family has, on both sides, she is as good a creature as ever lived. I beleeve she will passe for a handsome woman in France, though she has not yett, since her lying in, recovered that good shape she had before, and I am affraide never will. You will heare by this post, of the demelé that was betweene my Ld St Albans and M. de Chapel (Madame de Fiennes's husband), which is now made up. All I shall say of it, is that de Chapel was as much in the wrong as a man could be to his superior officer. Poor Oneale (the husband of Lady Stanhope) died this afternoon of an ulser in his gutts. He was as honest a man as ever lived. I am sure I have lost a very good servant by it. I have nothing to say more to you, upon our publique businesse, till I have an answer from you, of my last letter by the post, only that I expect with impatiency to know your mindes there, and then you shall finde me as forward to a strict frindship with the King, my brother, as you can wish. You will have heard of our takeing of New Amsterdame, which lies just by New England. 'Tis a place of great importance to trade, and a very good towne. It did belong to England heeretofore, but the Duch by degrees drove our people out of it, and built a very good towne, but we have gott the better of it, and 'tis now called New Yorke. He that took it, and is now there, is Nicols, my brother's servant, who you know very well. I am yours. C. R."

On the 4th of November, Henrietta wrote from Paris :—

" I have shewn your last letter to the King, who has ordered me to tell you in answer to what you write touching the Dutch, that if you will agree to treat his subjects in England as the English, he consents that the English in France should be treated as French, excepting the fifty *sous*." This was a tonnage exacted from all foreign ships leaving French ports, according to the treaty made between France and Holland in 1662.

" I am not clever enough to know what this means, but these are the King's own words which I repeat to you. If this is what you want, reply as soon as you can, for if you do not quickly end all this, you will not gain time, as you both appear to wish, and this will drag on to infinite lengths ! It is so late, and I am so sleepy that I will add nothing more but that I am your very humble servant."

Madame's next letter speaks of her sister-in-law, Queen Marie Thérèse's dangerous illness, which had thrown the Court into a great state of alarm. An attack of fever brought on a premature confinement, and for some weeks the Queen's life was in imminent danger. There were prayers in all the

Paris churches. The Queen-mother, who was herself in a very precarious condition, went in solemn state to the Church of Les Feuillants to pray for her daughter-in-law's recovery, and Louis XIV.'s distress almost equalled that of his brother of England, on a similar occasion. Mademoiselle describes the crowds which thronged the sick chamber, and takes care to record the vexation of the Queen, on seeing Madame with her hair elegantly dressed and decked out in yellow ribands, a mark, in her eyes, of great disrespect and want of feeling, Marie Thérèse eventually recovered, but the baby, a little girl who was christened Marie Anne, and had Madame for her godmother, died in December. On the 12th of November, Henrietta wrote :—

"I sent you word by the last post of the Queen's illness, which has much increased since then, owing to the frightful pains in her limbs, which keep the fever high. The King seems much distressed, although we are assured there is no danger at present, either for her or her child. I think you had better send some one to inquire after her, for this is not a little illness which will be over to-day or to-morrow. I have no leisure to say more. I will write more fully by Mr Sidnei, who leaves to-morrow, and will only tell you now that I am your humble servant."

On the 28th she wrote to Charles by the Marquis de Ruvigny, brother-in-law to Lord Southampton, who was sent to England by Louis XIV., on a special mission to report on the state of feeling towards France, and supply information on points in which Comminges had failed to satisfy the King's mind. "I could not let Ruvigny start without this letter, to assure you again, what he will also tell you, how much your friendship is wished for here, and how necessary it is to France. Profit by this, in God's name, and lose no time in obtaining a promise from the King not to help the Dutch. You understand that he cannot bind himself publicly, owing to his engagements with them, although we all know these are only worth what he chooses to make them. For, as with everything else in this world, it is necessary to keep up a good

M

appearance. You must, therefore, content yourself with a
private agreement, which is likely in fact to be more lasting,
and I promise to see that this is done in good faith, for I fear
the contrary so much, in anything that I am mixed up with,
that I will have nothing to do with it, unless I see that this is
the case. Tell Ruvigny, I beg, how well I have spoken of
him to you, for he is the most honest of men. I do not think
you need me to tell you this, nor yet that I am your very
humble servant."

Charles, on his part, now sent his old friend Charles
Berkeley, Lord Fitzhardinge, on a confidential mission to
Paris, and was well pleased with the reception which the
King gave him, as we see from the following letter :—

" WHITHALL,
" 21 Nov. Monday, 1664.

" The Parlament being to meet on thursday next, gives me
so much businesse, to put all thinges in a good way at there
first comming together, as I have only time to tell you that C.
Berkeley arrived heere late last night, so as yett I have not
had full time to receave an account of the successe of his
negotiation. I shall only tell you now the great satisfaction
I receave, in the obligeing reception he had from the King, my
brother, which I am sure I will returne with all imaginable
kindnesses, and I hope there will not be many steps more
before the intier frindship be made betweene us. Pray tell
Monsieur I am as sensible of his frindship and kindnesse as I
ought to be, but that I have not now time to tell it him in
writting till the next post. For yourselfe, I am to much
obliged to you to say anything of it in so short a letter, nor
indeed can I ever diserve it from you. You have my hart,
and I cannot give you more.   C. R."

Madame replied by the hands of another gentleman of the
Court, who was about to start for London, and had begged
the favour of a line from her pen.

" This gentleman asks me to recommend him to you, and
is a very worthy person. He goes on the same errand as
Ruvigny, and I see that in this affair you are doing what is

desired here, as indeed it is best, since it is always well to oblige people in small matters. I am very sorry to have nothing more to say, by such a safe channel, when, I have no doubt, I shall long to tell you a hundred things another time when the insecurity will make it impossible. Here people say the Dutch will never dare sail this winter, and all they want to do is to gain time, in hopes that all the supplies on board your ships will be exhausted, and the great expense of fitting them out again will force you to make peace. I see by your last letter that Fitzhardinge has been very expeditious, and that you have not yet had time to speak with him. I hope when you have you will do what I ask in the letter I sent by him, which is assuredly the best way of coming to a good understanding with the King. You see how little great treaties are kept, but this kind of thing, on the contrary, must be inviolable as a compact made between two friends and brothers."

Monsieur, who at this time declared himself warmly in favour of England, had lately written to congratulate his brother-in-law on the advantage gained by his sailors over the Dutch on the coast of Guinea. Madame now wrote on hearing a similar report :—

> "PARIS,
> "ce 10 Décembre.

" It is said here that your fleet has taken forty Dutch ships, but, as you do not mention it, I fear it may not be true. I gave your letter to the King, who showed it to me. I also gave him the messages that you sent. He receives all your advances so well that I doubt not but he will respond to them in course of time. The Queen is much better, but as for the little Madame, she has suffered from such violent convulsions during the last ten days that her death is hourly expected, so the congratulations you are going to send on her birth will, I fear, have to be changed into condolences for her death which is all that your humble servant has to say for the present."

CHAPTER XIV

Arrest of De Vardes—Madame's last Interview with the Comte de Guiche—
Verdict of contemporary writers on her Character—Madame de La Fayette's
Vie de Madame Henriette—Madame a Patron of Art and Letters—Her
Friendship with Molière, Racine, La Fontaine, Bussy, and others.

WHILE Madame was conducting these important negotiations
between the two countries, and surprising experienced diplomats
by her tact and ability, she had a still more difficult task to do,
in setting herself free from the tangled web which falsehood
and intrigue had wound about her. De Vardes was still at
large, in spite of all the King's promises, and, as yet, even
Madame had not fathomed the abyss of his iniquities. An
unexpected incident suddenly revealed them to her. Since
his return to Court that summer, the Comte de Guiche had
vainly sought an opportunity of meeting the Princess.
Madame refused either to see him, or to read the despairing
letters which he addressed to her. In vain he implored the
Comtesse de Gramont to intercede for him, and paid her daily
visits that winter, in the hope of meeting Madame at her house.
This lady had, on her arrival from England, been received in
the most cordial manner by Henrietta, who welcomed the fair
Englishwoman as her brother had desired, and honoured her
with gracious marks of her friendship. But all Madame de
Gramont could obtain, on behalf of the Comte de Guiche, was
a message from Henrietta, to the effect that she recognised
his innocence of the false charges which had been brought
against him, and was grateful for the honourable way in which
he had behaved. A strange chance gave him the opportunity
which he had so long sought in vain. One evening Monsieur
and Madame were present at a masked ball given by the

Duchess de la Vieuville. They came without attendants, in a hired coach, the better to conceal their identity. As they entered the house, they fell in with another party of masked guests. Monsieur gallantly gave his hand to one of the ladies, Madame accepted the arm of an unknown cavalier. Suddenly she caught sight of the hand that was offered her, and recognised the maimed fingers of the Comte de Guiche, whose hand had been partly shot off in battle. At the same time, the familiar perfume of Madame's hair made the Count aware that she was his partner. They mounted the staircase in silence, and for some moments neither of them was able to speak a word. But the Count soon gathered courage, and in a few moments told Madame all. Now, for the first time, she realised the blackness of De Vardes's treachery, and the scandalous way in which she had been duped. She, on her part, explained all that had passed, and thanked the Count for his loyalty and obedience to her wishes. But Monsieur approached, and, fearful of exciting suspicion, the Count left the ball-room. Madame turned hastily to join her husband, and, catching her feet in her gown, she fell down a flight of steps. De Guiche, who was lingering on the staircase, caught her in his arms, and was just in time to save her from a dangerous fall. From that moment Madame resolved that De Vardes should no longer go unpunished. The effrontery with which he spoke of her in public soon gave her the excuse she needed. She appealed indignantly to the King for redress, and wrote a passionate letter to her brother, imploring his powerful help.

> " PARIS,
> " *ce* 17 *Décembre.*

" I have begged the ambassador to send you this courier, that he may inform you truly of the affair which has happened about Vardes, but having written it to the Queen, my mother, you will allow me to refer you to her letter, for the whole story. Here I will only say that the thing is so serious, I feel that it will influence all the rest of my life. If I cannot obtain my object, it will be a disgrace to feel that a private individual has been able to insult me with impunity, and if I do, it will be a warning to all the world in future, how they dare to attack

me. I know that you were angry that he was not punished
for the first affair, which makes me ask you this time to write
a letter to the King, saying that, although you feel sure he will
give me every possible satisfaction, and finish as well as he has
begun—for it will never do to let him see that we are displeased with him—yet, out of love for me, you cannot help
asking him to do so (if you do not think this expression too
strong), and that if it had not been one of his own servants who
is in fault, you would not have asked him for justice, but
would have done it yourself. But you will judge better than
I can what to say, for, as I have already told you, it is a business
which may have terrible consequences if this man is not exiled
All France is interested in the result, so I am obliged to stand
up for my honour, and leave you to judge what might happen !
I hope that the consideration in which you are held here may
settle all this. It will not be the first debt that I shall have
owed you, nor the one for which I shall be the least grateful,
since it will enable me to obtain justice in future. I end by
assuring you that I am your most humble servant."

Charles hastened to assure his sister that she might rely
on his assistance, and although he makes no further allusion
to the subject of her letter, the result proved that he was as
good as his word. A fortnight later, Lord Hollis, writing
home, informs his master that "the Marquis de Vardes has
been ordered to surrender himself to the Bastille, to expiate
some unbecoming words of which it is said that Madame had
complained to His Majesty." But since De Vardes's friends
went to see him at the Bastille, and boasted that all Madame's
influence would never obtain his banishment, the King soon
afterwards exiled him to the little town of Aigues-Mortes, and
forbade him to return to Court. A still more decisive
triumph, however, was in store for Madame. In spite of the
generous treatment which the Comtesse de Soissons had
received at her hands, this intriguing lady could not forgive
Madame for having robbed her of her lover. In her jealous
anger, she vowed vengeance, and by way of retaliation, told the
King that the Comte de Guiche had advised Madame to take
possession of Dunkirk in her brother's name, and that, in order

to effect this object he had placed the regiment of guards which he commanded at her disposal.

Fortunately Louis asked Madame if this were true, and Henrietta easily proved the story to be an impudent calumny of Madame de Soissons. This time the King's anger was thoroughly roused, and determined, once for all, to put an end to these perpetual intrigues, he banished the Comte and Comtesse de Soissons from Court, and imprisoned De Vardes in the citadel of Montpelier. Here this dangerous character remained for two years, and nineteen more passed away before he was allowed to show his face at Court again.

Thus Madame's honour was at last fully vindicated and her enemies met with their deserts. But one more chapter of the tale remains to be told. True to her resolve, Henrietta refused to see the Comte de Guiche again. But she sent him word through his father, the Maréchal de Gramont, of the mischievous reports which had reached the King's ears, and advised him to be perfectly frank and open with his master. The old Maréchal now took alarm, and although his son was ill of a fever, he insisted on his leaving Court at once. But the Count would not go without a last sight of Madame, and in spite of his weak state of health, he borrowed the liveries of one of La Vallière's servants and stood in this disguise in the court of the Palais-Royal, to see Madame pass by in her chair, on her way to the Louvre. He even ventured to draw near and speak to her, but when he had to take leave of her, his strength failed, and he fainted away. Madame's chair passed on, and they never met again. So the pitiful little romance ended.

The Comte de Guiche went to Holland, where he covered himself with laurels in the coming campaign. He fought desperately in a naval battle with the English, and when the Dutch man-of-war on which he served was blown up, only saved himself by plunging into the sea and swimming to shore. Afterwards, he returned to France, where he lived happily with the wife whom he had so long neglected, and wrote letters full of fine sentiments and eloquent phrases to the virtuous Madame de Brissac. In 1672, he became the hero of the famous Passage du Rhin. That day he dashed into the river at the head of his troop of cavalry, swam the stream and carried the enemy's post under the King's eyes, a foolhardy exploit enough, as Madame de Sevigné remarks. But it succeeded, and De Guiche's name was on every lip. A year afterwards he died at Kreuznach, in the midst of another campaign, of a sudden illness brought on, it is said, by over-fatigue and grief at the loss of the King's favour. Madame de Sevigné has described, in her inimitable way, the painful sensation that was caused by his death, and the pathetic interview, in which the Abbé Bourdaloue broke the news to his old father.

As for Madame, if the manner of the Count's farewell cost her a pang, she did not see the close of the little drama without a sense of relief. It had given her more pain than pleasure and had left her a sadder and a wiser woman. Madame de La Fayette, who heard every detail from her own lips, did not think that she ever entertained any very deep feeling for this daring knight, and was doubtful if his love for her was not rather a romantic devotion than *une grande passion*.

The Count's amours, contemporary writers agree, were of a distinctly Platonic nature. And Madame de Motteville remarks, that if his passion for Madame brought him great sorrows, his vanity probably deprived them of much of their bitterness. He had at least the satisfaction of being her acknowledged adorer, and of hearing his name linked with hers in the common talk of the Court. The same lady, who was one of Madame's severest critics, says decidedly that there was nothing criminal in this *liaison*, and that even the Queen-mother, while she blamed her daughter-in-law's thoughtlessness, never suspected her of a worse fault. The episode of Madame's so-called loves with the Comte de Guiche, supplied scandal-mongers with a fruitful theme. But their ribaldry met with no support from respectable writers. Even Manicamp, who wrote the famous libel, *Les Amours du Palais-Royal*, which made so much noise at the time, does not accuse Madame or her lover of anything worse than a foolish flirtation, carried on under very romantic circumstances, in the most high-flown language. Bishop Burnet, it is true, does his best to blast Henrietta's character, in what Swift has called

those " pretty, jumping periods " of his, but the mere fact that
this Princess was a Catholic and tried to win her brother over
to her own faith, was enough to make him paint her in the
blackest of colours.   And anyone who examines the memoirs
and letters of the Court, will see at a glance that his insinuations are groundless.   The worst that her enemies can say of
Henrietta is that she did not object to being adored.   The
Marquis de La Fare, who was never honoured with Madame's
confidence, and was intimate with her bitterest enemy, the
Comtesse de Soissons, gives it as his opinion that she was
vertueuse mais un peu coquette.   And this verdict is confirmed
by all the best authorities, amongst others, by her successor,
the blunt and outspoken princess, who became Monsieur's
second wife.   In her *Memoirs*, this honest but eccentric
lady repeatedly records her conviction that the world
had been unjust to Madame.   " I think," she writes in one
place, "that Madame had more misfortunes than faults.   She
had to do with wicked people, about whose conduct I could
tell a great deal if I chose.   Madame was very young, beautiful, agreeable, full of grace and charm.   From the time of her
marriage, she was surrounded by the greatest coquettes and
most intriguing women in the world, who were the mistresses
of her enemies.   I think people have been very unjust to her."

As Henrietta herself, when she first married, told Madame
de La Fayette, of all the ladies about her, there was not one
whom she could trust.   Certainly the position was full of
danger for a Princess of her youth and character, and if she
did not fall into worse difficulties, it was only due to her natural
goodness of heart   But from this time, a marked change was
noticed in her.   She was only twenty now, but the lessons of
the last few years had not been wasted on her.   Madame de
Motteville remarks, that once De Vardes, the author of all
these intrigues, had been finally banished, Madame seemed to
wish to alter her behaviour.   " She lived on better terms with
the Queen, her mother-in-law, and took her part in the necessary diversions of the Court, with no wish but to make herself
pleasant to all.   As she had much genius and penetration, and
could talk well on every subject, those who had the honour of
knowing her best, noticed that she was beginning to recognise,

by her own experience, how little the pleasures she had once
sought so eagerly, were capable of satisfying the human heart,
but she hardly grasped that truth in all its fulness ; as yet she
only saw it dimly and from afar."

It was during the following summer, a few months only
after the Comte de Guiche's final departure, that Madame,
being confined to her rooms by illness, and unable to take part
in the usual gaieties of the Court, told Madame de La Fayette
the story of his love.   The details were then fresh in her
mind, and as her friend expressed surprise at some of the
adventures which had befallen her, Madame suddenly exclaimed :—" Do you not think this would make a very pretty
story ?   You write stories so well, do please write this one,
and I will tell you all the details."   Madame de La Fayette
entered warmly into Henrietta's idea, and promised to do her
best.   Together they sketched out the plan of the story, and
Henrietta took a child-like pleasure in composing a novel of
her own " *un roman a elle*."   But she recovered her health and
the fancy passed.   It was only four years later, after the
birth of her second daughter, Mademoiselle de Valois, that the
idea came back to her mind.   This was just after her mother's
death.   Monsieur had accompanied the Court to Chambord,
and Madame de La Fayette remained almost alone with Henrietta at Saint-Cloud.   Together they set to work on the book.
Madame de La Fayette wrote down each morning what
Henrietta had told her the evening before, and then showed
her what she had written.   The task was by no means an
easy one, and Madame de La Fayette, more careful of Henrietta's reputation than this Princess herself, often found it
difficult to reconcile truth with propriety.   But Madame was
delighted.   The romantic bent of her nature was gratified.
She liked to feel herself the heroine of the tale, and took keen
interest in its progress, dictating some pages, correcting others,
and laughing merrily over the passages which gave her friend
the most trouble.   One day, when Madame de La Fayette
was summoned to Paris, she herself took up the pen, and
wrote several pages of the narrative.   But the King came
back, and Madame left Saint-Cloud to join her husband at
Paris.   The story was once more thrown aside, and when

Madame de La Fayette took it up again, a year later, Henrietta was dead and her broken-hearted friend was left alone to pen the few sad pages which tell the tale of her tragic end.

The details of Court intrigues and gallantries which fill Madame de La Fayette's book are of little interest now. What is really valuable is the portrait which she gives us of Madame herself. We see her in the light and grace of her youth, presiding at those Court *fêtes* which were never complete without her, rewarding the victor in the ring with one of the smiles that turned the heads of the wisest and the best, or else entertaining a brilliant company in the lighted saloons of the Palais-Royal, while foolish Monsieur struts up and down exulting over the number of his guests, all unconscious that they have come for Madame's sake. We see her foremost in dance and song, leading the masque under the forest trees of Fontainebleau, or gliding over the waters on summer nights to the sound of Lulli's violins. And we see her, too, in the more intimate moments of her life, at her beautiful home of Saint-Cloud, enjoying the society of one or two chosen friends, with that freedom and absence of constraint in which she delighted. There, among the green lawns and sunny terraces where her memory still lives, she loved to linger with her ladies, while Monsieur went off on his daily excursions to Paris. There she consoled herself for his ill-temper and jealousy by reading her favourite authors aloud with some companion who shared her tastes. Or else, laying her fair head on Madame de La Fayette's knee, she would pour out the fears and sorrows that vexed her, and speak of her unhappiness, with that air of sweetness which made her even more charming in her sadder moments. There, too, on summer evenings she loved to wander, arm-in-arm with one or other of her friends, listening to the music of the waterfalls and enjoying the fragrant scent of the flowers. And there, long after her death, it was said that she might be seen at midnight sitting, robed in white, at the foot of her favourite cascade.

Many were the distinguished visitors who came to see her in this lovely spot. The serious side of her nature attracted the ablest scholars and deepest thinkers of the Court. The two greatest soldiers of the day, Condé and Turenne, were both numbered among her friends. Turenne especially, whose rough exterior hid so true and loyal a soul, was deeply attached to Madame. His natural shyness and modesty kept him away from Court, and made him shrink from any kind of public recognition, but he was intimate with the Arnauld family, with the men of Port-Royal, and the members of Madame de Sevigné's circle. Another veteran whom Madame honoured with her friendship, and whose religious turn of mind had drawn him in the same direction, was the good old Maréchal de Bellefonds. But there was hardly a man of note in France, at this period, who was not brought into some connection with Madame. La Rochefoucauld and Madame de Sevigné became intimate with her, through Madame de La Fayette. Another accomplished scholar, M. de Tréville, was one of her most devoted friends. This brilliant gentleman held the honourable post of Captain of the Musketeers in Monsieur's household, and had the reputation of being at once the best Greek scholar and the wittiest man at Court. To talk like Tréville, to be as learned as Tréville, was the highest compliment you could pay a man. Bossuet, Arnauld and Nicole were among his closest friends. He helped Sacy with his translation of the New Testament, and was one of the editors of *Pascal's Pensées*. The death of Madame snapped the last link which bound him to the Court. That day he turned his back upon the world, and joined his friends at Port-Royal.

This famous society was, in those days, the centre of intellectual life in France. With the venerable Arnauld d'Andilly for its patriarch, and his children and brother and sister for its leading members, Port-Royal gathered together all the foremost scholars and deepest thinkers of the day. A succession of important publications issued from it walls, and to be stamped with the mark of Port-Royal was of itself a passport to fame. The piety and learning of the recluses attracted visitors from all parts. Madame de Longueville built herself a house at Port-Royal des Champs. Mademoiselle, Madame de Sevigné, Madame de La Fayette, all visited the convent, and came away deeply impressed. "This Port-Royal is a Thebaïd!" exclaims Madame de Sevigné!

"a paradise, where all that remains of Christian piety in the world has found a refuge." Madame de Sablé made herself a home within the precincts of Port-Royal de Paris and held *salons* there, which recalled the Saturdays of the hotel Rambouillet. Madame de Sevigné and Madame de La Fayette, herself a member of the old society and described by Scarron as *toute lumineuse, toute précieuse*, Mademoiselle de Scudéry, the author of Cyrus and Clélie, Madame de Suze, and Madame de Brégis came there to meet Arnauld and Pomponne, St. Cyran and Tréville, Sacy and Nicole. Madame herself was often present at these *réunions*, and both she and Monsieur, who had little enough in common with the thinkers of Port-Royal, were on intimate terms with Madame de Sablé. Monsieur, indeed, at one time kept up a correspondence with this cultivated lady, and many of his notes to her are preserved in the Bibliothèque Nationale. Among them we find the following note which was addressed by Madame herself to Madame de La Fayette, begging her to excuse her absence from one of those *réunions* as she has a bad cold, and is well aware of Madame de Sablé's fear of infection.

Tuesday Morning, 1666.

"My cold has become so much worse since yesterday, that I dare not go to Madame La Marquise de Sablé's house to-day, for, even if she were not afraid of me, the sight of me would certainly make her ill, and in order to avoid both these inconveniences, I think it wiser to put off my visit till Thursday. Do not think that I fail to keep my appointment out of laziness. I am really afraid I should alarm her! Find this out for me, and send me a line to l'Abbaye au Bois, where I am going to see Mademoiselle d'Elbœuf."

Gondrin, the excellent Archbishop of Sens, whose learning and virtues had earned for him the name of Jansenist, was another friend whom Madame met in these circles, and who lent her his help and advice in some of the most difficult moments of her life. A very different personage, Madame de Sevigné's troublesome cousin, Bussy, Comte de Rabutin, found his way into this coterie, by right of his wit, if not of

his virtue. This famous *bel-esprit*, who enjoyed the reputation of having the most dangerous tongue in France, knew
how to make himself agreeable to Madame, and when he had
forfeited the King's favour, and offended everyone at Court
by the impudence of his sarcasms, he implored her to intercede for him.   Henrietta consented with her usual good-
nature, and while mass was being celebrated in the royal
chapel on the following morning, she approached the King,
and begged him to grant Bussy an audience, assuring him
that he was a very worthy man, and had been unjustly calum-
niated.   Louis replied that this might be very true, but that
he made jests of every one, adding with a smile, that Madame
herself would be fortunate if she escaped.   Here mass ended,
and with it the conversation.   Afterwards Bussy found out
from Louvois, that he had been accused to the King of speaking ill of Madame.   "Why, she is the best of my friends!"
he replied, "if I may venture to speak in such a manner of so
exalted a lady."   Madame herself, he adds, only laughed at
the charge, and used her influence on his behalf to such good
purpose, that Bussy was pardoned, and allowed to retain his
post at Court, on promise of better behaviour in future.   His
gratitude was unbounded.   "I was as much obliged to
Madame," he writes in his *Memoirs*, "as if she had saved my
life, and although I knew she had a natural disposition to do
good to everyone, yet the honour she did me, and the manner
in which she treated me, made me think that she worked with
more zeal for me than for others.   To tell the truth, she saw
that I was much attracted to her, and greatly admired her
good qualities, for she was, both in mind and person, the most
charming princess that ever lived."   Unfortunately, Bussy
soon fell into disgrace again, owing to the treachery of his
mistress, who published a scurrilous pamphlet, *L'Histoire
Amoureuse des Gaules*, which he had only destined for private
circulation.   In April 1665, he was sent to the Bastille, and,
after a twelvemonth's imprisonment, was banished to his
estates in Burgundy, where he pined away, during his long
years of exile, and solaced himself by corresponding with the
wiser and more fortunate friends whom he had left at Court.
But he never forgot Madame's kindness, and lamented her

death, in common with all of those who had any love for letters, or any admiration for genius.

Henriette's taste for the drama, her keen interest in literature, and her generous appreciation of artistic excellence in every form, naturally attracted men of distinction to her side. "Need I remind you," exclaimed Bossuet, in a fine passage of his *Oraison*, "of that excellent judgment in art and letters, which made all those who succeeded in pleasing Madame, feel satisfied that they had attained perfection?" There was one group of men of letters whom she honoured in an especial manner with her patronage. This was the little band of poets who spent their evenings together in a garret of the Faubourg Saint Germain, and by day sought the Muses in the forest shades of Fontainebleau, or along the wooded banks of the Seine. As one of their number, Racine, wrote to his friend, La Fontaine, when he recalled their happy rambles together in the beautiful environs of Paris,—

> "Tantôt Fontainebleau les voit (*les Muses*).
> Le long de ses belles cascades,
> Tantôt Vincennes les reçoit,
> A l'ombre de ses palissades !
>
> Elles sont souvent sur les eaux
> Ou de la Marne, ou de la Seine,
> Elles étaient toujours à Vaux,
> Et ne l'ont pas quitté sans peine."

Each of these distinguished men found a kind friend and discriminating patron in Madame. Molière was honoured with many marks of her favour. On the 28th of February 1664, she stood sponsor to his first-born child, a boy, named Louis after the King, who was his godfather. And when the first performance of *Tartuffe* had roused a storm, and angry priests were saying aloud that Molière deserved to be burnt at the stake, Madame took the author under her protection, and caused the condemned play to be repeated before the King at her own house at Villers-Cotterets. Molière brought her his works to read, and listened with interest to her criticisms, if he did not always follow them. Such intelligent sympathy was too rare not to be valued by the poet. He has told us himself, how tired he was of the thankless task of seeing his plays performed before fools, and what strange pleasure it gave him to meet with a single understanding soul. Madame appreciated the finer side of his nature, the deep undercurrent of seriousness which ran through all his laughter, and shared to the full his hatred of false appearances and artificiality. This sympathy led her to understand his *Misanthrope*, that great work, written in a bitter and desponding moment of his life, in which he pours out all the weariness and discontent of his soul, his wail over the vanity of effort and the folly of human nature. The play was not a success at the time, and failed to attain the popularity of Molière's other works. But Madame recognised its truth and power from the first. She listened attentively when the poet read her his new play, and we can imagine the quick response of her heart, when he reached the famous passage where Alceste contrasts the *fadeurs* and conceits of fashionable love verses with the simple charm of the old song :—

> " Si le roi me donnait
> Paris sa grande ville,
> Et qu'il me fallut quitter
> L'amour de ma mie,
> Je dirais au roi Henri,
> Reprenez votre Paris,
> J'aime mieux ma mie, ô gué,
> J'aime mieux ma mie."

" *Voilà ce que peut dire un cœur vraiment épris.*"

But there was one line of the play to which she took exception :—"*Un grand flandrin, qui crache dans un puits, pour faire des ronds.*" This she begged Molière to alter. But the poet refused, with characteristic independence, unwilling to alter his own conception of his " original " in the slightest degree, and the passage remained. None the less, he retained the deepest sense of Madame's kindness on this occasion, and has left a lasting proof of his gratitude in the dedicatory epistle of his *École des Femmes*, one of the most charming and characteristic specimens of the kind, that has ever been written.

" *To Madame.*

" MADAME,—I am the most embarrassed man in the world when I have to dedicate a book, and I am so little accustomed to the style which is held proper for the epistle dedicatory, that I do not know how to begin. Any other author would be able to say a hundred fine things to Your Royal Highness on the title of my play—*L'École des Femmes*—and the offering which he would ask leave to lay at your feet. But, Madame, it is here that I must confess my weakness. I do not understand the art of discovering affinities between such remote objects, whatever good examples my comrades may have given me. I do not see what your Royal Highness has to do with the comedy which I offer her. No doubt, it is easy enough to praise you. Here, Madame, the material is all too abundant. Whichever way we look at you, we see glory piled upon glory, qualities heaped upon qualities. You are respected by all the world for your rank and birth. You are admired by all who see you for your graces of mind and person. Your soul is yet more beautiful, and if we may venture to say so, inspires all who have the honour of approaching you with love. I speak of that charming sweetness with which you temper the pride of your exalted rank, of that winning kindness, that generous affability which you show to all the world. These last qualities are those especially which are best known to me, and concerning which I feel that the time will soon come when I shall no longer be able to keep silence. Once more, Madame, I cannot enter here on these widely-known truths. To my mind they are too far-reaching and too excellent to be enclosed in an epistle, or to be mingled with trifles of this kind. When all has been said, I see nothing, Madame, but simply to dedicate my comedy to you, and to assure you, with all possible respect, that I am, Madame, Your Royal Highness's most humble, most obedient and most grateful servant.

" J. B. MOLIÈRE."

This was written in March 1663, when Madame was not yet nineteen years of age. *L'École des Femmes*, which had

been first acted at Christmas 1662, and afterwards repeatedly
performed at the Louvre and Palais-Royal, met with extraordinary success, and became the most popular of all Molière's
plays.

The second poet of the group, La Fontaine, was well
known to Madame, through Madame de La Fayette and La
Rochefoucauld, both of whom were among his most constant
patrons. His *Contes* of 1665, and his *Fables* which appeared
in 1668, with a dedication to the Dauphin, were widely read
and often quoted in her circle, but the *Epithalamium*, which
he composed in her honour, is the only trace we find in his
works of any direct connection with Madame. Of her kindness to his comrade, Boileau, a pretty little annecdote is told.
He had lately written his clever poem, *Le Lutrin*, inspired, it
is well known, by a quarrel as to the removal of an old reading-
desk in the choir of the Sainte-Chapelle. This dainty bit of
satire had been read to Madame, while still in manuscript.
A few days afterwards, as Madame was following the King
and Queen to mass, in the chapel of Versailles, she caught
sight of Boileau among the crowd of courtiers, and beckoning
him to approach, with one of her charming smiles, she
whispered the following lines from his own poem in his ear :—

> " Soupire, étend les bras, ferme l'œil et s'endort."

This graceful act attracted general notice, and the poet,
who was then slowly struggling towards fame, went home
charmed with so delicate and spontaneous a compliment to
his Muse.

But of these four friends, it was Racine who owed the
most to Madame. He had been educated at Port-Royal, and
was early introduced to her by his friends at Court. She
gave the young poet the help of her support and encouragement in the beginning of his career, and defended his first
works against the prejudices of the old school and the ex-
clusive admirers of Corneille. " Racine," said Madame de
Sevigné, " will never go very far." Voltaire remarks, that she
was as much mistaken, as when she said that coffee would
soon go out of fashion ! Madame was of a different opinion.
She made the poet read his works, in her presence, to a select

audience of her friends, and the tears which she herself shed
over the sorrows of *Andromaque* were proudly recalled by
Racine in the dedication of his first great tragedy.

" MADAME,—It is not without reason that I place your
illustrious name at the head of this work. What other name
could I choose, to dazzle the eyes of my readers, than that of
her whose presence has already enchanted my audience ? It
is well known that Your Royal Highness has deigned to take
my tragedy under her protection, that you have helped me
to enrich the theme with fresh beauties. Above all, it is no
secret that you honoured the first reading of my drama with
your tears. Pardon me, Madame, if I venture to boast of
these fortunate beginnings, which console me for the sternness
of those who will not allow their hearts to be touched. They
may condemn my *Andromaque* as much as they will, now I
can appeal from the subtleties of their imagining, to the heart
of Your Royal Highness. But, Madame, I know that you
judge the merits of a work, not alone by the heart, but by the
light of an intellect which cannot be deceived. Could we put
on the stage a story which is not known to you as well as to
us ? Could we invent a plot of which you would not at once
detect the secret ? And could we possibly conceive sentiments as elevated, and as tender as are the thoughts of
your soul ? It is well known, Madame, that in the exalted
station, where nature and fortune have placed you, you do
not despise the more obscure glory of men of letters. The
society of the Court regards you as the arbiter of all that is
beautiful. And we, who seek to please the public, need no
longer take the rules of the learned for our guide. All we
have to do is to please Your Royal Highness. This, no
doubt, is the least of your many excellent qualities. But it
is one of which I can speak from experience, without depart-
ing from the profound veneration with which I remain Your
Royal Highness's most humble, most obedient and most
faithful servant.   JEAN RACINE."

In this instance, at least, the example which Madame had
set, was followed by the whole nation. The first representa-

tion of *Andromaque* in 1667, was received with the greatest
enthusiasm, and the young poet's reputation was made.   Two
years afterwards, Henrietta, only a few months before her
own death, suggested the story of Titus and Berenice, as the
subject of a drama, both to Corneille and Racine.   The two
poets set to work in obedience to her commands.   The secret
was so well kept, that neither was aware that his rival was
employed on the same theme until the two works were
finished.   *Bérénice*, says Voltaire, was a duel, of which the
whole world has heard the result.   This time the younger
poet bore off the laurels, and not only Madame, but the whole
Court hailed the success of Racine's tragedy with acclamation.

This fine taste and genuine love of literature redeemed
Madame's character from frivolity, and distinguished her
from all the other ladies of Louis XIV.'s Court.   " She had,"
says Bussy, " more greatness and delicacy of taste, in things
of the mind, than all the ladies of the Court put together, and
her death is therefore an infinite loss."   And Madame de
Scudéry wrote in almost the same words.   " All persons of
wit and merit have had a great loss in Madame.   It is certain
that she had more mind than any other lady at Court, and that
she alone knew how to recognise real worth."   Sainte-Beuve
remarks justly how far superior Madame was, in this respect,
to that other charming Princess who brightened the close of
the great reign, her own grand-daughter, the lamented Duchess
of Burgundy.   Marie Adélaide was a merry child, whose high
spirits and light-hearted gaiety made her the pet and plaything
of all, but she belonged to another generation of Frenchwomen,
whose conduct was regulated by the standard of a debased
and licentious age.   She had a passion for cards, and loved
boisterous games.   Madame's tastes were of a more refined
and elevated character.   In her gayest moments, she never
forgot what was due to herself, and her lively imagination
lent new charm to the pastimes of the Court.   With her the
best days of the *grand siècle* passed away.   The pleasures of
the Court lost their culture and brightness, and sank into a
joyless and vulgar dissipation.   The *fêtes*, remarks Madame
de Sevigné, became dull and spiritless, the ballets were

abandoned. There was no one left to lead them. The King himself never danced in one again, after Madame's death, and for the next ten years they were altogether abandoned. " There can be no doubt," wrote La Fare, long afterwards, " that-in Madame, the Court lost the only person of her rank, who was capable of distinguishing true merit. Since her death, all has been gambling, confusion and bad manners."

IN January 1665, a new ballet, which had for its subject the
Birth of Venus, was given at the Palais-Royal. Benserade
composed the verses, and the Duc de Saint-Aignan assisted
Madame in the preparations. Henrietta herself represented
the Goddess of Beauty, and appeared, in the opening scene,
rising from the sea on a throne of mother-of-pearl, attended
by twelve fair Nereïds, among whom were La Vallière and
Mademoiselle de Sevigné. Monsieur, as the Day-star, accompanied by four Hours, then called her to ascend to the home
of the gods on Olympus, and the Queen of Love and Beauty
rose, gently wafted through the air to the strains of sweet
music, chaunted by the best Court singers, in the guise of
Tritons. In the next scene, Venus received the homage of
the gods, heroes, philosophers and poets of antiquity in turn.
Last of all, the King appeared as Alexander, leading Madame,
as Roxana, by the hand, and the two danced a stately measure
while the chorus sang fresh hymns in their praise. This ballet
was repeated several times during the winter, until Madame
fell ill and was glad to depute one of her maids-of-honour,
Mademoiselle de Fiennes, to take her part. She was ailing
all that spring, but her activity of body and mind seemed to
be greater than ever, and she was engaged in a perpetual interchange of letters with her brother on the subject of the proposed treaty between France and England.

On the 15th of December 1664, Charles wrote the following letter :—

"I wish very much that the treaty of commerce were finished, that then we might enter into that of the stricte alliance which I am very impatient of, for I assure you my owne inclination carryes me to it, and I am confident we shall finde both our accounts in it. I beleeve my friendship to France is and will be more considerable then that of the Hollanders in many respects, and you may have it, if you will. The house of Commons hath this day settled the severall rates upon the countyes for the raysing of the five and twenty hundred thousand pounds, and there is a bill preparing for that purpose, so as that matter is as good as done. Since my last to you, we have taken many more Duch ships; the truth is, hardly any escapes us that passe through the chanell. I beleeve we have taken already above fouer-score, and every day there comes in more. They brag very much that they will eate us up in the Spring, and so they did some two monthes agoe, but as yett we are all alive. By the letters from Paris, I perceeve that the blazing starr hath been seen there likewise, I hope it will have the same effect heere as that in Germany had, and then we shall beate our neighbouring Turks, as well as they beate theres. I will say no more at this time, but that I am intierly yours. C. R."

The victory over the Turks, to which Charles alludes, was that of Montecuculi, who had just defeated the Grand Vizier Ahmed Kouprouli in the battle of St. Gothard. The comet was at the time exciting much attention on both sides of the Channel, and causing much alarm among the prophets of evil. A French writer describes it as having a head as large as a plate, bristling all over with nails, and with a tail as long as three arms, turned now east, now west. Madame de Sevigné, writing to M. de Pomponne, describes how she is sitting up till three o'clock, in hopes of seeing the phenomenon, over which all the astrologers and wise men are disputing. Was it a presage of good or evil, she wonders? But the appearance of another blazing star, higher in the sky, two days before Christmas, very much disconcerted the wise men, who could not decide whether this were a new comet, or merely the old one appearing again in a different part of the heavens. Charles returns to the subject in his next letter.

"WHITHALL,
"26 December 1664.

"I have receaved yours by my Ld Rochester but yesterday, Silvius haveing given me your other three dayes before, and will not faile upon the first occasion, to do what you desire with the precaution you wish." (This was Madame's letter of the 17th of December, on the subject of De Vardes's arrest.) "I send you heere a printed paper, which will clearly informe you of the state of the quarrell between me and Holland, by which you will see that they are the agressors and the breakers of the peace, and not we ; I pray reade it with care that you may be fully instructed, for I do not dout but Van Benning-hen (the Dutch Ambassador at the French Court) will use all sortes of artes to make us seeme the agressors, and I would be glad that you might be able to answer anything that may be objected in that matter. We have seen heere the Comett, but the wether has been so cloudy, as I never saw it but once. It was very low and had a taile that stood upwards, it is now above twelve days since I saw it, but upon Christmas eve and the night before, there was another seene very much higher than the former. I saw it both nights and it lookes much lesser than the first, but none of the Astronimers can tell whether it be a new one or the old one growne lesse and got up higher, but all conclude it to be no ordinary starr. Pray inquire of the skillfull men, and lett me know whether it has been seen at Paris. This new one was seen heere, the 23rd and 24th of this month, old style, and had a little taile which stood north-east. I have no more to trouble you with, but that I am yours.   C. R."

On the 19th, Madame had written as follows :—
"I have sent Bonnefond, who is my Master of the Horse, to buy some horses. Be so good as to give him the neces-sary passport." This was an errand on which Madame's servants were frequently employed. Passes for her horses into France were constantly granted by the King, some-times for six, sometimes for twelve horses, on one occasion

for as many as twenty-three at a time. She continues :—" I must tell you that my Lord Hollis has informed me of the articles which you wish to uphold. The first I think very reasonable, but as regards the second, in which you ask that past treaties may be cancelled, the King cannot in honour do this, and if you wish for some pledge of this kind, it must be of a private nature between you and him, for it would be unjust to demand it in any other way. I think you know the Dutch are sending a man here. I tell you this, as I know these comings and goings concern you, and will let you know if I hear any more particulars. I tell the Queen all the news, which she will no doubt give you, and so I will only ask your pardon for not having thanked you before this for the honour you do my son, in promising to be his god-father, and remain your very humble servant."

On the 11th of January 1665 she wrote again, and answered her brother's questions, both as regards the treaty and the comet.

" I have read the paper you send me very regularly, and am glad to hear what is happening, in order to know what I am to reply. I tell my Lord Fitzhardinge the reason why there are many things I cannot speak of now, but I expect this will not last, and you will find it out first. The last time I wrote, I begged you to tell me what people think of the comet in England, and, two hours afterwards, I received yours, in which you asked me the same question. I must tell you then, that assemblies have been held at the Jesuits' Observatory, to which all the wise men went and all the foolish ones too. They disputed according to their belief, but no two of them think alike! Some say it is the same star that has come back, and others that it is an altogether new one, and as one would have to go there to find out the truth, I suppose the question must remain undecided, as well as the stuff of which it is made, which is also a matter of great dispute. This is all that my ignorance permits me to tell you, but I daresay it is enough to satisfy your curiosity, since *Messieurs les savants* are no doubt everyone of them fools, or nearly so, which is all that will be told you to-day by your very humble servant."

The negotiations between the two Kings dragged on all
through the year. Charles was anxious to prove the Dutch
to have been the aggressors in the war with England, and
maintained that Louis XIV. was therefore not bound, by the
Treaty of 1662, to help them. Louis, on his part, was by
no means anxious either to violate his engagements with
the Dutch, nor yet to quarrel with England. His policy was
to gain time, and so we find first one difficulty, then another
arising, before a single article of the Treaty can be concluded.
But since M. de Comminges plainly inspired Charles II. with
distrust, Louis resolved to send the Duc de Verneuil and M.
Courtin as Ambassadors to England, with the special object
of restoring peace with Holland. The *Célèbre Ambassade*,
as this deputation was called, set out with great pomp early
in April, but, as will be seen, proved as ineffectual as all other
attempts at mediation. "My fleet has already set sail, my
people are in a rage," remarked Charles to Courtin; "what
more is to be said?" after which, catching sight of Lord St.
Albans in the passage, his Majesty called out to him,—"Do
come here; here is a little man I can neither convince nor
silence!" With these words he hurried off, on the plea that
it was supper time. The astonished Ambassador duly reported
this conversation, and remarked in a letter to Lionne that,
"whereas the King, our master, can order his subjects to do as
he pleases, the King of England is bound to obey his." Meanwhile, Charles wrote to his sister on the 5th of January:—

"I have little to say to you at this time, expecting that
the Treaty of commerce will be finished, that then we might
enter upon the strict alliance. I perceive that Van Benninghen
does use all possible artes and trickes, to make me appeare
the aggressour, but if you have read over the printed paper
I sent you, you will clearly finde the contrary, and that 'tis
the Dutch hath begun with us, which now playnly appeares
by what de Rutter hath done in Guiny, and I am sure there
is nothing in the King of France's treaty that oblieges him
to second them, if they be the attaquers, so that except he
has a minde to helpe them, he is in no wayes oblieged to it
by treaty. For, by the Treaty, he is only to defend them in

case they be attaqued, and they are now the attacquers, so that we only defend ourselves. I say this to you, because the Ambassadour heere, came to me by order from his master, and sayd many thinges to me, from him, upon the subject of Holland, a little too pressing, and not in the stile Charles Berkeley was spoken to, in that matter when he was there, and I cannot chuse but observe that Monsieur de Cominges is much more eloquent when there is anything to be said that lookes not so kinde towards me, than when there is any kindnesse to be expressed. I wish with all my hart that there were a good occasion for Charles Berkeley to make another voyage to you, for my inclinations are to give my frindship to France, but if that cannot be had, I am not so inconsiderable but that I can make very considerable frindships elsewhere. The truth of it is I am presst at this time very much, and am offered very advantageous conditions, but I preferr the frindship with France in the first place, in case I can have it, and I assure you one of the great reasons why I do so, is because you are there. I write all this only to your selfe, though you may make what use of it you please, so as you do not use my name, for I would not be thought to seeke any bodys frindship, who is not ready to meet me halfe way. The wether is so colde, as I can hardly hold a penn in my hand, which you may perceeve by my scribbling, and I am affraide you will hardly reade this letter, my dearest sister, I am intierly yours.   C. R."

Charles's next letter begins with an allusion to Henrietta's own troubles, and to the suspicions which De Vardes and the Comtesse de Soissons had tried to instil into the King's mind. But he soon resumes the old subject.

"WHITHALL,
"12 *Jan.* 1665.

"I hope by this time that the K. of france is returned to the same freedome he has alwaise used towards you; I am sure you ought to do all you can to keepe him very kinde to you, which I do not doute but you will, it being so necessary for the condition you are in. Mon^r de Cominge was with me again yesterday, to presse me concerning the businesse of

Holland, and I tould him I would not faile to give the King, my brother, the true state of that matter, and that my ambassadore there had already given Mon^r de Lionne those papers, which would cleerly make it appeare that the Duch were the aggressors, which now is evident by what de Rutter hath done in Guiny, who had his orders to take our ships before we had made so much as the least stop of any of there ships, and you may tell the K., my brother, that I will lett him know what my pretentions are, than Van Benningen may not have the least pretence to say that I desire warre for warre sake, for I know that he does use all sortes of artes to make me the agressore, and does not sticke to affirme matters of fact which are not true, and which will be proved to be so. I am sure, if I can have what is iust and reasonable, I shall not desire the efusion of blood, nor wish to runn the hazards of a warre, though I may say that, reasonably speaking, the advantage lies on our side for many reasons, which are visable enough.   The Duch Ambassadore did yesterday, in discourse with me say, that de Rutter had orders from the States to goe for Guiny, which he never acknowledged before, and I believe it came out before he thought of it.   I have put Holmes into the tower for his takeing of Cape Verd without orders, and I am certaine they can have no pretence that we have done any thing like an act of hostility but that, and that was done by a privat Captaine without authority.   There was a particular article in the treaty in case of such accidents, which the Duch have absolutely broake, by sending de Rutter thither, and providing an other fleete which was to have followed, if they durst have come out.   In fine, I do not dout, but to make it evident to the King, my brother, that he is no way obliged to favour them, they being the attacquers, and if there be any kindnesse to be showed, I hope I may reasonably expect it, before those who used France so unworthily in the treaty at Munster.   You may make what use you thinke fitt of this letter, to the king, my brother, and I will as soone as I can lett him know, what in iustice I expect from the Duch, and so I will end with assuring you that I am yours.   C. R."

The complaints about Bremen, to which Charles alludes

in his next letter, seem to have been a mere pretence for
delay, and Ruvigny wrote to Lionne that, after diligent
researches had been made, all that could be discovered was
that the cities of Hamburg, Lubeck and Bremen had been
asked for a description of their ships, in order that they might
not be mistaken for Dutch men-of-war.

"WHITHALL,
"19 *Jan.*

"I have received yours of the 20 and you have reason to
wonder that you have been so long without heareing from me,
but I have had nothing to say, and it has been so colde heere,
as it did not invite one to write nothing, and I did not write
to you by Bonnefond, because I thought he would be long
upon the way with his horses. I shall not say much to you
now, because Ruvigny will be despatched in two or three
dayes, and by him you shall heare at large from me, only I
cannot chuse but observe to you now, that I see that
Mon^r Comminge does me all good offices there, by foretelling
my intentions in as ill a sence as he uses to doe. My
Ld Hollis writes something to me about my giveing commissions to the Citty of Bremen, which the K., my brother, sayes
he will be satisfied in, before he goes on with our treaty,
w^cb is so great a dreame to me, as I know not from whence
this fancy proceedes, except it be from Mon^r de Comminge,
whoe, I am confident, you will finde in the end hath done me
as many ill offices as it hath layne in his power to doe, and I
do wonder that, after all the advances I made by C. Barkly, I
should find the treaty go on slower then it did, my Ld Hollis
haveing receaved not yett an answer to his last paper, which
is now almost two months agoe. After all this, when
Ruvigny returnes, you shall find my minde not changed, but
that I will be as sincere in that matter as I promised you to
be, and if there be any thing altered in my condition, since
we first talked of this matter, it is for the better, and so good
night for 'tis late.   C. R."

Three days later, we have another letter, in which the King
tells his sister of an important advantage gained by the
English ships over the Dutch, off Cadiz.

" In my last, I tould you that I would not enlarge my selfe upon the matters betweene me and the king, my brother, till the returne of Ruvigny, to whome I have now fully opened my minde in all particulars, which I would not do to Mon^r de Comminge, because I am most confident, by all the observations I can make, he does not desire there should be a good correspondence between us, and if the advances I now make have not the successe I wish, I must conclude there is no inclination to have a frindship with me. I shall not enlarge my selfe upon the particulars because Ruvigny will do it better by word of mouth, to whome I referr you. Since the losse of my two ships at Giberaltar, I have had some good fortune to recompense it, for Cap. Allen, with but seven of my ships, hath mett hard by Cadiz the Duch Smirna fleete of 30 ships, has taken three of them and sunke two, and if the wether had not been very bad, they would not have escaped so well. I do not yett know of what valew the ships are which are taken, but they write from Holland that that which is sunke was worth one hundred thousand pounds, and if there Admiral had not been so very neere the Porte, he had been sunke likewise, for he gott in with 7 foot watter in holde. They behaved themselves very poorly, for they had 4 men of warr to convoy them and many of there marchants had 30 guns a peece, which might have made good resistance if there hartes had not failed them, and two of our seven had but 24 guns a peece. I will not trouble you more at this time, only expect a returne from Ruvigny with impatiency. I am intierly yours. C. R."

On the 9th of February, Charles writes again, in his liveliest vein :—

" I must, in the first place, aske you pardon for haveing mist so many posts, the truth of it is, which betweene businesse and the little mascarades we have had, and besides the little businesse I had to write, with the helpe of the cold wether, I did not think it worth your trouble and my owne to freeze my fingers for nothing, haveing sayd all to Ruvigny that was upon my harte. I am very glad to find by yours that you are so well satisfied with what he brings, it lies wholy on your part now to answer the advances I have made, and if all be not as you wish, the faute is not on my side, I was this morning at the parlament house, to passe the Bill for the five and twenty hundred thousand pounds, and the commissioners are going into there severall countryes, for the raysing of it according to the Act. We are useing all possible diligence in the setting out the fleete for the spring. My L⁴ Sandwich sett saile two dayes since, with 18 good ships, to seeke out a squadron of the Duch fleete, wᶜʰ we heare was seene upon the north coast of England, and if he had the good fortune to meete with them, I hope he will give a good accounte of them. I am very glad to heere that your indisposition of health is turned into a greate belly, I hope you will have better lucke with it then the Duchesse heere had, who was brought to bed, monday last, of a girle. One part I shall wish you to have, which is that you may have as easy a labour, for shee dispatched her businesse in little more than an houer. I am afraide your shape is not so advantageously made for that convenience as hers is, however a boy will recompense two grunts more, and so good night, for feare I fall into naturale philosophy, before I thinke of it. I am Yours.		C. R."

The child to whom the Duchess of York had just given birth, was the Princess Anne, afterwards Queen of England, The cold, to which Charles alludes so frequently, was very severe that winter, the Seine was frozen over, and Madame de Comminges's return to France was delayed by the state of the roads, which made travelling impossible. Her wardrobe had been packed and sent off already, so that the poor lady remained for a whole fortnight, without any clothes excepting her travelling suit, and was obliged to keep her room for want of suitable apparel. Luckily, a thaw set in by the end of January, and she reached Paris in blooming health, as we learn from Madame's next letter.

" *20th Feb.* 1665.

" Madame de Comminges has arrived so well and fat that, if I had no other reason for desiring to go to England,

this would make me wish it with my whole heart. Even
Mirabeau (Madame de Fiennes) says, she should hang herself, if she did not hope to go back there some day!
She has tried to execute your commission, which agreed
so well with the style of a letter that you sent me, that
I have spared her the trouble. The Ambassadors are very
busy preparing to start. Do not forgot to reply to the request which has been addressed to you by the Queen and
Lord Fitzhardinge, for they only await your answer to set
out. To-morrow there is to be a ball here, although it is
Lent, to bid them farewell."

Madame's next letter is occupied with one of Lord Hollis's
usual grievances. An English merchant at Bordeaux had a
quarrel with a rude Dutchman, of the name of Oyens, who ·
called the King a pirate, and the Duke of York a captain of
thieves, and made use of many other coarse expressions, upon
which Hollis appealed to the French authorities for the man's
punishment, and Henrietta, after her wont, tried to pour oil
on the troubled waters.

> " PARIS,
> " 3 *March.*

" The King has ordered me to tell you of a thing which has
happened at Bordeaux, and in which my Lord Hollis has
asked for justice. You must know then that three or four
persons, walking in the port, began to discuss the Dutch war.
One of them, an Englishman, said you would never make
peace, unless you received compensation for the expenses of
the war. They then asked the opinion of a Dutchman, who
said his country was not rich enough for that, and proceeded
to call you and the Duke of York bad names. My Lord
Hollis insists that this is a point of honour, although no one
as a rule cares for what people say in the streets. All the
same, the King begs me to tell you, that if you wish it, the
men shall be sought out and punished in any way you desire.
M. de Verneuil has been rather unwell, but I do not think
this will retard his journey. I will tell him the honour you do
him, and end this letter in assuring you that I am your very
humble servant."

Charles replied promptly :—

" WHITHALL,
" 27 *Feb.* 1665.

" I am sorry thet my L⁴ Hollis has asked iustice upon a point of honour that I should never have thought of ; you know the old saying in England, the more a T; is stirr'd, the more it stinkes, and I do not care a T. for anything a Duch man sayes of me, and so I thinke you have enough upon this dirty subject, which nothing but a stinking Duch man could have been the cause of, but pray thanke the King, my brother, and desire him not to take any kinde of notice of it, for such idle discourses are not worth his anger or myne. I have been all this day at Hamton-court, and it is so long since I have been a-horse back, as with this smale dayes journey I am weary enough to beg your pardon if I say no more now, but that I am yours. C. R."

Madame was never idle where the honour of her brother was concerned, and when news reached her ears that cruelties had been inflicted on Frenchmen by his sailors, she hastened to draw his attention to these reports, in order that she might contradict them with greater force.

" DE PARIS,
" *ce* 22 *Mars* 1665.

" I have heard of the cruelty of the Dutch in Guinea, which is frightful, if it is true. It is also reported that your people have made some Frenchmen prisoners, and tortured them cruelly, to make them confess they were going to Holland, but I maintain that this cannot be true, or at least that it is done without your approval, and that so generous a soul as yours would never allow such treatment of your enemies, far less of Frenchmen who are your friends. Write me word, I beg, of what has happened and whether, if this is true, you have taken care it should not happen again, since nothing is more worthy of you than to use your power to make yourself at once beloved and feared, and to prevent all the horrors which too often accompany war. I end by assuring you that I am your most humble servant."

Charles replied, in a letter dated the 26th of March (O.S.)

" There is no such thing as that newes you heard of Guiny ;
at first it looked like truth, for a sea man, pretending to be a
Swede, came to me, and made a very particular relation of it,
and afterwards took his oath of it before the Admiralty, but
upon some contradictions, he gave him selfe in examining, we
found him to be a Duch man, who thought by this invention
to gett some money, but at last he was founde out, and has
been whiped through Cheapside for his periury.   I could wish
that what you write to me, concerning the treatment of some
French sea men by ours, were as false.   I have receaved a
memoriall this day about it from the french Ambassadour, and
have given orders that, if it be founde to be true, it be severely
punished.   I do assure you I am extreamly troubled at it,
there shall be very seveare iustice done.   I am going to Port-
mouth tomorrow, for 4 or 5 dayes, for the ordering of some
thinges there, and have no more time lefte me now, only to
assure you that I am intierly yours.   C. R."

A short letter which Henrietta addressed about this time
to Henry Bennet, afterwards Lord Arlington, on his appointment to the office of Secretary of State, is interesting as a
proof of her anxiety to be on good terms with her brother's
ministers.

" I would not have written to you so soon, since the Ambassadors start on Monday, and will not only give you all the
news, but business enough to occupy you for a long time to
come, but the new honour which the King has done you,
obliges me, as one of your friends, to assure you that no one
is better pleased than I am, or wishes you the continuance of
his favour more warmly than I do."

On the 8th of April, she wrote another letter to her
brother, which threw light on Louis XIV.'s ambitious projects,
and reveals the secret plans which governed his whole policy.

" Madame de Fiennes having told me that you would be
glad to see a pattern of the vests that are worn here, I take
the liberty of sending you one, and am sure that on your fine
figure it will look very well.   M. de Verneuil will arrive so

soon after this letter, and as I do not think he will succeed in making peace with Holland, and that I do not think it desirable for the King to take their parts, I beg of you to consider if some secret treaty could not be arranged, by which you could make sure of this, by giving a pledge on your part that you would help in the business he will soon have in Flanders, now the King of Spain is ill, and which will certainly be opposed by the Dutch, but will not be contrary to your interests. Think this over well, I beg of you, but never let anyone know that I was the first to mention it to you, only remember there is no one in the world who would so willingly serve you, or who wishes for your welfare as heartily as I do. My enemies here look so suspiciously on all I do, that soon I shall hardly venture to speak of your affairs! So, when you wish me to say something, send me word, and when I have a message to give from you, I shall have a right to speak on the subject."

We do not possess the King's reply to this confidential letter, and a little note which he wrote on the 22d of April is the only one that belongs to this month.

"This is the second letter I have writt to you to-day, therfore it is likely it will be the shortest, and the only businesse of it is to accompany the bearer, Jack Russell, who commandes my Regiment of gardes, who is goeing to Burbon for his health. I have nothing to add, only that he is a person I am very kind to, and a very honest man, and I desire you to looke upon him according to this carracter, and so I am yours.

"C. R."

CHAPTER XVI

1665—1666

THE war now began in good earnest. The English fleet—
"the finest sight in the world," wrote Comminges, sailed out
of the Thames, under the Duke of York's command, and a
battle was daily expected. On both sides of the Channel
the movements of the rival fleets were eagerly watched, and
news of their first encounter was impatiently awaited.
Madame grew terribly anxious as the days went by. On
the 27th of May she wrote to her brother in an agitated
frame of mind, from Saint-Germain, where the Court was
spending the summer.

"I would not answer the letter which you sent me by
M. de Sainton, by the post, because our letters are so often
opened: I would perhaps have spoken to the King, as it
were on my own account, about all that, but I have been
prevented by the prospect of a battle which is sure to be
furious, and is likely to change the face of affairs. If he had
given me a positive reply, everything might be altered before
you received this letter, for by the last news from Holland,
we hear that their fleet has left port, and that in consequence
a battle is certain. This, I confess, is a thing which makes
me tremble. Whatever advantage you may have, it is, after
all, Fortune which decides most things in this world. I
cannot bear to think that this little handful of miserable
creatures should dare to defy you. It is pushing glory rather
far, but I cannot help it. Everyone has his private fancy,

212

and mine is to be very much alive to all that concerns you!
I hope you will not blame me, and this will show you once
more that there is no one who loves you as well as I do."

Charles, on his part, showed his habitual coolness.

On the eve of the expected fight, he writes in his gayest
strain to his sister, and sends her the latest composition of
his favourite guitar player, Francesco Corbetta. This was the
Italian musician mentioned in Gramont's memoirs, who had
made guitar playing so fashionable at the English Court.
"Lords and ladies alike raved over his genius and tried to
imitate his example. Hardly had he composed a sarabande
than all the world played it. God knows the universal
scraping that was heard wherever you went." A year before,
Corbetta had paid a visit to Paris, but had been so ill on his
arrival, that he had been unable to appear before Madame,
and had begged leave to return to Whitehall without delay.
The Maréchal d'Humières, who was now on his way back
from England, was a valiant soldier and a great friend of
Turenne and Madame de Sevigné, which rendered him
acceptable both to Madame and her brother.

"WHITHALL,
29 *May* 1665.

"By that time this letter comes to your handes, I believe
Mon͏ʳ d'Humières will be with you, and I pray be kinde to
him upon my score, for I take him to be very much my
frinde, and as worthy a man as I do know; he will informe
you how all thinges are heere, and I do not give him the
commendation upon an ordinary score of civility, but upon
the confidence of his being as good a frinde where he applyes
himselfe as ever lived, which, in this age, is no little virtue,
there being so few persons in the world worth a frindeship,
and I will answer for him that he will not make me ashamed
of the good opinion I have of him; he expresses to me, upon
all occasions, how much he is your servant, for which you may
easily beleeve I do not love him the lesse, and I am confident
you cannot finde a man in all France worthyer of your good
opinion and trust then himselfe. The Ambassadors have
given me this day propositions in writing from the Hollanders,
in order to the composing of the differences now betweene

us; I have not yett had time to consider them, and to make answer to them, but I hope in a few dayes my brother will meet with there fleete, and make them much more reasonable then they are at present, I have had no letters from my brother this day, but I beleeve he will be ready to sett saile in two or three dayes, and then I beleeve a Battle will follow very quickly. I have heere sent you some lessons for the guittar, which I hope will please you ; the Comte de Gramont did carry over with him others, which it may be you have, and as Francesco makes any more that pleases me, I will send them to you, I have no more to-day at present but that I am intierly Yours.   C. R."

In her next letter from Saint-Germain, Henrietta mentions her mother-in-law's dangerous illness. For some time past Anne of Austria had suffered from cancer ; she had consulted every doctor, and, according to Gui Patin, tried every quack remedy in turn, with the effect of doing her malady more harm than good.   Twice over during the course of this summer she was thought to be dying, and received the last sacraments.   "The Queen," wrote Hollis in August, "holds out, but the doctors give no hope of improvement.   It makes a sad Court, and it will, I fear, soon be a sadder one."

" 30 Mai 1665.

" Although the illness of the Queen, my mother-in-law, is the cause of great distress here, and you will see from my letter to the Queen the state she is in, and understand the general consternation, I will not fail to speak to the King, and urge him to give you a positive answer to your last letter. And at least, if he does not write, I shall be able to get some idea of his sentiments, which is, it seems to me, what you wish most to obtain, in order to know where you are.   This is the pleasure of having to do with honest persons ! Ever since you have let me into your secrets, I am on thorns when I do not see my way clearly what to report.   I hope you will send me some positive orders, when you find a safe messenger."

Charles replied in a short note dated the 1st of June :—

" I send this bearer, George Porter, with no other errand then upon the subject of the Queene mother's indisposition, who I feare, by the nature of her disease, and what I finde by the letters from thence, will not long be in a position to receave any compliments. This bearer will tell you of our fleete being gone to seeke out the Dutch, and you know him so well as I neede say nothing more to you. He will play his owne part, and make you laugh before he returnes, which is all the businesse he has there, except it be to assure you with how much kindnesse I am Yours. C. R."

Suddenly, a report reached Paris that a great naval battle had taken place, in which the Duke of York's ship had been blown up, and he himself had been drowned. The shock was too much for Madame, after the last week of painful suspense. She was seized with convulsions, and became so dangerously ill that Lord Hollis wrote to the King : " If things had gone ill at sea, I really believe Madame would have died." Happily, the next posts brought the true version of the great victory which had been won by the Duke of York off Lowestoft, on the 3d of June. The flagship of the Dutch admiral, Opdam, had been blown up, and he had perished in the explosion, together with 500 of his men. Seventeen other vessels had been sunk, or taken prisoner, and the remnants of the fleet had taken refuge on the coast of Holland. The good news was hailed with great rejoicings in England, and Comminges complained that his windows were broken by the mob, because they were not illuminated. The victory, however, had cost England many brave lives. Both Lord Falmouth, as the King's trusted servant, Charles Berkeley, had lately become, and Lord Muskerry were killed, fighting gallantly at the Duke of York's side, on board the *Royal Charles*. The King alludes to the death of the former, in the letter which he hastened to send his sister.

" WHITHALL,
" 8 *June* 1665.

" I thanke God we have now the certayne newes of a very considerable victory over the Duch ; you will see most of the particulars by the relation my Lord Hollis will shew you,

though I have had as great a losse as 'tis possible in a good
frinde, poore C. Barckely.   It troubles me so much, as I hope
you will excuse the shortnesse of this letter, haveing receaved
the newes of it, but two houers agoe.   This great successe does
not at all change my inclinations towards France, which you
may assure the K., my brother, from me, and that it shall be
his faute if we be not very good frindes.   There is one come
from Dunkerke, who says that there were bonefires made on
sonday last for the great victory the Duch had over the
English.   Methinks Mon^r de Mourpeth might have had a
little patience, and then it may his rejoiceing might have been
on our side ; pray lett me know the meaning of this.   My
head does so ake, as I can only add that I am entierly Yours.

"C. R."

Madame's joy was unbounded on receiving this good
news.   Even Monsieur was stirred, and wrote a warm note of
congratulation to his royal brother-in-law on the 19th of June.

"Never before," he says, "have I felt how deeply your
Majesty's affairs concern me, as in these three last days,
during which we have been in mortal anxiety as to the results of the battle which has taken place.   Since the opening
of the war has been so fortunate, we need have no fear as to
its ultimate issue.   The good news only reached us this
evening, so I hasten to express my joy to you, and at the
same time my satisfaction at hearing that M. le Duc d'York
is safe.   I will say no more at present, but that if my wishes
are fulfilled, Your Majesty will enjoy every kind of prosperity."

As soon as Madame was able to put pen to paper, she
wrote the following joyful letter to her brother, one of the
longest that we have from her hand.

"DE SAINT-GERMAIN,
"22 *Juin* 1665.

"We cannot delay any longer, Monsieur and I, to send
you this gentleman to congratulate you on your victory, and
although I know you will easily believe my joy, I must tell
you how much it has been increased, owing to the repeated
frights we had received from the false reports of the merchants,
who all wish the Dutch well.   But, on the other hand, the

whole Court and all the nobility appear most anxious to show
that your interests are as dear to them as those of their own
King. Never has such a crowd been seen here, as Monsieur
and I have had to congratulate us on this occasion! And indeed you should be grateful to Monsieur for the interest
which he has taken in the whole thing, and for the way in
which he stands up for all that concerns you. The Comte de
Gramont was the first to bring us the news yesterday. We
were at mass, and there was quite a sensation. The King
himself called out to his ministers who were in the tribune :
'We must rejoice!' which I must say surprised me not a little,
for although at the bottom of his heart he wishes you every
possible success, I did not think he would care to declare this
in public, owing to his engagements with the Dutch. But I
hope that the result of this success will be to give you a
second, by enabling you to bring the war to an end in so
honourable a way that thirty more such victories would not
add to your glory. I assure you this is the opinion of all your
friends here, who are very numerous, and also that of common
sense, since now you have shown, not only what your power
is, and how dangerous it is to have you for an enemy, but
have also made your subjects see how well you can defend
their interests and greatness; you may now show the world
that your true desire is for peace, and triumph by clemency
as well as by force. For this is what gains hearts, and is no
less remarkable in its way than the other, besides being a
surer thing than trusting to the chances of war. And even if
the result of a long war were certain, you will never be in a
position to derive more advantage from success than you are
at present, when you might win over people, who, I can assure
you, ardently desire your friendship, and are in despair at
feeling that their word is already pledged. I have spoken
of this several times, and always find the King most reasonable, and since I do not think your feelings have changed, I
have good hopes of such a result as your best friends would
desire. But if I am so strongly on the side of peace, do not
think that it is from a sense of fear, as is the case with most
women. I can assure you I only desire your good, and since
you have nothing more to win by force, you must seek glory in

another way, and try to secure friends, of whom none can be more important than the King, without entering on a perpetual war of chicanery. This is what I most passionately desire.

"I cannot end without expressing my sorrow at the death of poor Lord Falmouth, whom I regret as much for the sake of the friendship you felt for him, and which he so justly deserved, as for his goodness to me. Indeed, I had to weep with all my heart for him, on the very day when the news of your victory gave me the greatest joy. I can assure you, by what I knew of his sentiments, he would have been of my mind as to peace, and now that your honour is satisfied, this must be the right step to take. If I dared, I would recommend the elder Hamilton to you, and you could not give the Privy Purse to anyone who deserves it better. I hope you will tell him that I have recommended him to you. His sister (the Comtesse de Gramont) begged me to do this, and is really one of the best women I ever knew in my life. As for the Comte de Gramont he is the most English of men, and shows this every day in a thousand ways. He was mad with joy when the news came. This letter is too long by half. I beg your pardon, but indeed I am so happy, I hardly know what I am about, and I could not help telling you, not only all I have heard, but all I think of as to the future consequences which are likely to spring out of these events."

The rejoicings over the victory in London were damped by the rapid spread of the plague, which attacked the city with such violence that summer. By the end of June, people were already dying by thousands. The Court moved to Hampton Court and the French Ambassadors, after declaring that the London fog suffocated them, were terror-stricken at the approach of a worse foe. They moved to " Kinstaun " (Kingston), but even here they were not safe, as the chief of the *Ambassade Célèbre* himself wrote home: " Yesterday I—the Duc de Verneuil—while taking my daily walk along the road, found the body of a man who had died of the plague." Their next move was to Salisbury, where they were much impressed at the sight of the very fine church, in the hands of the Protestants, with as many pillars as hours, as many windows as

days, as many gates as months in the year. But here again
the plague followed them. First one of the King's servants
fell ill, then a man dropped down dead not two hundred paces
from their door. "A bad habit," wrote Courtin "which is, I
fear, beginning to spread." Madame de Sablé, a great vale-
tudinarian herself, sent the Ambassadors disinfectants, but
even the use of these could not allay their terror, and when
they heard that the number of the dead in London had
reached eight thousand two hundred and fifty-two persons
during the first week of September, they begged earnestly to
be allowed to return home.

Early in July, the Queen-mother left London, the King
accompanying her on her journey down the mouth of the
Thames. She had long been suffering from a bad cough, and
had wasted away so rapidly that her doctors pronounced a
journey to France to be the only hope of saving her life.
She arrived in Paris to find that her daughter had been
prematurely delivered of a still-born babe, a few days before,
at Versailles. "Madame," wrote Hollis, "had gone to Versailles
with the King, to divert themselves for a day or two, and on
Thursday morning was surprised, for she fell in labour and
was delivered of a daughter who is dead, but the God be
praised, very well." And a few days later he wrote that the
Queen-mother was daily expected at Versailles, and that
Madame was very well and "longing for her coming." The
event had taken everyone by surprise. The King was
awakened in the middle of the night, and the curé of Versailles was hastily summoned. By the King's order the child
was buried privately at Saint-Denis, and the Queen Marie
Thérèse, Mademoiselle informs us, was much concerned that
she had not first insisted on the baptism of the lifeless infant.

As soon as his wife was out of danger, Monsieur accompanied the Court to Saint-Germain, and Henrietta Maria remained at the bedside of her dearly-loved daughter. By the
end of three weeks, Madame had sufficiently recovered to
accompany her mother to Colombes, where she remained till
the end of August, when Henrietta Maria went to drink the
waters of Bourbon.

"Madame is perfectly recovered," wrote Lord St. Albans,

who had accompanied his royal mistress to France, "and is a most excellent person ; very beautiful, full of wit and infinitely considered in this Court."

All the while she kept up a brisk correspondence with her brother, and left no stone unturned to conclude the treaty of alliance between the two Kings, which she so earnestly wished for. A long letter which she wrote from her bed, on the 5th of July, is missing, but Charles II.'s reply gives a full account of the situation. He sets forth his own motives and conduct plainly, and makes no secret of his vexation at the continual delays and temporising policy of his brother of France. A breach between the two countries, he foresees, is imminent, and his only concern is for Madame herself, whose difficult position he realises perfectly, and whom he compassionates with more than his usual affection. The letter, it must be owned, does credit both to the head and heart of this much-reviled monarch.

"HAMTONCOURT,
"13 *July* 1665.

"My going with the Queene as farr as the mouth of the river, the businesse I mett with there about the fleete, my hasty returne hither, and the dayly trouble I have had with neighbours' collations and the Irish Bill, is the reason you have not heard from me in answer to so many letters, and to congratulate your health after such a misfortune to your childe. But now at last I have sett my selfe downe to give you a full answer to your letter of the 5th, which indeede requires it, and I should be wanting to the care and concernement I have for you, if I should not cleerely lett you know my minde, in the negotiation now depending heere with France, that you may governe your selfe accordingly. You remember very well the severall and pressing advances I made by you, the last yeare, afterwards by Ch. Berkely, and at last by Ruvigny, for the perfecting our treaty and entring into a strickter alliance with france then ever, which were all in appearance so well accepted, that I may truly say I lost many oportunityes of strengthening my selfe with other aliances abroad, to be in a state of embracing that, which, upon the comming of the Ambassadores,

I looked would have been compleated ; instead of which, all
I have heard from them (after I had accepted there mediation)
hath been ouvertures towards an agreement with Holland, but
upon propositions which they who made them to me could not
but undervalewe, and declaring themselves tide by a treaty to
helpe the Hollanders, wh: was disowned when the treaty
was the first made, and now cannot be produced to be appealed
unto. If this be the true state of the case (as I dare say you
will agree it to be), where is my faute ? would any body advise
me to make any advances towards a peace, after all the expense
I have been at to support the warre, and such a successe in it,
upon such weake invitations ; it is most certaine, they who
propose it do not thinke I ought to agree to it, and standers
by say these Ambassadores are kept here only till France can
agree with Holland upon what termes they shall helpe them,
on which, if they agree, I shall be necessitated to take part
with Spaine, and to your exception thereunto, lett me minde
you that, according to the course of the World, those are better
frinds who see they have neede of us, then whose prosperity
makes them think we have neede of them ; and whatever be
my fortune in this, I should runne it cheerfully, if my concernement for you did not perplex me, who I know will have a
hard part to play, (as you say) betweene your brother and
brother-in-Law, and yett methinkes it is to early to dispaire of
seeing all thinges well agreed betwixt us, and though that
should not happen so quickly, it must be your part to keepe
your selfe still in a state of contributing thereunto, and haveing
a most principle part therein, which will not be a hard taske to
your discretion and good talent ; and be assured the kindnesse
I have for you, will in all occasions make me mindfull of what
I owe you, and of reserving the obliging parts for you, and
leaveing the contrary for others if there should be any such.
And this would be enough in answer to your long letter, if
lookeing it over againe, I did not finde you endeavouring to
perswade me the King, my brother, is no way guilty towards
me of censuring my actions, I do verily beleeve it and should
do so, though I should furnish him occasion for it, that being
an action infinitely belowe the opinion and caracter I have
alwayes figured to my selfe of him, which may also serve to

assure you these reports have never made any impression in me, to the preiudice of our frindship. I will conclude this long letter, assuring you the kindnesse and frindship I have for you is as entire as ever, and that no alteration or change in my affaires shall make any in that.   C. R."

At the same time Courtin wrote home that the King of England felt sure that Madame had misunderstood Louis XIV. She had, it appears, told her brother that the King of France was under the impression that his Majesty could not enter into any treaty without the sanction of Parliament, a mistake which Charles begged him to correct.

The Queen-mother, Henrietta Maria, now joined her efforts to those of Madame, and did her utmost to prevent a breach of the peace between France and England. Hollis reports how he paid a visit to Colombes on the 22d of August, and met the King of France there.

" I was yesterday at Colombes, to take my leave of the Queen-mother, before her departure for Bourbon. The King of France came to Colombes, whilst I was in her presence. At last he thought proper to notice me, and gave me a little salute with his head, and truly, my lord, I answered him with just such another, because I knew his ambassadors in England are welcomed in different style. I did before him entertain myself all the while with the Prince de Condé, who is very affectionate in all that concerns his Majesty, but this by the way. Soon after, the King of France and the Queen-mother went alone into her bed-chamber, and our Princess, Madame, went in, after they had been there at least an hour. When the King of France went away, I had an interview with the Queen-mother afterwards, and took the boldness to ask her how she found things. She said, they had been all the time within talking over these businesses of Holland, and that Louis XIV. told her he had made King Charles some propositions, which were very fair ones, which, if he refused, he must take part with the Hollanders. The next morning, though pouring with wet, the Queen-mother set off towards the baths of Bourbon."

The tone of this letter shows us that the Ambassador was

still as punctilious and ready to take offence as ever. A little later, his dignity was grievously offended by an insult offered him by the servants of the Princesse de Carignan, who, armed with clubs, stopped his coach on its way to the Louvre, and followed Madame's carriage to the palace gate. This revival of the old quarrel for precedence roused the fiery spirit of the stern old Puritan, and Henrietta tried in vain to appease his anger. He refused to accept the apologies that were offered him, and became absolutely intractable. It was impossible to make further use of him, but negotiations were still carried on that autumn by the Queen-mother and Madame, although Charles himself now saw plainly that war was inevitable. Two short letters which he wrote to his sister, while the Court was at Salisbury, are all we have of his correspondence during the remainder of 1665.

> " SALSBURY,
> " 5 *Aug.* 1665.

" I hope you will pardon my long silence, which I should not have been guilty of if I had stay'd long enough in one place to have writt to you since my coming from Hamton-court, butt I have been at Portsmouth about the fortifications there, and went thence to the Ile of Wight, which place I had never seen before, in order to the putting that Iland in a good posture. I hope the french Ambassadores are well satisfied with the answer I gave them upon what they proposed concerning the businesse with Holland. I have not had time to desire you to returne my thankes to the King of France for the kinde expressions he made me by G. Porter, and I assure you it shall be his faute if ever there be the least dispute betweene us. I have been a hunting all this day, and am so sleepy as I hope you will pardon the shortnesse of this, but you shall now heare constantly from me.   C. R."

> "SALSBURY,
> "9 *Sep.* 1665.

" I finde by yours of the 11 of Sep. that you are very much alarumed with the retreate of the fleete to Soule bay, but when you shall know that the fleete had no other businesse there but to take in some drinke, and to ioyne with twenty fresh ships

(whereof the *Soverine* is one), and stayd but seven dayes there.
It will in some degree satisfie those able seamen at Paris, who
iudge so sudenly of our want of conduct in Navall matters,
and in all neweses *il faut attendre le boiteux*. I am confident
my Ld Sandwich is some dayes before this, betweene the duch
fleete and home, with a better fleete then that which beate
them last time, and, if God will permitt it, I do not dout to
send you a good account and conclusion of this sumers campaigne. I have been troubled these few dayes past with a
collique, but I thanke God I am now perfectly well againe.
It hath been almost a general disease in this place. I am
goeing to make a little turne into dorset sheere for 8 or 9
dayes to passe away the time till I go to Oxford, beleeving
that this place was the cause of my indisposition. I am very
glad that Queene-mother is so well of her brest. Pray make
my compliments to her upon it. I do confesse myselfe very
fauty in my faileing so many weekes. I will repaire my faute
for the time to come, but the truth is I have been some what
indisposed ever since my being heere, and consequently out of
humour, but I beg of you to be assured that what failings
soever I may have, nothing can ever change me in the least
degree of that frindship and kindnesse I have for you. Pray
returne my compliments to Monsieur, with all imaginable
kindnesse.   C. R."

The violence of the plague was now abating, and by
November, people began to return to town. In October, the
Parliament met at Oxford, and the French proposals were
finally rejected. Arlington gave the Ambassadors a note to
this effect, on the 8th of November, and in December they
started on their return journey. The death of Philip IV. of
Spain, on the 17th of September, threatened to produce fresh
complications, but for the moment Louis XIV. contented
himself with advancing a formal claim to the sovereignty of
Flanders, in his wife's name, while he pressed on warlike preparations with renewed vigour. The actual outbreak of
hostilities was delayed by Anne of Austria's critical state of
health, and by the earnestness with which she implored her
son to avert the horrors of war. She lingered all through the

summer and autumn, and was able to be moved in a litter from Saint-Germain to Paris.

Both Monsieur and Madame were assiduous in their attentions to their dying parent, but during the intervals of her attacks, they followed their usual course of amusement. In September, they entertained the Court at Villers-Cotterets, and Mademoiselle describes the succession of hunting-parties, of balls and comedies, with which they amused their guests. Christmas and New Year were celebrated with greater splendour than ever. The *fête* given by Madame, on the eve of the Feast of the Three Kings, excelled all others that winter. Queen Marie Thérèse was absent, owing to her deep mourning for her father, but the King appeared in a suit of violet velvet, resplendent with pearls and diamonds, and was received by Monsieur and Madame in the great gallery of the Palais-Royal, hung with mirrors, and blazing with torches. Molière's *Médecin malgré lui* was performed that evening, between the banquet and the ball with which the evening ended. It became the popular play of the winter, and all Paris crowded to see it, greatly to the delight of Gui Patin, who chuckled over the feelings of the Court doctors when they heard the fits of laughter with which the King greeted the performance. " So the world laughs at doctors who kill folks with impunity." Four days afterwards, the Queen-mother became suddenly worse, and all hope of her recovery was abandoned. She received the last sacraments, and took a tender farewell of her children. She saw the King and Queen, Monsieur and Madame, each separately, and spoke to each of them in turn with the freedom of a dying woman. In these last days, her old affection for Madame revived. She left her the crucifix which she held in her last agony, besides many of her most valuable jewels, and settled the greater part of her fortune on her grand-daughter, the little Mademoiselle. On the night of the 20th of January she passed away, and the tolling of the great bell of Notre-Dame announced the news of her death. Monsieur, who had hardly left his mother's bedside, was the only member of her family present at the last, and was so deeply distressed that he refused to hear her will read, and retired at once with Madame to

P

Saint-Cloud. Shortly afterwards the King and Queen went to Versailles, leaving Mademoiselle to pay the last honours to her aunt's remains. "So these royalties," remarks Gui Patin, "practise the Gospel precept: 'Let the dead bury their dead.'"

The heart of the dead Queen was borne to her own Abbey of Val-de-Grâce, and her body was laid to rest in the royal vaults at Saint-Denis. Stately funeral services were held in both churches, and at Notre-Dame, where the royal family assisted, and Madame figured as chief mourner, wearing a train seven yards long.

Hardly had Anne of Austria breathed her last, than war was declared against England. On the 26th of January the Ambassadors received an intimation to this effect, and on the following day the official proclamation was publicly read with a great flourish of trumpets. Hollis, however, remained in Paris three months longer, and attempts at mediation were still carried on at intervals, by the Queen-mother and Madame. On the 15th of January, Henrietta wrote to her brother from Paris as follows :—

"PARIS,

"15 <i>Janvier</i> 1665.

"Monsieur has sent you a long letter, with a last attempt at mediation. As for me, I confess that I do not care to attempt what is useless, so that I only pray God to guide you in all your actions to do what is best. After this, I must tell you that the Queen, my mother-in-law, is very ill. Her fever has increased very much during the last week, and the doctors are greatly alarmed. A curious adventure has just happened here. La Feuillade and the Chevalier de Clermont fought on the Pont-Neuf, because the latter accused the other of speaking ill of him to the King and Monsieur, saying that he had cheated the Maréchal de Gramont at play. As a matter of fact, La Feuillade had defended him against others who said this, which makes people think there must be more than we know of behind this. Clermont, being the instigator, has been banished as guilty of duelling, and the other is safe, because witnesses say that he only defended himself. As a matter of fact, one is a fool who has ruined himself by gambling, and the other may think himself very fortunate. My Lord St. Albans will be sorry for the sake of our friend, M. l'Abbé de Clermont, brother of the Chevalier, who is in despair, and with good reason. This is all your humble servant has to say."

Charles replied to this letter, as well as to Monsieur's friendly attempt at intervention, in the following terms :—

" HAMTONCOURT,
" 29 *Jan.* 1666.

" I did intend to have answered last weeke yours and Monsieur's letters, upon the subject of doing good offices betweene me and France, but that I found, by the letter the Queene writt me of a later date, that mediations of that kinde were not sesonable at this time, France being resolved to declare for Holland, so that I only write now to Monsieur a letter of condolance upon the death of Queene-mother, which I sure you, gave me an equall share in the losse. I have been two dayes in this place, and do intend for to go to Whithall this weeke, for to dispatch all my preparations against the spring, which are allready in very good forwardnesse. We had some kinde of an alarum, that the troopes which Mon^r de Turene went to reviewe, were intended to make us a visite heere, but we shall be very ready to bid them welcome, either by sea or land. I have left my wife at Oxford, but hope that in a fortnight or three weekes to send for her to London, where already the Plague is in effect nothing. But our wemen are afraide of the name of Plague, so that they must have a little time to fancy all cleere, I cannot tell what kind of correspondence we must keep with letters, now that France declares war with us ; you must derect me in it, and I shall observe what you iudge convenient for you, but nothing can make me lessen in the least degree, of that kindnesse I alwayes have had for you, which I assure you is so rooted in my hart, as it will continue to the last moment of my life.
" C. R."

This was followed by another affectionate little note,

prompted by the King's concern for his sister's health, which again gave cause for anxiety. After this, we have a long interval, during which, as Charles feared, the pleasant interchange of letters between the two was suspended by the war, and it was only on very rare occasions that a safe messenger could be found.

" WHITHALL,
" Last of Feb. 1666.

" I was in great paine to heare of the fall you had, least it might have done you prejudice, in the condition you are in, but I was as glad to finde by your letter, that it had done you no harm. We have the same disease of Sermons that you complaine of there, but I hope you have the same convenience that the rest of the family has, of sleeping out most of the time, which is a great ease to those who are bounde to heare them, I have little to trouble you with this post, only to tell you that I am now very busy every day in prepareing businesse for the Parlament that meetes a fortenight hence. Mr Mountagu has had the sciatique, but is now pretty well. I thanke you for the care you have taken of the snuffe, at the same time pray send me some wax to seale letters, that has gold in it, the same you seald your letters with before you were in mourning, for there is none to be gott in this towne, I am entierly Yours.   C. R."

The epidemic of sermons, which had lately set in with fresh severity, was the course preached before the Court, on week-days in Lent, in the chapel of Saint-Germain. The rules of Court etiquette required Madame's presence, and besides hearing these sermons, she had to listen to all the long funeral orations, which were delivered during the same month, in honour of the Queen-mother. But there was one preacher who occupied the pulpit of Saint-Germain, during the Sundays in Lent, of whose eloquence Madame never wearied. This was Bossuet, the newly-appointed Dean of Metz. He had preached an Advent course at the Louvre in December 1665, at which Madame had been present, and the deep impression then made upon her is recorded, by the Court gazetteer, in a letter which he addressed to her on the subject. From this time, that friendship between Madame and Bossuet began, which was destined to exert so marked an influence on her character during the last years of her life, and to become memorable by the sublime oration which the great Bishop was to pronounce over her grave.

The Chevalier de Lorraine becomes Monsieur's Favourite—Excellent Influence of
Cosnac, Bishop of Valence—Libel of Manicamp—Copies destroyed by the
Bishop—His Admiration for Madame, and Character of this Princess in his
Memoirs—Peace of Breda.

THE Queen-mother's death that winter caused but a brief lull
in the Court festivities. The return of the Carnival season
became the signal for the revival of gaieties, and Molière's
Amour Médecin was acted at Saint-Germain, before the King.
After Easter, hunting - parties and masques began again.
Expeditions to Versailles were planned, in which the King
was accompanied by a few of his favourites, and "the God of
Love," the Court chronicler observes significantly, "never
failed to be of the party." With the death of his mother,
Louis had thrown aside the last pretence at concealment.
The son whom La Vallière had borne him, two years before,
was brought up at the Tuileries, and treated with royal honours, and the deputations from the Parliament and Courts of
Law, who came to Saint-Germain, to present their condolences
on the Queen-mother's death, were amazed to see the King's
mistress present among the ladies in attendance on the Queen.
Marie Thérèse resented this bitterly, but her tears failed to
move the King, who had listened with such remorse to his
mother's dying exhortations, and when Madame, in compassion for her sister-in-law, ventured to take her part, she only
drew the King's displeasure upon herself.

"The Queen of France," writes an English correspondent,
a few months later, "perceiving Mademoiselle de la Vallière
big with child, hath forbid her to appeare before her any
more, and disgraced some of her ladyes of honour, who deluded

her Majestie, that there was nothing but a meere frindship betweene the King and her. The King is much irritated against Madame."

Fortunately for Henrietta, this coldness on her brother-in-law's part soon disappeared, but she had too many causes of trouble in her own home to remain long at peace. Already the Chevalier de Lorraine, a younger brother of M. d'Armagnac, the Grand Écuyer, had won Monsieur's affection, and began to acquire that influence over him which was to prove so fatal to Madame's happiness. This worthless man, who had nothing to recommend him but his cherub face, and who had long carried on a scandalous intrigue with Madame's maid-of-honour, Mademoiselle de Fiennes, had, by degrees, gained an absolute mastery over Monsieur's mind, and governed him and his whole household. But, for a time, this evil influence was kept in check by the presence of another and a better friend. This was Daniel de Cosnac, Bishop of Valence. A man of great talent and ambition, this prelate was as much distinguished by his restless activity as by the independence and honesty of his character. Madame de Sevigné, who knew him well, and valued his friendship highly, describes him as a person full of great thoughts, but so frank of speech, and so hot of temper that, in conversation with him, it is necessary to be as cautious as when you are driving a shying horse. This fiery spirit often interfered with Cosnac's advancement, but, although little of a courtier, "*ce fou d'évêque*," as Voltaire calls him, was the truest and most loyal of servants. In his youth he had played an active part in the Fronde, and had exerted great influence over the Prince de Conti, to whose household he belonged, but, on his master's marriage, he embraced a new career, and became Bishop of Valence. During the next four years he devoted himself with admirable zeal to his new duties, and although, as Grand Almoner to Monsieur, he officiated at his marriage, the new Bishop was seldom seen at Court. But his restless spirit thirsted for the more stirring scenes of his old life, and when he was summoned to Paris in 1665 to attend a General Assembly of the Clergy, an unexpected opportunity of acquiring influence at Court presented itself. On the death of the Queen-mother, to whose regard he owed his post in her son's household, the Bishop followed Monsieur to Saint-Cloud, as in duty bound, to offer his condolences. He found Monsieur genuinely distressed at his mother's loss, and, full of good intentions, determined, in fact, to lead a nobler and more useful life. Cosnac was not slow to seize his opportunity. Up to this time, Monsieur's weak and frivolous character had only inspired him with contempt. Now, it seemed to him, a change for the better had come over him, and he resolved to use all his influence to make him reform his ways. For the moment, Monsieur was delighted with his new adviser. He consulted him on all occasions, and followed his instructions carefully. This change in his habits was generally noticed. "Monsieur le Duc d'Orléans," wrote Gui Patin, "is learning mathematics, and people say he is to command the army in the coming campaign." Acting under Cosnac's advice, he asked the King to give him the government of Languedoc, which had become vacant by the Prince de Conti's death in February. This Louis XIV. refused, determined, as he had always been, never to put power into his brother's hands, and Monsieur retired in a very bad humour to Villers-Cotterets. Cosnac, however, soon induced him to return to Court. He advised him to cultivate the King's good graces carefully, and to avail himself for this purpose of Madame's influence with Louis XIV. For a while the plan worked admirably. The King treated his brother with marked kindness, and admitted him to the Royal Councils. Monsieur lived on better terms with his wife, and was well pleased with Cosnac, with himself, and every one.

About the same time, the Bishop was able to render Madame a service which she never afterwards forgot. A copy of a pamphlet, called *Les Amours du Palais Royal*, printed in Holland, professing to give a true version of the loves of Madame and the Comte de Guiche, was brought to the King by his minister, Louvois. Louis privately showed it to Madame, and warned her to keep it from her husband's eyes. The libel, as has been already mentioned, was the work of Manicamp, a friend of the Comte de Guiche, and its contents were of a very harmless nature. But many of the details were evidently the result of personal observation, and this air of reality may well have excited Madame's alarm. In her fear lest the pamphlet should fall into Monsieur's hands, she sought the aid of Cosnac, as the ablest and most trustworthy of Monsieur's servants. The Bishop rose to the emergency at once. Without a moment's delay, he sent a confidential agent to Holland, a son of the doctor, Gui Patin, who bought up the whole edition of 1800 copies and obtained an order from the States, prohibiting the further publication of the pamphlet. These copies were delivered to Monsieur's faithful valet, Mérille, who burnt them in Madame's presence. The original MS., however, seems to have escaped destruction, since, a hundred years later, the libel was published in an edition of Bussy-Rabutin's *Histoire Amoureuse des Gaules*. Bussy has, accordingly, been frequently taxed with the authorship, an act of ingratitude of which he deserves to be acquitted. Monsieur, after his habit, not only declined to defray the heavy expenses which had been incurred by Cosnac on this occasion, but availed himself of the zeal that he had shown in Madame's service, to borrow further sums. "The whole affair," remarks the Bishop, "cost me a great deal of trouble and money, but, far from regretting this, I was only too well paid by the thanks which Madame bestowed upon me."

Soon afterwards, the Bishop left Court to attend to the affairs of his distant diocese. But he had made himself indispensable to Monsieur, who urged him to return to him as early as possible. And he took with him a deep, lasting impression of Madame's charm and greatness of soul. She had won his heart, after her usual habit, and from this time, the proud and impetuous prelate was her most devoted servant. Her figure plays a prominent part in the *Memoirs* which he compiled in exile, shortly after her death, and to their pages we owe some of the most interesting glimpses that we possess of Madame, at this period of her life. His narrative forms a valuable supplement to Madame de La Fayette's volume. The author of *Zaïde* is always cautious and guarded in her expressions, careful, as becomes a Court lady, not to lift the veil which shrouds the domestic life of

these royal persons, or to show us Monsieur in his true
colours.   Cosnac, bishop and priest though he be, has no
such delicacy.   He ignores rank, and has little or no respect
of persons.   The true qualities of the different personages,
with whom he is brought into contact, are brought out vividly.
The King's imperious will and impatience of contradiction,
the force of character which impressed even men like Cosnac,
who did not enjoy his favour; Monsieur's absurd love of
trivialities, his ignorance and fickleness, are clearly revealed.
Above all, he has given us the best portrait that we have of
Madame's person and character, and the fullest and most
accurate account of her death.   When the news of that
lamentable event reached him in his banishment, he was overwhelmed with grief, and by way of consolation he took up
his pen and tried to draw a faithful picture of the lamented
Princess whose image was still present to his mind.

"Madame," he wrote, "had a clear and strong intellect.
She was full of good sense, and was gifted with fine perception.   Her soul was great and just.   She always knew what
she ought to do, but did not always act up to her convictions
either from natural indolence, or else from a certain contempt
for ordinary duties, which formed part of her character.   Her
whole conversation was filled with a sweetness which made
her unlike all other royal personages.   It was not that she had
less majesty, but she was simpler and touched you more easily,
for, in spite of her divine qualities, she was the most human
creature in the world.   She seemed to lay hold of all hearts,
instead of treating them as common property, and this
naturally gave rise to the mistaken belief that she wished to
please people of all kinds, without distinction.   As for the
features of her countenance, they were exquisite.   Her eyes were
bright without being fierce, her mouth was admirable, her nose
perfect, a very rare thing! since Nature, unlike Art, does its
best in eyes, and its worst in noses!   Her complexion was
white and clear beyond words, her figure slight and of middle
height.   The grace of her soul seemed to animate her whole
being, down to the tips of her feet, and made her dance better
than any woman I ever saw.   As for the inexpressible charm
which, strange to say, is so often given to persons of no posi-

tion, ' *ce je ne sais quoi*,' which goes straight to all hearts, I have often heard critics say that in Madame alone this gift was original, and that others only tried to copy her. In short, everyone who approached her agreed in this, that she was the most perfect of women." The shrewd, calculating man of the world becomes eloquent as he recalls the infinite grace, the sweetness and gentleness, which made this brilliant Princess the most human, the most lovable of women. But, as he goes on, the memory of all that he has lost becomes too much for him. He breaks off abruptly, and ends with the words :—" I have no more to say of this Princess, but that she was the glory and honour of her age, and that this age would have adored her, had it been worthy of her."

When Cosnac came to Madame's help in this serious matter, the Court had already moved to Fontainebleau for the summer. Warlike preparations absorbed the King's attention. A camp was formed at Fontainebleau, where Lauzun figured, to Mademoiselle's admiration, at the head of the royal dragoons, and the Court ladies accompanied the King to reviews at Compiègne and Vincennes. Louvois and Turenne were both of them busy in raising fresh bodies of troops. But there was a general impression abroad that these forces were not intended to invade England. A detachment of French troops was sent indeed into Holland to oppose the advance of Charles II.'s ally, the Prince-Bishop of Munster, and the French fleet, under the Duc de Beaufort, was ordered to join De Ruyter's navy. But before they met the English fleet, a violent tempest scattered the French ships and forced them to take shelter in the port of Brest. In England the national hatred of France was fairly roused. " The English," said Gui Patin, " I hear no longer dress *à la Français*, but *à l'Espagnol* and *à la Moscovite*, not that, so far as I can see, this will hurt us much." And Sir George Savile, from the quiet shades of his home in Sherwood Forest, wrote in his usual witty strain to Sir William Temple, His Majesty's Minister at the Hague :—" His Majesty of France doth not declare war like '*un honnête homme*,' therefore I hope he will not pursue it like a wise one. I do not despair but that the English, who used to go into France for their breeding

may for once have the honour to teach them better manners.
In the meantime, we have great alarm the *Monsieurs* will invade
us, which makes everybody prepare for their entertainment,
and I hope they will neither find us so little ready, or perhaps so
divided as they expect. Your Bishop is, I fear, likely to be over-
matched, so we must rely on the oak and courage of England
to do our business." For the present the oak and courage of
England, had enough to do, to hold their own against the
Dutch, and several fiercely-contested battles between the rival
fleets took place at sea in the course of the summer. The
honours of war, however, remained with the English, who
were led by Prince Rupert and the Duke of Albemarle.
Meanwhile, at the Queen-mother's request, negotiations were
resumed between Louis XIV. and Lord Hollis, who still remained in France. The death of his wife at Paris, in January,
had left the Ambassador "a sorrowful man," and had "added
much to the desire he felt to be gone." Before the end of
March his baggage had been all packed and sent on board
the boat, and he himself was living in two hired rooms, suffering, moreover, acutely from the gout in his feet. But still, at
Madame's urgent entreaty, he lingered on, and lent a reluctant
ear to the fresh proposals for peace which were made at
Henrietta Maria's suggestion. But these proposals were by no
means acceptable to Charles, as he intimates in a letter, which
he sent to Madame by an equerry who was buying horses for
her in England.

                              "WHITHALL,
                                "2 *May* 1666.

"There are few occasions could be unwelcome to me, when
they give you a pretence to make me happy with a letter from
you, I do assure you that, if there were no other reason but
this constraint which is upon our commerce of letters, I should
use all my endeavours to have a good inteligence betweene
me and France, but I do feare very much that the desire to
peace is not wished for there, as it is on my part, for else my
Ld Hollis would not have been stoped so long to so little
purpose, there being lesse proposed at the conference then I
refused last yeare, which certainly does not shew any great

inclination to an agreement, but rather to amuse me, and certainly they must thinke me in a very ill condition to accept of such propositions as were offred to my Ld Hollis, in which I beleeve they will finde themselves mistaken ; however, I shall alwaies be very ready to harken to peace, as a good Christian ought to do, which is all I can do to advance it, for I have long since had to ill lucke with the advances I made to that end, as I can now only wish for peace, and leave the rest to God. I am goeing to-morrow to see the fleete, which will be ready very speedily, and I do assure you, tis much better in all respects then it was the last yeare, and the great want the Hollanders have of seamen, we are in no danger of, for we have more and better seamen then we had the last yeare. I will be very carefull of the choice of your horses, my Ld Crafts (Crofts) has promised me two, which he assures me will fitt you, and I will looke out for others, when I can light upon them, for if I had had any good of my owne, you should not have stayd so long but the plague of horses has been in my stable, and I shall have much ado to mounte my selfe with so much as jades for this summer's hunting, the scarsity of good ones is so great at this present. I will say no more, but only to assure you that nothing can alter that passion and tendernesse I have for you, and to beg of you that you will continue your kindnesse to me, for I am truly Yours.

"C. R."

After that there is another gap in the correspondence, and we find no mention of the Great Fire of London, which took place that September. On the 18th of October, however, Charles again resumes his pen. This time, Lord St. Albans, after repeated consultations with Henrietta Maria and Madame at Colombes, had been sent to London, to renew negotiations. The Dutch, aware of the King of England's want of money, refused to agree to an armistice, so Louis determined to come to a private agreement with Charles.

" WHITHALL,
18 Oct. 1666.

" It seemes to me by that which my Lord St. Albans sayes to me, that this commerce may at present begin againe, and

continue, even till the next campaigne; it was a great displeasure to me, to finde it forbidden, and by so much the
more, that as I do not thinke this to be an eternall warr, I
should be very glad that you should have part in all the
thinges that may conduce to the ending of it. I was likewise
very glad to learne that the King, my brother, makes professions still of haveing as just a sence in this subject as I
have, that is to say, beleeveing it nether good for him, nor for
me, and desireing an end of it, as much as I do; but allowe
me to tell you that in this occasion 'tis not enough to speak
in generall termes, esptially after haveing given so much
place to doute of his intentions, to reestablish the trust, it
were very good to speake more particulaly what that shall
be. You may assure your selfe I shall corresponde on my
side as farr as reason ought to guide me; this is all I shall
trouble you with at present, only to tell you the ioye I have
to assure you my selfe with how much tendernesse and kindnesse I am yours.   C. R."

Communications were now carried on between the two
Kings through Queen Henrietta Maria, and in the end a secret
treaty, signed by both monarchs, was placed in her hands at
Colombes. By this agreement the islands of the Antilles were
restored to England, and Charles pledged himself to lend no
assistance to Spain for the space of a year. A congress was
summoned to meet at Breda in the spring, and the Dutch
agreed to send commissioners to settle the terms of peace,
which had been already secretly arranged between Louis XIV.
and Charles II. "Peace is signed in reality," wrote the
French King, on the 8th of May 1667, "and all the plenipotentiaries who meet at Breda will have to do, is to draw up
the treaty on paper." Two months later the Peace of Breda
was signed, between England on the one hand, and France,
Holland and their ally, Denmark, on the other, and Louis
XIV. found himself at liberty to pursue the schemes of conquest which had so long floated before his eyes.

CHAPTER XVIII

Death of the Duc de Valois—Invasion of Flanders—Monsieur joins the Army and
distinguishes himself in the Field—Illness of Madame—Visit of the Duke
of Monmouth—Intrigue of Lorraine—Disgrace of the Bishop of Valence.

NEITHER war, nor preparations for war, could interrupt the
festivities of the Grand Monarque's Court in these early
years of his reign. He himself was never so busy, never so
much absorbed in conferences with his ministers and generals,
as not to find time for the brilliant shows with which he loved
to dazzle the eyes of his subjects. The Court spent the
autumn and winter at Saint-Germain, where balls and pastoral
plays followed each other in rapid succession, and the
splendour and profusion displayed was greater than ever
before. These *fêtes* were marked by the re-appearance of
La Vallière, who had given birth to a daughter, afterwards
the Princess de Conti, in October, and was still the object
of the King's devotion. She drew a large diamond at the
King's lottery, and figured once more in a Court ballet
which was in preparation that November. Here Madame,
as usual, was the moving spirit. Suddenly, in the midst of
the rehearsals, news reached Henrietta of her son's dangerous
illness. She was passionately fond of the little Duke, a
singularly handsome and engaging boy of two years old, and
hastened without delay to Saint-Cloud, where Madame de
Saint-Chaumont was nursing him with the most devoted
care. For some time past, the little Prince's health had
given cause for anxiety, but the present attack was said to be
brought on by teething. His new teeth, however, came
through at the end of a few days, and the child recovered.
Madame brought him to Paris, and since her doctor, M.

Esprit, declared himself perfectly satisfied with the little
Prince's condition, his mother returned, at the end of the
month, to Saint-Germain.   There, on the 2d of December, the *Ballet des Muses* was performed.   Molière's genius
had again been called into requisition.   He composed
" Le Sicilien " as an interlude, and introduced Turks and
Moors on the stage, by way of novelty.   This time Madame
appeared as a Shepherdess with her crook, holding her
favourite little white-and-tan spaniel, Mimi, in her arms, and
the following verses, written by Benserade, were recited in
her honour :—

> " Non, je ne pense pas que jamais rien égale
> Ces manières, cet air et ces charmes vainqueurs :
>   C'est un Dédale pour tous les cœurs.
> Elle vous prend d'abord, vous entraîne, vous tue,
> Vous pille jusqu' à l'âme, et puis, apres cela
>   Sans être émue,
>   Vous laisse là !
> Mais la témèrité découvre la ruine,
> Pour la jeune bergére osant plus qu'il ne faut ;
>   Son origine
>   Vient de trop haut :
> Qu' içi tous les respects les plus profonds s'assemblent
> Dans un cœur ; un tel cœur n'en a pas à demi,
>   Tous les loups tremblent
>   Devant Mimi."

Mimi was the pet dog who appears with Madame, in
several of the portraits painted by Mignard, about this
period, and who, we are told, by Madame de Sevigné, was
so jealous of anything that robbed him of his mistress's
notice, that he would run away and hide, whenever she
took up a book.   The day after this performance Madame
was again summoned to Paris, by the news of her little boy's
relapse.   He had caught a cold which brought on an attack
of fever and convulsions, and his state was so alarming that
Monsieur insisted his christening should take place at once.
It was then the custom to sprinkle the Princes of the royal
line with water, at their birth, but to defer the administration
of the full baptismal rites until the age of twelve.   On the
7th of December, the ceremony was performed in the Chapel

of the Palais-Royal. The Bishop of Valence, who had arrived in Paris a fortnight before, officiated, and the child received the name of Philippe Charles. Mademoiselle represented the Queen of France, who could not leave Saint-Germain, on account of her approaching confinement, and the Duc d'Enghien stood proxy for Charles II. But the poor child became rapidly worse, and died on the following evening. His body lay in state all the next day, and the King himself came to show his grief and sympathy by sprinkling holy water on the bier, followed by all the princes of the blood, and an immense concourse of people. The event was regarded as a national calamity, owing to the delicacy of the King's only son, and the hopes which had been entertained of this promising child. Olivier d'Ormesson, the great lawyer, deplores his loss in his journal, but remarks, with a touch of Gui Patin's sarcasm, that people say, if the Duc de Valois had been the child of a *bourgeois*, instead of the son of Monsieur, he would not have died. The poor little Prince's heart was borne to the Val-de-Grâce, and on the night of the tenth of December, a stately procession of princes and nobles, bearing lighted torches, followed his remains to their last resting-place in the tomb of the Kings at Saint-Denis. Crowds flocked to the funeral, and the Bishop of Valence's eloquent discourse drew tears from all who were present.

The loss of this precious child was a terrible blow to Madame. Cosnac tells us that she was in despair. Monsieur seemed much distressed for a day or two, after which, his sole anxiety was to secure the reversion of the allowance which his son had received from the King. Louis XIV. showed his sister-in-law much sympathy, and sent the following graceful little note to Charles II. :—

"SAINT-GERMAIN,
"23 *Dec.*

" The common loss we have had in the death of my nephew, the Duc de Valois, touches us both so closely that the only difference in our mutual grief is that mine began a few days sooner than yours. LOUIS."

The whole Royal Family spent Christmas quietly together at Saint-Germain. But when the Queen had given birth to another daughter, on the 4th of January, the King became impatient to resume his usual round of *fêtes*, and, at his desire, Madame consented, reluctantly, to allow the *Ballet des Muses* to be performed at the Palais-Royal, on the 12th of January 1667. She was weary of *fêtes* and sick at heart, but the King's word was law. In the absence of the Queen, her presence was required, and she yielded to the pressure of a stern necessity. Balls and concerts now began again, and the Carnival was celebrated by a series of banquets and masquerades at Versailles. The park was thrown open to the public, and all who came in masks were allowed to join in the dancing. The letters of the period are full of the beauty and brilliancy of the *fêtes*, of the magical effect of the illuminated gardens, and of the regal hospitality with which the guests were entertained. "The *Fête* of Versailles must have cost millions, it is said. All Paris was there, and 4000 partridges were served at supper." Bussy-Rabutin's mouth watered when he read of these wonders, and he sighed over the hard fate which kept him in the country. "Was there ever a King so great alike in peace and in war?" he exclaims. But there was another side to the picture. "Here, in Paris," wrote Olivier d'Ormesson, "there are few masques, and few people who have the heart to be joyful." And Gui Patin draws a striking contrast between the magnificence of the Court and the poverty of the peasantry, and laments the heavy burdens which excessive taxation has entailed on the country.

"Never before, in the memory of man," he writes, "was the world so poor or so wretched, and yet the town is full of fools who run about in the streets in masks. All around me people complain loudly of their misery. And I, who have all my life offered up the Wise Man's prayer—give me neither poverty nor riches—am forced to tremble when I see such disorder. Well, this Carnival at least is over! The doctors complain that they have no patients and no money. Only comedians have a good time of it. *Tartuffe* is all the rage. All the great world goes there. We need not wonder. Human life is like nothing so much as a comedy."

No sooner was the secret treaty with Charles signed, than Turenne marched to the frontier at the head of an army of 50,000 men.

"Paris is a desert," complained Madame de Sevigné, on her return from the country, that spring. "All the youth of France is gone to fight in Flanders, and I shall go back to the country, preferring solitude there to empty streets here."

> "En attendant que nos guerriers
> Reviennent couronnés de lauriers."

On the 16th of May, Louis XIV. himself joined the army, and a few days afterwards Monsieur followed him to Péronne. Since the death of the little Duc de Valois, Cosnac had regained his old influence with his master. Monsieur consulted him on every occasion, listened to his advice, and took his remonstrances in good part. But his folly and pettiness tried Cosnac's patience almost beyond endurance. At one time, he was inclined to listen to proposals that were made him by some Neapolitan nobles, and put himself at the head of a revolution which they were plotting against the Spaniards; but when he was told that Naples was close to Vesuvius, and was therefore sometimes exposed to the danger of an eruption, he promptly gave up the idea. Now, however, he assured Cosnac that he was going to appear in a new light, as a worthy grandson of Henri Quatre. "Follow me to the camp," he said, "and you will see how well I can fight." On the day of his departure, he took a tender farewell of Madame, and was gratified at seeing her ladies shed tears. She was again expecting to become a mother, and remained at Saint-Cloud, where she received frequent visits from Queen Henrietta Maria, and watched the course of the campaign with the utmost eagerness. She was greatly delighted when news reached her, that her husband had been seen in the trenches at Tournay and Douay, and had distinguished himself by his valour and coolness under fire. The warlike Bishop was always at his side, and took care that the Court gazetteers should record his master's prowess. "What!" said the King one day, when he visited the camp before Tournay, "do I see M. de Valence in the trenches!" "Sire," replied Cosnac, "I

have come here, to be able to tell others, that I have seen the
greatest King upon earth exposing his person to the same
risks as a simple soldier." Nevertheless, Louis was not over
well pleased to see the credit which his brother had acquired,
and was inclined to look with suspicion on this bold adviser.
But Monsieur's military ardour proved of short duration.
Before long, he became more occupied with the decoration of
his tent and the hanging of crystal chandeliers and mirrors,
than with active warfare, and he was delighted when a bad
report of Madame's health gave him an excuse to return
home, and receive the laurels which he had earned in the field,
from the fair hands of her ladies.

On reaching Saint-Cloud, he found Madame very dangerously ill, from the results of a miscarriage. During ten days
she hovered between life and death, and on the 12th of July,
Monsieur wrote the following note to Charles II.:—"Madame
begs me to ask Your Majesty's pardon for not writing by
this post, but she has not the strength to sit up, since the
accident which happened to her a week ago, after which she
was thought to be dead during a quarter-of-an-hour. This
has obliged me to leave Douay, before the entrance of the
King, my brother, to whose arms the town surrendered three
hours before my departure."

A few days afterwards, the King of France himself paid a
visit of inquiry to Madame. He had left the army to take a
short rest at Compiègne, and brought the Queen back with
him to show her to the new subjects whom he had conquered
in her name. With her went all the ladies of the Court, chief
among them La Vallière, whom the King had just raised to
the rank of Duchess, and Madame de Montespan, whose more
striking beauty and superior powers of conversation were
rapidly gaining the King's affections. The whole campaign
bore the appearance of a triumphal progress. One city after
the other opened its gates to his victorious army, and the
sight of all this splendour was well calculated to impress the
quiet Flemish burghers. "All you have heard of the glory
of Solomon, and of the Emperor of China," wrote one of
Bussy's correspondents, "is not to be compared with the pomp
of warlike array which surrounds the King. The streets are

full of cloth of gold, of waving plumes, of chariots and superbly-harnessed mules, of horses with gold and embroidered trappings, and of sumptuous carriages." And another writer remarks :—" La Vallière is playing the Grand Duchess at the camp, and Monsieur is gone with fine courage to join the King at Arras."

As soon as Madame was out of danger, Monsieur did indeed return to the army, accompanied by his faithful Bishop. He was present at the surrender of Oudenarde, and appeared in the trenches at the siege of Lille. It was even whispered that Monsieur was to receive the post of Lieutenant-General of the army, and the King really promised him the command of an expedition to Catalonia, which was planned to take place in the spring. Unfortunately, one day the Chevalier de Lorraine appeared in camp. The sight of him renewed all Monsieur's old infatuation. From that moment, Cosnac saw that all his efforts were doomed to failure. Monsieur could talk and think of nothing else but his favourite, and when the Chevalier was slightly wounded, he left the camp to spend whole days in his company. After the surrender of Lille, the King, satisfied with the conquests which he had effected, left the command of the army to Turenne, and returned to Paris with the Queen. Monsieur joined his wife at Villers-Cotterets, where her mother had brought her for change of air after her long illness. He received a warm welcome, and his mother-in-law was especially cordial in her congratulations on the distinctions that he had won. For a few days he occupied himself harmlessly enough, although, much to Cosnac's disgust, in ranging chairs and tables in battle array, and sticking mirrors up as outposts. But in a little while, the Chevalier de Lorraine appeared on the scene, and there was an end of all peace. Monsieur ran to meet him with transports of joy, and would never leave his side. He informed Cosnac of his intention to keep his favourite henceforth about his person, and to have no secrets from him. Accordingly, on his return to Paris, the Chevalier de Lorraine was installed in the best rooms of the Palais-Royal, and admitted into Monsieur's closest confidence.

Soon the Bishop began to feel the ill effects of his master's foolish passion. Monsieur complained that Cosnac was too much attached to Madame's service, and too intimate with her faithful servant Madame de Saint-Chaumont. He accused him of plotting against the Chevalier, and set spies to watch his movements. In vain Madame assured her husband if the man had a fault it was that of serving him with too much zeal and loyalty. The Bishop resolved to take his leave without delay and return to his diocese. Even Madame's entreaties could not shake his determination, grieved as he was to desert her at this critical time. He obtained a parting audience from the King, in which he explained himself with his accustomed freedom, and observed to the Duc de Luxembourg as he left the royal presence : " I have just seen a great man who has disgusted me more than ever with the *petit maître* it is my misfortune to serve ! " Louis's reply was a very gracious one, and he afterwards told the Maréchal de Gramont, that his brother had never had but one able man in his service, and that he had been unable to keep him long. So Cosnac left Court, but not without a parting promise to Madame that he would return at the earliest opportunity. Fortunately Henrietta had the support of her mother's presence in the trials that were fast thickening about her. She paid frequent visits to Colombes, where the Queen-mother led a very retired life during the summer, while she spent the winter at the Hotel de la Bazinière, a fine house in Paris, which had been lent her by the King's orders. Madame's correspondence with her royal brother had been actively renewed since the cessation of the war with England. Unfortunately her own letters to Charles during this period have perished, and the last we have from her pen is dated January 1666. Three only of the King's belong to the year 1667.

The first of these was addressed to her during her illness at Saint-Cloud, and contains little but an apology for his neglect, in leaving so many of her letters unanswered. The second was written a month later, in answer to an appeal which Henrietta had made him on behalf of her old friend, Miss Stewart, who had incurred his displeasure by marrying the Duke of Richmond. The King's own passion for the beautiful maid-of-honour was so well known, that when the

Queen's death seemed imminent, his marriage with Miss
Stewart had been confidently expected.   But although
Hamilton tells us that she was blest with as little wit as she
had great beauty, and seemed well content to accept the
King's homage, "la belle Stuart" had kept her reputation
unsullied, and, to her honour, refused all the presents offered
to her by her royal lover.   The position, however, was a
difficult one, and when the Duke of Richmond, who had long
been dying of love for her, laid his hand and heart at her feet,
she, according to Hamilton, left Court, and was privately
married to him.   Charles II.'s anger was great at what he
considered this breach of friendship.   For some time he refused to admit the Duke and Duchess to his presence, and not
even Henrietta's intercession could induce him to forgive his
old favourite.   But this severity, as we shall see, did not last
very long, and the influence of "that fantastic little gentleman,
Dan Cupid," soon regained its old power over the good-
natured monarch.

"WHITHALL,
"27 *July* 1667.

"I have been so faulty to you in matter of writing, as it
is impudence to expect pardon from you.   The truth is, I am
gotten into such a vaine of hunting and the game lies so farr
from this towne, as I must spende one day intirely to kill one
stagg, and then the other dayes I have a great deale of
businesse, so that all this, with my lazynesse towards writing,
has been the cause of my faulte towards you.   I am but iust
now come from hunting, and am very weary, but I am resolved for the future to be very punctuall in writing to you
so that in time I hope to merritt your pardon, for though I
am fauty to you in letters, I am sure there is nothing can
love an other so well as I do you.   C. R."

"WHITHALL,
"26 *Aug.* 1667.

"I do assure you I am very much troubled that I cannot
in everything give you that satisfaction I could wish, especially in this businesse of the duchesse of Richmonde, wherein
you may thinke me ill natured, but if you consider how hard

a thing 'tis to swallow an injury done by a person I had so
much tendernesse for, you will in some degree excuse the
resentment I use towards her; you know my good nature
enough to beleeve that I could not be so severe, if I had not
great provocation, and I assure you her carriage towards me
has been as bad as breach of frindship and faith can make it,
therfore I hope you will pardon me if I cannot so soon
forgett an injury which went so neere my hart. I will not
now answer the letter you writt by your watterman who fell
sick upon the way, and so I had the letter but some dayes
since, but will expect a safer way to write then by the post.
I beleeve Ruvigny will be heere in two or three dayes, and
the other gentleman whos name I cannot reade in your letter.
The peace was proclaimed heere on saturday last, and so I
will end my letter, and will only add the assurance of my
being intierly Yours.   C. R."

The next letter deals with a graver subject. The Lord
Chancellor, Clarendon, had been deprived of his office, and
condemned to banishment, by a recent vote of Parliament.
During his tenure of office, he had made many enemies, and
of late years he had forfeited the King's favour by endeavouring to set limits to his extravagance, and to the
increasing rapacity of his mistresses. He was also supposed
to have privately countenanced the Duke of Richmond's
marriage, a step which Charles could not forgive. But
Madame had been greatly alarmed and distressed on hearing
of Clarendon's fall, and had, it seems, expressed herself with
some warmth on the subject, in writing to the King. Charles
replied in the following terms :—

" WHITHALL,
" 30 Nov. 1667.

" If you looke upon our condition heere, as it is reported
by common fame, I do confesse you have reason to have
those aprehensions you mention in your letter by this bearer ;
the truth is, the ill conduct of my Ld Clarendon in my
affaires has forced me to permitt many inquiryes to be made,
which otherwise I would not have suffred the parlament to
have done, though I must tell you that in themselves they

are but inconvenient apearances, rather than real mischives.
There can be nothing advanced in the Parl : for my advantage, till this matter of my Ld Clarendon be over, but after
that I shall be able to take my mesures to with them, as you
will see the good effects of it ; I am sure I will not part with
any of my power, nor do I beleeve that they will desire any
unreesonable thing, I have written at large to the Queene, in
the particular of my Ld Clarendon, which I could not do but
by a safe way, and I dout not that you will in that matter,
and many others, have informations very farr from the truth.
I will add no more, only thanke you for your kindnesse in
being so free with me, which I pray continue upon all occasions, and be assured that I am entierly Yours.   C. R."

All that autumn, Madame remained in weak health, and a
note written by Monsieur to Charles II., on the 20th of
October, informed him that for six days she had suffered so
acutely from headaches, that she was unable to leave her bedroom, and lay there with closed shutters all day. The remedies
prescribed by the doctors had given her no relief, and she
had been bled in the foot with no effect but that of increasing
her pains. Soon afterwards, however, she was able to appear
on horseback, at the royal hunting-parties held at Versailles,
in honour of St. Hubert's Feast, and rode at the head of her
ladies with her usual grace and spirit.

A description of her, which was sent home by Philip, the
second Earl of Chesterfield, when he visited Paris, is interesting, in spite of its flowery language, as showing the impression made by her upon this acute observer and keen judge of
womanhood, in these last years of her life. It was written at
the request of the Countess of Derby, the daughter-in-law of
her mother's old friend, Charlotte de la Trémouille, whom he
addresses as follows :—

"Since our correspondence hath outlived our inclination,
and that you are pleased to command me to send you the
portrait or description of Armida, though I am very unable
to perform as hard a task, yet I will endeavour it with great
fidelity. Your ladyship knowes that sometimes very ill
painters doe draw as like as the greatest masters. Armida

whom all the world so much admires, is a princess who, at
the first blush, appears to be of the greatest quality, and has
something in the looks besides her beauty, so new and unusual, that it surprises the beholders. Her stature is rather
tall than otherwise, her shape is delicate, her motions graceful, her eyes are sparkling and yet compassionate, and do not
only penetrate the thoughts of others, but often also express
her own, teaching, as it were, a language yet unknown to any
but the blest above. Her breasts seem two little moving
worlds of pleasure, which, by the reflection of her eyes, fire
the hartes of all that see them, and yet so sweet an inno-
cency shines in her composure, that one would think she
neither knew or had ever heard the name of sin. Her lips
do always blush for kissing of the finest teeth that were ever
seen, and her complexion is unparalleled. The freedom of
her carriage and the pleasantness of her discourse would
charm an anchorite, yet there is something of majesty so
mixed with all the rest, that it stifles the breath of any unruly
thought, and creates a love, mingled with fear, very like that
we owe to a deity. Her wit is mostly extolled by all that
hear her, for she has not only a peculiar talent in finding apt
similitudes, and in the quickness of her repartee, but in the
plainest subject of her discourse, she finds out something new
and unexpected which pleases all her auditors. But now as
to her mind; though always generous, it is so changeable, as
to other things, that it seems incapable of lasting friendship;
for she is never long satisfied with herself, or with those who
endeavour most to please her."

Lord Chesterfield, it is plain from this last sentence,
judged Madame as a casual acquaintance, who had seen her
shine in society, but was never intimate with her. Cosnac
and Bussy, La Fayette and Bossuet, have a very different tale
to tell. She was, they all agree, the truest and the best of
friends.

The Court now returned to Paris for Christmas, and the
presence of a new guest at the winter *fêtes* gladdened Henrietta's heart. This was her brother's illegitimate son, the
young Duke of Monmouth. For some years he had been
recognised at the English Court, and was treated with great

kindness by the Queen and the Duchess of York. The King's affection for him was well known, and he now sent him to Paris, with the following recommendation, to his sister's care.

"WHITHALL,
"14 <i>Jan.</i> 1668.

" I beleeve you may easily guesse that I am some thing concerned for this bearer, James,[1] and therefore I put him into your handes to be directed by you in all thinges, and pray use that authority over him as you ought to do in kindnesse to me, which is all I shall say to you at this time, for I thinke he will not be so soone at Paris as the post, and have no more to trouble you now, only to assure you that I am intierly yours. C. R."

Henrietta, as might be expected, responded warmly to her brother's request. She welcomed her nephew affectionately, received him in the Palais-Royal, and gave a series of balls and *fêtes* in his honour during that carnival. The handsome youth who danced so well, and was distinguished by his graceful manners, soon became very popular at Court, and was on the best of terms with Madame. He taught her to dance the English country dances, which Charles II. so often called for in his revels at Whitehall and Hampton Court, and made himself agreeable to her in a thousand ways. But his presence soon aroused her husband's jealousy, and the mischievous Chevalier de Lorraine took care to fan the flame. Monsieur complained to his wife that she conversed with the Duke in English, and preferred her nephew's society to his own. Madame, in return, complained of his favourite's insolence, and of the airs which he gave himself in her house. She had, it must be owned, good cause to resent the Chevalier's conduct. He had openly seduced her maid-of-honour, Mademoiselle de Fiennes, and when Monsieur, in a fit of jealousy, drove the wretched girl out of his house without a word to Madame, Lorraine had the face to say that he had

---

[1] The words "Duke of Monmouth" have been here added in red ink and a different handwriting.

sacrificed his mistress to his friendship for Monsieur. For some time Madame refused to admit him to her presence, and when Monsieur insisted on his return, told him plainly what she thought of his favourite. She poured out the same grievances in secret to Madame de Saint-Chaumont, who still retained the post of governess to her young daughter. This lady, indignant, as all Madame's servants were, at the Chevalier's behaviour to their mistress, took her complaints to the King, who blamed his brother severely for allowing his favourite such license. Upon this, Monsieur turned sulky, and carried off Madame, much against her will, to Villers-Cotterets, where she had to spend some weeks with only Lorraine and himself for her companions.

This was the state of things which the Bishop of Valence found on his return to Court, immediately after Easter. The cold reception which Monsieur gave him, convinced him that it would be useless to continue in his service, and it was only Madame's earnest prayer that prevented him from resigning his office on the spot. "In God's name, Madame," he said, "let me go out honestly by the door, and save Monsieur the trouble of throwing me out of the window!"

His words were but too true. After spending a week at Saint-Germain, where the Court then was, he returned to Paris. There he received a message from Monsieur, ordering him to give up his post of Grand Almoner and leave Paris at once. In vain both Madame and her mother, Queen Henrietta Maria, who had a great regard for the Bishop, used all the arguments in their power to induce Monsieur not to dismiss this faithful servant in so abrupt a manner. He refused to hear reason, and after a vain appeal to the King, Cosnac left Paris. Nor did the malice of his enemies end here. Lorraine's powerful friends joined with the ministers, Colbert and Louvois, who had no love for the Bishop, in persuading the King that he was a dangerous person, and he received an order, through the Archbishop of Paris, not to return to Paris without His Majesty's permission. The injustice of the whole proceeding rankled deeply in Cosnac's heart. What, he asks indignantly, in a letter to a friend, were the crimes to which he owed his disgrace?

" I have tried to the best of my power to serve Monsieur well, to make him a great Prince, honoured and respected by all. I have tried to help him to make himself useful and agreeable to his Majesty, I have desired that he should love and consider Madame as the greatness of her soul and the goodness of her heart deserve. And I have tried to make him just and kind to the servants who are faithful and active in doing his bidding. These are the only cabals of which I have been guilty."

But, in his disappointment and solitude, he had one great consolation in the sympathy of his friends. Chief among these was Madame. She could not forgive herself for having, as she felt, caused his ruin, and she did all in her power to soften the ill-treatment which he had received at her husband's hands.

" In my distress," he writes, " I received letters from Madame, so full of kindness, so generous and touching, that they sometimes made me feel there could be no prosperity as sweet and gracious as disgrace."

He goes on to quote one of these letters which reached him in Paris on the day after he left the Palais-Royal :—

" You have always seen me so much attached to Monsieur's interests by inclination, as well as by duty, that if I could not distinguish his real from his pretended friends, you might have reason to doubt my friendship in his conduct towards yourself. But as this is not the first time that the misfortune of private individuals has proved stronger than the justice of princes, I hope you will regard these events as a trick of destiny, which is not to be resisted, and understand that the fatality which has cost you Monsieur's favour, does not extend to me, for I shall ever retain the same esteem I have always felt for you, and shall do my utmost to prove this by my actions."

True to her word, Madame did not forget the servant whose only fault, as Monsieur himself acknowledged, was that he had been too zealous in her service. She kept up constant communication with him, through Madame de Saint-

Chaumont, and interceded repeatedly with the King on his behalf. But Louis XIV. was inflexible. Some imprudent words of Cosnac, when he heard that Monsieur had asked the King to banish him, were repeated to him:—"Tell Monsieur," the Bishop had said, "that he will find it easier to obtain my dismissal, than it was to get himself made Governor of Languedoc!" The King, who was aware of Cosnac's share in soliciting this post for Monsieur, regarded these words as a breach of confidence, and was confirmed in his prejudice against the independent prelate. But he never failed to recognise Cosnac's merit, and in after years, when Madame had long been dead, and the old intrigues were forgotten, he honoured the Bishop with repeated marks of his favour, and told him plainly that, personally, he had never borne him any grudge, but that he had been obliged to gratify his brother's caprice.

CHAPTER XIX

The Triple Alliance—Conquest of Franche-Comté—Court intrigues in France
and England—Lady Shrewsbury and Madame de Mazarin.

EARLY in the year 1668, Sir William Temple succeeded in
concluding that Treaty of union between England, Holland
and Sweden, which became known by the name of the Triple
Alliance. The object of this Treaty, as is well known, was
to oppose the French King's schemes of conquest, which
began to excite the alarm of all Europe. The very day on
which the Treaty was signed, Charles II. wrote the following
letter to his sister :—

> " WHITHALL,
> " 23 *Jan.* 1668.

" I believe you will be a little surprised at the treaty I have
concluded with the States, the effect of it is to bring Spaine
to consent to the peace, upon the termes the King of France
hath avowed he will be content with, so as I have done nothing
to prejudice France in this agreement, and they cannot wonder
that I provide for my selfe against any mischifes this warre
may produce, and finding my propositions to France receave
so cold an answer, which in effect was as good as a refusall, I
thought I had no other way but this to secure my selfe. If
I finde by the letters that my Ld St Albans is come away,
I do intend to send somebody else into France, to incline the
King to accept of this peace. I give you a thousand thankes
for the care you take before hand of James, I will answer for
him that he will be very obedient in all your commands, and
your kindnesse to him obliges me as much as tis possible, for
I do confesse I love him very well ; he was, I beleeve, with

you, before your last letter came to my hands. You were misinformed in your intelligence concerning the D^{esse} of Richmond. If you were as well acquainted with a little fantastical gentleman called Cupide as I am, you would neither wonder, nor take ill, any suden changes which do happen in the affaires of his conducting, but in this matter there is nothing done in it. I do not answer Monsieur's letter by this post, because I have not yett spoken with M. de St Laurens,[1] to whom the letter refers me, so I shall only desire you to remember me very kindly to him, and be assured that I am entierly yours.   C. R."

"WHITHALL,
"30 *Jan.* 1668.

"I cannot thanke you enough for your goodness and kindnesse to James. His letter to me is almost nothing else but telling how much he is obliged to you and Monsieur for your care of him, and since you have taken the trouble of lodging him at the Palais-Royal, I am sure he cannot be better. I am very glad that you have put the thought of going to the army out of his head, for it were not proper that he should apeare in any army, now that I have become a mediataur, by the treaty I have lately made with Holland, and I am now despatching an envoyé to the King of france in order to the mediation, which I hope will hinder Monsieur's iourney into Catalogna, and save him from a hott campaigne, and this is all I will trouble you with at present, only againe thanke you for your kindnesse to James, and beg of you to be assured that my kindnesse and tendernesse to you is more then I can expresse.   C. R."

"WHITHALL,
"4 *Feb.* 1668.

"I have dispatched this bearer, Sr John Trevor, into France as my envoyé extraordinary, with power to negociate the Peace between the two crownes, according to the treaty I

---

[1] A member of Monsieur's household, whose office it was to introduce Ambassadors into his and Madame's presence. He was devoted to his mistress, and highly esteemed by Madame, both for his own merit and as a personal friend of Cosnac.

lately made with the States of the united provinces, I have given him orders to communicate all things with that freedom to you as I ought to do, haveing that kindnesse for you which I cannot in words sufficiently expresse. I hope he will not finde his worke difficulte, since I presse nothing but the conditions of peace, which the King of France offred to agree with Spaine upon. Mon^r de St Laurans will part from hence, in two or three days, by him I will write more to you, and so I am intierly Yours. C. R."

"WHITHALL,
" 10 *Feb*. 1668.

" I cannot enough thanke you for your kindnesse to James. I hope he is as sensible of your goodnesse to him as I am. I do not intende to call him yett away from you, except Monsieur should go to the army, but in that case I thinke it will not be decent for him to stay at Paris, when everybody will be in the feilde, and on the other side, as matters stande, it will not be convenient for me that he should goe to the army, for divers reasons, which I will not trouble you with in this letter. But I hope there will be no neede of Monsieur's going thither. I went this day to the parlament, to acquaint them with the League I had latly made, and to put them in minde of my debts I had contracted in this last warr, and to give me some mony at this present. They have put of the consideration of it till friday, and then I hope they will behave themselves as they ought to do. I have dispatched Mon^r de St Laurans this day to you, who I finde as much an honeste *homme* as you tould me he was, so as I have not any more to say to you now, but to assure that I am intierly yours.

"C. R."

The winter campaign to which Charles alludes in these letters was the brilliant expedition of Louis XIV. and Condé, which resulted in the conquest of the whole province of Franche-Comté from the Spaniards in less than a month's time. But the intervention of the Triple Alliance forced Louis to consent to peace. Ralph Montagu had been appointed Ambassador to France in March 1668, and had been wel-

R

comed by Madame with the warmth of an old friend. Sir John
Trevor was also sent to Paris to propose terms of agreement
between France and Spain, and on the 22d of April 1668,
plenipotentiaries from both countries met at Aix-la-Chapelle,
where the Peace was eventually concluded. Louis XIV. gave
up his newly-conquered province on condition of retaining the
towns of Spanish Flanders which he had taken in the previous
campaign. But his ambitious designs were only put off for
the moment, and the conquest of Holland itself was already
present to his mind. To detach Charles II. from the Triple
Alliance now became the chief object of his policy, and in
the negotiations which were shortly resumed between the two
kings, Madame once more found herself called upon to play a
leading part. A note which Louis XIV. addressed to his
sister-in-law, during his winter campaign, is of interest as a
proof of the affectionate regard in which he held her.

"À DIJON,
"<i>le</i> 5 <i>Fevrier</i> 1668.

"If I did not love you so well, I should not write to you,
for I have nothing to say, and I have given my brother all
the news there is to tell. But I am very glad to be able to
assure you once more of what I have already told you, which
is, that I have as much affection for you as you can possibly
desire. Be persuaded of what this letter confirms, and please
present my compliments to Mesdames de Monaco and de
Thianges."

During this spring, in spite of the delicate state of her
health, which Charles so often mentions with anxiety in his
letters, Madame kept up an active correspondence, not only
with her brother, but with several leading Englishmen at his
Court. She writes to Buckingham, Arlington and James
Hamilton, all in turn, and knows everything that is happening
at Whitehall. Nor does she hesitate to give Charles good
advice, and reproach him freely for his indolence and extravagance.

We learn, from the King's letter of March 5, that dis-
quieting rumours as to the state of affairs in England had

reached her. She was especially concerned to hear of the great influence which Buckingham had obtained over her brother. Charles, as usual, took her advice in good part, if he did not profit by it, but tried to excuse himself, and lay the blame on his late minister, Clarendon.

"I am extreamly troubled that Trevor carried himselfe so like an Asse to you. I have sent him a chideing for it. I can say nothing for him, but that it was a faute for want of good breeding, which is a disease very much spread over this country. I receaved your long letter of the 7th inst. now, wherein I perceave you are very much alarmed at my condition, and at the caballs which are growing heere. I do take your concerne for me very kindly, and thanke you for the councell you give me, but I do not thinke you have so much cause to feare, as you seeme to do, in your letter. There is no doute but a house of Commons will be extravagant enough when there is neede of them, and 'tis not much to be wondred at, that I should be in debt, after so expencefull a warr as I have had, which undoubtedly will give me some trouble before I gett out of it. I will not deny but that naturally I am more lazy then I ought to be, but you are very ill informed if you do not know that my Tresury, and in deede all my other affaires, are in as good a methode as our understandings can put them into. And I thinke the peace (13. February 1668) I have made betweene Spaine and portugal and the defensive league (23. January 1668) I have made with Holland, should give some testimony to the world that we thinke of our interest heere. I do assure you that I neglect nothing for want of paines. If we faile for want of understanding, there is no helpe for it. The gentleman by mistake gave hamilton's letter to my Ld Arlington, who read it, without looking upon the superscription, and so brought it to me. I assure you that my L^d of Buckingham does not governe affaires heere. I do not doute but my Ld Clarendon, and some of his frinds heere, will discreditt me and my affaires as much as they can, but I shall say no more upon that subject, for, if you knew how ill a servant he has been to me, you would not doute but he would be glad things should not

go on smouthly, now he is out of affaires, and most of the
vexation and trouble I have at present in my affaires I owe
to him. The Parlament have voted me three hundred
thousand pounds for the setting out of a fleete, and are now
finding out the meanes of raising it. You will heare great
complaints from La Roche, who was taken in the ship called
the *Ruby* last yeare, but Trevor will lett you know the truth,
and then you will see that I have reason to complaine. I will
add no more to this long letter, only againe thanke you for
your good councell, which I take very kindly from you, as
a marke of your concerne for me, but pray do not be
alarumed so soone by politique coxcombes, who thinke all
wisdome lies in finding faute, and be assured that I have all
the kindnesse and tendernesse for you imaginable.

" C. R."

The next few letters are chiefly taken up with the latest
Court gossip. The Duchess of Richmond's attack of smallpox, an event which had the effect of restoring her to the
King's good graces, the hopes of an heir to the Crown that
were once more entertained, the scandal caused by Lady
Shrewsbury's intrigues with Harry Killigrew and Buckingham,
and by the attack on her first lover as he left St James's, his
consequent flight abroad, and the Duke's famous duel with
her husband; these and similar topics, which were the common
talk of the day, fill the pages which run so glibly off the
King's pen. At the same time, he takes a lively interest in
what is passing at the French Court, in the controversy as to
whether a certain lady paints her face or not, in the sudden
flight of the Duchesse de Mazarin from Paris. This " famous
but errant beauty," as Evelyn calls her, was the same Hortense Mancini whose hand Charles himself had once sought
in marriage, and who was, before long, to come and take up
her permanent residence at his Court. Her quarrels with her
husband had long made her notorious, and a judicial separation was pending when, one night, she suddenly left her home,
and travelled to the frontier in the disguise of a man. When
she reached the gates of Paris, she discovered that her money
and jewels had been forgotten, upon which she returned, with

the utmost coolness, to fetch them before she continued her journey to Italy. This feat made the Merry Monarch remark that, in point of discretion, the Duchess had surpassed my Lady Shrewsbury! He goes on to observe that wives do not like devout husbands, a sarcasm which, as well as another phrase in his letter of the 14th of May, was evidently aimed at the pious Duc de Mazarin and the Marquis de Montespan, who had given way to a just burst of indignation on discovering his wife's intrigue with Louis XIV. All this is mingled with affectionate advice to Madame about her health, and the careful diet which she ought to observe, a precaution in which he seems to put more faith than in either Sir Theodore Mayerne's pills or the masses that were said daily by order of Queen Henrietta for her daughter's recovery.

"WHITHALL,

"10 *March* 1668.

"I am very sorry that your health obliges you to go to bourbon, but undoutedly 'tis the best course you can take to establish your health againe, which is that which you ought to thinke of in the first place. I am sure I am more concerned for it then for anything in this world, and if I had no other reason but gratitude, I ought to love more than I can expresse. My L^d of Buckingham is so affraide, that you should thinke that he is the cause that Killigrew does not return hither, since you have desired him to forgive what is past, as he has againe desired me to tell you, there is nothing of what relates to him in the case; as in truth there is not, but he has offended so many of the Ladyes relations in what concernes her, as it would not be convenient for him to shew his face heere. The truth is, both for his owne sake and oure quiett heere, it will be no inconvenience for him to have a little pacience in other countries. The parlament goes on very slowly in there mony, but they advance something every day. How ever I am prepareing my ships to goe to sea for the summer guarde; we expect Don John every day heere, in his way to Flanders. I hope his only businesse will be for the conclusion of the peace, which I wish may have a happy conclusion for many reasons. This bearer, Tom Howard, will lett you know of all things heere, so I shall not add any more, but to assure you that I am, with all imaginable kindnesse, Yours. C. R."

"WHITHALL,
"4 Aprill 1668.

"I send this expresse back againe, with the returne of what he brought from Trevor and Van Benninghen, the particulars of which he will acquainte you with, so as I will only add upon that matter, that I hope the peace will follow. I receaved yours of the sixth since the post went, so as I could not say anything to you then. I cannot tell whether the duchesse of Richmond will be much marked with the small pox, she has many, and I feare they will at least do her no good ; for her husband, he cannot alter from what he is, lett her be never so much changed ! But to turne my discourse to a matter which I am more concerned with than anything in this world, I see by your letter to James Hamilton that you are consulting your health with a Physisian, which I have a very ill opinion of in that affaire, which is your selfe. I must confesse I have not much better opinion of those you were governed by before, not beleeving they understand the disease you have so well as they do heere. I have therefore sent Doctor Fraser to you, who I will dispatch to-morrow, who is well-acquainted with the constitution of your body, and I beleeve is better verst in those kind of diseases, than any man in Paris, for those kinde of obstructions are much more heere than in France, and this is all I shall trouble you with at this time, but that I am intierly yours. C. R."

"WHITHALL,
"7th May 1668.

I have so often asked your pardon for omitting writing to you, as I am almost ashamed to do it now, the truth is, the last weeke I absolutely forgott it till it was to late, for I was at the Duchesse of Richmond's who, you know, I have not seene this twelve monthes, and shee put it out of my heade that it was post day. She is not much marked with the smale pox, and I must confesse this last affliction made me pardon all that is past, and cannot hinder myselfe from wishing her

very well, and I hope shee will not be much changed, as soone
as her eye is well, for she has a very great defluction in it, and
even some danger of haveing a blemish in it, but now I
beleeve the worst is past. I did receave your letter by Fitz
Gerald the same day that the physisians were doing the very
prescriptions you advise in your letter, but now that matter
is over, for my wife misscaried this morning, and though I am
troubled at it, yett I am glad that 'tis evident she was with
childe, which I will not deny to you; till now, I did feare she
was not capable of. The Physisians do intend to put her into
a course of physique, which they are confident will make her
holde faster next time. Ruvigny did tell me some dayes
since of that matter concerning my Ld Sandwich, which I
can say nothing to, till I heare from hence, only, if he has done
what you are informed of, I am sure he is inexcusable, and
shall answer for it severely when he comes home, for I never
did nor never will permitt my ambassadore to give the place
to any whatsoever. I am very glad you are so well pleased
with Trevor, for I have a very good opinion of him, not only
of his ability to serve me, but likewise of his inclination and
faithfulnesse to do it; he shall know the obligation he has to
you, and when 'tis a fitt season, the effects of it also. I will
not go about to decide the dispute betweene Mam's masses
or Mr de Mayerne's pills, but I am sure the suddenesse of
your recovery is as neere a miracle as anything can be, and
though you finde your selfe very well now, for God's sake
have a care of your diett, and beleeve the planer your diett is
the better health you will have. Above all, have a care of
strong brothes and gravy in the morning. I aske your
pardon for forgetting to deliver your message to James (the
Duke of Monmouth), but I have done it now; he shall answer
for him selfe, and I am sure he has no excuse, for I have
often put him in minde to acknowledge, upon all occasions,
the great obligations he has to you for your goodnesse to him,
which I assure you he expresses every day heere. If he does
faile in writting, I feare he takes a little after his father, and
so I will end this long trouble with the assureing you that I
cannot expresse the kindnesse and tendernesse I have for
you.   C. R."

" Trevor was very much in the right to assure you that I would not take it ill that you did that part of *charité* for my Ld Clarendon, for my displeasure does not follow him to that degree as to wish him any where but out of England. I see Monbrun does not change his humour; he allwayes tould every lady heere that his daughter was not painted, as was beleeved as much as he is in france; for her two other qualities, I can only say that if she be as truly his daughter as I am confident she was honest heere, he may be beleeved, for I am very confident no lady heere tooke the paines to aske her an indecent question. The truth is, James did maintaine for some time that she was not painted, but he was quickly laffed out of it. I am sorry to finde that cucolds in France grow so troublesome. They have been inconvenient in all countries this last yeare. I have been in great trouble for James his wife, her thigh being as we thought sett very well, for three dayes together. At last we found it was still out, so that the day before yesterday it was sett, with all the torture imaginable; she is now pretty well, and I hope will not be lame. I have been to sea, and am but newly returned, so as I have not time to add any more, but that I am entierly Yours.   C. R."

" You have, I hope, receaved full satisfaction by the last post in the matter of Marsillac, for my Ld Arlington has sent to Mr Montagu his history all the time he was heere, by which you will see how little creditt he had heere, and that particularly my Ld Arlington was not in his good graces, because he did not receave that satisfaction, in his negociation, he expected, and that was only in relation to the Swissers, and so I thinke I have sayd enough of this matter, and shall give you now a particular account of my wife with that plainenesse you desire . . . and if you desire any more of this kind, I will be instructed farther by the wemen, and send it to you. The accident which befell the Prince of Toscane, and the french

ambassadore heere made a great noise, but my Lady Shrews-
buryes businesse with Harry Killigrew has quite silenced the
other. My L^d chiefe Justice is inquireing after the matter,
and what the Law will do I cannot tell, but the Lady is retired out of her house, and not certainly knowne where she is.
And so, my dearest sister, good night, for 'tis late, and I have
nothing to add but that which I can never tell you too offten,
how truly and passionately I love my dearest Minette.

"C. R."

"WHITHALL,
"14 *June* 1668.

"The bearer and James Hamilton will tell you all that
passes heere. The suden retreate of Madame Mazarin is as
extraordinaire an action as I have heard. She has exceeded
my Lady Shrewsbury in point of discretion, by robbing her
husband! I see wives do not love devoute husbands, which
reason this woman had, besides many more, as I heare, to be
rid of her husband, upon any tearmes, and so I wish her a
good journey. I finde, by the letters from Trevor, that they
are allarumed in france, that I intende something against Den-
marke, with the fleete that I am now setting out. I do
assure you there never was any such intention, for I am now
sending most of the great ships into harbour, which are now
only a charge, the peace at Aix being concluded, and I shall
have this summer at sea only the ordinary summer guarde. I
shall say no more to you now, only desire you to have the
same goodnesse for James you had the last time, and to chide
him soundly when he does not that he should do. He
intendes to put on a perriwig againe, when he comes to Paris,
but I beleeve you will thinke him better farr, as I do, with his
short haire, and so I am intierly yours. C. R."

The Duke of Monmouth's first visit to Paris had been
interrupted by a sudden recall to England, owing to his wife's
accident. Now that she was restored to health he returned to
France towards the end of June, and was present at the *fêtes*
given at Versailles that summer. But Henrietta, mindful of
Monsieur's jealousy on the last occasion, had thought it well

to give her brother a warning to this effect before the Duke's departure. This is the "ridiculous fancy" to which Charles alludes in the next letter, in which he deplores, with good reason, the trifling causes that were allowed to make poor Madame's life miserable. The subject on which he desired his son to confer with her was evidently her wish to pay her brother a visit, "which, if it comes to pass, will be the greatest happiness to me imaginable." But this meeting, which both the brother and sister desired so ardently, was not to take place for more than two years.

" WHITHALL,
" 22 *June* 1668.

" I did not receave your letter by Church till yesterday, and am very sorry that the occasion of your iust trouble continues. Ruvigny was gone before I receaved your letter, so as I could not say anything to him ; therfore you must give me new directions what I am to do. I understand your letter of the 26, and by it perseave the ridiculous fancy that comes in to some people's head, but I cannot chuse but be troubled at it, when I consider what small occasions furnish matter to give you unquiett howers. I did order James to speake with you about one part of the commands you layd upon Trevor, which, if we can bring to passe, will be the greatest happynesse to me imaginable. I have had but little time yett to speake with Trevor, so, as for publique affaires, I deferr speaking of till I returne from sheerenesse, where I am going this afternoone, and shall not be heere againe till the end of the weeke, which is all I shall say at this time, only to assure you that I am, with all the kindnesse imaginable, Yours.

" C. R."

CHAPTER XX

1668

THE great *fête* of Versailles took place on the 18th of July It was nominally given by Louis XIV. to celebrate the conclusion of the Peace of Aix-la-Chapelle, but in reality to do honour to his new mistress, Madame de Montespan. Madame de Sevigné, who was among the three hundred ladies invited to the King's table, has described its splendour, and La Fontaine, in his fable of Psyche, has painted the wonders of the vast gardens, which on that day were thrown open to the public. Architects and landscape gardeners had been busily employed in extending the grounds, and new porticoes and grottoes, adorned with countless statues, had arisen in all directions. Visits were paid to the beautiful orangery, which La Fontaine calls a very garden of Hesperides, to the menagerie, with its rare birds from Asia and Africa, to the famous grotto of Thetis, the *chef d'œuvre* of the sculptor's art. There, on a colossal *bas-relief* cut in the rock, a golden sun, the King's favourite device, was seen setting in the waves of the sea, surrounded by Tritons and Sirens, that gushed with streams of water, while life-size statues of Apollo and the Muses adorned the sides of the grotto. This singular creation was destroyed by Louis XIV. before the end of his reign, in order to build a new wing on to the palace. But, at the time of this *fête*, it was one of the great sights of the place, and excited the admiration of all the visitors, including La Fontaine and his friends. The afternoon was spent in drives over the park, songs and dances under the trees beguiled the hours till nightfall. Then Molière's new play, *Georges Dandin*, was performed in the theatre, with musical interludes composed by Lulli, and, after a sumptuous banquet in the great gallery, a superb display of fireworks took place. While the King led the dancing within, the magical effect of illuminated fountains and gardens enchanted the crowds without. The Duke of Monmouth left Paris the next day for England, where Charles II. was eagerly awaiting his description of these brilliant scenes. On the 8th of July, O.S., he wrote to Madame.

"WHITHALL,
"8 *Jully* 1668.

"I cannot say much to you yett, in answer to the letters you have writt to me, concerning the good correspondence you desire there should be betweene the King of France and me. I am very glad to find, by your letters as well as Trevor's relations, the inclinations there is to meete with the constante desire I have allwayes had, to make a stricter alliance with France then there has hitherto been, and pray say all to the king you ought to say from me, in returne of the kindnesse he expresses towards me, and when M. de Colbert comes, I hope he will have those powers as will finish what we all desire, and be assured that whatsoever negociation there is betweene France and me, you shall alwayes have that part in it as they shall see the valew and kindnesse I have for you. One thing I desire you to take as much as you can out of the king of France' head, that my ministers are any thing but what I will have them, and that they have no parciallity but to my interest and the good of England.

"I shall not say any thing upon the letter you writt to me by Mon^r de Boisiolly, till I have a more sure way to write then by the post, only I cannot chuse but say that I am sorry there can be so much impertinence in the world, as I see upon that subject. We are heere in great expectation of the relation of the entertainment at Versailles, I hope James will be the first mesenger that will bring it, and so I am yours.

"C. R."

Colbert de Croissy was a brother of Louis XIV.'s minister, who had now been sent as ambassador to England. The letter in which Charles announces his arrival contains an interesting allusion to Madame's domestic troubles. After Monmouth's departure, Monsieur seems to have changed his conduct for the better, and to have become ashamed of his childish behaviour. But the true cause of all these dissensions, the Chevalier de Lorraine, still exerted his evil influence over Monsieur, and as long as he remained under her roof, Henrietta knew that she had no hope of peace or happiness in her home. Under the circumstances, Charles's advice was probably the best which could be given her. She determined to tolerate the Chevalier's presence for the moment as a necessary evil, but to take the first opportunity she could find of freeing herself from this insupportable personage.

> "WHITHALL,
>
> "3 *August* 1668.
>
> "I have received so many letters of yours by James and his company, as you will not expect a punctuall answer to all the particulars by this post, and besides, there are many thinges which I will expect to answer by a surer way then the post. I am very glad to finde by you, and what James sayes to me, the inclination and intention the king, my brother, has to enter into a stricter frindeship with me. I am sure I have all the inclinations towards it, that ether he or you can desire in that matter, and when Mon^r Colbert comes, he shall find nothing wanting on my part. I wish with all my hart, that the propositions which Ruvigny sent, long since when he was heere, had receaved that answer which I might reasonably have expected. They would have then seene, that whatsoever opinion my ministers had been of, I would and do alwayes follow my owne judgement, and if they take any other mesures then that, they will see themselves mistaken in the end. I will say no more to you now, but expect Mon^r Colbert, and I assure you the kindnesse I have for you will always make me do all I can to have a very good understanding with the country where you are, for there is nothing more at my hart then the letting you see, by all the wayes I can, how truly I love you. C. R."

" I take the occasion of this bearer to say some thinges to you, which I would not send by the post, and to tell you that I am very glad that Mon^r begins to be ashamed of his ridiculous fancyes; you ought undoutedly to over see what is past, so that, for the future, he will leave being of those fantasticall humours, and I thinke the lesse *éclairecissement* there is upon such kind of matters, the better for his frind the Chevalier. I thinke you have taken a very good resolution not to live so with him, but that, when there offers a good occasion, you may ease your selfe of such a rival, and by the carracter I have of him, there is hopes he will find out the occasion himselfe, which, for Mr's sake, I wish may be quickly. Mr Colbert is come, and I saw him in privat last night, we only discoursed in generall termes about what he comes, so as I can only tell you that I sayd those thinges concerning you as I beleeve he will acquaint his master with by to-morrow post, by which you will perceave the valew and kindnesse I have for you. I shall write to-morrow, to you, by the post, so I will add no more, but that upon all occasions, you may be most assured, that I will lett you see how truly I am Yours.   C. R."

" WHITHALL,
" 2*d Sep.* 1668.

" You judge very well, when you conclude that I am satisfied with Mon^r Colbert, and I wish with all my harte that france had been as forwarde in there intentions towards us when Ruvigny was heere, as I see they are now. I should not have been so embarrassed with the ties I am now under if the offers I then made had been accepted : my inclinations are still the same, and I hope in the end to bring all things to what I wish, but there are two impediments in the way, which at least do retarde the inclinations there is, on both sides, to have an intier union. The first is, the great applycation there is at this time in France to establish trade, and to be very considerable at sea, which is so jealous a point to us heere, who can be only considerable by our trade and power by sea, as any steps that France makes that way, must continue a jealousy betweene the two Nations, which will, upon all occasions, be a great hinderance to an intire frindship. And you cannot chuse but beleeve that it must be dangerous to me at home to make an intire league, till first the great and principale interest of this nation be secured, which is trade. The other difficulty is the treatyes I am entred into of late, which I am sure the King, my brother, would not have me violate upon any termes, since he has given me the good example of being a martire to his word. But when I have sayd this, I do beleeve we are not so tied, as if we receaved satisfaction ; on the principal matter of the sea, there is scope sufficient for a very neere alliance. I am sure, as my inclinations carryes me to it, so I will use all my endeavours to bring it to passe. I have had some discourses with Mr Colbert upon the subject of this letter, and have enlarged my selfe more fully to him than I can do in a letter, and now I must tell you that I am very well satisfied with him, and thinke him as proper an Ambassadore for this place as could have been chosen. I have, upon all occasions, lett him know the kindnesse I have for you, and that, if I had no other inclination to France but your being there, it would be a sufficient motive to make me desire passionatly a stricte union with them.

"I am going to-morrow to Bagshott to hunt the stag, and shall not be heere againe till saturday come sennight, intending likewise to take Portsmouth in my returne, to see the fortifications that have lately been made there, and what is farther to be done. The Comte de Chappelles will tell you of all the little newes heere, so as I shall not trouble you with it. I have been so civill to him as I could, both upon your recommendations and the kindnesse Monsieur has for him, and besides that, he hath a great deale of merritt of his owne, and I hope he is not ill satisfied with us heere. I hope you will not finde faute with the shortnesse of this letter, and if you are but as sleepy at the reading of it as I am at the writing, I am certaine you will thinke it long enough, and therefore, my dearest sister, I will only assure you that I am intierly Yours. C. R."

The negotiations now proceeded briskly. First of all, the Treaty of Commerce was to be drawn up, after which a Treaty of Alliance was to be concluded between the two Kings. Louis XIV. took care to pave the way by the promise of liberal gifts to Charles II.'s favourites, and when Buckingham's emissary, Sir Ellis Leighton, came to Paris with letters from the King, he bestowed a present worth 2000 pistoles upon him. Madame de Monaco, whose departure for her husband's principality is mentioned by Charles, was Madame's intimate friend, the Comte de Guiche's sister. This lady had long enjoyed Louis XIV.'s friendship, but recently she had been involved in an intrigue with Lauzun, which had aroused the King's jealousy, and made her think it wiser to retire from Court for a while.

" WHITHALL,
" 14 Sep. 1668.

" At my returne from Portsmouth, I found two of yours, one by the post, and the other by Mr Lambert, with the gloves, for which I thanke you extreamely. They are as good as is possible to smell, and in the other letter, you accuse me most justly for my failing towards you, which I do ingeniously confesse, as most people do, to their gostly father, and as offten fall into the same sinn againe. I hope I shall not be so fauty for the time to come, haveing now done stag hunting for this yeare, which now and then made me so weary, as with the naturall lazinesse I have towards writting, . gave me occasion to misse offtener than otherwise I would have done. The reason why I begin with the treaty of commerce is because I, must enter first upon those matters which will render the rest more plausible heere, for you know that the thing which is neerest the harte of the Nation is trade and all that belongs to it. But I shall not enter farther upon this matter now, because I have done it fully by de Chapelles, who will be with you before this time. And, you may be sure, that I will continue my care to lett them see the power you have over me, and how much my kindnesse to you adds to my inclination to live allwayes very well with France. I am very sorry that Mme de Monaco goes yett farther distance from England. Since she thinkes the *douceurs* I sent her in your letter not enough, if she comes with you into England, I hope to serve her at a neerer distance then I can do at Monaco. I do intend to go to Newmarkett the last day of this month, at which place, and at Audely End, I shall stay neere a month. My wife goes to the latter of these places at the same time, which is all I will trouble with at this time, but to assure you that 'tis impossible to have more kindnesse and tendernesse then I have for you. C. R."

"WHITHALL,
"3 *Oct.* 1668.

"I have received yours of the 7th from Vincenes but just this moment, as the post is goeing away, and therefore can say nothing to you now. The paper in your letter, referring to a treaty which I never saw, it being made when I was P. of Wales, and at a great distance from the King, my father, I shall imediatly looke out for that treaty, but for feare I shall not be able to finde a copy of it heere, it being made in a disorderly time, pray gett a copy of it, and send it imediatly hither, that so there may be no time lost. In the meane time, I shall only add, that I am very glad to see the King, my brother, so ready to make a good frindship with me, and pray assure him, that nothing can be more welcome to me than a strict frindship betweene us. I have no more time left me, only to assure you that I am intierly Yours.
"C. R."

"WHITHALL,
"17 *Oct.* 1668.

"I hope you will pardon the faute I am in towards you, in point of writing to you of late, when you consider the multitude of businesse is now upon my hands by the altera-tion I have made, and the Parlament now sitting, and though there anger may make them a little froward to particular persons, yett in the end I dout not but they will do what they ought to do towards me. For Harry Killigrew, you may see him as you please, and though I cannot commende my L^{dy} Shrewsbury's conduct in many things, yett Mr Killi-grew's carriage towards her has been worse then I will re-

S

peate, and for his *demelé* with my L^d of Buckingham, he ought not to brag of, for it was in all sorts most abominable. I am glad the poore wrech has gott a meanes of subsistance, but have one caution of him, that you beleeve not one word he sayes of us heere, for he is a most notorious lyar, and does not want witt to sett forth his storyes pleasantly enough. I am very glad that Monsieur is so well recovered. Pray make my compliments to him with all imaginable kindnesse. I shall write to you by the Duchesse of Richmond, with greater freedome then I am willing to do by the post, for feare of miscarrying, and so will say no more to you now, but the assuring you of the constant tendernesse and kindnesse I have for you.   C. R."

"WHITHALL,
"14 *Decem.* 1668.

" He that came last, and delivered me your letter of the 9th, has given me a full account of what he was charged with and I am very well pleased with what he tells me. I will answer the other letter he brought to me very quickly. I am sure it shall not be my faute if all be not as you can wish. I will send you a cypher by the first safe occasion, and you shall then know the way I thinke most proper to proceede in the whole matter, which I hope will not displease you. I will say no more by the post upon this businesse, for you know 'tis not very sure.

" I do intende to prorogue the Parlament till October next, before which time I shall have sett my affaires in that posture as there will not be so many miscarriages to be hunted after, as in the last sessions. I beg your pardon for forgetting, in my last, to thanke you for the petticote you sent me, 'tis the finest I ever saw, and thanke you a thousand times for it. I can say no more to you now, for I am calld to goe to the Play, and so I am intierly yours.

                              "C. R."

The King's next letter contains an allusion to an incident which had made a great noise at the French Court, and was by no means pleasing to Madame. A strange adventurer, the Chevalier de Rohan, who had already distinguished himself by helping Madame de Mazarin in her nocturnal flight, now came forward as the avenger of Madame's wrongs. He dared the Chevalier de Lorraine to fight, and struck him in the presence of witnesses, in order to compel him to accept his challenge. Henrietta, alarmed at the prospect of a duel on her account, appealed to Louis XIV., who sent the Duc de Noailles to reconcile the angry knights, and Louis de Rohan was forced to own himself in the wrong.

> "WHITHALL,
> "27 *Decem.* 1668.

"You must yett expect a day or two for an answer to what Leighton brought, because I send it by a safe way, and you know how much secrecy is necessary for the carrying on of the businesse, and I assure you that nobody does, nor shall, know anything of it heere, but my selfe and that one person more, till it be fitt to be publique, which will not be till all matters are agreed upon. In the meane time, I must tell you that I receaved yours of the 26th of this month, and the 2 of Jan : just now, and am very glad that the Chevalier de Rohan has that mortification put upon him, by your desire, for it will make others have a care of their behaviour towards you, and I do not wonder that the princesse de bade makes her selfe so well beloved, for she cannot chuse but be well natured, comming from such a mother as she does. I must confesse, I would rather have had you stayd some monthes before you had been with childe, for reasons you will know shortly, but I hope it will be for your advantage, and then I shall be glad of it. I shall say no more now, only wish you a good new yeare, which, if it proove as happy to you as I wish, you will have no reason to complayne.   C. R."

In this letter, Charles insists on the secrecy necessary to the success of his plans. Neither Colbert nor Montagu were to be admitted into what he calls "the great secret." Their share in the negotiations was strictly limited to the Commercial Treaty, which they were engaged in drawing up, with all the minute care and attention necessary for the preservation of mutual interests. Meanwhile, the correspondence respect-

ing the Secret Treaty was conducted entirely by Madame.
For some time Charles would not admit any of his own
ministers into his confidence, but by degrees, Arlington and
Buckingham were allowed a partial acquaintance with the
substance of the Treaty.   Of the French ministers, only
Lionne and Louvois were in the secret, while Turenne was
afterwards consulted on certain points on which his military
knowledge was required.   The articles of the Treaty, as
Charles very well knew, were not likely to meet with popular
approval in England, and the greatest caution would be
necessary in their execution.   In the first place, Charles was
to join the French King in the invasion of Holland, and co-
operate with his forces, both by sea and land, on condition
of receiving large yearly subsidies as long as the war lasted,
and an ultimate share in the spoils of the conquered provinces.

In the second place, the King of England agreed to make
a public confession of his conversion to the Roman Catholic
faith.   Louis XIV. promised to pay down a large sum of
money, and to give him further supplies of men and money,
in case his action should produce troubles among his subjects.
The question whether Charles himself was sincere in his
intention of abjuring Protestantism, has been much disputed.
There seems to be no doubt that his personal sympathies were
entirely in favour of the Roman Catholic faith.   It was the
religion professed by his mother and sister, the two persons
whom he loved best.   And he had long ago come to the
conclusion, as he told the French ambassador, that no other
creed agreed so well with the absolute authority and divine
right of kings.   The Duke of York had already privately
declared himself a Catholic, and, early in 1669, Charles
secretly acknowledged himself a member of the same Church,
in the presence of his brother, Lord Arundel and Sir Thomas
Clifford.   But no one was better aware of the difficulties which
lay in the way of any public declaration of his belief.   He
knew the fanatical feeling of his subjects against Popery, and
had no wish, as he expressed it, to be sent on his travels a
second time.   Accordingly, the policy which he pursued was
to defer his public profession of Catholicism for the present,
hoping, by this means, to gain time and money, without finally

committing himself to a step which might entail his ruin.
But, in order to discuss all these questions fully, a meeting
with his sister was desirable.   Henrietta herself had long
wished to pay a visit to England, and Charles was exceedingly disappointed to hear that her state of health would
delay her journey for the present.   As for Madame's share in
the negotiations, it is easy to understand the satisfaction
which she felt in effecting a closer union between the two
Kings, to whom she was so closely related.   The hope of
seeing the brother, whom she loved so dearly, embrace that
faith which she had been taught to regard as the only hope
of salvation, was, in her eyes, a still deeper cause of happiness.
It is impossible to blame her, as many writers have done, for
the eagerness which she showed in the pursuit of these ends.
We are, on the contrary, rather inclined to admire the talents,
the courage, and the unwearying perseverance with which
this Princess of five-and-twenty conducted these delicate and
important negotiations, without ever losing sight of the great
issues that were at stake.

CHAPTER XXI

1669

Secret Negotiations continued — The Abbé Pregnani sent to England — Madame corresponds with Buckingham and Arlington — Last Letters from Charles II. to his Sister.

AMONG all the envoys who were employed in these prolonged negotiations, and who went to and fro with letters from Charles II. and Madame during the course of the next year, none had a stranger part to play than the Italian astrologer, the Abbé Pregnani. This Theatine monk had already attracted great attention by telling fortunes in Paris, and had cast the Duke of Monmouth's horoscope, and that of the chief personages at Court, during the past summer. He was now sent to England with a double object. On the one hand, his presence afforded a safe channel of communication between the two Kings, while on the other, as Lionne explained to Colbert, his astrological forecasts were intended to impress the English Court with the advantage of the French alliance. Pregnani was accordingly introduced by Monmouth to the King at Newmarket, and proceeded to cast his horoscope. But Charles was of too shrewd and incredulous a nature to be taken in by arts of this kind. "Cattle of this sort," he tells his sister plainly, are little to his taste. The less you have to do with them the better. But he treated the would-be astrologer with his usual good-nature, and was much amused when certain predictions, which Pregnani had ventured to make as to the winning horses at Newmarket, proved false. On the 20th of January, Charles wrote the following letter, in answer to one which the Italian Abbé, whose name and capacity were not yet known to him, had brought from France.

278

"You will see, by the letter which I have written to the King, my brother, the desire I have to enter into a personall frindship with him, and to unite our interests so, for the future, as there may never be any jealousys betweene us. The only thing which can give any impediment to what we both desire is the matter of the Sea, which is so essenciall a point to us heere, as an union upon any other security can never be lasting, nor can I be answerable to my kingdomes, if I should enter into an alliance, wherein there present and future security were not fully provided for. I am now thinkeing of the way how to proceede in this whole matter, which must be caried on with all secrecy imaginable, till the particulars are farther agreed upon. I must confesse, I was not very glad to heare you were with childe, because I had a thought by your making a journey hither, all things might have been adjusted, without any suspicion, and as I shall be very just to the King, my brother, in never mentioning what has past betweene us, in case this negociation does not succeede as I desire so I expect the same justice and generosity from him, that no advances which I make out of the desire I have to obtaine a true frindship between us, may ever turne to my prejudice. I send you, heere inclosed, my letter to the King, my brother, desireing that this matter might passe through your handes, as the person in the world I have most confidence in, and I am very glad to finde that Mon^r de Turene is so much your frinde, who I esteeme very much, and assure my selfe will be very usefull in this negociation. I had written thus farr, when I receaved yours by the Italian, whose name and capacity you do not know, and he delivred your letter to me, in a passage, where it was so darke, as I do not know his face againe if I see him; so as the man is likely to succeede, when his recommendation and reception are so sutable to one another! But to returne to the businesse of the letter, I assure you that there is no league entered into as yett with the Empereur. The only league I am in, is the garanty I am engaged in with the Hollanders upon the peace at Aix, which is equally bindeing towards both the Crownes. I thinke Mr de Lorraine deserves to be punished for his unquiett humour, but I wish the King, my brother, do not proceede too farr in that matter, least he gives a jealousy to his neighbours, that he intends a farther progresse than what he declared at first, which might be very prejudiciall to what you and I wish and endeavour to compasse. And you shall not want, upon all occasions, full informations necessary, but we must have a great care what we write by the post, least it fall into hands which may hinder our design, for I must againe conjure you, that the whole matter be an absolut secrett, other wise we shall never compasse the end we aime at. I have not yett absolutely contrived how to proceede in this businesse, because there must be all possible precautions used, that it may not *éclater*, before all things be agreed upon, and pray do you thinke of all the wayes you can to the same end, and communicate them to me. I send you heere a cypher, which is very easy and secure, the first side is the single cypher, and within such names I could thinke of necessary to our purpose. I have no more to add, but that I am entierly Yours.   C. R."

Louis XIV.'s intended expedition against the Duke of Lorraine, to which Charles here alludes as already exciting the alarm of the other European powers, was deferred for the present, and the conquest of that principality did not take place until two years later.

On the 12th of February, Madame addressed a long letter to Sir Ellis Leighton, which was intended to soothe Buckingham's offended pride, and assure him of the French King's good-will, and confidence in his assistance in these negotiations. The Duke had got wind of the large share which Madame had in the business, from his sister, Lady Mary Villiers, who, as maid-of-honour to the Queen-mother, was aware of the frequent conferences that were held at Colombes between Louis XIV. and his sister-in-law. His indignation was great at the moment, and he declared loudly that he had been duped by Charles and his sister ; but the costly presents which were offered him by the French ambassador, and a few judicious compliments from Madame, soon allayed his childish vanity.

"I have shown your letter," wrote Henrietta, "to the King, who assures me that, even before seeing it, he was convinced of the Duke's good intentions, zeal and activity on his behalf. He is equally aware that all Crofts's advances, on behalf of Lord Arlington, must be regarded with suspicion, since the man's attachment to the Dutch and his inclination towards Spain are too well known, and the King is convinced that he can only rely on the Duke's help in the matter. So certain is he on this point, that he has told me he would give up the whole thing if the Duke were to change his feelings. He will send his Ambassador word, next Wednesday, to act on these principles, and not to put any trust in the proposals and promises that are made to him from this quarter, but to abandon himself entirely to the Duke's judgment, and never mistrust his good-will, even if he does not mention the subject for weeks. I forgot to tell you, that you need not fear lest the Ambassador should entertain jealousy of Ruvigny, or of any one else, for that he wishes the Duke to have the sole glory of success, and will never put any trust in Arlington's proposals. The sooner you can induce the King, my brother, to be open with the Ambassador, the better it will be, as regards the Duke's wish to engage all parties so far in the affair that there can be no withdrawal. Or, if he prefers it, he might send you back here, or anyone else whom he may choose, since the King begs me to let him know, that all who come from him, about this business, will be welcome."

This proof of confidence naturally flattered Buckingham, who wrote again on the 17th, in answer to another note which she had sent him, saying that he had obeyed her orders, and seen Colbert, but had not dared to discuss the subject with him, without his master's leave.

"I have burnt your note," he adds, "and beg you to believe, that the strongest desire I have in this world is to obey you. For the love of God, do not be impatient, and consider that in a place where measures must be taken to gain the goodwill of the people, one cannot act with so much dispatch as might be wished."

But the confidence which Charles II. and Madame placed in Buckingham was less absolute than he supposed. The

King urged the need of caution, with regard to the Duke, repeatedly on his sister, and never allowed him to hear a word of the religious question, which formed so important an article of the treaty. The Duke of York, having lately informed the King of his own change of religion, was now admitted into the secret, as well as another Roman Catholic peer, Lord Arundel, who was now sent to Paris with Sir Richard Bellings. Charles now adopted a cipher in his correspondence with his sister, but a key, which has been preserved in the French Archives, explains the meaning of most of the numbers which he employs. The interpretation, however, is not always easy, and, if the key is correct, different figures often stand for the same word.

On the 7th of March he wrote again, on the eve of going to Newmarket :—

" WHITHALL,
" 7 <i>March</i> 1669.

" I am to go, to-morrow morning, to Newmarkett, at three a clocke, and kept this expresse till now, to know what the King, my brother, would do with Douglas his regiment, which I perceave, by yours that I receaved this day, does not go to Candie, which I take as a great marke of the King, my brother's, kindnesse to me, and pray lett him know so much from me, and assure him that it was not anything for Douglas his sake, that I desired so earnestly his stay, but for reasons which he shall know within very few dayes. I have dispatched this night the Earl of St. Albans to Lord Arundel, who is fully instructed as you can wish. You will see by him, the reason why I desired you to write to nobody heere, of the businesse of France, but to my selfe ; he has some private businesse of his owne to dispatch before he leaves this towne, but he will certaynely sett out this weeke. But pray take no notice of his haveing any commission from me, for he pretends to go only upon his owne score, to attend the queene. You need not feare anything concerning Hamilton, for there is nobody as like to burne there fingers but those who medle in businesse, and he does not come in that trap. But I see you are misse informed if you thinke I trust my L^d of Ormond lesse

than I did. There are other considerations which makes me
send my Ld Robarts into Ireland, which are too long for a
letter. I am not sorry that Sr Will: Coventry has given me
this good occasion, by sending my L^d of Buckingham a
chalenge, to turne him out of the Councill. I do intend
to turn him allso out of the Tresury. The truth of it is,
he has been a troublesome man in both places, and I am
well rid of him. You may be sure that I will keepe the secrett
of your profett. I give little creditt to such kinde of cattle,
and the lesse you do it the better, for if they could tell anything 'tis inconvenient to know one's fortune before hand,
whether good or bad, and so, my dearest sister, good-night,
for 'tis late, and I have not above three howers to sleepe this
night.   C. R.

"I had almost forgott to tell you, that I find your frind,
l'Abbé Pregnany, a man very ingenious in all things I have
talked with him upon, and I find him to have a great deale of
witt, but you may be sure I will enter no farther with him
than according to your carracter."

Charles probably means that he has no intention to trust
the Italian with any secrets of state, and will only have deal-
ings with him in that capacity of astrologer, in which he was
best known to Madame. The King's next two letters, written
from Newmarket on the 12th and 22d of March, give an
amusing account of the Abbé's experiences there.

"I have had very good sport heere since Monday last, both
by hunting and horse-races. L'Abbé Pregnany is heere, and
wonders very much at the pleasure everybody takes at the
races, he was so weary with riding from Audly End hither, to
see the foot-match, as he is scarce recovered yett. I have been
a fox hunting this day and am very weary, yett the wether is
so good, as my brother has perswaded me to see his fox-
hounds runn to-morrow, and at night I am to lye at Saxum,
(Lord Croft's), where I shall stay Sunday, and so come hither
gaine, and not returne to London, till the latter end of next
weeke. This bearer, my Ld Rochester, has a minde to
make a little journy to Paris, and would not kiss your hands
without a letter from me; pray use him as one I have a very

good opinion of ; you will find him not to want witt, and did behave him selfe, in all the duch warr, as well as any body, as a volunteer. I have no more to add, but that I am intierly yours. C. R."

"I came from Newmarkett, the day before yesterday, where we had as fine wether as we could wish, which added much both to the horse matches, as well as to hunting. L'abbé Pregnani was there most part of the time, and I believe will give you some account of it, but not that he lost his money upon confidence that the Starrs could tell which horse would winn, for he had the ill luck to foretell three times wrong together, and James beleeved him so much, as he lost his mony upon the same score. I had nqt my cypher at Newmarkett, when I receaved yours of the 16th, so as I could say nothing to you in answer to it till now, and before this comes to your hands, you will cleerly see upon what score 363 (the Duke of York) is come into the businesse, and for what reason I desired you not to write to anybody upon the businesse of 271 (France), 341 (Buckingham) knows nothing of 360's (Charles II.), intentions towards 290, 315 (the Catholic religion), nor of the person 334 (Charles II.) sends to 100 (the King of France), and you need not feare that he will take it ill that 103 (Lord Arundel) does not write to him, for I have tould him that I have forbid 129 (Arundel) to do it, for feare of intercepting of letters, nor indeed is there much use of our writing much upon this subject, because letters may miscarry, and you are, before his time, so fully acquainted with all, as there is nothing more to be added, till my messenger comes back. You have councilled Monsieur very well in the matter of Mr de Rohan, I never heard of a more impertinent carriage then his. I had not time to write to you by father Paterique, for he tooke the resolution of going to France but the night before I left this place, but now I desire you to be kinde to the poore man, for he is an honest a man as lives, and pray direct your phisisian to have a care of him, for I should really be troubled if he should not do well. What you sent by Mercer is lost, for there are letters come, that informes of his setting saile from havre, in an open *challoupe*, with intention to come to portsmouth, and we have never heard of him since, so he is undoutedly drownd. I heare Mam sent me a present by him, which, I beleeve, brought him the ill lucke, so as she ought, in conscience, to be at the charges of praying for his soule, for 'tis her fortune has made the man miscarry! and so, my dearest sister, I am yours, with all the kindnesse and tendernesse imaginable. C. R."

"WHITHALL,
"25 *Aprill* 1669.

"I find by 405 (Arlington) that he does beleeve there is some businesse with 271 (France), which he knowes nothing of; he tould 341 (Buckingham) that I had forbidden you to write to him, by which he beleeved there was some mistery in the matter, but Buckingham was not at all alarumed at it, because it was by his owne desire that I writt that to you, but how 371 (Arlington) comes to know that, I cannot tell: It will be good that you write some times to 393 (Leighton) in generall termes, that he may not suspect that there is farther negociations then what he knowes of, but pray have a care you do not say any thing to him, which may make him thinke that I have imployed any body to 152 (the King) which he is to know nothing of, because by the messenger he may suspect that there is something of 290, 315 (the Catholic religion's) interest in the case, which is a matter he must not be acquainted with. Therfore you must have a great care, not to say the least thing that may make him suspect any-thing of it. I had writt thus farr before I had heard of your fall, which puts me in great paine for you, and shall not be out of it, till I know that you have receaved no prejudice by it. I go to-morrow to Newmarkett for 6 dayes, and shall be, in the meanetime, very impatient to heare from you, for I can be at no rest when you are not well, and so, my dearest sister, have a care of your selfe, as you have any kindnesse for me.
"C. R."

The premature confinement, which had nearly cost Henrietta her life, two years before, had rendered the utmost caution necessary, now that she was again expecting the birth of a child. She had been well enough to take part in the Carnival *fêtes*, and had figured, for the last time in her life, in a royal ballet, as Flora, the goddess of Spring. Crowned with roses, and clad in a white robe, wreathed with flowers, she had received the homage of the four quarters of the globe. These, led by Louis XIV. as Europe, had all in turn saluted her as their Queen. But after that, she had been obliged to resign herself to a quiet life, and often spent whole days in bed. The fall, however, which Charles mentions, produced no evil consequences, and on the 10th of May, Monsieur, writing from Saint-Germain, where the Court spent the summer, was able to give a good account of his wife's health.

"There is so little news at this moment, that I have only trifles hardly worth mentioning to tell you. What people talk of mostly here, and what we are told has made a great noise in England, through the report of the Spanish Ambassador, is the camp at Maisons, two leagues from here. The King has assembled 6000 men, merely for his own amusement, and by no means to besiege Cambray, as we hear they are saying in Flanders. The number of men would be too small for so strong a place, and I can assure you that no one dreams of such a thing. What other news we have here, chiefly concerns ladies and excursions of pleasure. The best thing I have to tell you, is that your sister is very well, considering her condition, and that she has not suffered from her fall. For such a dull letter this one is long enough! I beg your pardon for troubling you, and hope you will believe no one could be more truly yours than I am."

Madame seems to have devoted this enforced leisure, which was so distasteful to her natural vivacity, almost entirely to her English correspondence. She wrote two or three times a week to her brother, and at intervals addressed letters to his ministers, Buckingham and Arlington. In his next letters, Charles insists again on the need of secrecy, and altogether refuses to admit the French Ambassador, Colbert, to the knowledge of what he calls "the main business." He also tries to remove his sister's distrust of Arlington, who, although in the first place averse to an alliance with France, had now adopted the King's views and was, by degrees, to be admitted to a larger share of his confidence.

On the 6th of May, the King writes :—

" WHITHALL,

" 6 *May* 1669.

" You cannot imagine what a noise Lord St. Albans' comming has made heere, as if he had great propositions from 152 (the King of France), which I beate down as much as I can. It being preiudiciall, at this time, to have it thought that 360 (Charles II.) had any other commerce with 126 (Louis XIV.) but that of 280 (the Treaty of Commerce), and in order to that, I have directed some of the councill to meat with 112 (Colbert), which in time will bring on the whole matter, as we can wish, and pray lett there be great caution used on the side of 271 (France) concerning 386 (Charles II.'s) intentions towards 126 (Louis XIV.) which would not only be preiudiciall to the carrying on of the matters with 270 (Holland), but also to our farther designes abroade, and this opinion I am sure you must be of, if you consider well the whole matter. I beleeve Mr Montagu has, before this, in some degree satisfied you concerning my Ld Arlington, and done him that justice to assure you that nobody is more your servant than he, for he cannot be so intierly myne as he is, and be wanting to you in the least degree, and I will be answerable for him in what he owes you. I finde the poore Abbé Pregnany very much troubled, for feare that the railleries about fore-telling the horse matches may have done him some prejudice with you, which I hope it has not done, for he was only trying new trickes, which he had read of in bookes, and gave as little creditt to them as we did. Pray continue to be his frind so much as to hinder all you can any prejudice that may come to him upon that score, for the man has witt enough, and is as much your servant as is possible, which makes me love him. My wife has been a little indisposed some few dayes, and there is hopes that it will prove a disease not displeasing to me. I should not have been so forward in saying thus much without more certainty, but that I beleeve

others will write it to Paris, and say more than there is, and
so I shall end with assureing you that 'tis impossible to be
more yours than I am.   C. R."

A month later, Charles wrote another long letter, expressing his cordial dislike to the Dutch, and his readiness to join
in any enterprise against them.   He further describes his
preparations for fortifying the ports, and making sure of the
fleet, and speaks of satisfying the claims of these holders of
Church lands, in a way which looks as if he were seriously
contemplating the establishment of the Roman Catholic religion in England.

" WHITHALL,

" 6 June 1669.

" The oportunity of this bearers going into France gives
me a good occasion to answer your letters by my L⁴ Arlington,
and in the first place to tell you that I am secureing all the
principall portes of this countery, not only by fortifying them
as they ought to be, but likewise the keeping them in such
handes as I am sure will be faithfull to me upon all occasions,
and this will secure the fleete, because the chiefe places where
the ships lye are chattam and portsmouth.   The first of
which is fortifying with all speede, and will be finished this
yeare, the other is in good condition already, but not so good
as I desire, for it will coste some mony and time to make
the place as I have designed it, and I will not have lesse care
both in Scotland and Ireland.   As for that which concernes
those who have church lands, there will be easy wayes found
out to secure them, and put them out of all aprehension.
There is all the reason in the worlde to joyne profitt with
honour, when it may be done honestly, and the King will
finde me as forward to do 299 (Holland) a good turne as he
can desire, and we shall, I dout not, agree very well in the
point, for that country has used us both very scurvily, and I
am sure we shall never be satisfied till we have had our
revenge, and I am very willing to enter into an agreement
upon that matter whensoever the King pleases.   I will
answer for 346 (Arlington) that he will be as forward in

that matter as I am, and farther assurance you cannot expect
from an honest man in his post, nor ought you to trust him,
if he should make any other professions then to be for what
his master is for. I say this to you, because I undertooke
to answer that part of the letter you writt to him upon this
subject, and I hope this will be full satisfaction as to him in
the future, that there may be no doute, since I do answer
for him: I had writt thus farr when I receaved yours by
Ellwies, by which I perceave the inclination there still is of
trusting 112 (Colbert) with the maine business, which I must
confess, for many reasons, I am very unwilling to, and if
there were no other reason than his understanding, which, to
tell you the truth, I have not so great an esteeme for, as to
be willing to trust him with that which is of so much concerne. There will be a time when both he and 342 (Montagu)
may have a share in part of the matter, but for the great
secrett, if it be not kept so till all things be ready to begin,
we shall never go through with it, and destroy the whole
businesse. I have seen your letter to 341 (Buckingham) and
what you write to him is as it ought to be. He shall be
brought into all the businesse before he can suspect anything,
except that which concernes 263 (Charles II.), which he must
not be trusted with. You will do well to writ but seldome
to him, for feare something may slip from your penn which
may make him jealous that there is something more then
what he knows of. I do long to heare from 340 (Arundel)
or to see him heere, for till I see the paper you mention
which comes from 113 (Lionne) I cannot say more then I
have done. And now I shall only add one word of this
bearer, Monsr de la hilière, who I have founde by my
acquaintance with him since his being heere, to have both
witt and judgement, and a very honest man, and pray lett
him know that I am very much his frind, and if att any time
you can give him a good word to the King of France, I shall
be very glad of it. I will end this with desireing you to
beleeve that I have nothing so much at my harte as to be
able to acknowledge the kindnesse you have for me. If I
thought that making many compliments upon that matter
would persuade you more of the sincerity of my kindnesse

T

to you, you should not want whole sheetes of paper with nothing but that, but I hope you have the iustice to beleeve me, more then I can expresse, intierly Yours.   C. R."

Lord Arlington, to whose correspondence with Madame the King here alludes, himself wrote her a long letter about this time, defending his conduct proudly, and showing how much he resented the imputations which had been cast upon his loyalty.

"If Your Royal Highness complains of the general terms in which my letter is written, I have, with submission, much more reason to complain of the particular terms of yours ; and assuredly your correspondents in this Court must have given a false description of me to your Royal Highness, otherwise you would never have thought of treating me in this way. I have been all my life a good servant of the King, my master, and such I will die, by the grace of God, and I would not, for all the wealth of the world, act any other part than that of a good Englishman. Moreover, the King will bear me witness, that in two or three remarkable conjunctures I have pleaded the part of France more earnestly than any of his ministers, but it was when I thought its friendship would be the most useful to him. I have done the same, in other cases, for Spain and Holland, when the same reason seemed to necessitate it, but always (thank God!) without expecting or receiving any benefit for myself. You now see, Madame, my temper, and if such a man can be agreeable to Your Royal Highness, I entreat you most humbly to accept me as your most humble and most obedient servant, who honours you with profound veneration, as being the beloved sister of my master, and also, as I firmly believe, the most accomplished Princess in the world. I might add to this my interest in serving Your Royal Highness well, knowing how much the King loves you, and how he prizes your affection. I conclude by reminding Your Royal Highness that His Majesty has been so good as to answer for me, and that thus all other cautions would be no only superfluous, but derogatory to the royal warrant which you have already received for me.   ARLINGTON."

On the 7th of June, Charles writes again, once more impressing the greatest possible secrecy on his sister, and repeating his old arguments against admitting the French Ambassador or any one else into the secret.

"I writt to you yesterday by Mr de La hilière upon that important point, whether 112 (Colbert de Croissy) ought to be acquainted with our secrett, and the more I thinke of it, the more I am perplexed, reflecting upon his insufficiency, I cannot thinke him fitt for it, and therefore could wish some other fitter man in his station, but because the attempting of that might disoblige 137 (Colbert, the French minister), I can by no meanes advise it; upon the whole matter I see no kinde of necessity of telling 112 (Colbert de Croissy) of the secrett now, nor indeede till 270 (Charles II.) is in a better redinesse to make use of 297 (France) towards the great businesse. Methinkes, it will be enough that 164 (Colbert de Croissy) be made acquainted with 360 (Charles II.'s) security in 100 (the King of France's) frindship, without knowing the reason of it. To conclude, remember how much the secrett in this matter importes, and take care that no new body be acquainted with it, till I see what 340 (Arundel) brings 334 (Charles II.) in answer to his propositions, and till you have my consent that 164 (Colbert de Croissy), or anybody else, have there share in that matter. I would faine know (which I cannot do but by 366) (Arundel) how ready 323 (France) is to breake with 299 (Holland). That is the game that would, as I conceive, most accomodate the interests both of 270 (England) and 207 (France). As for 324 (Spain), he is sufficiently undoing himselfe to neede any helpe from 271 (France), nay, I am perswaded the medling with him would unite and make his councells stronger; the sooner you dispatch 340 (Arundel), the more cleerly we shall be able to judge of the whole matter. One caution more, I had like to have forgotten, that when it shall be fitt to acquainte 138 (Colbert de Croissy) with 386 (Charles II.'s) security in 152 (the King's) frindship, he must not say any thing of it in 270 (England), and pray lett the ministers in 297 (France) speake lesse confidently of our frindship then I heare they do, for it

will infinitely discompose 269 (Parliament) when they meete
with 334 (Charles II.) to beleeve that 386 (Charles II.) is tied
so fast with 271 (France), and make 321 (Parliament) have a
thousand jealousies upon it. I have no more to add, but to
tell you that my wife, after all our hopes, has miscarried
againe, without any visible accident. The physicians are
divided whether it were a false conception or a good one, and
so good night, for 'tis very late. I am intierly yours.

"C. R."

On the 24th of June we have another letter, in which the
King expresses his impatience for Lord Arundel's return, and
promises to write more fully to Abbé Pregnani, who was
setting out the next day, not without a somewhat diminished
reputation for soothsaying.

" WHITHALL,
" 24 <i>June</i> 1669.</div>

" It will be very difficulte for me to say anything to you
upon the propositions till 340 (Arundel) returne hither, and if
he makes many objections, which it may be are not alltogether
reasonable, you must not wonder at it, for, as he is not a man
much versed in affaires of state, so there are many scruples he
may have, which will not be so heere, and I am confident,
when we have heard the reasons of all sides we shall not differ
in the maine, haveing the same interest and inclinations. And
for 372 (Arlington) I can say no more for him than I have
already done, only that I thinke, being upon the place, and
observing every body as well as I can, I am the best judge of
his fidelity to me, and what his inclinations are, and, if I
should be deceived in the opinion I have of them, I am sure I
should smarte for it most. I shall write to you to-morrow by
l'Abbé Prégnany, so I shall add no more now, and, in truth, I
am just now going to a new play that I heare very much com-
mended, and so I am Yours.   C. R."

So, in a strain singularly characteristic of the writer's
mingled levity and seriousness, the correspondence comes to
an end. For neither the letter which "the poore Abbé" is to
bring, nor yet any other addressed by the King to his sister,

remains in the French Archives. The correspondence, which was no doubt carried on more actively than ever, during the course of the next twelve months, here breaks off abruptly, just when it promised to become most interesting. We look, not without a sense of regret, at the fourth page of the worn brown paper, where the accustomed words, " For my Dearest Sister," meet our eye, and close the pages with strangely mixed feelings. Many are the curious glimpses of the King, which they have given us from time to time, many the scraps of precious information they supply as to the men and manners of the day. But it is, above all, as a true and vivid record of the deep and enduring affection which he had for Henrietta, that we now value them. They remain a living witness of the faithful love which survived all shocks and separations, and bound this royal brother and sister together unto the end. And no one can read them without thinking of Charles II. more kindly than before.

CHAPTER XXII

Birth of Madame's younger Daughter—Death of Queen Henrietta Maria—Bossuet's
Funeral Oration—Madame de La Fayette's *Vie de Madame Henriette*—
Arrest of Cosnac, and Dismissal of Madame de Saint-Chaumont.

EARLY in June, Madame retired to Saint-Cloud, and spent the rest of the summer there. Monsieur went to and fro from Saint-Germain, where the Court remained until the birth of the Queen's second son, the little Duke of Anjou, on the 2d of August. Henrietta's solitude was brightened by frequent visits from her mother, whose own health was failing fast, and became a cause of great anxiety to her daughter, as the spring deepened into summer.

On the 23d of August, the Queen-mother paid a last visit to Saint-Cloud. Four days later, Madame gave birth to a daughter, much to her own disappointment and that of Monsieur, who expressed his regret in the following note to his friend, Madame de Sablé :—

" Were it possible, Madame, that you should have had so bad an opinion of me as to think I had forgotten you, this would indeed be an additional grief to me in my present disappointment, and I may say, without any flattery, that I should be more sorry to lose your friendship, than I am at having only a daughter, when I had hoped to have sons, and have not one."

Montagu announced the news to his royal master in the following note, dated August 28 :—" Madame has put a stop for this time to my Lord Crofts his journey, by being brought to bed of a daughter last night at twelve o'clock. I saw her to-day. She is very well."

Before Madame had recovered her strength, she received the sad news of her mother's sudden death. This took place on the 10th of September, at Colombes. Henrietta Maria had been too suffering during the last week to visit her daughter, but, at Madame's earnest request, she allowed the King's doctor, Vallot, and M. Esprit and M. Yvelin, first physicians to Monsieur and Madame, to hold a consultation with her own doctor, as to her state of health. The result of this consultation was that Vallot recommended the Queen to take a grain of opium, in order to allay the continual cough and pains in the side that disturbed her rest. According to Father Cyprian's account, Henrietta Maria at first objected to this, saying that her old doctor, Mayerne, had always warned her against taking any narcotic. "Besides," she said, with a smile to her ladies, "an astrologer told me, years ago, a grain would be the cause of my death, and I fear that M. Vallot's prescription may be that fatal grain." Her objections, however, were over-ruled. She took the opium pills when she retired to rest on the night of the 9th, and in the morning was found in a dying condition. Father Cyprian hastened to administer the last sacraments, but the Queen never recovered consciousness, and passed quietly away. "She could not sleep," observes Mademoiselle, in her caustic style, "so the doctors gave her a pill to send her to sleep, which it did so effectually that she never woke again."

The account of Henrietta Maria's death, given by Lord St. Albans, differs considerably, it must be owned, from that of Père de Gamaches, and is probably the more accurate version. The following letter, in which this faithful servant announced the death of his mistress to Charles II., was written from Colombes, early in the morning of the 10th of September, a few hours after the Queen had breathed her last :—

"If that whiche hath happened here could, or ought to be, concealed from you, my hand would not be the first in giving you notice of it. It hath pleased God to take from us this morning, about three o'clock, the Queene, your mother, and, notwithstanding her long sicknesse, as unexpectedly and with as muche surprise as if she had never been sicke at all. On Saturday last she had a consultation of physicians—M. Vallot, M. Duquesne, M. Esprit, and M. Yvelin. The resul

of the consultation was to give her, towards night, in order to
the quieting of the humoures in her body, from whence they
consider the great disorder came, with some rest, a grayne of
laudanum.   About 10 o'clock, she was in too much sweate to
venture the grayne of laudanum, and the resolution was taken
not to give it.   She caused, thereupon, her curtaines to be
drawne, and sent us all away, just as she used to doe for
severall nights before, fearing herself noe more than she had
donne, nor, indeed, inspiring in any of us the least imagination of that which immediately followed.   Not being able to
sleep of herself, she called to her doctor, Monsieur Duquesne,
for the grayne, and he, contrary to his former resolution, and,
he sayeth, to his opinion when he did it, suffered himself to
be over-ruled by the Queen, and gave it her in the yolk of an
egge.   She fell presently asleep ; he, sitting by her, perceiving
her to sleep too profoundly, and her pulse to alter, endeavoured, by all the meanes he could, to wake her and bring her
to herself, but could effect neither by all the generall remedies
used in such cases.   She lasted thus till betweene 3 and 4
o'clock, and then died.   That which doth further concearn
this matter, I shall give my Lord Arlington an account of.
God of Heaven give you all necessary resolution in it.

"ST. ALBANS."

A messenger took the news post haste to Monsieur at
Saint-Germain, and, after paying a hurried visit to Colombes
at six in the morning, he returned to Saint-Cloud, and broke
the sad tidings to his wife.   Madame's grief was excessive,
and there was a wide-spread feeling of indignation against
Vallot, whose advice was supposed to have hastened, if it had
not been the actual cause of, the Queen's death.   Gui Patin,
as might be expected, is eloquent on the occasion, and cannot
find words strong enough to express his contempt for the
Court doctors and their little grains!   "Quacks like these,
who pretend to be wiser than others, often become poisoners.
God in His mercy preserve us from them all !" he exclaims,
and, after this pious ejaculation, he goes on to quote an
epigram which had just been composed on the poor Queen's
death :—

> " La croirez-vous, race future,
> Que la fille du grand Henri,
> Eût en mourant même aventure,
> Que feu son père et son mari.
> Tous trois sont morts par assassin,
> Ravaillac, Cromwell et médécin.
> Henri d'un coup de bayonnette,
> Charles périt sur un billot,
> Et maintenant meurt Henriette,
> Par l'ignorance de Vallot."

On the day after her death, the heart of the Queen was borne in solemn procession to the convent of Chaillot, where she had always hoped to end her days, and delivered by Abbé Montagu to the keeping of the Abbess and her nuns. Two days afterwards her corpse was buried at Saint-Denis with royal honours, Mademoiselle appearing as chief mourner, followed by all the princes and princesses of the blood.

Hardly had his mother-in-law breathed her last, than Monsieur hastened to lay claim to her possessions in his wife's name, as the only one of her children residing in France. Madame refused to take any part in his action, and declared her readiness to await the intimation of her brother's pleasure. Commissioners were sent over from England to take formal possession of the late Queen's effects in Charles II.'s name, and a curious inventory, drawn up by Sir Thomas Bond and Dr. Jenkins, is preserved among the French correspondence at the Record Office. The jewels and pictures, including many valuable paintings by Titian, Holbein, Correggio, Vandyke, and Guido, which had belonged to Charles I., were eventually removed to England, but most of the furniture, and those pictures that were fixed in the walls, were allowed to remain at Colombes for Madame's use. A note is added, saying, "What Madame cares not to have is to be distributed among the Queen's women, at the discretion of the Lord Commissioners." And one picture, a " Noli me Tangere " by Guido, over the mantelpiece of the Queen's room, is "to be taken away unknown to Madame." The house and lands at Colombes were formally handed over to Madame, by the English Ambassador in his master's name, for her sole use and benefit, as His Majesty's free gift. At the same time,

Montagu presented her with a set of pearls, which she had been in the habit of wearing in her mother's lifetime, and which was said to be of priceless value, "the pearls being all of the best and finest." The furniture of Henrietta Maria's rooms in the convent at Chaillot was given by Charles II. to the Abbess and nuns of that community. Abbé Montagu, the Queen's Grand Almoner, was appointed to the same office in Monsieur's household, and poor old Father Cyprian became Almoner to Madame. He lived to survive the *petite princesse*, who had been the darling of her mother's heart, and only died in 1679, more than eight years after Henrietta's own tragic end. At the time of the Queen's death, one of her English grandchildren, the Duke of York's little daughter, Anne, was staying at Colombes, to be under the treatment of a French physician for a complaint of the eyes from which she suffered. Madame now took the child into her own nursery, and the little Princess was brought up with her young cousin, Marie Louise, and treated with the greatest kindness by her aunt. A general mourning for Queen Henrietta was ordered, both in England and France, and the royal proclamation, issued by Louis XIV., called on all loyal subjects to mourn for the King's aunt, as the last surviving child of the *Grand Henri*.

After paying Madame a visit of condolence, the King and Queen, accompanied by Monsieur, went to Chambord, and Henrietta was left to lament her loss alone at Saint-Cloud. It was then that Madame de La Fayette, in the hope of beguiling her lonely hours, and diverting her thoughts from the deep sadness into which the death of her mother had plunged her, once more took up the half-written story of her early married life. As they recalled those brilliant days of her youth, Madame's spirits revived, and before long she became amused and interested in the progress of the story. Another and still more distinguished personage, who paid Madame frequent visits at Saint-Cloud at this time, was the Abbé Bossuet. Her mother's regard for this eloquent preacher naturally drew her to seek a closer acquaintance with him. Twice over in the Lent of that year, when Bossuet was preaching at the Chapel of the Oratory, in the Rue St Honoré, Madame had been there to hear him, and it was only the suddenness of her

mother's end, which had prevented him from being present at
her death-bed. Now Madame sent for him to Saint-Cloud,
and from that time he paid her constant visits, and had long
conversations with her on religious subjects. Her friend and
companion, Madame de La Fayette, had, we know, the
highest opinion of Bossuet, and rejoiced to see her Princess
find pleasure in the company of so excellent a man. " M. de
Condom," she says, writing after Bossuet had been appointed
to the vacant see, "is one of my greatest friends. He is the
most honest and straightforward of men, the gentlest and the
frankest speaker who has ever been known at Court."

One short note from Madame's pen belongs to this
period. It has a peculiar interest, as the only one of all her
letters that bears her signature. It is addressed to Cardinal
de Retz, and is a reply to a letter of condolence on her
mother's death, which she had received from this old hero of
the Fronde, who had been so true a friend to the English
royal family in their darkest hours.

" A SAINT CLOUD,
" <i>ce 2 Octobre.</i>

" *Mon cousin*, even if you had not all the reasons that you
give me for the concern that you show in my recent loss, I
am too glad to believe that consideration for me alone would
have prompted your kind words. These are my feelings,
little as I know you. You can imagine what they would be
if all the merit, of which Madame de La Fayette tells me
daily, were better known to me. It will not be my fault if
we are not better friends before long. Meanwhile, I value
your kindness as it deserves, and hope that you are persuaded
of my regard for you and believe me to be, my cousin, yours
very affectionately.   HENRIETTE ANNE.

" *A Monseigneur le Cardinal de Retz.*"

By the end of the month, the Court returned to Saint-
Germain, and Monsieur and Madame were present at a solemn
funeral service, in memory of the Queen-mother, that was
held at Chaillot on the 16th of November. Abbé Montagu
officiated, but, by Madame's express wish, Bossuet delivered

the funeral oration. There, in the presence of the overflowing
congregation which thronged the convent church, and
numbered many of the most august names in France and
England, the great preacher recalled the virtues, the misfortunes, the heroic courage which had marked the *Reine
malheureuse.* "O wife, O mother, O Queen incomparable,
and worthy of a better fortune!" There, too, he reminded his
hearers of the royal child, who, born in the midst of civil
war, had been snatched from the hands of the rebels, by the
devotion of Lady Morton, and restored to her mother's arms,
to become her consolation in sorrow, her joy in exile and
ruin. Little did Bossuet himself, or those who heard him,
dream that the next time they met, it would be to lament the
Princess, who, in all the bloom of her youth and beauty, sat
listening to his words that day. An Englishman, Dr. Jenkins,
who was present on this occasion, gives an interesting account
of the service at Chaillot and of the sermon which that day
made so deep an impression on the whole audience. "The
funeral oration," he writes, "for so may the sermon be called,
was by Monsieur l'Abbé de Bossuet, lately nominated to the
Bishoprick of Condom, to the perfect satisfaction of all that
heard him, who, when he came to that long scene of Her
Matie's affliction, forgott not one remarque of that incomparable
magnanimity which she showed, from her first embarquing in
the Low Countries and her landing in the North of England,
to her leaving of Exeter and the Kingdome. Nor was he
less eloquent or less particular in these yet greater agonies
and desolation that soon after followed, and lasted till His
Matie's most happy Restauration, being, in all particulars
mindfull of the justice his narrative did owe to the Memorie
of our late, and the Majestie of our present, Souverayne." The
sermon which Dr. Jenkins admired so much, was published at
Madame's request, a few months afterwards, and widely
circulated. Bussy, who received a copy from Madame de
Sevigné, justly pronounced it to be a masterpiece of
eloquence. The admiration which it excited was the greater
from the contrast between this noble sermon and the feeble
eulogy of the dead Queen that was pronounced four days later,
at Saint-Denis, by the Cordelier, Faure, Bishop of Amiens.

As a former tutor of the King, he had been selected to occupy
the pulpit at the funeral service which was held there on the
20th of November. Monsieur and Madame, with their little
daughter Mademoiselle, the King and Queen and the whole
Court, were all present at this imposing ceremony.

"The music performed by Lulli and his orchestra was
superb," writes Oliver d'Ormesson, one of the deputies chosen
to represent the Parliament on this occasion. "The *Dies iræ*
was sung in a new and most beautiful way, but the Bishop of
Amiens' *oraison* was very poor indeed—in fact, he acquitted
himself even worse this time than at the Queen-mother's
funeral." Five days afterwards, a third funeral mass was
performed at Notre-Dame, and attended as before by Madame.
She and Monsieur then joined the Court at Saint-Germain, and
here, during the following Advent, she attended the course of
sermons that was delivered by her friend Bossuet in the Royal
Chapel. She needed all the consolation she could find, for
one sorrow after another seemed to darken her life, and, as it
were, to force upon her soul the conviction of that vanity of
earthly joys, which was the great preacher's favourite theme.
"The night cometh when no man can work. Repent, for
the kingdom of Heaven is at hand." This was the burden of
his cry all through that Advent. One Sunday especially, in
the presence of Madame, he spoke solemnly of the nearness
of death. He reminded his hearers, in touching words, of the
young and the beautiful who were dying around them, every
hour of their lives, and startled many by the impressive way
in which he uttered the words—"Now is the axe laid to the
root of the tree." Six months from that day, Madame was in
her grave.

In the midst of the sorrows which had come to her, and
the pressure of political business, Henrietta had not forgotten
her absent friend, the exiled Bishop of Valence. Her efforts
to obtain his pardon from the King, or to interest her powerful friends on his behalf, had so far proved in vain. But a
bright idea had suddenly come into her head. She would
avail herself of the influence which her brother's conversion
would give him with Pope Clement, to obtain a dazzling reward
for Cosnac, in the shape of a Cardinal's hat! The vision of

this Cardinal's hat is always floating before her eyes. It is the theme of her letters to the Bishop, and the subject of her conversations with his good friend, Madame de Saint-Chaumont. In vain Cosnac humbly replies that the idea is absurd, impossible. Madame is hurt, almost angry with him, for doubting her word, or her power to obtain what she desires. On the 10th of June, she had written to him, from St Cloud, in the following terms :—" In your grief for the injuries which you have received, it might well add to your sorrow, if your friends did not seek for consolations to help you bear your misfortunes. Madame de Saint-Chaumont and I have resolved that the best thing we can do, is to get you a Cardinal's hat. This idea may, I understand well, appear visionary to you at first, since the authorities on whom these favours depend, seemed so little inclined to show you any good. But, to explain this enigma, you must know that among an infinite number of affairs, which are now in course of arrangement between France and England, the last-named country is likely, before long, to become of such importance in the eyes of Rome, and there will be so great a readiness to oblige the King, my brother, in whatever he may wish, that I am quite certain nothing that he asks will be refused. I have already begged him, without mentioning names, to ask for a Cardinal's hat, and he has promised me to do this. The hat will be for you, so you can reckon upon it. If only I could have obtained your return to Court, we could have taken means to facilitate the business, but however far off you may be, I will not cease to work for this end, and shall be glad to hear your ideas on the subject, and to find out the best way of making the thing acceptable here. I leave Madame de Saint-Chaumont to tell you the rest, and only ask you to believe, that as I have under-taken this joyfully for your benefit, so I shall persevere in the design, with all the resolution necessary to bring it to a happy conclusion."

What chiefly impressed Cosnac in this proposal was Madame's kindness and thoughtfulness. In spite of repeated assurances, and even reproaches, both from Henrietta and Madame de Saint-Chaumont, he owns that he never could put any faith in the Cardinal's hat, or speak of it without a smile.

On the 19th of September, before Madame had recovered
from the effects of her confinement and the shock of her
mother's death, she wrote another letter on the same subject.
She begins by a mysterious allusion to some fresh intrigues of
Chevalier de Lorraine and his companions against her, which
had happily failed, but the manuscript quoted in Cosnac's
Memoirs was illegible, and the sense of the passage remains
obscure. " I see, by your letter, that you have been informed
of the strange treatment which I have met with in this State,
where it was hitherto supposed that it was dangerous to harm
others, but ordinary rules do not apply to those persons.
One proof of this lies in their eagerness to disown their
designs against me, which would in itself be a sufficient revenge
to gratify me, were it not that Monsieur is mixed up in the
thing. This distresses me as much as it has always done, and
I cannot bear to recognise his faults, although he has so many
that by this time I ought to be used to it. As for the business
which I mentioned to you, I mean the affair of the hat, all is
progressing according to my desire. I have received fresh
assurances from the person on whom it depends, and I see
nothing to hinder it now, unless it is your ill-luck. But I
hardly think even this can be bad enough to make the person
who has made me this promise break his word. I only wish
it were as easy to bring you here for the Assembly of Clergy.
Your friends agree with me that, till then, it would be useless
to make any further efforts for your return. But I continually
beg M. le Coadjuteur de Reims (Le Tellier, a son of the
minister) to induce his father to approach the King on this
subject. He promised me an answer, but the death of the
Queen, my mother, has prevented me from seeing him. The
loss of your brother has grieved me very much for your sake
and you will always find me as grateful to you as I ought
to be."

A few weeks after this, the Bishop received pressing
letters from Madame, urging him to pay a visit to Paris, or, if
this were impossible, to some place in the neighbourhood,
where she might meet him and discuss the whole thing. The
death of her mother had left her without a single friend,
whose advice she could ask on the important affairs with

which the two Kings entrusted her, and Louis XIV. would
on no account let Monsieur into the secret. In her loneli-
ness, it was only natural that she should turn to this old
servant, whose ability was well known, and whose loyalty
was above suspicion. And, as Madame de Saint-Chaumont
intimated in her letters to Cosnac, her mistress was anxious
that he should, if possible, accompany her to England, and
thought that his presence might facilitate the success of her
application for the Cardinal's hat. Besides this, the Bishop
retained in his possession three letters addressed by the
Chevalier de Lorraine to Mademoiselle de Fiennes, which had
been seized by one of Madame's attendants, when the unfortunate girl was driven out of the house by Monsieur.
These letters, containing as they did many insolent expressions against her husband, Madame was anxious to have, in
hopes that Monsieur's eyes might thus be opened to his
favourite's true character, or, if need be, that she might lay
them before the King as the best proof of the Chevalier's
misconduct. And knowing, as Cosnac did, how often letters
were opened by Louvois's spies, he did not dare entrust these
important documents to the post. But in spite of all these
reasons, Cosnac was still reluctant to undertake the journey
in open defiance of the royal command. He knew the strict
watch that was kept upon his movements by Louvois's
orders, and feared to expose himself to the King's anger.
Still Madame insisted, and after sending him repeated
messages, she herself wrote a yet more urgent entreaty, ending with the words :—"You no longer care for me, my dear
Bishop, since you refuse to give me a consolation which I
cannot do without."

This last appeal decided Cosnac. He agreed to stop at
Saint-Denis, on his way to visit an Abbey near Orleans, and
promised to meet Madame at a friend's house, on the day of
the funeral service that was held there in memory of her
mother. In order to avoid recognition, he laid aside his
episcopal habit, and travelled in disguise to Paris. Unluckily
he fell ill on the journey, and, on reaching Paris, he took to
his bed, in a miserable lodging of the Rue St. Denis, and sent
his nephew to deliver the letters which he had brought with

him, to Madame de Saint-Chaumont at the Palais-Royal. Hardly had he done this, than the police, whose suspicions had been aroused by the secrecy of his movements, arrested him as a notorious forger, of whom they were in search. To their surprise, the supposed forger drew forth a crozier from under his pillow, and declared himself to be the Bishop of Valence. He was now removed to the prison of Fort l'Evêque, and, after spending a night there, received orders, from Louvois, to leave Paris without delay, for the remote town of l'Ile Jourdain, where he spent the next two years in solitary exile. The consternation of Madame was great when she heard of the disastrous fate which had befallen her friend. Monsieur was the first to inform her of his arrest. A secretary of the English Embassy, Francis Vernon, writing home on the 27th of November, observes:—" They say that Monsieur, in dressing himself before he went to St. Germain, broke the business to Madame, and said: ' Madame, ne savez-vous pas que M. l'Evêque de Valence est à Paris ?' She answered : she thought he would not be so indiscreet as to come contrary to the King's order. So he combed his head, and a little while after, he said : ' Oui Madame, il est vrai, il est à Paris, il est encore en prison.' Whereupon she expressed a passion, and said she hoped they would consider his character and use him with respect."

Poor Madame's passion increased, when she found that her faithful servant, Madame de Saint-Chaumont, was involved in the Bishop's disgrace. With great presence of mind, Cosnac had destroyed all the letters from Madame which he had in his hands at the time of his arrest. But one brief note from Madame de Saint-Chaumont escaped his vigilant eyes, and was seized by the police and brought to Louvois. Upon this, Louis XIV., convinced that there was some intrigue on foot between the Bishop and this lady, sent Turenne to Madame, with a note demanding her instant dismissal. This was a terrible blow to Henrietta, for Madame de Saint-Chaumont had been her own daily companion, and the governess of her children, ever since the birth of the little Mademoiselle, eight years ago. She had nursed

U

the infant Duc de Valois in his last illness with the utmost devotion, and was tenderly attached to the little Princess Marie Louise. But her prayers and tears could avail nothing. The King was inflexible, and Madame de Saint-Chaumont, taking a sorrowful leave of her mistress, retired to the country. After Madame's death she took the veil and joined the Carmelites of the Rue du Bouloi. Henrietta wished to give her place to Madame de La Fayette, but Monsieur preferred Madame de Clérembault, an eccentric but trustworthy lady, who discharged her office faithfully, if she could never console Madame for the loss of her beloved friend.

It seemed, indeed, as Madame wrote, that she was destined to bring trouble on the heads of all those who had the misfortune to love and serve her. To add to her distress, Lorraine boasted loudly that he had effected Madame de Saint-Chaumont's disgrace and Cosnac's ruin, and she became daily more convinced that he and Monsieur would not rest until they had driven away every friend in whom she could trust. In her despair she turned to her brother for help, and Louis XIV. was compelled to offer excuses to Charles II., through his ambassador, and to promise that the insolence of Monsieur's minion should not be allowed to go unpunished. On the 5th of December, Colbert de Croissy sent his master the report of a conversation, in which the King of England had expressed his great concern at the Bishop of Valence's imprisonment and exile, and the dismissal of his sister's wise and devoted servant, Madame de Saint-Chaumont, and had ended by declaring his conviction that the whole affair was the Chevalier de Lorraine's doing. A few days afterwards, Charles returned to the subject, and sent Leighton to the Ambassador, to insist on some reparation being made to his sister for the wrongs that she had suffered. Louis, in reply, promised to deliver Madame from the insolent favourite at the first opportunity, and consoled his sister-in-law, in the meanwhile, with constant assurances of his regard and sympathy.

On the 28th of December, Henrietta addressed the following letter to Cosnac, from Saint-Germain :—

" If I had not heard of you from your friends, who told me
of your letter, I should be very anxious about you, fearing
the journey would injure your health, but, from what I hear
of its improvement, I see, as I have often found myself, that
bodily health does not always depend upon peace of mind.   If
this were the case, I should hardly be alive now, after the grief
I have had in losing you, and your strength would not have
resisted the effects of so much fatigue, at the worst season
of the year, and of all the trials to which you have been
exposed.   Madame de Fiennes showed Monsieur your letter,
but I cannot say that it moved him as it ought to have
done.   He has long since lost the use of his native tongue,
and can only speak in the language which has been taught
him by the Chevalier de Lorraine, whose will he follows
blindly, and the worst is, I have no hope that he will ever
mend his ways.   You will understand how happy this
certainty is likely to make me, and what hours I spend in
bitter reflections !   If the King keeps the promises which
he daily repeats to me, I shall in future have less cause for
annoyance, but you know how little I have learnt to trust such
words, from a personage who is so obstinate in refusing to
forgive you, and who is able to do what he wills.   As for
good Père Zoccoli (Madame's Capuchin Confessor), he im-
plores me every day to be kind to the Chevalier de Lorraine,
and blames me for refusing to receive his insincere advances.
I tell him that, in order to like a man who is the cause of all
my sorrows, past and present, I ought at least to have some
esteem for him, or else owe him some debt of gratitude,
both of which are absolutely impossible, after the way in
which he has behaved.   Yet Monsieur refused to communicate
at Christmas, unless I would promise him, not to drive his
favourite away.   I did this to satisfy him, but at the same
time, I had the pleasure of letting him know, how much
wrong this intimacy did me, and what grief I felt at seeing
how little he cared for me.   Farewell, nothing can ever
diminish the esteem that I have for you."

And so, darkly and sadly enough for Madame, the year
1669 came to an end.

Arrest of the Chevalier de Lorraine—Monsieur retires to Villers-Cotterets—
Arrival of the English Envoys—Colbert induces Monsieur to return to
Court—He consents reluctantly to Madame's visit to England—Letters of
Henrietta to Madame de Saint-Chaumont.

WITH the opening of the new year, Charles II. renewed his
invitation to Madame in the most pressing manner. Even
before his mother's death he had written to Louis XIV.,
saying that a visit from Madame would be the best way to
effect the final completion of the Treaty, and on the 5th of
January he told Colbert that he passionately desired to see
his sister in the coming spring. Three weeks later, Lord
Falconbridge was sent to Paris, with an official request to
the same effect from his master. But when the English
envoy reached Saint-Germain, he found that Madame had
been suddenly carried off to Villers-Cotterets, after an angry
scene between the King and Monsieur.

From the moment of Madame de Saint-Chaumont's
disgrace, the Chevalier de Lorraine's insolence had become
daily more insufferable. He boasted of his supremacy in
Monsieur's house, and talked openly of a divorce between
him and Madame. On the 30th of January, Monsieur, who
was still as infatuated with his minion as ever, begged the
King to give the Chevalier the revenues of two Abbeys which
had fallen vacant by the death of the Bishop of Langres.
Louis met this request with a flat refusal, and when his
brother remonstrated, told him frankly that his favourite's
conduct was intolerable. Monsieur flew into a rage, and
vowed that he would leave Court at once, adding that, if he
had a house a thousand leagues from Saint-Germain, he would

go there on the spot, and never see his brother's face again.
The King replied by ordering the immediate arrest of the
Chevalier, who was taken by the royal guards to Pierre-
Encise, near Lyons, and there imprisoned. Monsieur fainted
on hearing of his favourite's removal, and, throwing himself
at the King's feet, implored him with tears to recall his order.
This Louis absolutely refused to do, upon which Monsieur
ordered his rooms to be dismantled, and left Saint-Germain
that same evening for Paris, taking Madame with him.

This incident excited general surprise, and Francis Vernon,
the Secretary of the English Embassy, describes the scene in
the following graphic terms :—

> " PARIS,
> " *Feb.* 1, 1670.

" On Thursday night there happened a novelty, something
extraordinary, at the Court at S. Germain. Monsieur
arrived here from Court, all in a passion, and the Chevalier
de Lorraine, his favourite, was sent to the Bastille. All was
in disorder. He had asked the King to give the Chevalier
some lands of the Bishop of Langres. Before the Bishop had
yet expired, he had said, I give it to the Chevalier de Lorraine.
The King heard of it, and was very angry at Monsieur
disposing of lands without his consent, and, to show his
resentment, said that the Chevalier should not have them.
Hee, speaking thereupon something freely, was sent to the
Bastille, upon which the Duke of Orleans was soe transported
with choler, that he went to the King and upbraide him, and
said he could never endeavour to do anything, but still he
was crosst. For his part, hee was weary of such a life, and
hee would leave the Court, and, after hee had soe said, ordered
his coach to be made ready, his guards to march, and that
evening left the Court, and came away to Paris, and to-day
intends to retire to Villers-Cotterets. But I suppose matters
will shortly be adjusted."

The dispute, however, was not arranged so easily as the
English secretary expected.

Monsieur's rage was unbounded, and Mademoiselle, who
had arrived at the Luxembourg the day before he and

Madame came to Paris, was shocked at the violence of his language, and at the unkindness with which he treated his wife. Madame, on her part, spoke very gently to him, and remarked that, although she had no great reason to like the Chevalier, she was much distressed at the pain which his arrest had given Monsieur. That evening, she wrote the following note to Madame de Saint-Chaumont:—

"De Paris,
"*le* 30 *Janvier*, 1670.

"You will need all your piety to enable you to resist the temptation, which the arrest of the Chevalier will arouse in you, to rejoice at the evil which has befallen your neighbour! You will soon hear how violently Monsieur has acted, and I am sure you will pity him in spite of the ill-treatment which you have received at his hands. But, even if I had time to tell you all that has happened, I would prefer to speak of the injustice that you do me, in ever thinking that I can forget you. I love you, and you must, I am sure, know this. I have never tried so hard to help anyone as I have tried to help you, and, as often as ever you wish, I am ready to tell you that I care more for you than for any of my friends. After this, do not judge what I wish to do by what I can do, and believe that my only wish is to find out how I can best please you. Time will show you the truth of my words, and you may rest assured that nothing can ever change the tenderness that I feel for you."

The next day, Monsieur carried his wife off to Villers-Cotterets, but before her departure she found time to send a note to Maréchal Turenne, one of the privileged few, it will be remembered, who were admitted into the Royal secrets.

"*Friday*, 3 *o'clock*.

"I only write to bid you farewell, for things have come to such a pass that, unless the King detains us by much affection and a little force, we go to-day to Villers-Cotterets, to return I know not when. You will understand what pain I feel from the step which Monsieur has taken, and how little compared with this I mind the weariness of the place, the unpleasantness of his company in his present mood, and a thousand other things of which I might complain. My only real cause of regret is having to leave my friends, and the fear I feel that the King may forget me.' I know he will never have to complain of me, and all I ask him is to love me as well in my absence as if I were present with him. With that, I shall rest quite content, as far as he is concerned. As for you, I will not let you off so easily. I pretend to be regretted by you, without counting the 100 pistoles which you lose by my absence, and, to speak seriously, you would be very wrong not to miss me, since no one is so truly your friend as I am."

But Louis XIV. did not interfere for the moment, and poor Madame spent the next month in the solitude of Villers-Cotterets, alone with her angry and unreasonable husband.

The day after his arrival, Monsieur wrote a long letter to the Minister, Colbert, complaining bitterly of the cruel treatment which his friend the Chevalier had received, and of the marked affront which he considered had been done him by this arrest. More than this, he declared that, when the King heard of his intention to leave Court, he had actually sent to ask Madame what steps she would take, thereby encouraging her to fail in the duty that she owed her husband. He ended with many protestations of his favourite's devotion to the King, and of his own deep attachment to the Chevalier, whom he called the best friend that he had in the world.

On receiving this angry epistle, Colbert hastened to Villers-Cotterets, in the hope that Monsieur would, by this time, have got over his first paroxysm of rage, and would be ready to lend a willing ear to his advice. But, to his surprise, Monsieur absolutely refused to return to Court unless Lorraine were recalled. It was now the King's turn to be angry, and, hearing that his brother kept up a daily correspondence with his captive friend, he ordered the Chevalier to be removed to the fortress of Château d'If, at Marseilles, and to be allowed no communication with his friends. So great was the scandal excited by this open rupture between the royal brothers, that the King actually informed his ambassa-

dors at foreign courts, of the steps which Monsieur's extraordinary conduct had compelled him to take, adding, however,
the expression of his fervent hope that his brother would
soon return to a sense of his duty. In Paris and the provinces alike, Lorraine's arrest and Monsieur's quarrel with the
King were freely discussed. Contemporary journals and
letters are full of the wildest reports, and the greatest sympathy was expressed for Madame. Her presence was sorely
missed at Saint-Germain, and Madame de Suze poured out
the lamentation of the whole Court in the following letter,
which she addressed to one of Madame's ladies at Villers-
Cotterets :—

"All the world is writing to you, and I am too anxious
not to be forgotten at Villers-Cotterets, to delay sending you
these few lines any longer. But expect nothing amusing or
lively from my pen ! We are too sad here even to try to be
agreeable, and, since Madame left us, joy is no longer to be
seen at Saint-Germain.

> "Les plaisirs, les jeux, les amours,
> Et les ris qui marchent toujours,
> Sur les pas de votre Princesse,
> Avec elle ont quitté la Cour.
> Resolus, qui qu'on les empresse,
> De n'y plus faire de séjour,
> Que cette incomparable Princesse,
> En ces lieux ne soit de retour."

"But in plain prose, for I confess I am tired of verse,
everyone here is very dull in Madame's absence, and unless
she returns soon, I cannot think what we shall do with
ourselves. Nobody thinks of anything else but of writing
to her, and the ladies of the Court are to be seen, pen in hand,
at all hours of the day. I hope you will soon return, and with
you the Graces, who always follow in Madame's train. She
alone can bring us back the Spring-time."

On the arrival of the English envoy, Lord Falconbridge
sent his secretary, Dodington, to Villers-Cotterets where he
had a long interview with Henrietta. "Madame," he writes,
"received me with all imaginable kindness, much beyond

what a man of my figure could pretend to, and did me the honour to give me a full hour's private discourse with her, and, perceiving that I was not unacquainted with her affairs, and flattering herself that I had address enough, or, at least, inclination, to serve her, she was pleased to tell me she had designed to see the King, her brother, at Dover, as this Court passeth by Calais to Flanders; that this King had received the motion with all kindness, and conceived the ways of inducing Monsieur to accomplish it, which was that both her brothers and my Lord of St. Albans should write to Monsieur to that effect, which they had done; but the letters, coming hither a day or two after the Chevalier de Lorraine's disgrace, Monsieur fell into so ill a humour with Madame, even to parting of beds, that the King of France had commanded the letters should not be delivered to Monsieur, until he was better prepared to receive such a motion. That, since his coming to Villers-Cotterets, he began to come to himself, and that she thought, if the King of France approved of it, that the letters might now be delivered, in order to which Her Highness gave one of these three letters into my hand, and desired that my Lord Ambassador Montagu would, presently on my return, dispatch away one to St. Germain, to get the King's permission that my Lord Falconbridge might bring them with him to Villers-Cotterets, and deliver them to Monsieur. The King of France is extraordinary kind to Madame, and hath signified it sufficiently in all this affair of the Chevalier de Lorraine, whom he disgraced on her account, and on hers also it is that Monsieur is now invited to Court, although he seems not to take notice of it. She is even adored by all here, and, questionlesse, hath more spirit and conduct than even her mother had, and certainly is capable of the greatest matters."

Madame's enforced banishment, however, was not to last long. Her presence was too necessary, at this stage of affairs, for Louis XIV. not to insist on her return, and, hearing that Monsieur was already tired of his solitude, he sent Colbert a second time to Villers-Cotterets. The day before his arrival, Lord Falconbridge himself paid Madame a visit, which he describes in his letter of the 25th of February.

"Madame's reception was obliging beyond expression She has something of particular in all she says or does that is very surprising. I found by her that, although Monsieur were at that time in better humour than he had of late been, yet he still lies apart from her; that she wanted not hopes of inducing his consent to her seeing of the King, my master, at Dover or Canterbury this spring, as this Court passes into Flanders, nor is this King unwilling to second her desires in that particular; and, to say the truth, I find she has a very great influence in this Court, where they all adore her, as she deserves, being a princess of extraordinary address and conduct."

The next day Colbert arrived, bringing with him a present of jewels, laces, perfumes, diamond garters, gloves, and twenty purses, each containing 100 louis d'or, which the King sent to Madame with a message, saying that, since she had been absent from the Court Carnival, he had drawn tickets for her at the lottery, and that her good fortune had won these prizes. A very neat compliment, adds the English secretary, Vernon, and one which added not a little to the worth of the gifts, that were already valued at 20,000 crowns. At the same time the French secretary of State, speaking in the King's name, requested Monsieur to return to Court, and informed him that the Chevalier de Lorraine had been set at liberty, and allowed to go into Italy, on condition that he should not present himself at Court. Monsieur was only too glad to avail himself of this offer, and on the same day, the 24th of February, he and Madame travelled to Paris in a carriage with Colbert and the English ambassadors. That evening, Monsieur went on to Saint-Germain, and Madame joined him there the following day.

Their return was welcomed with general rejoicing. Madame received fresh presents from the King, and was warmly received by the Queen, as well as by Mademoiselle and all the Court ladies. "The King," wrote Dodington, "hath presented Madame with a most magnificent present of jewellery, cabinets, plate, and I know not how many rich curiosities. She hath a great influence on this Prince, and is adored by all heere, as I told you in my last." But everyone noticed how thin and pale she looked, and Vernon tells us that the sadness of her expression struck many of those who knew her best. Even Mademoiselle's sympathy was aroused on her behalf. In these last months of Madame's life, these two Princesses were more closely drawn together than ever before. Henrietta especially seemed anxious to make friends with her cousin, and often spoke to her in affectionate words, which Mademoiselle afterwards remembered with emotion. "Until now we have not often met my cousin, and we have never been as intimate as we ought to be," she said to her one day, at Saint-Germain. "But you, I know, have a good heart. Mine, you will find, is not a bad one. Let us be friends." The Queen, too, now began to feel compassion for Madame, and showed her great kindness. Like everyone else, she was shocked at Monsieur's ill-nature, and at the vexatious tyranny with which he treated his wife, in spite of their apparent reconciliation. He often refused to speak to her during whole days, and went so far as to tell Mademoiselle, that he had never loved Madame for more than a fortnight after his marriage. In fact, he spoke of her in such outrageous language that at length his cousin felt compelled to remind him that he owed Madame more respect, and should, at least, remember that she was the mother of his children. Henrietta, on her part, spoke of her husband with more sorrow than anger. "If he had strangled me when he fancied that I had wronged him," she would say to Mademoiselle, "I could, at least, have understood it, but to go on teasing me as he does, all about nothing, this is really more than I can bear." "There was," Mademoiselle allows, "a great deal of truth and good sense in all that she said on this point." And, on the 10th of March, Henrietta wrote to Madame de Saint-Chaumont in the same strain. "I did not write to you from Villers-Cotterets, because I had no safe means of conveyance, and the post is too dangerous to be trusted with anything but mere compliments. While I was there, I received your answer to the letter in which I informed you of the Chevalier de Lorraine's disgrace, and am not surprised to find how calmly you take this revenge, which *le bon Dieu* has so promptly granted you. Monsieur still per-

sists in believing that it is all my doing, and forms part of the
promises which I made you. That is an honour of which I
am unworthy, excepting so far as wishes go, and I was not
guilty in this respect, if indeed it can be called guilt, to desire
the ruin of a man, who has been the cause of all my troubles.
In your piety, you seem even to have ceased to wish for
vengeance. That is a pitch of perfection to which I confess
I cannot attain, and I am glad to see a man, who had never
done justice to anyone, get his deserts. The bad impression
which he left on Monsieur's mind still lasts, and he never
sees me without reproaches. The King has reconciled us,
but since Monsieur cannot at present give the Chevalier the
pensions which he desires, he sulks in my presence, and hopes
that, by ill-treating me, he will make me wish for the Chevalier's return. I have told him that this kind of conduct will
never answer. He replies with those airs of his which you
know well. I fear the King is still displeased with you. Let
us hope that he will one day recognise your innocence, and
repent of the way in which you have been treated. But alas!
it is too late already, for your place is filled, and Monsieur is
so conscious, and so much ashamed of the injustice which
he has done you, that he will, I fear, never forgive you.
Another day, I will answer the letter which you wrote before
your last one, and will only now reproach you for ever dream-
ing that I could forget to defend you. I forget nothing
which concerns you, and you will always find me the most
constant and the tenderest of friends."

On their return to Saint-Germain, Monsieur and Madame
lodged in their usual rooms in the Château Neuf, but Henrietta also occupied a large saloon in the old Palace, where she
spent the afternoons, engaged on business with the King.
The chief difficulty now was how to overcome Monsieur's
opposition to his wife's visit to England. His obstinacy was
greatly increased by the mortification he felt at not having
been admitted into the secret before. When the King first
explained the state of affairs to him, he was surprised to
find that Monsieur had already been informed by the Chevalier de Lorraine of Madame's intended journey. Unable to
discover how the secret had transpired, Louis sent for

Turenne, who confessed, with some confusion, that he had mentioned Henrietta's intended visit to England to one of her ladies, Madame de Coëtquen, a princess of the house of Rohan, who would, he knew, be anxious to accompany her. The King laughed when he heard this, and said : " Then I am to understand that you love Madame de Coëtquen ? " " No, sire," replied the Maréchal, proudly, " but she is certainly a friend of mine." " Well," replied Louis, " what is done cannot be undone, but, for heaven's sake, tell her nothing more, for I am sorry to tell you she loves the Chevalier de Lorraine, and tells him all she hears, and the Chevalier repeats every word to my brother." Some time afterwards, Madame gently reproached the indiscreet lady-in-waiting who had been the cause of all this mischief, and Madame de Coëtquen, falling on her knees before her mistress, owned that she loved Lorraine too well, and implored her pardon with tears. For some time Monsieur remained obdurate, and would not yield either to threats or entreaties on the King's part. On the 22d of March, Lionne wrote to Colbert de Croissy from Saint-Germain :—

" I write in haste to tell you, that the King wishes His Britannic Majesty to know, that when he proposed Madame's journey into England to Monsieur, he replied, in as contrary a manner as possible, and with violent transports of rage, saying that he would not even allow Madame to go into Flanders. Your brother, in whom Monsieur has confidence, having spoken to him again about it yesterday, by His Majesty's order, found him a little softened and more willing to hear reason. The King will continue to try, by gentle means, to get his consent, and hopes he may prevail before very long."

A week later, Louis XIV. himself wrote to his Ambassador in England, saying that Monsieur had so far relented as to allow Madame to visit her brother at Dover, but that he insisted on crossing over with her, so that all the honour of the Treaty should not be carried off by her. Louis added that he had vainly tried to show his brother that the King of England would, naturally enough, wish to enjoy a little more of his

sister's company, and take her back with him to London, but
that Monsieur said, nothing would induce him to go there
himself, or to allow his wife to go beyond Dover. Madame
was by no means anxious for her husband's company in
England, and told Louis XIV. that his presence would only
put difficulties in the way of transacting business. She consented, however, to refer the matter to her brother, who found
excellent reasons for declining the honour which Monsieur
proposed to do him. In her letters to Madame de Saint-
Chaumont, Henrietta gives a full account of Monsieur's proceedings, which were as wayward and unreasonable as those
of a spoilt child. On the 26th of March she writes from
Saint-Germain :—

"It seems as if all the peace of my life had departed
with you, and as if the wrong which had been done you, had
left neither quiet nor repose of mind to those who were its
cause. It is true that I too have had to suffer, who am certainly not answerable for this, but the truth is, all that Monsieur does, concerns me so nearly, that it is impossible his
actions should not fall back upon me. He has been very
angry at the wish which the King, my brother, has expressed
that I should go and see him. This has driven him to lengths
which you would hardly believe, for, regardless of what the
world may say, in his wrath against me, he declares aloud that
I reproached him for the life he led with his favourite, and
many other things of the kind, which have been very edifying
hearing for our charitable neighbours. The King has worked
hard to bring him to reason, but all in vain, for his only object
in treating me so ill is to force me to ask favours for the
Chevalier, and I am determined not to give in to blows
(*coups de bâtons*). This state of things does not admit of any
reconciliation, and Monsieur now refuses to come near me,
and hardly ever speaks to me, which, in all the quarrels we
have had, has never happened before. But the gift of some
additional revenues from the King has now softened his
anger a little, and I hope that by Easter, all may yet be well.
I am, on the whole, content with what the King has hitherto
done, but I see that, from the ashes of Monsieur's love for the

Chevalier, as from the dragon's teeth, a whole brood of fresh favourites are likely to spring up to vex me. Monsieur now puts his trust in the little Marsan (another prince of the house of Lorraine) and the Chevalier de Beuvron, not to speak of the false face of the Marquis de Villeroy, who prides himself on being his friend, and only seeks his own interests, regardless of those of Monsieur, or of the Chevalier. All I can do, is to spend the rest of my life in trying to undo the mischief which these gentlemen have done, without much hope of remedying the true evil that lies at the root of all. You will understand how much patience I shall need for this, and I am quite surprised to find that I have any left, for the task is a very hard one. As for my journey to England, I do not despair that it may yet take place. If it does, it will be a great happiness for me. All these affairs have prevented me from mentioning your business, but not from thinking of you. Nothing in the world can ever hinder me from showing you fresh marks of my remembrance and tenderness. But, as you know, there are moments when all one can do is to hold one's peace and wait for a better chance. This alone is the reason why I will say nothing about your affairs, but, as I have already told you, no one could love you more tenderly than I do."

On the 6th of April she wrote again :—

" As for my reconciliation with Monsieur, you will see that the news which you heard respecting my journey is one of those too favourable judgments with which the world is kind enough to honour me, from time to time ; unfortunately, absolutely without foundation. I have indeed wished to see the King, my brother, but there has been no question of the Chevalier's return in all Monsieur's opposition to my journey. Only he still declares that he cannot love me, unless his favourite is allowed to form a third in our union. Since then, I have made him understand that, however much I might desire the Chevalier's return, it would be impossible to obtain it, and he has given up the idea, but, by making a noise about my journey to England, he hopes to show that he is

master, and can treat me as ill in the Chevalier's absence as
in his presence. This being his policy, he began to speak
openly of our quarrels, refused to enter my room, and pretended to show that he could revenge himself for having been
left in ignorance of these affairs, and make me suffer for what
he calls the faults of the two Kings. However, after all this
noise, he has thought fit to relent, and said he would make
peace if I would make the first advances. This I have done
gladly enough, through the Princesse Palatine (Anne de
Gonzague). He accused me of saying a thousand extravagant
things, which I should have been mad ever to dream of saying! I told him that he had been misinformed, but that I
was ready to beg his pardon, even for what I had not said.
Finally he became more tractable, and after many promises
to forget the past, and live more happily in future, without
even mentioning the Chevalier's name, he not only agreed
that I should go to England, but proposed that he should go
there too. I wrote at once to my brother, to make this proposal, but as yet I have had no answer, and none of this news
has yet been made public. Every one talks according to his
own ideas. All the world knows that I am going, but no one
imagines that Monsieur wishes to accompany me, after all
that he has said against the King, my brother, and his repeated
declarations that he would never let me go, in order to have
his revenge. You will confess that the version of matters
which you had heard, is altogether contrary to the true state
of things. Once for all, you may be certain that I shall never
do such an extravagant thing as to ask for the Chevalier's
return, even if this depended upon me, which is not the case.
As for your affairs, I have spent the last week in Paris, and
have, therefore, been unable to speak to the King. But do
not imagine for a moment that I consider the permission
which you ask, to stay within three days' journey of Paris, is
to be held in the light of a favour. I shall only ask for this
as a sign of your respect for the King, and as a thing which
cannot be refused, since the promise was made before you
left. It is to be hoped that, once this first step has been taken,
you will no longer be honoured with the importance of being
treated as a dangerous person, but will be able to go wherever

you like, whether for your affairs, or for your health. You
see that I agree with you on all of these subjects, and will do
everything that I can. You know this is not always what I
should like to do, and I will own to you that, however fair
things appear outwardly, I do not always see the kindness
which I hope for in certain quarters. When you would think
me happiest, I often meet with terrible disappointments, of
which I tell no one, because it is of no use to complain, and,
besides, I have no one whom I can speak to now. I have
lately wished for you back again, a thousand times a day, and
although you used formerly to reproach me with not telling
you what I felt, but I am sure I should have spoken this
time, if only I could have had you. But that, alas! is a
pleasure which I cannot hope for now. Be sure, at least, that
I shall always feel your loss, and shall never forget what you
have suffered for my sake, and what I owe to my love for
you."

Madame wrote this letter from the Palais-Royal, where
she had come to spend Holy Week and Easter. Here she
found consolation in the visits of Bossuet, who was then in
Paris awaiting the papal bull which should confirm his appointment to the Bishopric of Condom, in Paris. All that
winter, Madame seems to have been in constant correspondence with the eloquent preacher, whose words had stirred her
heart so deeply. He paid her frequent visits at the Palais-
Royal or at Saint-Cloud, recommended a course of serious
reading for her study, and was surprised to find her so intelligent and thoughtful. Madame, on her part, weary and disappointed as she was with the vanities of the world, turned
gladly to him for help, and listened with her usual sweetness
to his advice. " I am afraid," she said to him, " I have thought
too little of my soul. If it is not too late, help me to find the
way of salvation." It was then, in her gratitude to Bossuet
for his instructions, that she ordered an emerald ring to be
made by her jeweller, as a present for the Bishop. But the
ring was not ready until she had started for England, and it
was only after her death that Bossuet received this precious
memorial of her friendship.

On the 8th of April, her little daughter was christened by Abbé Montagu at the Palais-Royal. The child, who was now eight months old, received the name of Anne Marie, and bore the title of Mademoiselle de Valois. Mademoiselle, the young Dauphin, and the Duc d'Enghien, the son of the Prince of Condé, stood sponsors, and were afterwards entertained at supper by Monsieur and Madame, together with the King and Queen, and all the princes and princesses of the blood. "Yesterday," wrote Vernon, "the King came to Paris, much to the burghers' satisfaction, visited some churches, admired Val-de-Grâce, and was present at a gossiping in the Palais-Royal, where Madame's young daughter, ye Duchesse de Valois, was formally baptized." On the evening of the same day, Madame, with her usual thoughtfulness, wrote a kind letter to the exiled Bishop of Valence, who had formerly officiated on these occasions, assuring him of her sympathy and remembrance.

After the ceremony, the Court returned to Saint-Germain, and on the 14th, Madame wrote another long letter to Madame de Saint-Chaumont :—

"I was hoping for an opportunity of asking the King to give you the liberty of going where you like, but my good intentions have been hindered by some bad offices which have been done you. The King sent for your brother (the Maréchal de Gramont) and told him that he heard you were in Paris, and that he knew I meant to intercede for you, but begged I would do nothing of the kind, since it grieved him to be compelled to give me a refusal. Your brother replied, with the utmost earnestness, that these were all unkind inventions, which fell heavily on innocent persons, but that he would certainly beg me not to think of interfering on your behalf, so that I have said nothing, fearing that I should do more harm than good. It grieves me to feel that I can do nothing for you. This is one of my worst sorrows, and I cannot be happy until you are free to go where you will, and there seems to be a hope that I may once more have you with me. The Maréchale has been ill ; never before have I so earnestly wished for any one's recovery as I have for hers. If she had died, I have no doubt Monsieur would insist on giving her place to the daughter-in law (probably a member of the Lorraine faction), and all the fuss we had at Saint-Cloud on the subject would begin again. But, thank God! she has recovered, and I still flatter myself with the hope that one day you may succeed her, although La Comtesse remains his favourite, and is one of those respectable characters with whom Monsieur is always anxious to surround me. I have not spoken to you of the state of affairs, because of the insecurity of the post, and all the couriers are in M. de Louvois' service. Also, you know that Monsieur's sole complaint against you is that you knew too many of my secrets. So I have waited to reply to the letter which I received at Villers-Cotterets, but now that M. de Valence has sent me a trustworthy messenger, I must tell you that all is finally settled between the two Kings, and that there is very little left for me to do in England. From this, you would imagine that I might do whatever I liked! But although the King has been exceedingly good to me in some ways, I often find him very troublesome. He makes a thousand mistakes, and commits inconceivable follies, without the least intending it. For instance, I had begged him to allow Monsieur to grant certain pensions to the Chevalier, so as to put him into a good humour. He refused, saying that I only asked for this because I was so anxious to go to England, and that I need not distress myself on that score, for I should certainly go, since my presence there was necessary to him. He spoke to Monsieur, who was furious, as you know, and made all this noise about the journey. Meanwhile, the King, after promising me he would do nothing for the Chevalier, excepting at my request, releases Monsieur's favourite to appease him, and promises him these pensions on his return from his journey, providing I agree, and all this without saying a word to me. You will confess that a naturally honest mind finds all this very surprising, and that it becomes difficult to know how to act in these circumstances. I had asked the King to allow me to give Monsieur . . . (the words are effaced in the original). He refused, saying people would think that Monsieur's bad temper had been rewarded. Two days afterwards, he gives him more than I had ever asked for, and

allows Monsieur himself to go to England, without reflecting
what embarrassment this will 'cause my brother, who would
never consent to discuss affairs with him.   Naturally, when
this proposal was made, he met it with a decided refusal, saying that my brother, the Duke of York, could not come to
Calais while Monsieur was at Dover, and that one visit should
not take place without the other.   This refusal has renewed
Monsieur's irritation.   He complains that all the honour will
be mine, and consents to my journey with a very bad grace.
At present, his chief friends are M. de Marsan, the Marquis de
Villeroy and the Chevalier de Beuvron.   The Marquis d'Effiat
is the only one of the troop who is perhaps a little less of a
rogue, but he is not clever enough to manage Monsieur, and
the three others do all they can to make me miserable until
the Chevalier returns.   Although Monsieur is somewhat
softened, he still tells me there is only one way in which I
can show my love for him.   Such a remedy, you know, would
be followed by certain death !   Besides, the King has pledged
his word that the Chevalier shall not return for eight years, by
which time it is to be hoped Monsieur will either be cured of
his passion, or else enlightened as to his favourite's true
character.   He may then see what faults this man has made
him commit, and live to hate him as much as once he loved
him.   This is my only hope, although, even then, I may still
be unhappy.   Monsieur's jealous nature and his constant fear
that I should be loved and esteemed will always be the cause
of trouble, and the King does not make people happy, even
when he means to treat them well.   We see how even his
mistresses have to suffer three or four rebuffs a week.   What
then must his friends expect ? "

Madame alludes to the perpetual jealousies and quarrels
between the King's new mistress, Madame de Montespan, and
his old love, La Vallière, who still struggled with the chains
that bound her.   D'Effiat, whom Madame mentions as the best
of the "*Lorrains*," was the very one of the Chevalier's friends
who was afterwards suspected of having poisoned her.   In
point of fact there was little to choose between these men,
who were equally vicious and unprincipled, and who, after

embittering the first Madame's life with their intrigues, lived
to cause the second Madame almost as much annoyance.
Henrietta concludes this long letter by telling her friend
the latest arrangements which have been made for her
journey :—

4.

" The Comtesse de Gramont will accompany me to Dover,
as well as her brother, M. d'Hamilton. Everyone in France
wants to follow me, but the King, my brother, will not allow
this, and Monsieur is delighted to hear only a few persons are
to accompany me, fearing too much honour should be paid
me. I will see on my journey what can be done for this poor
M. de Valence, as to his Cardinalate. You may be sure that
I long to help him more than ever. I am going to ask the
King once more to-day if he may return to his diocese, but I
know not if I shall succeed. Perhaps the bearer of this will
be able to inform you if I have not time to tell you myself. I
hardly know how I have managed to write such a long letter.
I will finish by assuring you that I cannot console myself for
your absence, and that I am always saying, what I will repeat
once more, that I can never be happy without you."

As Madame says in her letter, Monsieur had at last
yielded with a very bad grace, but not until Charles II. had
sent another urgent request by a new envoy, Lord Godolphin,
upon which Louis XIV. told his brother angrily, that Madame's
journey was for the good of the State, and that he would hear
of no more refusals. A stay of three days at Dover, however,
was the utmost to which Monsieur would agree, and he
positively declined to allow his wife to visit London, although,
in hopes of conciliating him, Charles II. had sent word that
Madame should be received with the highest honours, and
should take precedence of the Duchess of York, and of every
other lady in England but the Queen. Louis XIV. did his
best to atone for Monsieur's churlishness by his attentions to
his sister-in-law. He presented her with 200,000 crowns towards the expenses of her household, and himself selected the
ladies and gentlemen who were to accompany her. " The
King," wrote Montagu, " is going to send Madame over with

a great suite and handsome equipage. All the ladies of
France, who wish to display their beauty, have begged to go
with her." But, although a few favoured individuals had been
privately informed of Madame's intended visit to England,
the secret was so well kept that even Mademoiselle remained
in the dark, and knew nothing until Charles II.'s envoys
came to meet the Royal party at Courtray, and requested
Madame to cross over, and pay the King, her brother, a visit at
Dover.

CHAPTER XXIV

1670

FOR some time past, great preparations had been made for the Court's journey into Flanders. The King had announced his intention of taking the Queen to visit her new subjects, but the true object of the journey remained concealed for the present. On the 28th of April the royal party set out. On the day of her departure, Madame wrote a last letter to Madame de Saint-Chaumont, taking a tender farewell of her absent friend.

"I should not think my journey could prosper if I began it without bidding you farewell. Never has anything been more wrangled over, and even now Monsieur refuses to let me stay more than three days with the King, my brother. This is better than nothing, but it is a very short time for all which two people, who love one another as well as he and I do, have to say. Monsieur is still very angry with me, and I know that I shall have to expect many troubles, on my return. You will believe this, when you recollect how I foretold all that would happen after my last *accouchement*, although I knew that there was nothing to be done. The same thing will happen now. Monsieur vows that, if I do not procure the Chevalier's return, he will treat me as badly as the meanest of creatures. Before his arrest he advised Monsieur to find means to obtain a separation from me. I told the King, who laughed at me, but since then he has owned that I was right, and that Monsieur had actually proposed this to him. So I

told him that he must see the necessity of never allowing the
return of this man, who would only do far worse in future. I
have no time to say more, and can only assure you that nothing will ever disminish my tenderness for you."

A few hours later, Madame started in the Royal coach,
resplendent with gilding and embroidery, and attended by a
brilliant escort of cavalry, with Lauzun at their head. The
other occupants of the state carriage were the King and
Queen and Madame de Montespan, whose triumph over her
rival was now complete. In the next came the boy Dauphin
and Mademoiselle, who had eyes for no one but the captain
of the Royal guard, and was satisfied that Lauzun eclipsed all
his peers. After them came a long train of carriages, with the
ladies of the Court and the attendants and furniture of the
Royal family. The way lay through Senlis, Compiègne and
Saint-Quentin, to Arras, and afterwards to Douay and Courtray.
Wherever a halt was made, rooms were furnished and meals
served, exactly as at Saint-Germain or Versailles. French
historians dilate on the splendour of the *cortège*, on the balls and
fireworks which everywhere greeted the King's appearance,
on the gold and jewels which he showered on the ladies of the
cities through which they passed. "The journey," Voltaire
writes, "was one continual *fête*, and among all the beauties of
the Court, Madame shone supreme, conscious that all this
glory was for her alone." The reality was hardly so pleasant
as these words might lead us to suppose. Mademoiselle,
blissful as she was in her lover's presence, draws a graphic
picture of the miseries to which the royal family, and the
members of their suite, were exposed on this journey. The
weather was very bad, the rain fell in torrents, drenching
spendid uniforms and nodding plumes. Half a league from
Landrécies, the Sambre had overflowed its banks, the bridges
were broken down, and the royal party had to spend the
night in a barn, much to the disgust of the Queen, who
grumbled at the soup that was offered her, and declared that
she could not lie down in the presence of her ladies. Madame
and Mademoiselle, with better sense, laughed at these new
experiences, and made light of the small inconveniences to
which they were exposed. They ate chickens without knives

and forks, and lay down to rest on mattresses, which the gentlemen-in-waiting spread on the floor of the barn. At four o'clock, when they were all fast asleep, Louvois brought word that the bridge was repaired, and the royal party went on to Landrécies.

And Madame de Fiennes, writing to Bussy from Paris, descants on the miseries which her husband, in common with the other members of the suite, experienced on this disastrous journey. She describes how they had to camp out in pouring rain, and sleep under dripping canvas, and how the new clothes and splendid equipages, which they had gone to such expense to provide, were ruined by the heavy rain and shocking roads. "I have just had a letter from Madame," she writes, on the 18th of May, "who says that they had to suffer the same inconveniences as the rest of the troops, and were kept 24 hours in their coach, without food or drink, on the edge of a river which had overflowed its banks. I know that she means a great deal by this, for the dear Princess tries to make light of what she has endured for my sake. She is very happy to think of going to England, but would have been better pleased if she could have gone to London, Dover being a very wretched place to spend three days in. But, as she says, we must not grumble in this world if we get half of what we desire."

Although she wrote cheerfully, Henrietta was both sad and suffering. Mademoiselle tells us that she was very much out of spirits, and could seldom touch anything but a little milk. Whenever they reached the end of the day's journey, she retired to her bedroom. The King often visited her, and treated her with the greatest kindness. Not so Monsieur. Whenever he travelled in the coach with her, he would say the most disagreeable things to her face, before the Queen and Mademoiselle. One day he remarked, with a smile, that an astrologer had once told him that he would have several wives, and that this prophecy seemed likely to be fulfilled, for that Madame would evidently not live long. "This seemed to me very hard," observed Mademoiselle, "and the Queen and I showed, by our silence, what we thought of his conduct to poor Madame." But Henrietta took it all

patiently, and was too much accustomed to her husband's
odious behaviour to pay him any attention. Happily, she
was spared Monsieur's company on the journey through
Flanders, for he took it into his head to ride through the
towns which his prowess had helped to conquer, sword in
hand, at the head of his regiment. On arriving at Courtray,
the English envoys met the Royal party with the news that
Charles II. was at Dover, and begged Madame to embark as
soon as possible on the fleet, under Lord Sandwich, which was
awaiting her orders in the port of Dunkirk. "Madame," observes Mademoiselle, "appeared extremely happy at this
news, while Monsieur was equally mortified. He tried to
stop her departure, but the King told him plainly that her
journey was undertaken in his interests, and at his command.
After that, there was nothing more to be said."

The Royal Family accompanied Henrietta as far as Lille.
Here M. de Pomponne, the French envoy at the Hague,
came to pay his respects to Madame, and had a long conversation with her on the evening before her departure. As
the son of Arnauld d'Andilly, the venerable patriarch of Port-
Royal, Pomponne was intimately connected with many of
Madame's friends, and he gladly availed himself of this opportunity to become better acquainted with this admired
Princess. And, like everyone else, he came away deeply impressed by her charms and talents. "I confess," he wrote
afterwards, "that I was surprised to find such grasp of mind
and capacity for business in a princess, whose womanly graces
seemed to have destined her to be the ornament of her sex.
I found that she was aware of the orders which I had received
not to enter into any solid alliance with the States, and
showed great indignation with Temple for his dislike of
France, a feeling that he could not hide. However, she
assured me that he would not long be able to oppose us.
From what the King had said to me of the hope which he
had of securing the friendship of the King of England, and
from what Madame confirmed, it was easy to see that the
journey of this Princess to London was not merely undertaken
for the simple pleasure of seeing the King, her brother."

The next day Madame set out for Dunkirk. The whole

Court came to bid her farewell, but Henrietta's joy at the prospect of seeing her brother was sadly marred by her husband's unkindness. When the time for parting came, she could not hide her tears, and Mademoiselle was shocked at the bitterness with which Monsieur spoke of his wife's influence with both the Kings, after she was gone.

A suite of no less than 237 persons accompanied Madame. Among her five maids-of-honour was Louise de Keroüalle, the daughter of a poor Breton gentleman of noble family, who had lately entered her service, and whose baby face was to make so profound an impression on Charles II. Besides the members of her household and a crowd of attendants, including doctors, chaplains, grooms and maids, she was escorted by the Maréchal de Plessis, the Bishop of Tournay, the Comte and Comtesse de Gramont, Anthony Hamilton, and a few other personages of high rank, whom the King had chosen to form her escort. On the evening of the 24th of May, this brilliant company embarked on board the English ships. At five o'clock the next morning, when the cliffs of Dover were coming into sight, a boat was seen rowing at full speed towards the fleet. Madame hurried on deck, and presently her eyes were gladdened by the sight of both her brothers, the King and the Duke of York, who, accompanied by Prince Rupert and the Duke of Monmouth, had come to welcome her. After a joyous meeting, they all landed at Dover, and conducted Madame to the Castle, which had been prepared for her reception, while the members of her numerous suite found lodgings in the town. "Madame is here in perfect health," wrote Colbert de Croissy, who had come to Dover to meet her. "The King of England has sent for the Queen and the Duchess of York, and is doing all he can to enliven this dreary place, and make it agreeable to Madame."

No time was lost in setting to work, but since it was plain that the original three days granted by Monsieur would not suffice to complete the negotiations, Louis XIV. wrote from Dunkirk on the 31st of May, saying that, with his brother's consent, Madame might prolong her visit for another ten or twelve days. The Duke of York had been summoned to London, owing to rumours of disturbances in the city, which proved happily untrue, but his absence rather facilitated the progress of affairs, which his zeal, as a newly-converted Romanist, might have hampered. Both Charles II. and Madame agreed that it would be desirable to defer any public declaration of the King's change of religion for the present. On the other hand, Henrietta urged her brother to join in an offensive as well as defensive alliance against the States, and did her utmost to remove the obstacles which still delayed the conclusion of the Commercial Treaty. "Commerce," wrote Colbert be Croissy to his master, "is the idol of Great Britain's worship." And the rights of the fleet was the one point on which even Charles II. was in earnest. By degrees, however, Madame's tact and cleverness succeeded in smoothing away these difficulties. She reconciled those old rivals, Buckingham and Arlington, and recovered her old influence over the Duke, without allowing him to become a party to the secret articles of the Treaty. On the 30th of May she told the French Ambassador that she had already changed her brother's mind, and that he was *almost* inclined to declare war against Holland on the spot. And she went so far as to suggest that the Maréchal de Turenne should be sent over, on pretence of escorting her home, to discuss the most advisable measures. But this idea was given up, as too likely to excite suspicion in both countries. The fears of the Dutch had already been aroused by Madame's expedition, but the secret of the negotiations was so well kept that Van Benninghen, who had been charged to keep a sharp watch on her proceedings, wrote home that the State need fear nothing, and that feasting and rejoicing were the order of the day at Dover.

On the 1st of June, six days after her landing, the Secret Treaty was signed at Dover by Colbert de Croissy on one hand, and by Lord Arlington, Lord Arundel, Sir Thomas Clifford, and Sir Richard Bellings on the other. Its chief articles are given by Mignet as follows:—"The King of England will make a public profession of the Catholic faith, and will receive the sum of two millions of crowns, to aid him in this project, from the Most Christian King, in the course of the next six months. The date of this declaration is left absolutely to his own pleasure. The King of France will faithfully observe the Treaty of Aix-la-Chapelle, as regards Spain, and the King of England will maintain the Treaty of the Triple Alliance in a similar manner. If new rights to the Spanish monarchy revert to the King of France, the King of England will aid him in maintaining these rights. The two Kings will declare war against the United Provinces. The King of France will attack them by land, and will receive the help of 6000 men from England. The King of England will send 50 men-of-war to sea, and the King of France 30; the combined fleets will be under the Duke of York's command. His Brittanic Majesty will be content to receive Walcheren, the mouth of the Scheldt, and the isle of Cadzand, as his share of the conquered provinces. Separate articles will provide for the interests of the Prince of Orange. The Treaty of Commerce, which has been already begun, shall be concluded as promptly as possible."

As soon as the Treaty had been signed, the French Ambassador crossed over to Boulogne, and there delivered it to his royal master. On the 14th of June the first ratifications were secretly exchanged between the two Kings. The direct object of Madame's journey having been thus accomplished, the remainder of her visit was spent in pleasant intercourse with the royal family. The mourning for the Queen-mother was still general, and Madame's grief for her mother was renewed by the sight of the familiar scenes and faces which recalled her presence. But she was too happy in the companionship of her brother, and in the society of her relatives and friends, to sorrow long. On the 29th of May, Queen Catherine arrived at Dover, and was soon on the most affectionate terms with her sister-in-law. Henrietta afterwards described her to Mademoiselle as "a very good woman, not handsome, but so kind and excellent that it was impossible not to love her." In the Duchess of York she welcomed an old friend, whose cleverness and good sense she warmly recognised. The Duchess, on her part, had good reason to be grateful to Henrietta for the kindness with which she had treated her daughter, the little Princess Anne, whom she insisted on keeping at Saint-Cloud with her own children.

The anniversary of the Restoration was celebrated with great rejoicings. One day the King took his sister to Canterbury, where a ballet and comedy were acted before her, followed by a sumptuous collation in the hall of St. Augustine's Abbey. On another day, the 8th of June, the royal party sailed in yachts along the coast, and went on board the fleet. "Many of our expeditions are on the sea," wrote a member of Henrietta's suite, "where Madame is as bold as she is on land, and walks as fearlessly along the edge of the ships, as she does on shore." Wherever she went, she won all hearts, and was adored alike by the Court and the people. But the hours flew by all too fast, and soon the time for departure came. Charles showed his grief by loading his sister with presents for herself and her friends. He gave her 6000 pistoles to defray the expenses of her journey, presented her with 2000 gold crowns to build a chapel at Chaillot as a memorial to her mother, and, on the eve of her departure, gave her another magnificent present of jewels. At the same time he begged her, with a smile, to leave one of her own jewels with him, as a parting souvenir. Henrietta at once bade her maid-of-honour, Mdlle. de Keroüalle, fetch her casket, and told the King to choose whatever he liked. Upon this, Charles took the fair maiden by the hand, and begged his sister to allow her to remain in England, declaring that this was the only jewel which he coveted. But Madame, to her credit, absolutely refused to grant this request, and told the King that she was responsible to Mdlle. de Keroüalle's parents for their child, and had promised to bring back the girl with her to France. Charles, however, did not forget the Breton maiden with the lovely face, and when, a few months later, Madame's death left her without a protector, he sent for Louise de la Keroüalle to England, and appointed her maid-of-honour to his wife. "Madame's death," wrote Bussy, "has been the cause of La Keroüalle's good fortune. If it had not been for that, she would hardly have found so exalted a lover in France."

On the 12th of June, Henrietta started on her homeward journey. As she set foot on the ship that was to bear her back to France, the poet Waller who, twenty years before, had

celebrated her rescue by Lady Morton, now presented her
with the following ode :—

> " That sun of beauty did among us rise,
> England first saw the light of your fair eyes ;
> In England, too, your early wit was shown ;
> Favour that language, which was then your own
> When, though a child, through guards you made your way,
> What fleet or army could an angel stay ?
> Thrice happy Britain ! if she could retain
> Whom she first bred within her ancient main.
> Our late burned London, in apparel new,
> Shook off her ashes, to have treated you ;
> But we must see our glory snatched away,
> And with warm tears increase the guilty sea ;
> No wind can favour us.   Howe'er it blows,
> We must be wretched, and our dear treasure lose !
> Sighs will not let us half our sorrow tell,
> Fair, lovely, great and best of nymphs, farewell."

The King and the Duke of York, who had returned to
bid his sister good-bye, accompanied Madame on board, and
sailed with her for some distance.   Then they were forced
to part.   Three times over Charles bade his sister a tender
farewell, and each time returned to embrace her once more,
as if he could not bear to let her go.   Henrietta wept
bitterly, and the French Ambassador declared he had never
witnessed so sorrowful a leave-taking, or known before how
much royal personages could love one another.   The sea was
smooth, the wind favourable, and before Madame's tears were
dried, the noise of the Calais guns, firing royal salutes in her
honour, woke her from her mournful dream.   That evening
she attended a service at the church of the Minimes, and the
next day heard mass at the Capuchins, before starting for
Boulogne.   Wherever she stopped she was received with
royal honours.   At Montreuil the Duc d'Elbœuf entertained
her splendidly.   At Abbeville an escort of the King's guards
met her and attended her to Beauvais, where the English
Ambassador, Ralph Montagu, was waiting to conduct her to
Saint-Germain.   The King and Queen had intended to meet
her there, but Monsieur positively refused to accompany them,
and Louis refrained from an act which would have made his

brother's absence more remarkable. All Monsieur would do was to meet his wife a few miles from Saint-Germain and bring her back with him to the château, where, on the 18th of June, her return was warmly welcomed by the whole of the royal family.

So Madame came back to France. The King treated her with the highest consideration, both in public and in private. He gave her a fresh present of 6000 pistoles towards her expenses, begging her to keep her brother's gift for her own use, and acknowledged his obligations to her in every possible manner. The Queen and Mademoiselle were delighted to see her, apparently restored to health, and looking as bright and beautiful as of old. "*Tant elle paraissait belle et contente.*" She had much to tell them about England, and spoke freely of her brother's kindnesses, and of the affection with which she had been received by her sister-in-law. Only the mention of her mother, says Mademoiselle, renewed her old grief for that lady, whom she had loved so well, and brought tears to her eyes. All the Court hailed her return with delight. She seemed to have brought back joy and sunshine with her. But Monsieur was in a more evil mood than ever. He sullenly refused to accompany the King when he moved to Versailles on the 20th of June. "This," Mademoiselle remarks, "was done out of spite to Madame." When the Queen and Mademoiselle parted from her, they both noticed how she struggled with her tears, and how at length they flowed fast, in spite of all her efforts. She now accompanied her husband to Paris, where the foreign ambassadors and chief personages at Court flocked to congratulate her on her return. Her journey to England had been the talk of all Paris, and all sorts of rumours were afloat. Oliver D'Ormesson and Gui Patin both dwell on the great consideration in which Madame was held by Louis XIV., and the extraordinary reception she had met with in England. And our friend Vernon writes :—

"There is all the buzzing and rumour in the world that Madame hath had a secret negotiation with His Majesty, that she hath made several presents at Court, and at last prevailed, and that the triple alliance is quite to be broken ; that indeed for a colour, things are to be continued in their ancient channel for a little while, but that at last the disguise is to be taken off, and the King of England to unite publicly with the King of France. These, because they are town news, and invented only to keep their tongues in use, it being an idle time and they having nothing else to busy themselves about ; I think, therefore, the less notice is to be taken of them."

On the 24th of June, Madame went to Saint-Cloud with her husband and children. There she enjoyed the beautiful summer weather, and the company of her friends. Tréville, Turenne, La Fare, La Rochefoucauld, Madame de La Fayette, Ralph Montagu and two other young Englishmen, then on a visit to Paris, Sir Thomas Armstrong and Lord Poulett were among those who saw her during that last week of her life. Together they talked of books and poetry, of England and of the pleasant days which she had lately spent there. Together they took long rambles in the gardens, then in all the glory of their midsummer loveliness. Madame sang and played the guitar to her friends. She talked with all her accustomed animation, and with more than her wonted charm. Her friends thought they had never seen her more brilliant and beautiful. But they did not know the perpetual troubles that vexed her heart, and were fretting out her very life. Monsieur would give her no peace. He persisted in declaring that the Chevalier de Lorraine's exile was her doing, and in telling her that he would never rest till his favourite had been recalled. On the 26th of June, she wrote a last letter to Madame de Saint-Chaumont :—

" I knew you would understand the joy which my visit to England gave me. It was indeed most delightful, and, long as I have known the affection of my brother, the King, it proved still greater than I expected. He showed me the greatest possible kindness, and was ready to help me in all that he could do. Since my return, the King here has been very good to me, but as for Monsieur, nothing can equal his bitterness and anxiety to find fault. He does me the honour

to say that I am all-powerful, and can do everything that I
like, and so, if I do not bring back the Chevalier, it is because
I do not wish to please him. At the same time he joins
threats for the future with this kind of talk. I have once
more told him how little his favourite's return depends upon
me, and how little I get my own way, or you would not be
where you now are. Instead of seeing the truth of this, and
becoming softened, he took occasion of my remark to go and
complain of you to the King, and tried, at the same time, to
do me other ill offices. This has had a very bad effect,
together with the letter which you wrote to my child, and
which, they pretend, was delivered to her secretly, and has,
I fear, increased the King's unfavourable opinion of you. I
have not yet had time to defend you, but you may trust me
to do the best I can for you, and to prove that I am not
unworthy of the friendship which you have so often shown
me. If I cannot do away with these unfortunate impressions,
I will at least try to remove the false reports by which they
have been occasioned. I have often blamed you for the
tender love you feel for my child. In God's name, put that
love away. The poor child cannot return your affection, and
will, alas! be brought up to hate me. You had better keep
your love for persons who are as grateful as I am, and who
feel, as keenly as I do, the pain of being unable to help you
in your present need. I hope that you will do me the justice
to believe this, and will remain, once for all, assured that I
shall never lose a chance of helping you, and of showing you
my tenderness. Since my return from England, the King
has gone to Versailles, where Monsieur would not follow
him, lest I should have the pleasure of being with him."

The very day that Madame wrote this letter, Monsieur
received an order from the King to bring his wife to see the
Queen. He consented with a very bad grace, and the afternoon and evening were spent at Versailles. Here Madame
had a long and animated conversation with the King, on the
subject of the Treaty with England. Unfortunately, Monsieur
entered the room while they were talking, and was much
offended because his brother refused to continue the discus-

sion before him. Again, at dinner, a young relative of
Madame de Montespan, M. de Tonnay-Charente, who had
been to England with Madame, and happened to be in waiting that day, began to describe the splendour of her reception
at Dover, and dwelt especially on the attentions which had
been paid her by the young Duke of Monmouth. No subject
could have been more unfortunate. Monsieur grew more and
more furious, and the King, after vainly trying to change the
conversation, rose from table, not without remarking, to
Madame, that the youth must have been born in Madagascar.

All this affected Madame visibly. Both the Queen and
Mademoiselle noticed how ill she looked, and saw the tears in
her eyes when she took leave of them. After her departure,
they both pitied her extremely, and the Queen was heard to
observe, " Madame bears death plainly written in her face."

The heat was very great all these days, and on the following morning Madame bathed in the Seine, contrary to the
advice of her doctor, M. Yvelin. Afterwards she felt very
unwell, and complained of sharp pains in her side. The
fatigue and excitement of her visit to England, where she
had not given herself a moment's rest, and the excessive heat
of the weather during her journey home, seemed sufficient to
account for this, and her doctors merely prescribed rest and
quiet.

On the afternoon of Saturday, the 28th of June, Montagu
paid her a visit at Saint-Cloud, and had a long conversation
with her, which was interrupted by Monsieur's entrance.
She spoke to the Ambassador of the recent negotiations
between the two Kings, and of the alliance against Holland
into which they had entered. And she told him, too, how
badly her husband had treated her since her return, and how
impossible it seemed to live happily with him. With these
thoughts in her mind she sat down early the next morning
and wrote a long letter to the Princess Palatine. A copy of
this letter was found in the papers of Cardinal de Retz, and
afterwards passed into M. Monmerqué's collection. It was
first published in the *Archives de la Bastille*, and has since
then appeared in M. Anatole France's introduction to Madame
de La Fayette's book. Anne de Gonzague, the wife of

Edward, Prince Palatine, had always been a friend of
Monsieur. In old days, it will be remembered, she had
helped to arrange his marriage with her young cousin, and
had lately done her best to reconcile him to his wife's visit
to England. "The Duke and Duchess of Orleans had
quarrelled," wrote Gui Patin, in April, "but the Princess
Palatine has helped the King to make peace between them."
And the English secretaries say the same in their letters
home. It was, therefore, only natural that Madame should
wish to give the Princess some account of her journey, and
should, with her usual frankness, unburden her heart to this
kind and sympathetic friend.

> "DE ST CLOUD,
> "29 *Juin*, 1670.

"It is only fair that I should give you an account of a
journey which you tried to render acceptable in the only
quarter where it could fail to meet with approval. I will
confess that, on my return, I had hoped to find everyone
satisfied, instead of which, things are worse than ever. You
remember telling me that Monsieur insisted on three things :
first, that I should place him in confidential relations with the
King, my brother; secondly, that I should ask the King to
give him his son's allowance; thirdly, that I should help the
Chevalier de Lorraine. The King, my brother, was so kind
as to promise that he would willingly trust Monsieur with his
secrets if he would behave better in future than he had done
with regard to my journey. He even offered to give the
Chevalier de Lorraine a refuge in his kingdom till affairs
should have calmed down here. He could do no more for
him. As for the pension, I have great hopes of obtaining it,
if only Monsieur will put an end to the comedy which he
still presents to the public gaze, but you will understand that
I cannot ask for this, after the way in which he behaved,
unless I can satisfy the King that our domestic peace will be
restored, and that he will no longer hold me responsible for
everything that happens in Europe. I have said all this to
him, expecting it would be well received, but since there is
no prospect of the Chevalier's immediate return, Monsieur
declares that all the rest is useless, and says I am never to

expect to be restored to his good graces until I have given him back his favourite. I am, I must confess, very much surprised at this behaviour on his part. Monsieur wished for my brother's friendship, and, now I offer it to him, he accepts it as if he were doing the King a favour. He refuses to send the Chevalier to England, as if these things could blow over in the next quarter of an hour, and scorns the offer of the pension. If he reflects at all, it is impossible for him to go on in this manner, and I can only suppose that he is bent on quarrelling with me. The King was good enough to assure him, on his oath, that I had no part in the Chevalier's exile, and that his return did not depend upon me. Unfortunately for me, he refused to believe the King, who has never been known to utter a falsehood, and it will be still more unfortunate if I cannot help him while it is yet possible. You see now, my dear cousin, the state of my affairs. Of the three things which Monsieur desired, I can obtain two and a half, and he is angry because I cannot do more, and counts the King, my brother's, friendship and his own advantage all as nothing. As for me, I have done more than I could have hoped. But if I am unhappy enough for Monsieur to go on treating me so unkindly, I declare, my dear cousin, that I shall give it all up, and take no more trouble as to his pension or his favourite's return, or his friendship with the King, my brother. Two of the three things are hard to obtain, and others might think them of great importance, but I have only to drop the subject, and maintain the same silence as Monsieur, who refuses to speak when I desire an explanation. As for the Chevalier's return, even if my credit were as great as Monsieur believes it to be, I never will give way to blows (*coups-de-bâton*). If Monsieur therefore refuses to accept the two things which he can have, and insists on getting the third, which must depend on the King's pleasure, I can only await the knowledge of Monsieur's will in silence. If he desires me to act I will do it joyfully, for I have no greater wish than to be on good terms with him. If not, I will keep silence and patiently bear all his unkindness, without trying to defend myself. His hatred is unreasonable, but his esteem may be earned. I may say that I have neither

deserved the first, nor am I altogether unworthy of the last,
and I still console myself with the hope that it may some
day be obtained. You can do more than anyone else to
help me, and I am so persuaded that you have my good and
Monsieur's at heart, that I hope you will still endeavour to
assist me. I will only remind you of one thing. If you let
a good chance slip by, it does not always return again. The
present moment seems to be favourable for obtaining the
pension, and the future is, to say the least, doubtful. After
this, I must tell you that your pension from England will be
paid shortly. The King, my brother, gave me his word for
it, and those persons whose business it is to see this done
promised to afford the necessary facilities. If you were here
we would take further steps to settle the business, for you
know that I was not sufficiently acquainted with the particulars of your affairs to do more than repeat what you had
told me. If I can give you any further proofs of my affection,
I will do so with all the pleasure in the world."

The authenticity of this long and interesting letter has
been disputed by many of the best French critics. Both in
style and sentiment, however, it agrees exactly with Henrietta's letters to Madame de Saint-Chaumont, and the following despatch from Ralph Montagu may be considered to
settle the question. This important note is preserved among
the French correspondence in the Record Office, but seems
hitherto to have escaped observation. Writing to Arlington,
a month after Madame's death, the Ambassador sends him
the letter which she had written a few hours before she died,
and which he feels sure the King will be glad to see.

" PARIS,
" 1st of August 1670.

" MY LORD,—I am to-morrow to goe to Saint Germain
to an audience, and this is only to send your Lordship this
enclosed, which is a letter that Madame, since her returne
from England, writ to the Princesse Palatine. It was writ
the morning she dyed. It is worth the King's seeing, because
it is soe well writ, and doth alsoe give an exact account of

everything that concerns her. There is nothing more worth troubling your Lordship with, from my Lord, Your Lordship's most faithful, most obedient servant,

" R. MONTAGU."

Here, then, we have the last words that were traced by Henrietta's pen. This letter, which was written so short a time before her death, contains a full and frank statement of the quarrel between herself and her husband. It is plain, as she told Madame de Saint-Chaumont, that Monsieur will be satisfied with nothing short of his favourite's return. But, at least, she will make one last attempt at conciliation, through this mutual friend. If that, too, fails, there will be nothing left but to bear his cruelty patiently, and wait in the hope that he may some day come to a better mind. So she writes on that bright summer morning. The tone of the letter is sad, almost hopeless. Life has proved too hard for her. She is utterly weary and out of heart. Health and spirits have failed her, and she is old and worn-out before her time The present is well-nigh intolerable. The future is dark and desperate. There is no one at hand to help her. Where, then, can she turn? And out of the deep of despair and misery, her cry goes up to Heaven, that cry with which she has turned to Bossuet—" I have thought too little of my soul. Help me, if it is not too late, to find the way of salvation."

Sudden Illness and Death of Madame at Saint-Cloud, on Monday, June 30.

AT ten o'clock on the evening of Saturday, the 28th of June, Madame de La Fayette arrived at Saint-Cloud. Madame had sent to tell her that she was ailing, and had begged her to spend Sunday with her. She complained of the pain in her side which had lately troubled her, but, after supper, she walked with her friend in the gardens, and sat on her favourite seat, by the Grande Cascade, in the moonlight. It was past twelve before they went indoors, and Madame retired to rest. She rose early the next morning, and probably wrote the letter to the Princess Palatine before leaving her room. After a long talk with Monsieur, she paid Madame de La Fayette a visit, and told her that she had slept well, but was very unhappy. "Yet the ill-humour of which she complained," adds Madame de La Fayette, "would have been thought charming in other women, so great was her natural sweetness, and so incapable was she of anger and of bitterness." Presently she went to mass, and, as she returned, leaning on Madame de La Fayette's arm, she said, in the gentle tone of voice peculiar to her, that she should not feel so cross if she could talk to her, but that she was tired of all the people about her, and could not endure their presence. After some conversation she went to look at the portrait of her child, the little Mademoiselle, which was being painted by an English artist, and then talked of her journey to England, and of her brother, the King. This revived her spirits, and another intimate friend of hers, the widowed Duchesse d'Épernon, having arrived, Madame talked to the

344

two ladies with her accustomed vivacity. Madame de La
Fayette had lately received a blow from the cornice of a
mantelpiece, which had fallen on her head. This strange
accident had excited as much amusement as compassion
amongst her friends, and Bussy had written a witty letter
expressing his regrets at hearing that a head so dear to
Madame should have been so unkindly used. Madame, on
hearing the story, insisted on unfastening Madame de La
Fayette's hair, to examine the wound, and exclaimed : " Why,
it might have killed you ! I wonder if you would have been
afraid to die ? " And, after a moment's reflection, she added
with a sigh : " As for me, I do not think I should be afraid
of death."

Dinner was served in Monsieur's rooms. He and
Madame's ladies were present, besides her two guests. The
meal ended, Madame lay down on cushions spread on the
floor, after her habit, keeping Madame de La Fayette close
at her side, and fell fast asleep, while Monsieur talked to the
ladies, and discussed his own portrait on which the English
artist was also engaged. Madame de La Fayette, who had
often seen the Princess in her sleep, then noticed for the first
time a strange alteration in her face, and, when Henrietta
woke up, Monsieur remarked how very ill she looked. She
passed out into a hall, where she spoke for some minutes
with Monsieur's treasurer, Boisfranc, stopping now and then
to take breath, and complaining of the pain in her side.
Monsieur had meanwhile gone downstairs, to start for Paris,
after his daily habit, but, meeting Madame de Mecklembourg
on the stairs, he brought her in to see Madame. Henrietta
welcomed this new guest warmly, and they conversed together until about five o'clock. A glass of iced chicory water,
for which Madame had asked, was handed to her by one of
her ladies, Madame de Gourdon. Hardly had she drunk the
water, than she was seized with a violent pain in her side, and
cried out, " Ah ! what a pain ! What shall I do ! I must be
poisoned." Her ladies hastened to her assistance. They un-
laced her gown, took off her clothes, and helped her to lie
down on her bed. Madame de La Fayette, grieved at seeing the tears in her eyes, kissed the arm that she was

supporting, and said that she feared she must be suffering
acutely, for she knew that she was always the most patient
person in the world.   Madame replied that the pain was
indeed frightful, and rolled to and fro in her agony.   Monsieur's chief doctor, M. Esprit, was hastily summoned.   He
declared that Madame was suffering from colique, and prescribed some ordinary remedies.   Still her pains only became
worse, and those about her were horrified to hear her ask for
her confessor, and say that she was certainly going to die.
Monsieur now entered the room.   She turned to embrace
him, and said, with a sweetness and charm that would have
melted the hardest heart : " Alas ! Monsieur, you have long
ceased to love me, but you have been unjust to me.   I never
wronged you."   Monsieur was deeply touched by these words,
and all who stood by burst into tears.

But still Madame complained of terrible pains.   Suddenly
she exclaimed again that she had been poisoned, and begged
that the water of which she had drunk might be examined.
At these words, Madame de La Fayette, who stood in the
alcove close to the bedside at Monsieur's side, looked narrowly
at him.   He seemed neither embarrassed nor yet distressed,
but merely said that, if this were the case, emetics had better
be sent for, and some of the chicory water given to a dog.
Madame Desbordes, Henrietta's oldest and most attached
servant, said that she had mixed the chicory water, and,
taking the bottle from a shelf, drank of the water out of the
same cup, in Madame's presence.   Monsieur's first valet,
Mérille, meanwhile brought an emetic which Madame
swallowed, but which only seemed to increase her pains.
Her exhaustion now became greater every moment, and she
said repeatedly that there was no help for it, for that she
knew she must die.   " It seemed," says Madame de La
Fayette, " that she felt confident she was dying, and, with
great calmness and courage, she prepared to meet her end.
The idea of poison had taken hold of her mind, and, seeing
that all remedies appeared useless, she no longer thought of life,
but only tried to bear her suffering patiently."

One of her attendants, Madame de Gamaches, now felt
her pulse, and, to her horror, declared that Madame had no

pulse, and that her hands and feet were growing cold and numb. Upon this, Monsieur became alarmed, and, when M. Esprit declared that this was commonly the case in similar attacks, and that he could answer for Madame's life, he replied angrily that M. Esprit had answered for the little Duc de Valois's life, but that the child had died, and that he now pretended to answer for Madame, while she too was dying. By this time, the Curé de Saint-Cloud had arrived. Madame made her confession quietly, and whispered a few gentle words in Monsieur's ear, after which he asked her if she would consent to be bled in the arm, as M. Esprit advised. "Let him do what he likes," she replied, "it is all the same, nothing can save me."

She had now been ill during more than three hours, and showed no signs of improvement. M. Yvelin, her own physician, and M. Vallot, the King's doctor, who had also been summoned from Versailles, held a consultation together, and agreed that there could be no danger. Monsieur repeated their opinion to his wife, upon which she replied calmly, but quite decidedly, that they were wrong, for that she knew there was no hope. The Prince de Condé now entered the room. Madame told him that she was dying, and hoped soon to be out of pain. But the doctors persisted in saying that she was better, and out of danger, and her ladies began to feel consoled. Madame d'Épernon and Madame de La Fayette both tried to cheer her, by saying that now, at least, Monsieur would treat her more kindly since the sight of her suffering had caused him so much distress. But all the while Madame herself said that she was no better, and declared that her pains were so great, she would put an end of her life if she were not a Christian. "I suppose it is wrong," she added, "to wish others harm, but I must say I wish the doctors could feel for one moment what I am suffering, and then they might, perhaps, understand my condition." She changed her bed, and was able to walk across the room, but began to get worse directly she lay down. One of the doctors now held a candle to her face, and when Monsieur asked if it hurt her eyes, she replied: "Ah! no, Monsieur, nothing hurts me now. I shall not be alive to-

morrow morning, you will see." A cup of soup was given
her, which only brought back her pains with increased
violence. Even the doctors now began to be alarmed. They
owned that the numbness of her limbs was a bad sign, and
feared the worst.

At this moment, the King and Queen arrived. The news
of Madame's illness had reached Versailles, and the King had
sent repeated messages of inquiry to Saint-Cloud. At nine
o'clock the Duc de Créqui arrived in haste, bringing him
word that Madame was dying. He had come straight from
her chamber, and declared that, whatever the doctors might
say, she had the look of a dying woman on her face. Louis
XIV. ordered his carriage, and said he would go to her at
once. *Madame se meurt*—the news flew like wildfire through
Versailles. Mademoiselle paints the horror and dismay with
which the words passed from lip to lip. She was walking in
the garden, on the banks of the ornamental water, with the
Queen, when a message from Madame herself was brought to
Marie Thérèse, begging her to lose no time if she wished to
find her alive. They set off immediately with the King and
the Comtesse de Soissons, once Madame's bitter enemy. On
the way, the Queen spoke of the horrible rumours of poison
which had got abroad, and was full of compassion for her
sister-in-law, and of indignation at Monsieur's unkindness.
Vallot, who met them on his return from Saint-Cloud,
informed the King that Madame's illness was merely an
attack of colic, and would soon pass off. But when they
reached the palace, their own eyes told them a very different
tale.

Madame lay there, stretched on a little bed, with her
nightdress unfastened and her hair loose. Her face was
deadly pale, her features drawn and sunken. "She had,"
says Mademoiselle, "already the air of a corpse." "You see
the state I am in," she said, as the King entered the room.
Louis spoke tenderly to her, and tried to cheer her with hopes
of recovery. But she shook her head, and told him the first
thing he would hear the next morning would be the news
of her death. She roused herself to embrace the King
and Queen, and spoke affectionately to them both. Then

she pressed Mademoiselle's hand, and said: "You are losing a good friend, who was beginning to know and love you." The King began to reason with the doctors. "Surely," he said, "you will not let a woman die without trying to save her." But they could only look at each other helplessly, and had not a word to say. The King returned to Madame's bedside and told her that, although no physician himself, he had proposed a dozen different remedies, but that the doctors were still of opinion that it would be wiser not to administer them at present. Madame shrugged her shoulders, and replied that she supposed she must die according to proper form. Louis could only embrace her, and bid her turn her thoughts to God.

Never before had the halls of Saint-Cloud, that palace of delight, witnessed so strange a scene. The doors were crowded with courtiers, with princes and princesses, ministers and ladies of rank, all coming and going, standing about in the passages, and waiting anxiously for the latest news. A few, frivolous even in the presence of death, were talking and laughing in under-tones. But most faces were full of sorrow. And, in the darkened chamber within, the King, with tears streaming down his cheeks, was clasping Madame in a last farewell. "Kiss me, sire," she said, "for the last time. Ah, sire! do not weep for me, or you will make me weep too. You are losing a good servant, who has always feared the loss of your good graces more than death itself."

On her other side stood the Queen in tears, and Monsieur, looking more bewildered than distressed, while Mademoiselle knelt at the foot of the bed, sobbing aloud. Many others, who had known Madame in the days of youth and joy, were there now. There was the great soldier, Condé, and his old rival, Turenne. There were her faithful friends, Madame d'Epernon and Madame de La Fayette, and there, standing apart, with a look of silent agony on his face, was Tréville, the brilliant and accomplished Tréville, the wittiest man in France; Tréville, who had adored Madame from afar, and would have given his life to save her. And there, too, strange companions in the chamber of death, were La Vallière and Montespan, the King's rival mistresses, who had both of them, in old days, been maids-of-honour to Madame, and who now came together to see her die.

There she lay, with all these familiar faces about her, strangely calm in the intervals of her agony, speaking kindly to each in turn, and talking naturally of her approaching end. From the first, she never had a hope of recovery, and did not once express regret at the cruel fate which snatched her away in the flower of her youth. Her presence of mind and thoughtfulness for others never left her. She took a kind farewell of the grey-headed Maréchal de Gramont, the father of the Comte de Guiche, and brother of Madame de Saint-Chaumont; and the fine old man bade her adieu in the most touching words. "You are losing a good friend in me," she said, and added that she had at first thought herself poisoned by accident. Then, catching sight of Tréville, who stood in the background overcome with grief, she said, "*Adieu, Tréville, adieu!*" The King now bade Madame farewell, and left the room, unable to restrain his tears. The Queen followed his example, after a last embrace, and Mademoiselle was so overwhelmed with grief that she left the room without daring to approach Madame. By this time they were all convinced that she was dying, and the King told Monsieur that a priest must be summoned without delay, since Madame had asked repeatedly for the last sacraments. Monsieur hesitated, and asked whose name would appear best in the *Gazette*. Fortunately, someone said that Madame had asked for M. de Condom. "He will do excellently," replied Monsieur; "Madame has often talked with him." And three couriers were despatched in haste to Paris to bring Bossuet to Saint-Cloud.

Meanwhile, Madame de La Fayette had already sent for M. Feuillet, a Jansenist canon of Saint-Cloud, whose apostolic fervour was highly esteemed by her friends at Port-Royal. The severity of his doctrines did not find favour at Court, and Boileau had styled him in his satire the reformer of the universe. One day in Lent, when Feuillet happened to be at Saint-Cloud, Monsieur, who was as scrupulous, when the fit seized him, in matters of religion as in questions of etiquette, asked him if he might eat an orange without breaking his fast. The priest replied : "Eat an ox if you like, Monsieur, but pay your debts, and lead a Christian life." The boldness of this answer had pleased Madame, and at this crisis Madame de La Fayette thought of him at once.

Feuillet entered the room at eleven o'clock, as the King and Queen retired.

"You see, M. Feuillet," said Madame, as he drew near, "the state to which I am reduced."

"A very good state, Madame," replied the austere priest. "You will now confess that there is a God in Heaven, whom you have never really known."

"It is too true," said Madame, sadly ; "till now, my God, I have never really known Thee !"

Here her own confessor, Padre Zoccoli, a Capuchin, fit for little, Monsieur had observed, except to ride in her coach, tried to interfere, but Madame stopped him gently, and said, with a smile at Madame de La Fayette, "Allow M. Feuillet to speak now, my father, and you shall have your turn next."

He then exhorted her to repent of her past sins, of the years which she had spent in selfish luxury, in frivolous pleasures and forgetfulness of God. He told her plainly that she had never known the true Christian faith, and she owned humbly that her past confession and communions had been worth little. By her own wish she made a general confession and then asked earnestly "that she might be allowed to receive Jesus Christ." Even the stern Jansenist priest was moved by her gentleness and humility. "God gave her," he wrote afterwards, "sentiments which surprised me, and made her speak in language altogether unlike that of the world. to which she belonged."

While Feuillet was still speaking, Ralph Montagu arrived. He had hastened to Saint-Cloud on receiving a summons which Madame de Mecklembourg had sent him, at Madame's request, and stood speechless with grief and horror at her bedside.

She turned eagerly to him.

"You see, I am dying," she said. "Alas ! how much I grieve for the King, my brother ! He is losing the person who loves him best in the whole world."

Many were the tender messages which she bade the
Ambassador convey to the brother whom she had loved so
well. She asked Montagu if he remembered their conversation the day before, and what she had told him respecting the
alliance with France and Holland, adding : " I beg you to tell
my brother that I only urged him to do this, because I was
convinced that it was for his own honour and advantage.
I have always loved him better than life itself, and now
my only regret in dying is to be leaving him."

Again and again she repeated these words in English,
and told Montagu not to forget them. The Ambassador then
asked her in English, if she believed herself to have been
poisoned.   Here Feuillet interfered, catching the word
poison.

"Madame," he said, "you must accuse no one, but offer
your life as a sacrifice to God."

Montagu repeated the question, but she only shrugged
her shoulders. Madame de La Fayette, however, heard her
say in a low voice, which did not reach the Ambassador's
ears :—

" If this is true, you must never let the King, my brother,
know it.   Spare him that grief at all events, and, above all,
do not let him take revenge on the King here, for he at least
is not guilty." She then told her maid, Madame Desbordes,
to give Montagu the casket that held her brother's letters, and
recommended her poor servants to the King's care.   Once
more she sent the most affectionate messages to both of her
brothers, and drawing a ring from off her fingers, bade
Montagu give it, with her last and tenderest love, to the King
of England.   She again thanked Montagu for all his zeal and
affection in her service and begged him to accept the 6000 pistoles which Charles II. had given her, as a token of her regard.
This he declined to do, but promised to distribute the money
among those of her servants, whose names she mentioned.

The Curé of Saint-Cloud now arrived, bringing the Host
with him.   Madame received the Viaticum with the greatest
devotion, and asked for the crucifix which had belonged to
her mother-in-law, Anne of Austria.   After that she wished to
see Monsieur, who had left the room, but who now came back,

weeping bitterly, and embraced her for the last time. She took leave of him, saying that she only wished to think of God. Some one who was present, observed that she seemed rather better.

"Alas!" said Madame, overhearing the remark, "they think I am better, because I have no longer strength to complain."

Another doctor of great repute, M. Brayer, who had been summoned from Paris by the King's orders, now arrived, and made a last effort to save her, by bleeding her in the foot. But this remedy proved as ineffectual as the others, and seemed only to increase her pains.

"*Mon Dieu!*" she cried, "when will these fearful pains cease?"

"What, Madame," said Feuillet, "are you already impatient? You have been sinning against God during twenty-six years, and you have only begun to do penance in these last six hours." Madame bowed her head humbly, and asked at what hour Christ died on the Cross.

"At three o'clock," replied the priest.

"Perhaps," she said gently, "He will allow me to die at the same hour."

Extreme unction was now administered, and at the same moment Bossuet arrived. A gleam of joy lighted up Madame's pale face as he entered, and she turned herself towards him.

"*L'espérance, Madame, L'espérance!*" were his first words, as he flung himself on his knees, and placed the crucifix once more in her hands.

"I put my whole trust in His mercy," she replied, joining her hands together. The few friends who were still present, Madame de La Fayette and Madame d'Epernon, the Maréchal de Bellefonds, Tréville and Montagu, fell on their knees while the great Bishop prayed for the passing soul with all the force and energy of his being.

"My heart is with you," Madame whispered, as she followed his prayers.

"You see, Madame," said Bossuet, rising from his knees, "you see what this life is. Thank God who calls you to Himself."

He paused, fearing to exhaust her rapidly failing strength.
But she signed to him to proceed.

"Go on!" she said faintly, "go on! I am listening!"

"You die, Madame," he asked her, "in the Catholic Apostolic and Roman Faith?"

"I have lived in that faith and I die in it," she replied in
a clear voice.

Her pains now returned with greater violence than ever,
and Bossuet bade her offer them to God, in union with those
of Our Lord on the Cross.

"That is what I am trying to do," she replied.

Holding the crucifix aloft before her failing eyes, the
Bishop spoke words of hope and comfort. "*There* is Christ,"
he said, "whose arms are stretched out to receive you! He
will give you eternal life, and raise up that suffering body in
the glory of His Resurrection."

"*Credo! credo!*" she replied fervently, and then sank back
exhausted.

The Bishop withdrew into the window seat, to give her a
few minutes' rest, and knelt there in silent prayer. Then
Madame, who was still perfectly conscious, remembered the
present which she had ordered for him, and with that delicacy
which marked all her actions, she whispered to one of her
maids, in English: "Give M. de Condom the emerald ring
which I have had made for him, when I am dead."

A few moments afterwards, she said to M. Feuillet, who
stood beside her.

"It is all over; call back M. de Condom."

Bossuet returned and noticed the change in her appearance at once.

"Madame," he said, "you believe in God, you hope in
God, you love God?"

"With all my heart," she murmured, and never spoke
again. The crucifix dropped from her hands, and as Bossuet
uttered the last prayers, *In manus tuas*, she died.

It was three o'clock on the morning of the 30th of June.

"Thus," writes the Bishop of Valence, "this great and
royal-hearted princess passed away, without ever having shown
the least sign of trouble or weakness in this awful surprise.

All she said and did was perfectly natural and without effort, and they who saw and heard her, know that she spoke from her heart. The whole of France, mourning as it does for her, is edified by the sight of her piety, and amazed at her great and heroic courage."

"I pray that God may receive her, in His mercy," adds the Jansenist priest, Feuillet, "and all you, who read these words, pray for her also."

Grief of the King and Court for Madame—Popular Feeling in England—The Suspicion that she was Poisoned becomes General—Letters of Montagu—Saint Simon's Version—Was Madame Poisoned, or was her Death due to Natural Causes?

THE summer morning which dawned on that night of agony was long remembered in France. The cry that broke from Monsieur's lips, the sobs and lamentations of Madame's servants, were but the first notes of the wail that went up from one end of the land to the other. "All the world," wrote an English secretary, "is in lamentation." There was grief and consternation everywhere. The King, on waking, heard the news of Madame's death, and Mademoiselle found him in floods of tears. Never in all his life, he said, had he known so great a sorrow. An hour later, Bossuet arrived, and told the King and Queen that Madame had died, as only a good Christian could die. He described how bravely and calmly she had met her end, and how, in that supreme hour, the sweetness of nature, which had marked her in life, had not once failed her.

"*Madame fut douce envers la mort, comme elle l'etait envers tout le monde.*"

For some time past, the Bishop told the King, Madame had frequently conversed with him on religious subjects. She had begged him to come and instruct her in these matters, at times when she could be alone, and now he had every reason to be thankful for the blessed state of mind in which she had died. Bossuet remained closeted for an hour with the King, and Condé told him afterwards, that he had never seen His Majesty so deeply moved.

The next day, Louis XIV. wrote a few lines with his own hand to Charles II.

"MY BROTHER,—The tender love I had for my sister was well known to you, and you will understand the grief into which her death has plunged me. In this heavy affliction, I can only say that the part which I take in your own sorrow, for the loss of one who was so dear to both of us, increases the burden of my regret. My only comfort is the confidence I cherish that this fatal accident will make no change in our friendship, and that you will continue to let me enjoy yours as fully as I give you mine."

At the same time, Lionne wrote a long despatch to Colbert de Croissy, giving a full account of Madame's death, and saying that His Majesty had decided to send the Maréchal de Bellefonds, who was present at Saint-Cloud during her last agony, and who had been honoured with her especial friendship, to give the King of England a more particular report of this distressing event.

"He will be better able, by word of mouth, to tell you in what condition he saw the King, who would not leave the bedside of the Princess until she was at the point of death. He will tell you what marks of love and tenderness passed between them, how many tears it has cost his Majesty, and he will describe the despair of Monsieur, the affliction and consternation of the whole Court, and of all Paris. If anything could give us consolation, in so terrible an accident, and so great a loss, which, for a thousand reasons, must be eternally lamented, it would be the manner of her death, which was as holy and Christian as it was resolute and heroic. Never was there seen deeper resignation to the will of God, and greater devotion in receiving the sacrament, than Madame showed, as well as more perfect trust in the Divine goodness. The Bishop of Condom, who assisted her in her passage from this world, has wonderful things to tell

us on the subject, and all who were present say that no one
ever showed greater presence of mind, or less fear of death.
She did not even weep while the King, Monsieur, the whole
Court and all her own servants, were in floods of tears. I
assure you, sir, that the King's grief has been, and is still, so
excessive, that I am very anxious for his health, He is going
to sleep at Saint-Germain to-night, saying that he cannot
remain in this house of pleasure while he is so overwhelmed
with grief."

But long before these letters reached England, Charles
II. had already heard the sad news. An hour after Madame
had breathed her last, Ralph Montagu wrote the following
letter to Lord Arlington, and sent it to London by Sir
Thomas Armstrong :—

" PARIS,
"*June* 30, 1670. *Four in the morning.*

" MY LORD,—I am sorry to be obliged by my employment,
to give you an account of the saddest story in the world, and
which I have hardly the courage to write. Madame, on
Sunday the 29th of this instant, being at St Clou with a
great deal of company, about five o'clock in the afternoon
called for a glass of chicory water that was prescribed for
her to drink, she having for two or three days after bathing
found herself indisposed. She had no sooner drunk this
but she cryed out she was dead, and fell into Madam
Mechelbourg's arms, desired to be put to bed, and have a
confessor. She continued in the greatest tortures imaginable,
till 3 o'clock in the morning, when she dyed ; the King, the
Queen, and all the Court being there, till about an hour
before. God send the King, our master, patience and
constancy to bear so great an affliction. Madame declared
she had no reluctancy to die, but out of the grief she thought
it would be to the King, her brother, and when she was in
any case for the torture she was in, which the physician
called *colique bileuse*, she asked for me, and it was to charge
me to say all the kind things from her to her brothers, the
King and Duke. I did not leave her till she expired, and
happened to come to Saint Clou an hour after she fell ill.

Never anybody died with that piety and resolution, and kept her senses to the last. Excuse this imperfect relation, for the grief I am in. I am sure all that had the Honour to know her will have their share for so great and general a loss. I am, my Lord, Yours," etc.

An hour later his secretary added the following lines :—

"The bearer will tell you that Madame fell sick of a colic about 4 in the afternoon, and died, a most lamented Princess, this morning at 3. Grief will not let me add more, but refer you for further particulars to his relation, who was present at St. Cloud."

At six o'clock, after taking a last look at Madame's lifeless face, the young Englishman rode off, post-haste, to Calais, and never stopped till he reached Whitehall, where he himself delivered the sad tidings to the King. At the first moment, Charles gave way to a violent outburst of grief and indignation. He shed torrents of tears, and passionately execrated Monsieur's name. But he soon recovered his composure, and prudently refrained from expressing his feelings in public. "Monsieur is a villain!" he exclaimed, "but, Sir Thomas, I beg of you, not a word of this to others." None the less, the horrible suspicion of poison, which Madame herself had shared, gained ground rapidly, and roused a storm of popular indignation. Buckingham raged like a madman, and was for declaring war on the spot. In the city, the mob rose tumultuously and shouted death to the French. The Ambassador's life was threatened, and a report reached Paris that a detachment of the King's guards had been sent to protect his house. Colbert himself became seriously alarmed, and wrote Lionne word of the evil rumours that were abroad. "The King of England," he repeats, "remains inconsolable, and his grief is increased by the general impression which has got abroad, that Madame was poisoned. Neither His Majesty, nor any other member of the Royal Family, have expressed their belief in this extravagant report; but three personages at Court declare aloud that it is true—Prince Rupert, because he has a natural

inclination to believe evil ; the Duke of Buckingham, because
he courts popularity ; and Sir John Trevor, because he is
Dutch at heart, and consequently hates the French."

The same sinister reports were widely repeated in France.
The crime was openly ascribed to the Chevalier de Lorraine,
and every detail was given with frightful accuracy. It was
said that he had sent a deadly poison from Rome, and that
D'Effiat, his accomplice, had rubbed it on the silver cup, from
which Madame drank the chicory water on that Sunday
afternoon. Montagu believed the story, and remained convinced of its truth until his dying day. So general was the
impression of foul play, that Louis XIV. ordered a post-
mortem examination, which was held on the evening of the
30th of June, in the presence of the English Ambassador.
An English doctor, named Hugh Chamberlain, a surgeon in
Charles II.'s service, named Boscher, Lord Salisbury, Abbé
Montagu and James Hamilton, were also present. Both the
English and French physicians agreed that no trace of poison
was to be found, and an official report, signed by the French
doctors present, declared that Madame had died of cholera-
morbus. Chamberlain and Boscher drew up separate statements, in which they expressed their opinion that death was
produced by natural causes, but Boscher distinctly said that
the operation had been conducted in the most unskilful
manner, "as if the surgeon's business were rather to hide the
truth than to reveal it." We learn, from Temple's letters,
that the English doctors were not altogether satisfied with the
result of the examination. Writing to Lord Arlington on the
15th of July, he expresses his satisfaction "that the sad and
surprising affliction of Madame's death shall at least be without that odious circumstance which was at first so generally
thought to have attended it," but remarks that, " where he is,"
it is no easy matter to succeed in allaying people's suspicions.
" These," he adds, " have been much increased by the Princess
Dowager's curiosity to ask her physicians' opinions upon the
relation transmitted hither to one of them from his brother,
who is the Dutch secretary at Paris, and pretends it came
from Dr Chamberlain, though something different from what
he transmitted into England. However it happened, it had

The Princess Henrietta of England.
Duchess of Orleans.

certainly all the circumstances to aggravate the affliction to His Majesty, which I am infinitely touched with, as with the sense of an accident, in itself so deplorable. But it is a necessary tribute we pay for the continuance of our lives, to bewail the frequent and sometimes untimely death of our friends."

Louis XIV. had, from the first, dreaded the effect which these reports would produce among his enemies in Holland, and had himself written to M. de Pomponne, as follows :—

"Your despatch of the 26th of last month requiring no special answer, I will only speak to you of the heavy blow which I and my whole family have just received from the hand of God, who has taken away my sister, the Duchesse d'Orléans. She was carried off by a violent colique, in the short space of seven or eight hours. This misfortune will not be regarded where you are with the sentiments which I must feel. I can only bow to the Divine Will, and seek what consolation I can find in the manner of this Princess's death, which could not have been holier or more Christian, and leaving Lionne to give you particulars of this fatal accident, I pray God to have you, M. de Pomponne, in His holy keeping.   LOUIS.

"*Saint Germain-en-Laye, 4th day of July* 1670."

At the same time, the King did his utmost to allay the angry feeling which Madame's death had aroused in England. The very day after the sad event, he sent Montagu word that he felt Madame's loss as deeply as if she had been his own wife, and begged him to assure his master that, " if there were the least imagination that her death had been caused by poison, nothing should be wanting, either towards the discovering or the punishing soe horrid a fact." A few days later he gave the Ambassador an audience, in which he showed him extraordinary marks of kindness and sympathy, and spoke of his sister-in-law in the tenderest manner.

By degrees the popular mind became calmer. Charles II. received Monsieur's envoy coldly, and refused, it is said, to read his brother-in-law's letter. And he spoke bitterly to Colbert, of the way in which Monsieur had treated his wife, and of the

Chevalier de Lorraine's scandalous behaviour towards her.
But he received the Maréchal de Bellefonds with the greatest
courtesy, and professed himself satisfied with the letters and
explanations which he brought with him.

No one could doubt the sincerity of Louis XIV.'s
grief, or the genuineness of his regard for Madame ; and if
Charles II. was less satisfied with Monsieur's conduct, he was
not disposed to visit his resentment on the King. On the 7th
of July, Colbert de Croissy was able to write home that any
suspicions which had arisen in the minds of the King of
England, and of the chief personages at Court, were now quite
dissipated, and the only feeling now remaining in England
was that of sorrow for the loss of so admirable a Princess.
Arlington dined at the Guildhall to pacify the citizens of
London, and the King sent Buckingham to France, to represent him at Madame's funeral, and to assure Louis XIV. of
his continued friendship. It was not in Charles II.'s nature
to sorrow long and deeply, even for the sister who had been
so dear to him. He observes, in a characteristic note to the
Duc d'Elbœuf, "I cannot help thanking you very warmly
for the sorrow which you express at my sister's death, knowing, as I do, how much she esteemed you. But, to say the
truth, my grief for her is so great that I dare not allow myself to dwell upon it, and try as far as possible to think of
other things."

Meanwhile, what with the rumours of poison that were
filling the air, and the enmity shown him by Monsieur, Ralph
Montagu had a difficult task to obey his master's orders, and
fulfil Madame's last wishes. His letters, both to the King
and Arlington, are full of interesting details, and their tone
shows that, in spite of the natural resentment which he felt at
being excluded from any share in the recent negotiations, he
had lost none of his old devotion for Madame. On the 6th
of July, he writes to Arlington :—

"I suppose by this time you may have with you the
Maréchal de Bellefonds, who, besides his *condoléances*, will
endeavour, I believe, to disabuse our Court of *what the Court
and people here will never be disabused of*, which is Madame's

being poisoned, which, having so good an authority as her
own saying it several times in her great pain, makes the report
much more credited. But to me in particular, when I asked
her several times, whether she thought herself poisoned, she
would answer nothing; I believe, being willing to spare the
addition of so great a trouble to the King, our master, which
was the reason why, in my first letter, I made no mention of
it, neither am I physician good enough to say she was
poisoned, or she was not. They are willing, in this countrey,
to make me the author of the report, I mean Monsieur, who
says I do it, to break the good intelligence between the two
crowns. The King and ministers here seem extremely affected
with the loss of Madame, and I do not doubt but what they
are, for they hoped upon her consideration to bring the King,
our master, to condescend to things, and enter into a friendship with this crown, stricter perhaps than they think he will,
now she is no more. What was begun, or what was intended,
I will not presume to search into, since your Lordship did not
think fit to communicate the least part of it to me, but I cannot help knowing the town talk, and I dare answer that all
the King, our master, can propose, will be granted here, to have
his friendship, and there is nothing on the other side the
Dutch will not do, to hinder our joining with the French.
All I desire, my Lord, is that, whilst I am here, I may know
what language to hold in conversation with the other ministers,
that I may not be ridiculed with the character I have upon
me. Whilst Madame was alive, she did me the honour to
trust me enough, to hinder me from being exposed to that
misfortune. I am sure that, for the little time you knew her
in England, you could not but know her enough to regret her
as long as you live; as I am sure you have reason. For I
never knew anybody kinder, nor have a better opinion of
another in all kinds than she had of you. And I believe she
loved the King, her Brother, too well, if she had not been
persuaded how well and faithfully you served him, to have
been so really concerned for you, as I have observed her to be,
upon all occasions, since there has been a good understanding
between you. As for my own particular, I have had so great
a loss, that I have no joy in this countrey, nor hopes of any

in another. Madame, after several discourses with me in her illness, which was all nothing but kind expressions of the King, our Master, at last told me she was extremely sorry she had done nothing for me before she died, in return of all the zeal and affection with which I had served her, since my being here. She told me that there were 6000 pistoles of hers in several places; she bid me take them for her sake. I told her she had many poor servants that wanted more than I, that I never served her out of interest, and that absolutely I would not take it, but if she pleased to tell me which of them I should give it to, I would dispose of it, according to her pleasure. She had so much presence of mind as to name them to me by their names, but the breath was no sooner out of her body, but Monsieur seized all her keys and caskets. I inquired next day where the money was. One of her women said it was in such a place, which happened to be the first 6000 pistoles the King, our master, sent her. For, just as that money came, it was designed to unpawn some jewels upon which she had already taken up the money; but two days before, the King of France gave her money with which she impawned them, so the money came clear in to her. I demanded the money upon this, from Monsieur, as money of mine, that was borrowed for Madame, as having been delivered by my servant to two of her women, who assured him (as they could not do otherwise) that that money came from me, for they never knew that the King, our master, had sent it her. Monsieur had, in this time, got away above half of the money. The rest I had delivered me, which I did to the uttermost farthing, in the presence of my Lord Abbot Montagu and two other witnesses, dispose to Madame's servants equally, as she directed. Monsieur has promised me the rest, which they are to have in the same manner, but if they are not wise enough to keep their council, he will certainly take it away from them. I could not have got it for the poor people any other way, and I believe the King will be gladder they should have it than Monsieur.

"*P.S.*—Since the writing of this, I am told, from very good hands, and one that Monsieur trusts, that he, being desired by the King to deliver up all Madame's papers, before he would do it he first sent for my Lord Abbot Montagu, to read them, and interpret them to him ; but not trusting enough to him, he employed other persons that understood the language to do it, amongst which Madame de Fiennes was one, so that most of the private thoughts between the King and Madame are, and will be, very publick. There were some in cypher, which trouble him extreamly; but yet he pretends to guess at it. And he complains extreamly of the King, our master, for having a confidence with Madame, and treating things with her without his knowledge. My Lord Abbot Montagu will, I hope, give you a larger account of this matter than I can, for though Monsieur enjoined him secrecy to all the world, it cannot extend to you, if there be anything that concerns the King, our Master's, affairs."

The papers which Monsieur had seized were Charles II.'s confidential letters to his sister, which have been fully given in these pages. On hearing of Madame's death, Charles had sent an express to the French King, begging him to take charge of them without delay. Louis, accordingly, sent a peremptory order to his brother, demanding immediate possession of Madame's private papers, and Monsieur was compelled to give them up, after having, as the Ambassador reports, done his best to decipher them, with the help of Abbé Montagu and Madame de Fiennes. So Charles II.'s letters to his sister found their way into the Depôt at Versailles, and have been preserved to this day among the Archives des Affaires Etrangères.

On the 15th of July, Montagu sent Lord Arlington the ring, which Madame had taken off her finger on her death-bed, to be presented to His Majesty, in fulfilment of her dying wish, and himself wrote a letter to the King, with a fuller account of Madame's last messages.

"SIR,—I ought to begin with begging your Majesty's pardon for saying anything to you upon so sad a subject, and where I had the misfortune to be a witness of the cruellest and most generous end any person in the world ever made. I had the honour on the Saturday, which was

the day before Madame dy'd, to entertain her a great while,
the most of her discourse being concerning Monsieur, and
how impossible she said it was for her to live happily with
him, for he was fallen out with her worse than ever, because
that, two days before, she had been at Versailles, and there he
found her talking privately with the King about affairs
which were not fit to be communicated to him. She told me
your Majesty and the King here were both resolved upon a
war with Holland, as soon as you could be agreed on the
manner of it. These were the last words I had the honour to
have from her, till she fell ill, for Monsieur came in and
interrupted her, and I returned to Paris the next day. When
she fell ill, she called for me two or three times. Madame de
Meckelburg sent for me. As soon as I came in, she told
me :—' You see the sad condition I am in. I am going to
die. How I pity the King, my Brother! For I am sure he
loses the Person in the World that loves him best.' A little
while after she called me again, bidding me be sure to say
all the kind things in the world from her to the King, her
brother, and 'thank him for all his kindness and care of me.'
Then she asked me if I remembered what she had said to
me the night before, of your Majesty's intentions to join with
France against Holland. I told her, Yes. ' Pray, then,' said
she, ' tell my Brother I never persuaded him to it out of my
own interest, or to be more considered in this country, but
because I thought it for his honour and advantage. For I
always loved him above all things in the world, and have no
regret to leave it, but because I leave him.' She called to me
several times to be sure to say this to you, and spoke to me
in English. I asked her then, if she believed her self
poisoned. Her confessor, that was by, understood that word,
and told her, ' Madame, you must accuse nobody, but offer up
your death to God as a sacrifice.' So she would never answer
me to that question, though I asked her several times, but
would only shrink up her shoulders. I asked her for her
casket, where all her letters were, to send them to Your
Majesty. She bade me take it from Madame Des Bordes,
but she was swooning and dying to see her Mistress in that
condition, and, before she came to herself, Monsieur had

seized on them. She recommended to you to help, as much as you could, all her poor servants. She bid me write unto my Lord Arlington to put you in mind of it, ‘And tell the King, my Brother, I hope he will, for my sake, do for him what he promised, *Car c'est un homme qui l'ayme, et qui le sert bien.'* She spoke afterwards a great deal, in French, aloud, bemoaning and lamenting the condition she knew your Majesty would be in when you heard the news of her death. I humbly again beg your Majesty's pardon for having been the unfortunate teller of so sad news, there being none of your servants that wishes you constant happiness with more zeal and truth than, Sir, Your Majesty's most humble and obedient servant,   RALPH MONTAGU."

In a letter to Lord Arlington, written on the same day, the Ambassador again alludes to his growing conviction that Madame had been poisoned :—

"Of the various reports since her death, that of her being poisoned prevails above all the rest, which has disordered the Ministers, as well as the King, to the greatest degree that can be. For my own particular, I have been so much struck with it, that I have hardly had the heart to stir out since; which, joined with the reports of the town, how much the King, our Master, resented so horrid a fact, that he would not receive Monsieur's letter, and that he commanded me home, made them conclude that the King was dissatisfied with this Court to the degree it was reported. So that to-day I am not able to express the satisfaction of the King and everybody to know that the King, our Master, was a little appeased. You may judge from this how much they value the friendship of England."

The relief of Louis XIV. and his ministers was evidently great, when they found that Charles II. was willing to drop the subject, and Lionne wrote joyfully to Pomponne at the Hague, that he might laugh Dutch and Spanish alike to scorn, since it was now plain that Madame's death would make no change in the friendship between the two Kings.

None the less, the belief that Madame had been poisoned by Lorraine and his friends, either with, or without Monsieur's knowledge, had taken hold of the popular mind, both in France and England. Burnet, who saw in this Princess the incarnation of Popery and of French influence, quietly remarks that Monsieur, no doubt, poisoned her because of her intrigues with the Comte de Guiche and M. de Tréville, a singular travesty of facts. Other contemporary writers suppose that Monsieur poisoned her out of jealousy of the Duke of Monmouth. But these statements, we need hardly observe, are absolutely devoid of foundation, and Monsieur may safely be acquitted of all share in the crime. Vicious and worthless as he was, cruel as his treatment of his wife had been, nature had not fitted him for the part of a great criminal. His cowardice was too abject, his terror of public opinion too excessive for him to have ventured on a crime, which would have made him infamous in the eyes of all Europe. Besides, his conduct on that memorable night was not that of a guilty man. Madame de La Fayette owns, that when Madame exclaimed she was poisoned, her first impulse was to look at Monsieur, but that, narrowly as she watched him, she could detect no sign of fear or confusion. Yet the story told by Saint-Simon in his *Memoirs* has gained acceptance among a large class of writers. According to his account, Louis XIV., being full of uneasiness as to the cause of Madame's death, ordered Monsieur's chief *maître d'hôtel*, Simon, to be secretly arrested, on the night of the 30th of June, and brought by a private staircase into his own presence. The King himself examined him, and charged him, on pain of instant death, to tell him if Madame had been poisoned. The wretched man owned tremblingly that it was so, and, on being further pressed, said that D'Effiat and Beuvron had obtained the poison from the Chevalier de Lorraine. "My brother, did he know of it?" asked the King, breathlessly. "No, sire," replied the servant, "we were not fools enough to tell him. He cannot keep a secret, and would have ruined us all." "That is enough," said the King, with a sigh of relief, and the man was set at liberty. But, from that time, Louis did not venture to make further inquiries, and the thing was hushed up. Saint-Simon goes on to say that, a few days after Monsieur's second marriage, to Elizabeth Charlotte, Princess Palatine, the King took the new Madame aside and informed her of these facts, adding, that he would never have allowed her to marry his brother had he been guilty of so monstrous a crime. Often as this version of the tale has been repeated, the story is, to say the least, highly improbable, and its sensational and dramatic character stamps it at once as a creation of Saint-Simon's brain. But there is no doubt that Monsieur's second wife firmly believed the first Madame to have been poisoned by Lorraine and D'Effiat. This eccentric lady had the greatest hatred of the whole *cabale des Lorrains*, as she called the Chevalier and his friends, and, when she quarrelled with Monsieur, was often heard to exclaim aloud that she knew they would poison her as they had poisoned poor Madame! She expresses her convictions on the subject in several passages of her correspondence.

"It is quite true that poor Madame was poisoned," she writes, in July 1716, "but without Monsieur's knowledge. To say the truth, he was incapable of such a crime. When these wretches conferred together, as to how they should poison poor Madame, they discussed whether they should tell Monsieur, but Lorraine said 'No, for he would never be able to hold his tongue, and even if he kept silence for a year, he would tell the King in the end, and we might all be hanged ten years afterwards.' They persuaded Monsieur that the Dutch had poisoned her in a cup of chocolate. The real truth is that D'Effiat rubbed the poison on a cup belonging to Madame, as a valet in her service himself told me, on that Sunday morning, while Monsieur and Madame were at Mass. As soon as Madame had drunk the chicory water out of that cup, she cried out, 'I am poisoned!' Others drank of the same water, but not out of that cup. The story is old, and reads like a page of romance, but it is never the less true." And elsewhere, in speaking of the Chevalier de Lorraine's debaucheries, and of the domestic broils which embittered Henrietta's life, she observes that Lorraine was banished as he deserved, but that his exile cost Madame her life.

The same conviction remained firmly rooted in Montagu's mind. When, in February 1672, only a year and a half after Madame's death, the Chevalier de Lorraine dared again to show his face at Court, the English Ambassador wrote an indignant letter home.

"If Madame were poisoned, as few people doubt, he is looked upon, by all France, to have done it, and it is wondered at, by all France, that this King should have so little regard to the King, our Master, considering how insolently he always carried himself to her when she was alive, as to allow his return." Lorraine's return to Court was a concession to Monsieur's weakness, on the King's part, for which Louis XIV. was no doubt to blame, even though he said repeatedly that it was done to gratify his brother, and made no secret of his own contempt for the Chevalier. But he could have hardly allowed the favourite's return, if he had really believed him to be guilty of Madame's death. Elizabeth Charlotte, it must be borne in mind, obtained her information entirely from servants, and was eager to believe the worst of a man whom she regarded as the cause of all the troubles of her married life.

There was, at that time, a common tendency to attribute sudden death to violent causes, a tendency that was no doubt increased by the lack of medical knowledge, and the incapacity of the Court doctors. The same suspicions were aroused in the case of Madame's own daughter, Marie Louise, the poor young Queen of Spain, who died exactly at her mother's age, and in a very similar manner, and again in that of her grand-daughter, the dearly loved Duchess of Burgundy. And Madame's health, always delicate, had been shattered by grave illnesses and frequent imprudences. Twice over, prema-ture accouchements had brought her to the point of death, and during the last few months of her life she was, as Made-moiselle remarks, almost always ill. That wise old doctor, Gui Patin, had long ago noticed the frequent cough from which she suffered, her extreme thinness and the hectic flush on her cheek. "The last day she was at Versailles, she looked," says Mademoiselle, "like a corpse, with a spot of rouge on each side of her face." Her constitution had been ruined by a life of continual fatigue and excitement, but that wonderful courage and spirit, which she showed in so remarkable a manner during the long hours of her death-agony, probably deceived those about her as to her true state of health.

In a separate report, which Vallot drew up, after the post-mortem examination, and presented to the King, he stated that for the last four or five years he had always had a very bad opinion of Madame's health, and feared that she might die suddenly ; but that, after the autopsy of her corpse, he could only say that it was a miracle she had lived so long. Even Gui Patin, with all his contempt for the Court doctors, agrees with their conclusions in this case, and rejects the idea of poison as a fabrication of the popular fancy.

"Here," he writes a month after, "they are still talking of that tragic event, the death of Madame la Duchesse d'Orléans. Many people believe that she was poisoned. But, as a matter of fact, her death was caused by a bad *régime* of living, as well as a naturally bad constitution. The popular voice, which likes to imagine grievances, and to meddle in things that it does not understand, should not be believed in such matters."

There can be little doubt that the old doctor was right. The chicory water which Madame drank, on that fatal Sunday afternoon, was mixed by her favourite maid, Madame Desbordes, who drank of it herself afterwards. According to Bossuet and Lionne, both Monsieur and Madame de Mecklembourg did the same, without any bad effects. It is very unlikely that Desbordes, or any other servant, would have allowed any powder to remain on the rim of the cup, from which her mistress was to drink, and it is still less probable that any poison would have been so prompt in its action, as to cause the violent pains which Henrietta felt the moment she had swallowed the draught.

Madame's death, grievous and lamentable as it was, may be safely ascribed to natural causes. That strange and sudden illness, which brought her life to a close at so early an age, was, in all probability, an attack of acute peritonitis, brought on by over-fatigue and by a chill, caught from bathing in the river in her already weakened condition. When we think of the continual strain to which her physical and mental powers were exposed, and of all the experiences and emotions which had been crowded into the last few years of her life, we need hardly wonder that she died before her time, sinking under a burden which she had not the strength to carry.

CHAPTER XXVII

1670

Conduct of Monsieur after his Wife's Death—Grief of Madame's Friends—Funeral
Services at Saint-Denis, Val-de-Grâce and Saint-Cloud — Bossuet's
Oraison.

THE cold and heartless conduct of Monsieur, after his wife's
death, naturally confirmed people in the belief that he was
not sorry to be rid of a Princess whose true worth he had
never known. Hardly had Madame breathed her last than,
as Montagu reports, he seized her letters and the money
which was to have been distributed to her servants, and went
off to Paris. There he devoted his thoughts wholly to the
mourning arrangements, and the reception of those official
visits of condolence in which he took so childish a pleasure.
Mademoiselle, who went to see him on Tuesday, at the Palais-
Royal, was surprised to find how little sorrow he showed.
He had dressed up his little daughter and her cousin, the
Princess Anne, in long trailing mantles of violet velvet, and,
with his usual ridiculous love of ceremony, insisted that
formal visits of condolence should be paid not only to these
children, but to his younger daughter, the baby Mademoiselle
de Valois, in her nursery. Two days after Madame's death
he retired to Madame d'Aiguillon's house at Rouille, where he
seemed to take his loss more to heart than he had done at
first.

"I believe," writes Vernon, "that he himself doubts where
he shall find a second wife whose qualities may come up to
those of her he has lost." But, as the English secretary
remarks, he soon got tired of "walking in the shade of melancholy," and in a fortnight's time he joined the Court at Saint

Germain, attired in the most elegant mourning, and apparently
in excellent spirits. "Monsieur," writes Vernon, on the 16th
of July, "is come from Rouille. I saw him yesterday at
dinner with the King. The King seems much more sensible
of our losse than he doe." Already he spoke freely of marrying again, and told his brother that he should like to make
Mademoiselle his wife, since, at her age, she would not be
likely to have a family, and he would thus secure the whole
of her large fortune. "Monsieur is in amours again," writes
Vernon early in August, "and if he be not shortly married to
Mademoiselle, all the world is in a mistake. He follows her,
he courts her, he is at her toilette, and waits on her as she
dresseth herself." But Mademoiselle was already in love with
Lauzun, and knew Monsieur too well now, to consent to become his wife at any price.

There were others on whom Madame's death had made a
deeper and more lasting impression. Tréville, who had seen
her die, and received her last farewell, never recovered from
the shock. When La Fare led him home, in the early dawn
of the June morning, he was so dazed with grief that his
friends trembled for his reason. After the funeral, he gave
up his post at Court, and left the world to become a recluse
at Port-Royal. Turenne felt the blow hardly less. Two years
before he had been brought over to the Catholic Church, by
Bossuet's influence, and now he had serious thoughts of joining the Fathers of the Oratory, and was only restrained from
taking the final step by the King's intimation that his services
at the head of the army would be shortly required. Madame
d'Epernon, who had spent that last Sunday at Saint-Cloud,
and who, with Madame de La Fayette, had remained at
Madame's bedside to the last, took the veil soon afterwards,
and joined the community of the Grandes Carmélites. And
in the same convent another witness of that tragic scene, and
another of Bossuet's converts, the King's forgotten mistress,
La Vallière, came, ere long, to end her days in penitence and
solitude, as Sœur Louise de la Miséricorde.

Never had the Court of the Grand Monarque received so
startling a warning of the vanity of this world's glory. In the
great preacher's words, Madame had faded away, as suddenly

as the flowers of the field. "In the morning our flower was blooming, with what grace we all know ; in the evening, it was cut down, dried up and withered." "You will hear from Corbinelli of the death of Madame," wrote Madame de Sevigné to Bussy de Rabutin, "and will imagine our horror in seeing her fall suddenly ill and die in eight hours' time. With her, we have lost all the joy, all the charm, and all the pleasures of the Court. Good-bye, my cousin, do not let us quarrel any more. I may have been a little in the wrong, but which of us does not sometimes make mistakes in this world?" And Bussy, insolent, gossiping Bussy, wrote back: "The death of Madame has afflicted me to the last degree. You know on what pleasant terms we used to be, and what kindness she showed me in my disgrace. If anything were capable of detaching those hearts who are the most attached to this life, it is the reflections which such a death inspires. Adieu, *ma belle cousine*, we will not quarrel any more." And he writes to Gramont, a month afterwards, "I can think of nothing but Madame's death. It haunts me as if it had happened yesterday." In his correspondence with Madame de Scudéry, the two friends can talk of nothing else. This accomplished lady takes advantage of the opportunity to send him a copy of *Pascal's Pensées*, in the hope that these Christian reflections may be profitable to the cynical Count. "Do not be angry with my little sermon," she says, "I preach it with the best intentions. The death of Madame has been a *terrible* sermon. She died with the most heroic courage. It is surprising to see a Princess of twenty-six, as young and beautiful as she was, go out of life as contentedly as some old beggar, who has spent his last years in the desert preparing to meet his end."

In reply, Bussy assures her that he has read Pascal with great admiration, even if he does not profess to follow his precepts, and that no one can regret Madame more deeply than he does. "I had," he repeats, "infinite esteem and affection for her." And when, many years afterwards, he recalls the chief events of his past life, for the benefit of his children, he speaks of Madame's death as a great misfortune for himself and a calamity for the whole of France. "Not only was she loved and honoured by all, for the sake of her cleverness and charm, but she was the most generous and the truest of friends. For the rest, this death was worth more to me than many sermons. A Princess, young, beautiful and happy, who could die at twenty-six with all the firmness and Christian faith of men who are old and sick of life—that was an example for the whole world, and God gave me the grace to lay it seriously to heart."

But every writer of the period records the same impression. "Never, since first dying came into fashion," said the witty Lord Rochester, "was anyone so deeply lamented." "The death of Madame," wrote the Comte de Choiseul, "is not a piece of news. It is a general and profound affliction." And Cardinal Barberini, from his villa on the banks of the lake of Nemi, wrote to Charles II. at Newmarket :—"I cannot sufficiently express my grief at the death of Madame d'Orléans, which is the greater and more general, because the rare qualities of this distinguished Princess were admired, not only by all France, but by the whole of Europe. She ought indeed to have lived many hundreds of years, if only to make the world better, by so beautiful an example of virtue."

Even that cold and impassive lady, Madame de Grignan, was deeply moved when the news reached her in her far-off Provençal home. "Do you remember," writes Madame de Sevigné, a year afterwards, "how upset you were by the news? how your mind seemed altogether out of place?" In the same letter, written from her country house in Brittany, on the anniversary of Madame's death, she adds : "Even here I have felt the end of Madame's year." And when, two years afterwards, France was dismayed by the death of the gallant and handsome young Prince de Longueville, who was slain at the passage of the Rhine, she remarks how quickly such sad events are forgotten here at Court, where no one has time to grieve, but adds : "The death of Madame lasted much longer." "Have you seen Madame de Monaco? and did you talk of Madame?" she asks another time, when her daughter was expecting a visit from Henrietta's old friend. And when, a year afterwards, Monsieur's marriage with the daughter of the Elector Palatine was arranged, Madame de Sevigné asks Madame de Grignan what she thinks of it, and observes : "You will understand how delighted he is to think of being married with great ceremony," but adds, with a sigh,—" Alas! if, instead of the new Madame, he could give us back the one we have lost!" But she goes with the rest of the world to pay her respects to the new Madame, and is well pleased on the whole with this singular lady. "Yesterday I went to the Palais-Royal, where I wept for Madame with all my heart. I was surprised at the wit of this one, not that she is in the least agreeable, but full of good sense, very obstinate and resolute. She has good taste, too, for she detests Madame de Gourdon." The latter was an attendant of the former Madame, who was supposed by many to have been implicated in her death, since she handed her the glass of chicory water. The second Madame, however, observes that, if she did not poison poor Madame intentionally, she told Monsieur all the evil that she could imagine, and rendered her mistress the worst offices possible behind her back.

As for Madame de La Fayette, she remained inconsolable, and rarely appeared at Court, although the King and the Prince of Condé both treated her with the highest consideration. She could not bear to visit those scenes which recalled poor Madame's memory so vividly, and where her absence had left a blank that no one could fill. "There are sorrows," she writes, "for which nothing can ever console one, and which leave a shadow over the whole of one's life." And, in a letter to her friend, Madame de Sevigné, written on the 30th of July 1673, she says: "Yesterday it was three years since I saw Madame die. I have been reading many of her letters over again. I am quite full of her." Her health was always delicate, and caused her so much suffering, that Madame de Sevigné used to wonder if it were worth while to have, "as Madame de La Fayette has, all the wit of Pascal, when it is accompanied with such inconveniences!" The only pleasure left her was the society of her faithful companion, La Rochefoucauld, and a few other intimate friends. Paris, she often said, seemed to kill her, and she had lost her taste for letter-writing, and did not care to put pen to paper. Yet she survived Madame twenty-three years, and only died in 1693.

There was another faithful servant of Madame, whose

regrets were still more bitter. This was Daniel de Cosnac, Bishop of Valence. On him, in his lonely exile, the blow fell with crushing force. A day or two before her death, Madame had begged his friend, Saint-Laurens, to write and tell him that her journey to England had been most prosperous, that the King, her brother, had renewed his promise to ask for a Cardinal's hat for the Bishop, and that, ere long, she hoped to see himself and Madame de Saint-Chaumont once more at Court. Cosnac was reading this letter when the news of her death reached him. He lived to become Archbishop of Aix, and to return to Court, and enjoy greater influence than ever before, but the horror of that moment was never forgotten.

" I cannot," he writes, "describe the state in which I found myself. Since men have been known to die of grief, it seems a crime on my part to have survived that day. All the terrible regrets which respect, esteem and gratitude could suggest, as well as those prompted by personal ambition and self-interest, passed through my mind a thousand times. My strength resisted the shock. . I was not even ill, but from that day, my life became so sad and dreary, that it was little better than a living death. I cared little for the loss of my fortune, and I had never put much faith in the hopes that had been held out to me of late. But to lose so great, so perfect, so good a Princess! No, if my heart had been really tender, it must have cost me my life! With her I lost all hope or desire of returning to Court, and, sick of the world, I turned my whole heart towards my sacred ministry."

While the flower of French society and the most cultured intellects of the day joined together in one common lamentation over Madame's untimely end, Louis XIV. prepared to pay her the last honours on a splendid scale. " I yield to no one," he had written to Colbert, "not even the King of England himself, in my grief and love for my sister." And now, as a testimony of his sorrow, he declared it to be his pleasure that Madame should be buried with the ceremonial usually reserved for the funeral of crowned heads. According to the *Court Gazette*, no royal burial had ever been solemnised with so much state before in France. During two days her corpse lay in state, surrounded by lighted candles,

and the King and Queen came to sprinkle it with holy
water. After that, the heart, enshrined in a silver casket,
was borne to the Abbey of Val-de-Grâce, by a long
train of ladies, with the Princesse de Condé at their head,
and there interred, in fulfilment of a promise which Madame
herself had made to the nuns. On the night of the
4th, the body was removed to Saint-Denis, by torchlight, followed by Mademoiselle and all the princesses of the blood.
Through the noble avenues of Saint-Cloud, across the Seine,
and up the silent streets of Paris, the long procession
wound slowly on its way, until about two o'clock in the morning, the gates of Saint-Denis were reached. There the coffin
was placed in the Abbey of the Kings, under a black velvet
canopy, and watched by Monsieur's guards night and day,
while the monks chanted masses for the repose of the dead.
The funeral had been originally fixed for the 25th of July, but
was put off until the 21st of August, to give more time for the
necessary arrangements, and the Bishop of Condom received
a command from the King to pronounce the funeral oration
on that day. A letter recording the fact, and giving some
other interesting details, was addressed by Bossuet himself to
some person residing at Dijon, whose name is unknown, but
who was, in all probability, his elder brother, Antoine Bossuet,
Treasurer of the States of Burgundy. This letter was copied
by Philibert de la Mare, a learned councillor of Dijon, in the
autograph MS. of his *Memoires,* now preserved in the library
of that city, and is published by M. Floquet in his *Etudes sur
la vie de Bossuet.*

"*July* 1670.

" I think you know that I was awakened, on Sunday night,
by order of Monsieur, to wait on Madame, who was at the
last extremity, and had asked eagerly for me. I found her
perfectly conscious, speaking and acting without the least
alarm or ostentation, without effort or violence, but so well and
naturally, with so much courage and piety, that I am still
amazed when I think of it! She had already received the
last Sacraments, even extreme unction, for which she asked
the Curé who brought her the Viaticum, and which she was
impatient to receive while she retained consciousness. I was

with her for an hour, and saw her draw her last breath, kissing
the crucifix, which she held pressed to her lips, as long as she
had any strength left. She was only insensible for a moment.
All she said to the King, to Monsieur and to those about her,
was short, precise and admirable. Never was there a Princess
more greatly admired, or more deeply regretted. What is the
most wonderful, is that from the moment she felt herself
doomed, she spoke only of God, without showing the least
signs of regret, feeling that her death would be acceptable to
Him, as her life has been glorious, owing to the love and trust
of two great Kings. She took all the remedies prescribed by
the doctors bravely, but never uttered a word of complaint at
their failure to relieve her, only saying that she must die in
due form. Her body was opened before a number of doctors,
surgeons and all kinds of people, because, when she was first
seized with violent pains after swallowing three mouthfuls of
chicory water, given her by her favourite and most devoted
attendant, she had exclaimed that she was poisoned. His
Excellency, the Ambassador of England and all the English
here, almost believed this, but the opening of the body proved
the contrary, since nothing was found in good condition but
the stomach and the heart, which are the first organs usually
attacked by poison. Also Monsieur, after giving Madame la
Duchesse de Meckelbourg, who was present, some of the same
water to drink, finished the bottle himself, to reassure
Madame. Accordingly, she was satisfied, and said nothing
more of poison, excepting that she had at first believed herself
to have been poisoned by mistake. Those were the very
words which I heard her say to M. le Maréchal de Gramont.
I took the news of Madame's death to Monsieur, who had
allowed himself to be led to his room down stairs, and found
this prince quite overcome, but tried to comfort him by telling
him of the Christian sentiments with which Madame had died.
I went to Versailles the same day, and saw the King, who,
although he had taken physic, commanded me to come and
tell him what I had seen. He had tears in his eyes, and his
heart ached, but he allowed me to speak to him, on this terrible accident, in the way that a man of my profession ought to
speak. M. le Prince seemed much pleased with what I had

said, and tells me that the King and all the Court are deeply
moved. His Majesty has sent me orders to pronounce the
funeral oration at Saint-Denis in three weeks' time. The day
before yesterday, Rose (the President Rose, an intimate friend
of Bossuet) told me that this good Princess had thought of me
on her death-bed, and had ordered a ring to be given me. I
hear now that she gave this order when I left her for a
moment to take a little rest. She soon recalled me, to speak
of God, and told me that she was just going to die. And, indeed, she died almost directly afterwards.

"J. B., *Evesque de Condom.*"

The ring, which Madame had left him, adorned with a
large emerald set with diamonds, was placed on Bossuet's
finger by the King himself, a few days after, and worn by
him when he pronounced Madame's funeral oration. Then,
as he spoke of this Princess's generosity and thoughtfulness
for others, of the enchanting grace with which she knew how
to give, he paused a moment and glanced at the ring he wore.
"I, too, have known it," he cried, and many of those present
caught the glitter of the emerald, which sparkled on his hand,
and understood his meaning. That ring he wore to his dying
day, and, thirty-four years later, we find it mentioned in an
inventory of his possessions that was taken after his death.

Two days before the funeral at Saint-Denis, Säintôt, the
King's Master of the Ceremonies, followed by heralds and
criers with bells, marched in procession through the streets of
Paris, and knocked at the doors of the Parliament and Council
Chambers, proclaiming aloud,—" All noble and devout persons
pray for the soul of the most high, puissant, virtuous and
excellent, Princess Henriette Anne d'Angleterre, daughter of
Charles I., King of Great Britain, and of Henriette Marie,
daughter of France, and wife of Philippe de France, only
brother of the King, who died in the château de Saint-Cloud,
on the 30th of June, for whose soul, the King commands
prayers to be offered, and Mass to be celebrated in the
Church of Saint-Denis de France, where her body now
reposes, at which place, next Wednesday afternoon, will be
said the vespers and vigil for the dead, and the next day, at

ten in the morning, her solemn funeral service will be held.
Pray, of your charity, for the repose of her soul."

On the morning of the 21st, an august assembly met in
the Abbey of Saint-Denis to pay Madame the last honours.
All the chief public bodies in the kingdom, the Parliament
and Courts of Law, the Assembly of the Clergy and the City
Corporations, were represented, and an immense concourse
of people thronged the doors of the great convent church.
The Queen herself was present in a tribune, with the King of
Poland, the English Ambassador, the Duke of Buckingham,
Lord Sandwich, Lord St. Albans, Lord Arundel, James
Hamilton, and the Comte and Comtesse de Gramont. The
Prince and Princesse de Condé, the Duc d'Enghien, the
Duchesse de Longueville, the little Prince de Conti, and the
Princesse de Carignan appeared as chief mourners, followed by
a long train of princes and princesses of the blood, and lords
and ladies. Last of all came the members of Monsieur and
Madame's household, bearing torches in their hands. A
mausoleum, surrounded with altars and silver urns, and
adorned with a crowd of mourning allegorical statues, among
which Youth, Poetry and Music were conspicuous, had been
erected in the centre of the choir. There the coffin rested,
covered with cloth of gold, edged with ermine, and embroidered with the arms of France and England, in gold and
silver. As soon as the assistants had taken their places, hundreds of flambeaux and wax candles, placed round the bier,
burst into flame, a cloud of incense rose from the altars, and
the Archbishop of Reims, assisted by other bishops, began the
mass, which was chanted by the King's musicians, accompanied by Lulli's violins.

"I do not think," said Madame de Sevigné, as she listened
to the surpassing sweetness of their strains, "there will be any
better music in heaven."

Then Bossuet, clad for the first time in his purple episcopal robes, and wearing his pectoral cross, mounted the pulpit,
and pronounced the text of his great *Oraison*. " *Vanitas
vanitatum, omnia vanitas.*" His hearers listened in breathless
silence as he spoke of the beauty, of the talents, of the
irresistible charm which had made this Princess adored by all.

He dwelt on her rare gifts of mind, on her fine taste in art
and letters, on the incomparable sweetness of her nature, on
the royalty of heart and soul which made this daughter
of Kings even greater than she was by birth. He extolled
the services which she had rendered to France, the love and
honour in which she was held by the two greatest Kings of the
earth.   And he recalled her famous journey to England,
upon which so much had depended, the success which had
crowned her efforts, and the joy and triumph of her return.
But when he spoke of that terrible night, which was still fresh
in the memory of his hearers, when he painted the sudden
horror with which the awful tidings fell like a thunder-clap on
the ears of the Court—*Madame se meurt, Madame est morte*
—the whole of that vast assembly broke into one sob, the
orator himself stopped and burst into tears.

But he recovered himself, and went on to show how, in the
presence of that awful catastrophe, the world seemed robbed of
its charm.   After this, what is life but a dream, health but a
name, youth but a fading flower, joy a mistake, and glory an
illusion?   *Vanity of vanities, all is vanity.*   Christians!"
he cried, " let us think of ourselves.   What more do we expect?
Shall the dead rise up to warn us?   If such fearful surprises
are needed to startle hearts deadened by the love of this
world, surely this example is great and terrible enough."

Among the Englishmen present at Saint-Denis that day
was Francis Vernon.   He has left us his impressions of that
imposing ceremony, and described the magnificence of the
scene and the eloquence of the Bishop of Condom.   But what
struck him more than all, were the extraordinary marks of
grief shown by those present, the tears and general wailing as,
one by one, the officers of Madame's household cast their
badge of office into her grave, and the coffin was borne into
the vault.

" On Thursday last," he writes, " was the solemnity of
Madame's funeral, at Saint-Denis, extraordinarily pompous
and magnificent.   In that kind, nothing was wanting ; all
symptoms of a public sorrow and affection were met together.
The Queen, which was an honour altogether new and un-
practised in former funerals, was there in person.   The King

of Poland was there. All the Court in general, ladies as well
as noblemen, assisted at the solemnity. The close mourners
and those who made the reverences and offerings were the
Prince de Condé, who led the Princess, the Duc d'Enghien,
who handed the Duchesse de Longueville, the little Prince de
Conti, who led the Princesse de Carignan. The Bishop of
Condom preached with an eloquence something transported
beyond his usual delicacy and sweetness. The hearse was
extreme richly adorned. All the officers of her family, with
great silence and mourning, cast the badges of their employment into her grave, and as her coffin was put in, there was
a general weeping, a circumstance something unusual at
these great ceremonies of the interment of princes, whose
deaths, as their lives, are made up rather of state and externall
shows."

So Henrietta of England was laid to rest in the crypt of
Saint-Louis, by the side of the mother whose loss she had so
bitterly deplored. But their ashes were not allowed to
remain in peace. A hundred and twenty years later, on the
16th of October 1773, an infuriated mob burst into the
sacred precincts, dashed the monument of the Kings to pieces,
and rifled the tombs of the dead. The first coffin then
brought to light was that of Henrietta Maria, the second
that of Madame. Their remains were buried, together with
all those of the Bourbons, in a trench on the north side of the
Basilica, known as the cemetery of the Valois. On the night
of the 20th of January 1817, they were solemnly exhumed,
in the presence of the Royal family of France, and buried
anew in the vault under the church. The names of the
royal personages, whose ashes were then restored to conse-
crated ground, were inscribed on a black marble tablet, and
the first we read among them are those of Henriette Marie
de France and Henriette Anne d'Angleterre.

During the same week, two other funeral services were
held in memory of Madame, and two other funeral orations
were pronounced by illustrious priests. One was at the
Abbey of Val de Grâce, where her heart had been laid. Here
l'Abbé Mascaron, one of the most distinguished of the Court
chaplains, preached the sermon in the presence of Monsieur.

He, too, paid an eloquent tribute to the beauty of Madame's character, and, in the words of Ecclesiasticus, described her as *Cor docile, cor splendidum et cor confirmatum.* " Nothing in this world," he said, "is more beautiful than the love of truth." That love it was which distinguished this great Princess in all her actions, and led her to seek instruction in those branches of study which are the most neglected by persons of her rank and age, and to take delight in reading, and in the society of cultivated men. This love of the best and highest, again made her lend a willing ear to the words of that great prelate who had touched her heart, and who, at her own request, paid her frequent visits, and conversed with her of those things which are eternal. Last of all, he spoke of the extraordinary courage and calmness with which she met her fate, of those dying words of hers, so strangely unlike the ordinary language of the Court, that even the priests at her bedside marvelled. " Children of the century," he cried in his final peroration, " hear and take warning. See how all your boasted riches and greatness, the pleasures on which you fix your heart, the objects of your desires, are but a shadow. *Dies meae sicut umbra praetereunt.* Hear the words of the great Princess whom we lament! ' Alas! my God !' she cries, with eyes fastened on the crucifix, ' why have I not known Thee before !' Hear her, as, with her last breath, she declares her submission to the will of God, her hope in His mercy, and learn from her how to die."

At the service held in her own church of Saint-Cloud, where her intestines were buried, Feuillet was the preacher. His sermon, inferior in point of rhetoric to those of Bossuet and Mascaron, was marked by a forcible and impressive eloquence of its own. Unlike them, he does not attempt to paint the charm and grace of her character, to speak of her sweetness and kindness of heart, of her wit and talents. He will only tell what he knows, and speak of what he saw on that strange and awful night. Watching by that death-bed, let the world learn the true meaning of life, there let us realise the sharp contrast that exists between the selfish and sinful laws, by which the men and women of the Court order their lives, and the Gospel of Christ. Let us pause and listen to the voice which speaks to us, as it spoke to her, asking "Whither are you going? What are you doing?" before it is too late and the doors are shut.

This, briefly told, was the lesson taught by the stern Jansenist priest, who stood by Madame's bedside and saw her die. His sermon was afterwards printed by the Queen's request, and published, together with a minute relation of Madame's last moments, written by Feuillet, and dedicated to Monsieur, in language characteristic of the author. " It is well that all men should know there is a God in Israel, whose arm is not shortened, Who is able still to save to the uttermost all who turn to Him in the hour of their death. That God, who worked such wonders in Madame's heart, may work the same in yours, Monsieur, and that you, too, may glorify Him by a holy life, is the earnest prayer and desire of a priest, who thinks he can show you no better mark of his profound respect than by telling you the plain truth."

Many years afterwards a tablet was placed on the walls of the church of Saint-Cloud, to the memory of Madame, by her only surviving daughter, Anne Marie, Queen of Sicily and Sardinia. It bore this inscription :—

> Içi repose une partie du corps de la très-haute, très-
> puissante et très-excellente Princesse,
> HENRIETTE ANNE d'ANGLETERRE,
> Fille de Charles I., Roi de la Grande Bretagne,
> et de Marie Henriette de France.
> Epouse de Philippe de France, frère unique du Roi Louis XIV.,
> Decédée au Château de St. Cloud, le 30 Juin 1670,
> agée de 26 ans.

The following sonnet, said to have been written by Madame de Brégis, is preserved on an old engraving of Madame's tomb, together with a quaint representation of the funeral pyre at Saint-Denis, with its statues and blazing urns, surrounded by a crowd of mourners :—

> " LE TOMBEAU DE MADAME.

> " Des pleurs, des pleurs sans fin, des plaintes éternelles,
> Des soupirs, des sanglots, des cris de déséspoir !
> Madame ne vit plus, et nous venons de voir
> Le terrible succèz de ses peines cruelles

" Aussi cette Beauté qui fit honte aux plus belles,
   Cet esprit admiré des maistres du scavoir,
   Cette grandeur supreme, et ce vaste pouvoir,
   N'estoient qu'un court passage à des douleurs mortelles.

" Mais ce moment fatal de soy plein d'horreur
   Devoit-il estre encor tout armé de fureur ?
   Falloit-il tant de maux pour perdre tant de charmes ?

" Ciel, qui l'avez permis, permettez ce transport,
   Faites régner vos loix, mais laissez-nous nos larmes
   Pour pleurer à jamais une si triste mort."

CHAPTER XXVIII

MADAME'S portrait was often painted, by many artists, in
different styles. Several of these works, oil paintings, miniatures and engravings, have been preserved. All of them are
interesting, and some are admirable specimens of workman-
ship, but not one is quite satisfactory as a likeness. In some
points they differ curiously from one another. The colour of
Henrietta's eyes, for instance, seems to have puzzled artists
and writers alike. Choisy describes them as black and very
bright. Madame de Brégis tells us they were blue. Her
testimony is borne out by Manicamp, the writer of the famous
libel, who knew Madame well, and had every opportunity of
studying her closely. After praising the dazzling pink and
white of her complexion, her rosy lips and pearly teeth, he
dwells on the rare beauty of her eyes, which he says are blue,
and at once sparkling and tender. In her portraits they are
sometimes hazel, sometimes grey, but more frequently of a
deep shade of blue. The colour of her hair in her pictures
again varies from dark-brown to the *blond cendré* described
by Manicamp. On the whole, Madame de Brégis's description
of Madame's eyes as blue, and her hair as a rich chestnut,
seems to have been the most accurate. But it is plain that
her face was a difficult one to paint, and that portraits seldom
do her justice. Her beauty depended more on expression
and colouring than on regularity of feature. No painter can
give the sparkle of the eye, the smile which lighted up her
whole countenance, the exquisite grace that distinguished her
among all other women.

The artist who painted her the most frequently, and who,

on the whole, succeeded best in rendering her peculiar charms, was Pierre Mignard. After spending many years in Italy, studying art among the French painters, who, with Nicolas Poussin at their head, made a little colony in Rome, Mignard returned to France in 1658, at the invitation of Louis XIV. In 1660 he painted a fine portrait of the King, and from that time his reputation was made. All the celebrities of the day sat to him in turn, all the ladies of the Court wanted to be painted, *en Mignardes*. He was employed to decorate the dome of Anne of Austria's new Abbey of Val-de-Grâce with frescoes, and to paint the galleries of Saint-Cloud and Versailles. On Lebrun's death, he became painter to the King, and Molière, who was a personal friend of his, paid him the greatest of compliments by describing Raphael and Michael Angelo as "*les Mignards de leur siècle.*" Madame honoured him with her patronage, and sat to him repeatedly, at different periods of her life. Two of his portraits of Madame are in the gallery at Versailles. A third is in our own National Portrait Gallery. All three are half-lengths, and in all three, Madame is represented wearing a low, flame-coloured gown, a broad lace collar or *berthe* fastened with a large pearl brooch, and a pearl necklace and earrings. Her hair is parted in the middle, and hangs in ringlets on either side of her face, frizzed up to the ears, in the style of which Pepys disapproved. And in her arms, gaily adorned with a crimson tassel, we see her pet dog, Mimi, the little spaniel who figured with his mistress in the *Ballet des Muses*, and was celebrated alike in Benserade's verses and in Madame de Sevigné's letters. Another remarkably fine portrait by Mignard, a three-quarters-length figure, which probably belonged to Lord Arlington, and is now the Duke of Grafton's property, was lent to the Stuart Exhibition in 1890. Here Madame is standing, with her face turned to the left, holding a crown and embroidered drapery in her hands. She wears the same amber-coloured gown, open in front and richly trimmed with pearl and jet ornaments, but has a red scarf twisted about her shoulders. The likeness of Henrietta to her father strikes us forcibly in all these portraits. Her hair is dressed in the French style, and the whole *pose* and air of the figure is

French, but the features resemble Charles I. far more than
Henrietta Maria. We see the charms which so many writers
have described, the dark and sparkling eyes, the skin of lilies
and roses, the beautiful neck and arms, the small rosy mouth
with the lips slightly raised at the corners. And the Duke of
Grafton's picture, at least, gives us something of the sprightly
air and bewitching manners which won the hearts of young
and old alike, and made such different men as Cosnac and
Monmouth, Buckingham and Turenne, her servants for life
and death. We recognise the sweet gentleness which was
the secret of her fascination, *cette douceur pleine de charmes*
which Molière praised, and La Fayette loved, which Bossuet
recalls three times over in his *Oraison*, and which had so fatal
an attraction for the Comte de Guiche. The eyes still seem
to seek ours, as if they would ask our sympathy ; the lips are
about to break into that enchanting smile which made her
the most charming of princesses.

Another portrait, almost exactly similar to the one in
the National Portrait Gallery, but ascribed to Rigaud, was
formerly at Saint-Cloud, where it perished in the fire of 1670.
One, by Nicolas de Largillière, belongs to the Earl of Home,
by whom it was lent to the Stuart Exhibition. This is a
whole-length, life-size picture, and represents Madame sitting
under a canopy, wearing a blue embroidered robe, lined with
ermine and trimmed with a deep lace collar, and holding a
small mariner's compass in her left hand. It is a good
picture and an evidently authentic portrait, but inferior in
point of character and expression to the Duke of Grafton's
Mignard. A half-length portrait, belonging to the Earl of
Ashburnham, and closely resembling the Mignard at Versailles, was also at the Stuart Exhibition.

These portraits all belong to the latter period of Madame's
life, and represent her in the bloom of womanhood, between
the ages of twenty-one and twenty-five. But there is a
second group of portraits, which belong to an earlier period,
and give a somewhat different impression of her appearance
and character. The first of these is a bust, which was lent
by Sir Charles Dilke to the Stuart Exhibition. It is ascribed
to Mignard, but differs in several points from this artist's other

portraits of Madame. Here again she wears a low, yellow
gown, and pearls on her neck and in her hair, but the eyes
are lighter and the locks are fairer than usual. The features
are the same, but the face is rounder and more childlike.
The expression is very sweet and gentle, but there is less
anxiety to please, less of the melting grace and seductive air
of the accomplished woman of the world, and more of the
fresh and simple charm of girlhood. There can be little
doubt that it was painted soon after her marriage, when she
was just seventeen, or even earlier. But what gives this
attractive picture additional interest, is the marked likeness
which it bears to the famous enamel miniature of Madame,
by Jean Petitot. This miniature, one of the finest specimens
of the master's art, was long in the possession of the painter
Zincke, who treasured it during many years, as a precious
example of Petitot's work, but finally parted with it to
Horace Walpole. At the sale of the Strawberry Hill collection in 1842, it passed, according to Propert, into Lady
Burdett-Coutts's collection. Another miniature of Madame,
by Petitot, is in the Duke of Devonshire's collection, and was
exhibited in 1890 at the Burlington Fine Arts Club. This
also bears a strong likeness to the Walpole enamel and the
Dilke picture, and has all the refinement of feeling and
mastery of his art which made Petitot famous. Two other
miniatures of Madame,. by inferior French artists, were also
exhibited at the New Gallery, in 1890. One of these, the
property of Lord Galloway, bears a certain likeness to
Petitot's enamels. The other belongs to the Duke of
Buccleuch, and was probably given by Madame herself to his
ancestor, the Duke of Monmouth. It is mounted in a silver
filigree frame, set with precious stones, and was evidently worn
as a pendant. Madame wears a spray of flowers in her hair,
and has a bright and animated expression, which gives the
work a value independent of its artistic merit.

Both Petitot's enamels, and Mignard's bust-portrait, bear
a striking likeness to two interesting engravings that we
have of Madame in her early youth. The first of these is
taken from a drawing by Claude Mellan, and forms the
frontispiece of the *Manual of Religious Instruction* drawn up

by Père Cyprien de Gamaches for his *petite Princesse*, and
published in 1655. Here, in spite of the ringlets and pearls
with which the youthful Princess is arrayed, she is still quite
a child, with round cheeks, and a serious expression on her
shy, young face, as in the days when she waited on the nuns
at Chaillot. The second belongs to a later period, and has
been repeatedly engraved from a portrait by Van der Werff,
a Dutch copyist, who is supposed to have worked from an
original drawing, taken by Claude Mellan about the time of
Madame's marriage. One version of this portrait, engraved
by J. Audran, forms the frontispiece of M. Anatole France's
edition of Madame de La Fayette's *Vie de Madame Henriette;* another was engraved by Jourdy, on a large scale, for
Vatout's *Palais - Royal.* This also is a bust-portrait, and
resembles the earlier engraving in the general shape and
character of the face. But the features are more regular, and
there is more of actual beauty. The graceful child has
grown up into a lovely maiden without losing any of her
innocent charm. Her gown is low, as in Mignard's portraits,
trimmed with a broad band of fur, and richly adorned with
pearls. So she may have looked on that evening at Fontainebleau, which Manicamp recalls, when, glittering with
jewels, and radiant in the light of her own beauty, she
entered the room, and all who were present exclaimed
there was no one in the world to be compared with
her.

Another interesting print in the British Museum is taken
from a full-length portrait formerly at Hengrave Hall. Here
Madame is represented, wearing a rich Court dress and head-
dress of feathers, in the act of taking a rose from a basket,
held by a child at her side. The pretty little girl, who offers
her the flowers, is Mary Bond, the daughter of Sir Thomas
Bond, Comptroller of Queen Henrietta Maria's household,
who afterwards married Sir Thomas Gage of Hengrave.
Lady Gage was fondly attached to Madame, and, at her own
death, left her grand-daughter a bracelet with several lockets,
given her by this Princess. One of these lockets contained
Henrietta's own portrait, painted in enamel, and "sette with
fourteene bigge dyamonds." Another held that of her pet

dog, Mimi, also painted in enamel, and "sette round with twenty little dyamonds."

In later years, Madame's portrait was painted more than once by her brother's favourite artist, Sir Peter Lely. Her picture belonged to the series of Beauties of Charles II.'s Court, which he painted, at the Duchess of York's suggestion, for the Queen's bedroom at Windsor. In James II.'s catalogue, the names of these ladies are given as follows :—The Duchess of Cleveland, the Duchess of Richmond, Mrs Middleton, Lady Northumberland, Lady Sunderland, Lady Falmouth, Lady Denham, and her sister, Miss Brooks, Lady Rochester, the Comtesse de Gramont, and Madame d'Orléans. Ten of these portraits are now at Hampton Court. That of Madame alone is missing. But a picture of her by Lely, perhaps the one originally painted for this series, was presented by Charles II. to the city of Exeter after his sister's death, and may still be seen in the Guildhall of her native town. It has been photographed expressly for the present work, by the kind permission of the Mayor of Exeter, and our plate is the first engraving ever made from this touching and interesting picture. Madame is represented as still in mourning for her mother, in a plain white satin robe, with a black veil on her head. The thin, pale features show traces of failing health, and wear the sad expression which had become habitual to her, in these last days of her life. An inscription on the frame records the dates of her birth and death, with the words :—" This portrait was presented by King Charles II. in 1672, painted by Sir Peter Lely." Madame probably sat to the painter on her visit to Dover, in which case this portrait has the additional interest of being the last that was ever taken. The Earl of Crawford also possesses a portrait of Madame, by Lely, which is said to have been given by Henrietta herself to Lady Ann Mackenzie, daughter of Colin, Earl of Seaforth, and wife of that faithful follower of Charles II., Alexander Lindsay, first Earl of Balcarres. But the picture is in the painter's later style, and, if Madame is the person represented, must have been copied from an earlier study.

Another very fine portrait of Madame, by Lely, hangs in

the Queen's private apartments at Buckingham Palace. Here she is represented as the goddess Pallas Athenè, armed with helmet and spear, much in the same manner as Miss Stewart figures on the penny, in the guise of Britannia. It was in the character of Pallas, it will be remembered, that Madame appeared in the *Ballet des Arts*, on that memorable occasion which Madame de Sevigné recalls with such enthusiasm in her old age. Another portrait of her as Pallas, painted by Mignard, was bought by Walpole at the sale of Lady Suffolk's pictures at Marble Hill, and was sold in 1842, with the rest of the Strawberry Hill collection. This was not the only time in which Henrietta was painted in fancy dress. She appears as Flora, in a white robe, wreathed with flowers, in a group of the Royal Family, painted by Nocret, at Versailles. In the same gallery there is a full-length picture of her, clad in classical draperies and wearing golden sandals on her feet. This was painted by Antoine Matthieu in 1664. A three-quarters-length of the same picture is at Cassiobury, in the Earl of Essex's collection, and was exhibited, at South Kensington in 1866, as the portrait of Lucy Walters. In both pictures, Madame holds a medallion of her husband in her hands. There is also an old engraving, taken from a picture belonging to Lord Poulett, early in the present century, in which Madame is represented wearing a jewelled crown, surmounted with a cross, and a long veil flowing over her hair. We do not know on what occasion she wore this costume, but Lord Poulett was in Paris at the time of her death, and is mentioned as one of the last guests whom she received at Saint-Cloud. The print bears a strong resemblance to Mignard's later portraits, and is no doubt genuine, although the original seems to have disappeared.

A word must be added regarding Madame's daughters. Both of these children grew up to womanhood, and lived to become Queens. Marie Thérèse, the wife of Louis XIV., took charge of the little Mademoiselle, who was eight years old at the time of her mother's death, and the child was brought up with her cousin, the young Dauphin, until, a year later, Monsieur married again. The lady chosen to fill Henrietta's place was Elizabeth Charlotte of Bavaria, the daughter of Madame's own first cousin, the Elector Palatine. Monsieur had little to do with the choice of his second wife, and his marriage was entirely arranged by Louis XIV., with a view to securing the reversion of the Elector's rights on the Palatinate. The new Madame was, in all respects, a strange contrast to the Princess whom all France remembered with such infinite regret. Saint-Simon describes her as badly shaped, badly dressed, and badly disposed towards everything and everyone. Another contemporary speaks of her as rude, satirical, and gifted with an originality that no one is tempted to imitate. She strode through the Palais Royal in top-boots, with a high hat on her head, and a hunting whip in her hand, and shrieked and raged at the top of her voice when she lost her temper. But this *vilaine altesse royale* was not without her merits. She had, as Madame de Sevigné soon discovered, plenty of good sense and feeling. She won the King's respect if she did not always comply with his wishes, and the Court poet, Benserade, remarked wittily, how strange it seemed that a second Madame, so utterly unlike the first, should be still more highly esteemed by Louis XIV. than the one whom he had adored. And if Monsieur's vices, and the absolute empire which his old favourite, the Chevalier de Lorraine, assumed over him from the moment of his return, destroyed the peace of her home, the orphan children of Henrietta found in her an excellent step-mother. From the first, she took the little Mademoiselle, Marie Louise, for her companion, and treated the child, who was only ten years younger than herself, more as a sister than a daughter. Her letters abound in tender memories of this charming young Princess, who had inherited so much of Madame's beauty and sweetness. Contemporaries describe the bright eyes and arched brows, the rosy lips and chestnut hair that recalled her dead mother. She had, Madame de Sevigné tells us, the same "*jolis pieds qui la font si bien danser.*" None of all the Royal children was so great a favourite at Court, no one blushed so prettily or laughed so merrily. Yet this winning child was doomed to a sad end.

"Do not take your daughter so often to Court," said la Grande Mademoiselle to Monsieur, with her accustomed frankness. " If you do, she will never be happy anywhere else." But the warning was thrown away on Monsieur, who had already made up his mind that his daughter should marry the Dauphin. They had been companions from childhood, and, as they grew up, they played and danced together. Marie Louise was the Dauphin's partner at every ball and *fête*, and he took the greatest pleasure in her company. But such a marriage did not suit the policy of Louis XIV. He had made up his mind that Mademoiselle should marry Charles II., the feeble and imbecile King of Spain, and the poor young Princess was sacrificed to his ambitious plans. In vain she threw herself at her uncle's feet, and begged to be allowed to remain in France. Louis was inflexible. " I make you Queen of Spain," he said, " could I do more for my own daughter?" " Ah, sire !" she is said to have replied, "you might have done more for your niece." The marriage was celebrated with great pomp at Fontainebleau, in May 1679, and Monsieur's thoughts were too much absorbed in the jewels he wore on his coat, to heed his daughter's tears.

" No one could help weeping," writes Madame d'Osna-brück, better known as the Electress Sophia of Hanover, who was among the wedding guests, "at the sight of this amiable little Princess, who loved France so well and could not bear to leave her home, and the whole Court resounded with cries and groans." The Dauphin, being, as Elizabeth Charlotte of Orléans remarks, the true son of his mother, soon consoled himself, but this kind stepmother was full of compassion for the poor child's fate. " I should pity her with all my heart if she were not going to be so great a Queen," she writes, at the time of the wedding. And afterwards she comes to the conclusion that Spain must be the most horrible country in the world, and the people there the silliest and most tiresome that ever lived. " I really pity that poor child," she adds, " for having to live there. The little dogs she took with her are her only comfort. She may not even smile in public, or speak to her old servants, and all her French maids have begged leave to come home." The King himself, that ugly baboon, as Madame d'Osnabrück calls him, adored his young wife, and did all in his power to make her happy. But the rigid fetters of Spanish etiquette were too hard for her. She pined for her old home, and drooped like a caged bird, cut off from joy and freedom. At length, after ten years of this gilded captivity, a death, as sudden and strange as that of her mother, set her free. Madame de Sevigné describes the painful sensation at the Court of France when, on the 17th of February 1689, the news reached St. Cyr, where the King and Madame de Maintenon were assisting at a performance of Racine's *Esther*. The King rose and left the hall in tears. Madame d'Orléans shrieked aloud, and all the Court shared their grief for the poor young Queen. "*Cela sent bien le fagot !*" was Madame de Sevigné's own comment. By a strange fate, it had been the Chevalier de Lorraine who led Marie Louise to the altar at her wedding, while another of her mother's bitter enemies, the Comtesse de Soissons, accompanied her as lady-in-waiting to Spain, and was accused of having poisoned her. But the charge was never proved, and had probably no better foundation than in the case of Madame. When she was dead her half-witted husband sank slowly into complete torpor of body and mind. A little while before his own death, he went down into the vault where the coffins of his ancestors lay, and gazed once more on the face of the young Queen, whose presence had brightened his dreary existence. "*Mi reyna, mi reyna,*" he sobbed, "before the year is out I will come to you." He left no children, and Louis XIV. claimed the crown for his grandson, the young Duke of Anjou, who became Philip V. of Spain.

A happier lot was in store for Madame's younger daughter, Anne Marie, Mademoiselle de Valois. She was only two years old when Monsieur married again, and had never known her mother, but she was brought up with the greatest care by her eccentric stepmother, who loved this Mademoiselle of the big mouth, as she commonly calls her, as dearly as if she had been her own child. In 1684 she married Victor Amadeus II., Duke of Savoy, afterwards King of Sicily and Sardinia; but Elizabeth Charlotte still retained the liveliest affection for her step-daughter, and wrote weekly letters to the "good Queen," whose virtues and angelic goodness she is never tired of praising. This second Madame was the most indefatigable correspondent, and devoted one day of the week to each of the different countries where members of her family lived. On Sunday she wrote to her own friends in Hanover, on Monday to Spain, on Tuesday to Savoy, and so on throughout the week, reserving Saturday for making up her arrears. Many of her letters, which often filled as many as twenty sheets, have fortunately been preserved, and, as her judgments are always delivered without the smallest respect of persons, they are often very entertaining. She does not scruple to speak of Louis XIV.'s Queen as a great goose, and generally alludes to Madame de Maintenon as *cette vieille sotte*. Neither does she make any attempt to hide her contempt for her husband and his unworthy minions. " Those are the men," she says repeatedly, "who poisoned poor Madame, and have brought the wrinkles to my brow." But she flatters herself that she has taught the Chevalier de Lorraine to keep in his place, or, as she puts it, has given *ce drôle* a lesson that will last him the rest of his life. And she does not pretend to conceal her satisfaction, when he is cut off by a fearfully sudden death, in the midst of his wicked courses.

Monsieur himself died of a fit of apoplexy at Saint-Cloud in 1701. His wife survived him more than twenty years, and lived to see her son become Regent of France, on the death of Louis XIV. The good Queen of Sardinia died in 1728, after having lost both her daughters in the flower of their youth. The elder one was Marie Adelaide, Duchess of Burgundy, whose son, Louis XV., succeeded his great-grandfather on the throne of France. The younger one, Marie Louise, another bright and intelligent Princess, became the wife of Philip V., King of Spain. By her talents and force of character she acquired great influence in state affairs, but, to the grief of her husband and subjects, she died in 1714, at the same age as Madame. Her two sons reigned in turn, but left no issue.

On the death of our Queen Anne in 1714, the eldest prince of the House of Savoy claimed the crown of England, by reason of his descent, through his mother, from Charles I., but as he professed the Roman Catholic religion, his claim was set aside in favour of the House of Brunswick, and the son

of the Electress Sophia ascended the throne of the Stuarts.
This branch of the House of Savoy is not yet extinct, and,
at the present time, a direct descendant of Madame, Marie
Thérèse, Princess of Modena, and wife of Prince Louis of
Bavaria, is the actual representative of the line of Charles
the First.

THE END.

COLSTON AND COMPANY, PRINTERS, EDINBURGH.

www.ingramcontent.com/pod-product-compliance
Lightning Source LLC
Chambersburg PA
CBHW021330110726
47900CB00005B/1417